D. Bruce Foster

THIS WAY TO PARADISE

Book Two of the Alex Randolph Series

Visit D. Bruce Foster's website at www.dbrucefoster.com

Macdougall Press

Printed in the United States of America

ISBN-10: 0615922724
ISBN-13: 978-0615922720 (Macdougall Press, LLC)

To Ali & Brian

ACKNOWLEDGMENTS

In many ways, the writing of a work of fiction is a collaborative effort between writer, editor, and first readers. It is the latter who with fresh perspectives let the writer know what works and what doesn't work; who provide the writer with confidence that the story is ultimately headed in the right direction—a liberating concept that I can tell you allows the words to flow much more freely off the fingertips onto the keyboard.

First among these is my wife, Jan, whose instincts are unfailingly correct as the first draft of each chapter comes off the printer, warm in her hands. She often seems to know and understand the characters better than I do. Along with my daughter, Allison Fortmann, we spend hours talking about the characters as if they were real people, some of whom we love and others whom we love to hate.

Marie Beck, my talented editor and friend, lets me get away with nothing, forcing me to make the case for the development of each character and viciously striking every cliché. Her story line suggestions invariably have a powerful impact on the quality of the finished product. Working with her is sheer pleasure, and to Marie goes my enduring thanks.

It was perhaps inevitable that some of my first readers would be colleagues, and so I offer my thanks to Drs. Scott Card, Vicki Ellis, Ed Foster, and Kittsey Reihard—all well-read—for their thoughtful analysis. They made it a far better book. Linda Gill Thompson, Rae Hamilton, and Wendy Scott are all themselves talented writers and offered valuable insight, along with George Dress, Mary Alice Baumgardner, and Miles and Anna Cole. It was Anna who suggested that the villain in book two should be a deranged female with sharp claws.

Invaluable technical advice was provided by Chief Barry Keller and Officer Mike McGovern of the Washington Township Police Department, ace automotive mechanic, Tom Houpt, Forensic Investigator David Foehner of the Maryland Office of the Chief Medical Examiner, and attorneys Katherine Kravitz of Barley Snyder and Sun Choi of Metropolitan Law Group.

To the extent that *This Way To Paradise* succeeds as a work of fiction, credit in large measure is due to these friends.

D. Bruce Foster
December 2013

PROLOGUE

South Shore of Lake Okeechobee, Florida
August 12th, 1996

S PENT, HE COLLAPSED ONTO HER TINY FRAME, her breath coming in short gasps under his dead weight. She lay staring at the sagging ceiling above her, tracing the water stain lines with her eyes, trying not to think about her breathing.

After what seemed an eternity, he finally raised his head, sending a suffocating stench of tobacco and alcohol to her nostrils. For a long moment he tried to bring her face into focus, then gave up, grunted, and clumsily rolled off her. He stood by the bed swaying unsteadily, staring down at her naked body as if unsure what to do next. Finally he turned and staggered down the trailer's narrow hallway to the bathroom.

She lay motionless except for the heaving of her chest, fearing that any movement might trigger his return. Sweat trickled down the little valley between her breasts in the oppressive Everglades heat.

She knew what was coming next. The urine splashed and the toilet flushed. He hit the wall twice as he stumbled to the kitchen. She heard the vacuum release as he popped the tab on a beer can and the springs creak as he collapsed onto the vinyl sofa.

As she waited for the snoring to begin, she dreamed of his death, as she had for many months. Not just any death, but an agonizing death at her own hand as she looked directly into his eyes. And when his eyes closed and he slipped away to hell, her mother could go with him.

Eventually his snoring rumbled down the hallway. She slipped out of bed, gathered her clothes, and quietly made her way to the moldy bathroom.

The cold water of the shower raised goosebumps on her skin. Hurriedly she scrubbed away every trace of the snoring man, determined to escape the trailer before her mother returned from grocery shopping, her mother's euphemism for completing her drug-running errands. The girl knew that she was the price her mother paid for a place to live and a ready supply of crack cocaine from the scum on the sofa, and she hated her mother for it.

When she was younger she used to dream that her father—whoever he was—would come home and rescue her, but not so much any more. That was little girl thinking.

I'm getting older now. Some day soon I'll make them pay, she promised herself.

She dried her skin, pulled on a halter top and shorts, and slipped out of the trailer into the humid night air. It was the night before Mary Anne Hampton's thirteenth birthday.

CHAPTER ONE

Baltimore County, Maryland
June 6th, 2011

T HEY SAY THAT MANY THINGS ARE LIKE riding a bicycle—once you've learned how to do it you never forget. But I wasn't at all sure it was going to be that easy on my first day back on the job after a little three-month vacation.

Actually it wasn't exactly a vacation, more like a convalescence, necessitated by a minor security event in the ER that resulted in a bunch of broken ribs and removal of my spleen, an organ for which I had considerable affection.

I wasn't really back on the job either, at least not on my old job, because I got fired from that. Well, not exactly... they just didn't renew my contract. *They* refers to John F. Salzman, the esteemed CEO of Americus Health Systems, with whom I did not see eye to eye and who did not consider me to be an asset to his corporation. Americus is a non-profit health system that owns four hospitals in the greater Baltimore region, including Mason-Dixon Medical Center, my little country hospital in the northern part of Baltimore County on Middletown Road.

John was a bit disappointed when I got beat to a pulp in the ER and ended up on his payroll with extended leave and workman's comp long after my official termination date. However, that doesn't really matter now because after the board discovered that John had run up a little personal expense account of over $450,000 for private jets and hospital conferences in exotic places, they concluded that *he* wasn't an asset to the corporation.

So now we have a new CEO who offered me back the position of chair of emergency medicine for the second time. Although I am not often complimentary of administrative types, this, I thought, was a very good decision. I also have to give the board of trustees some credit on this one because they thought outside the box and hired a doc for the position of CEO.

It may seem odd to you that a hospital—where physicians heal the sick—would not normally consider a physician as a candidate to run the place. But, in fact, that would be anathema to most boards of trustees. Trustees and administrators generally believe physicians to be Neanderthals when it comes to the complexities of organizational dynamics. But in this case, the board hired Harvey Mays, MD, a distinguished gastroenterologist and Mason-Dixon's former chief of staff, as CEO, thereby exploding all of my dearly held beliefs that boards of trustees are themselves all Neanderthals.

I pulled my '95 Jeep Wrangler into an empty parking space and walked toward the ambulance entrance. I was excited about being back to work. Convalescing for three months and doing nothing productive had left me a little bit loony, although my girlfriend considers this to be a persistent state.

I flashed my security badge at the reader on the brick wall, but nothing happened—no little green light—and the sliding glass doors didn't open. My badge was apparently still *persona non grata* at Mason-Dixon. So I walked around the building to the public ER entrance and made my way through the lobby. A guard stood at the security station wearing a gun belt and Taser. This was a new one for Mason-Dixon. The light bulb must have gone on after three people died, a nurse took a bullet in the chest, and I got my ribs kicked in.

Eileen Probst was sitting on a stool behind the reception counter. She flashed a wide smile. "Dr. Randolph, you're back!" she said, buzzing me through the secure entrance door to the staff locker rooms.

I changed into blue scrubs, thinking about my grand entrance back into the ER and preparing myself for the cheers and acclamation that would go up upon my appearance at the nursing station.

But there were no cheers when I pushed through the ER door. In fact, the nursing station was deserted. This was not a good sign. It usually meant that all the nurses were tied up someplace, typically working to keep some poor soul from crossing the river Styx.

Rebecca Franklin, RN—our resident marathon runner—careened around the corner of the nursing station counter to the Omnicell medication dispenser and started frantically pushing buttons on the machine.

"I think Lynn could probably use your help in Fifteen, Alex," she said unceremoniously. So much for my rousing welcome-back party.

I walked into Bed Fifteen, our resuscitation room, where barely controlled chaos reigned. Lynn Saylor, MD, a tall, lanky brunette in a ponytail, was bent over the head of a motionless middle-aged man. She held a bright metal laryngoscope in her hand, attempting to put a tube through the man's mouth into his trachea that would allow a ventilator to breathe for him. He had been stripped from the waist up and his skin was mottled with a purplish hue.

The room was crammed with nurses in motion: connecting monitors, pulling off clothes, and attempting to start IVs. My eyes instinctively went to the overhead color monitor screen. The EKG line showed a heart rate only in the thirties, with a very wide waveform—an ominous heart rhythm that frequently precedes death.

"Need some help in here, Lynn?" I asked.

"Hello, lover. Welcome back." Lynn likes me. In clipped, rapid-fire sentences she gave me the rundown. "The medics tell me this guy was having coffee with his wife, developed back pain, and just collapsed. He's got no blood pressure. We don't have an IV yet. Maybe you could get a central line in him."

A central line is a catheter with three different internal lumens, or tubes, that gets threaded into the central veins near the heart. This is the functional equivalent of plugging a garden hose into the circulatory system through which you can pour a ton of fluid, blood, or medicine very fast.

Two nurses, one on each leg, tugged off pinstriped gray slacks and then red silk boxer shorts. The dying man now lay naked on the table, his ample belly spilling over to the sides of the stretcher. He smelled of cologne.

I had two choices here. I could put a central line under his collarbone, or thread one into the femoral vein in his groin. The head of the bed was packed with people working on his airway, so my fingers went to his groin, feeling for a pulse that would give me the location of the femoral artery. The femoral vein—my target—would be just a centimeter to the inside of the artery.

I could feel the faintest of pulses intermittently, but I couldn't be sure whether I was feeling pulses from his femoral artery or the pulse in my own fingers. I would have to make my best guess as to where the vein lay.

Jen Wilke tore open a central line tray from which I picked up a wicked-looking syringe with a four-inch-long steel needle that I would use to find the vein. Jen sloshed his groin with brown betadine antiseptic solution, my fingers felt for a pulse again and I slid the razor-sharp needle edge into the skin at a 45-degree angle.

Lynn called out, "I've got the tube!" The endotracheal tube was in place. Score one for Lynn.

I pulled back on the syringe plunger, but no blood returned into the syringe. I pulled the needle back, redirected it and pushed in again. This time a gush of purplish blood surged into the syringe. *Ah, sweet. I can still do this.* Score one for me.

I quickly unscrewed the syringe, leaving the needle in place, and threaded a long flexible steel guide wire into the vein. Over the guidewire went the central venous catheter, and, *voila*, we were in.

"OK. Hang three liters of saline and run 'em all wide open. And give him a milligram of epi," I said to nobody in particular. We didn't know why this guy was on death's door, but near the top of the list of differential diagnoses was bleeding from somewhere internally, so a first step in trying to resuscitate him would be expanding the volume of fluid in his circulatory system in case bleeding was the problem.

The milligram of epinephrine, better known as adrenaline, would increase the vigor of his heartbeat and perhaps raise his blood pressure.

Now to figure out what in the hell was wrong with him. Maybe he was bleeding from his gastrointestinal tract.

Still wearing gloves, I lifted one of his legs, lubricated my index finger with gel, and slid it into his rectum. I met resistance from a mass of soft stool and removed the finger. No blood on the glove. He wasn't bleeding from his GI tract.

"Heart rate's coming up," called out Rebecca. "He's got a good femoral pulse now."

My hand went to his belly. It was harder than I expected. As I gently probed, the outlines of a large mass gradually became apparent to my fingers. It had a faint pulse that correlated with the heartbeats on the monitor screen.

"He's got a pulsatile mass, Lynn," I said.

"That makes sense," she replied. Sudden onset of back pain, followed by cardiovascular collapse. Almost certainly I was feeling an aortic aneurysm, a weak spot in the wall of his major abdominal artery that was expanding and finally had ruptured, pouring blood out of his circulatory system into the cavity of his belly, and likely spelling the end of his days on earth.

"I need four units of uncross-matched O-pos blood, and two units of fresh frozen plasma," I called out. "And tell the blood bank we want them *now*."

Lynn was already pulling a cart with a large video screen and a zillion dials to the bedside. This was an ultrasound machine, a unit that sends out waves of sound like sonar on a sub, allowing the operator to visualize structures beneath a handheld probe. It's what the obstetricians use to show expectant mommies cute little pictures of their baby sucking its thumb.

Lynn squirted a big blob of gel onto his belly and placed the probe just above his belly button. Slowly she eased the probe back and forth, adjusting some dials until a large tube appeared on the screen: his aorta. But this was not a cute sonogram. Below his belly button the tube expanded into an ugly, ragged bulge about eleven centimeters wide and eight centimeters long.

"Yep, that's it. He's got a triple-A," she said. In ER-speak, a *triple-A* is not the association you call when your car gives up the ghost in the middle of nowhere. It's an *abdominal aortic aneurysm*, a ticking time bomb that one day ruptures, ending this mortal life unless you can keep the victim alive long enough to get them to an OR. Even then, the mortality rate is about fifty percent.

"We're gonna need a surgeon," Lynn barked. "Call the OR and tell them to get ready. What's this guy's name? Any family here?"

"His wife's in the family counseling room," said Jen. "Name's Stern. Franklin Stern."

It was Lynn's case, so I let her keep working on Mr. Stern, while I walked down the hall to the family counseling room to give the bad news to Mrs. Stern. I never know what to expect on these little forays into the depths of the human heart, but they are always unvarnished and free of pretense. I briefly rapped on the door and pushed it open.

Seated on a love seat in the softly lit, warmly appointed room was an attractive blond woman in black running tights and sneakers. An ample amount of cleavage bubbled out from several layers of low-cut pink tops. This young lady did not look to me to be Mr. Stern's wife.

"Hi, I'm Dr. Randolph," I said, reaching for her hand. She shook my hand firmly and said, "I'm Amanda Stern, Dr. Randolph."

"And you are…"

She finished my sentence. "Franklin Stern's wife." *Wow.*

"Mrs. Stern, can you tell me what happened to your husband this morning?"

"Is he alive?" she asked quietly.

"Yes, he's still alive. But it would help us if you could tell me what you saw this morning." She gathered herself for a moment, took a deep breath, and then began to speak.

"Well, he was fine, just fine. He and I were having coffee before he went to work, and I was getting ready to go for a run. He was fixing another cup of coffee when he said his back was killing him. And then he sat down and turned white, and he started sweating, and a minute later he put his head down on the table. I said 'Frank, are you all right?' And he didn't answer me. So that's when I said to myself, 'I have to call 911.' I couldn't get him awake after that."

She paused and looked at me again. "What's wrong with him?"

8

"Well, Mrs. Stern, we've figured out what happened to your husband. He has an abdominal aneurysm that is leaking. Have you ever heard of that term?"

She looked off into the distance for a long moment, lost in thought, and then returned to my eyes. "Yes. His brother died of that," she said matter-of-factly.

I stood and put my hand on her shoulder. "Mrs. Stern, we're going to do everything we can to save your husband. We've figured out what's wrong, we've got blood running, and we've put a tube into his lungs to allow us to breathe for him. We're going to get him to the operating room as fast as possible. But it's going to be touch and go. He's very deep in shock. I'm not sure that we will be successful in saving him, but we're going to try like hell."

Time stands still for no man. Twenty minutes later Mr. Stern was fighting for his life in a third floor operating room, and I was trying to enter my first set of orders in three months into the computer. I clicked on the line displaying the name *Kohl, Alberta*.

Mrs. Kohl was a sweet, silver-haired lady whose dog on a leash had run circles around her until she was tied up like a mummy. Alberta said she teetered for a moment, and then toppled over like Saddam Hussein's statue. This was not good for her left hip and shoulder, which I thought were almost certainly fractured.

Entering Alberta's orders into the computer was my second challenge of the day in trying to get back on the bike. My fingers were slow and I couldn't remember where certain sets of orders could be found in the labyrinth of algorithms.

Little Lisa Turano, RN, mother of three, wife of homicide detective Frank Turano, and Mrs. Kohl's nurse today, stood at my shoulder with her arms folded and watched as I struggled to find the button to click for simply ordering an IV.

"A little slow today, aren't we?" she asked. She reached down and took control of my mouse. In three quick clicks she was at the IV button. "Is that what you were looking for?" Lisa is very nurturing.

"I knew that," I said.

In about a minute—an eternity in computer time—I had figured it out again. Little red icons for lab and x-ray popped up behind Alberta's name on the giant patient tracker screen hanging over the nursing station.

"Are you going to put in some pain meds, too?" she asked impatiently. ER nurses, in general, are very unassertive.

"Sure, I was going to do that."

I navigated to the medications section and found the button for Dilaudid, 0.5 mg IV. A moment later, a red *MED* icon flashed onto the screen.

"There you go," I said triumphantly, "...piece of cake." I leaned back in the chair, folded my arms and sighed. Although wobbly, the bike was upright, and the wheels were turning. It felt good.

It was late morning before I finally had a chance to pick up the phone and call the OR to see how Mr. Stern was doing. Something was nagging me about that name. It sounded familiar to me.

I got through to the circulating nurse in the OR and she gave me a brief rundown on the progress of the surgery. "Well, he's still alive," she said. "We've been through twelve pints of blood and they still have an hour or so to go, but it looks like the bleeding is finally under control." *Looks like Mr. Stern's number was not up today.*

And then it dawned on me. *No. It can't be.*

I jumped on the Internet and typed in a couple of search words. Google had the answer in an instant. I clicked on the first entry and a website popped up with a photo of a stern-looking Mr. Stern in better days. The header said "Stern, Healy, Watson & Craig—Protecting Your Loved Ones Since 1975."

I leaned back and stared at the screen. Franklin Stern. He and I actually had a little date coming up—in a courtroom—where Mr. Stern would attempt to convince a jury of my incompetence and gross negligence in the case of *Robert S. Kline vs. Alexander B. Randolph, MD.*

CHAPTER TWO

South Shore of Lake Okeechobee, Florida
August 29th, 1998

P EERING THROUGH THE VENETIAN BLINDS OF the back bedroom, the girl watched as her mother's taillights receded out the gravel lane to the highway. Thursday nights no longer made her stomach churn. After two years she knew how to do this. Hours of porn videos had been instructive. Gradually she had learned that if she took the initiative, she could turn these evenings to her advantage.

Quietly she peeled out of her clothes and from a drawer selected a pair of white bikini panties and an old, oversized white tank top. She pulled them on and turned to assess her appearance in the full-length mirror, tugging at the loose top here and there until it fell exactly right on her breasts.

Her auburn hair shined, perfectly framing an elegant face with a wide mouth and deep-set eyes. Over her shoulder she could see the bikini disappear into the crevice between flawless buttocks set atop long, slender legs. From the side she saw a flat belly and a generous glimpse of softly rounded breast. Nipples protruded proudly through the frayed tank top. Even at barely fifteen, Mary Anne Hampton knew that she was a striking beauty who was desired by men.

Satisfied, she ran her fingers through her hair, turned, and walked down the narrow hallway to the kitchen to complete her task.

As she passed the man slumped on the couch watching TV, his eyes widened and followed the girl's gently swaying buttocks. She opened the refrigerator door, popped a can of Budweiser and curled up in his lap, holding the can to his lips. Even in his fog, the man could smell the sweetness of her youth. She smiled as he ran his hands over her smooth legs, as if in a trance. Watching his eyes, she parted her knees slightly, allowing him to stare intently at the puffy crotch of her panties.

"Do you like what you see?" she asked sweetly. She traced the outline of his stubble-covered jaw with her finger. "I could buy more of these for you if I had a little cash."

His liquor-laden breath hit her full in the face as he stared dumbly at her for a moment, and then began to fumble for his wallet. She grasped the fifty-dollar bill between thumb and forefinger, dramatically lifted her hand high, and then, with a smile, let the money flutter to the floor. Steeling herself against the taste, she placed her mouth fully over his and thrust her tongue between his teeth. It was more than the man could bear.

With both hands he shoved the tank top high and hungrily sucked on her right breast. She grimaced and gently stroked his head as he bit into her nipple, sending intense waves of pain coursing to her brain. When she could no longer stand the pain, she pushed his head away and holding his face with both hands said, "I need you inside me now."

Dragging him down the narrow hallway by the hand, she kneeled on the bed, raising her buttocks high and allowing him to rip her panties down her thighs. This was her favored position. Here she could neither see him nor smell him.

He fumbled, unable to find her opening, so she reached between her legs and guided him to avoid the bruising thrusts. As he wildly pumped, she willed herself to relax and imagined, as she had before, that the boy on the other side of the trailer park was thrusting into her. As her daydream evolved, she felt her body begin to respond, and she allowed the sensations to wash over her.

She lay collapsed on the bed with her panties around her ankles for nearly twenty-five minutes, until she was certain that he was asleep on the sofa in the kitchen. Quietly she showered and then dressed.

As she tiptoed down the hallway under cover of the clattering air conditioner, she smelled smoke. He lay sprawled over the far metal arm of the sofa in his underwear, snoring deeply, one arm falling to the floor. On the Formica-covered table before him lay an empty plastic bag and a straw. He had snorted a line of cocaine.

She slowly walked around the sofa, searching for the source of the smoke. Beneath his dangling fingertips, a cigarette lay smoldering on the carpet.

The idea came to her in a flash. Returning to her bedroom, she quietly pulled a change of clothes from a drawer, and quickly stuffed them into a plastic bag along with an embroidered cheerleading patch she ripped from her bulletin board. She took one last look around the room, grabbed a ragged cloth doll from her bed, and tiptoed back to the kitchen.

Above the sink hung a roll of paper towels. She quietly tore off two sheets, walked toward the sofa, and then hesitated. What if he wakes up? He would kill her.

Grabbing a dirty glass from the counter, she filled it with water, and biting her lower lip, slowly tiptoed back to the sofa. If he awoke, she could tell him she was putting out the burning carpet.

She rolled up the two sections of paper towel into tubes and then laid them end-to-end from the cigarette leading to the floor-length drapes hanging from the window behind the sofa. With several soft puffs of her breath, the end of the paper towel next to the cigarette burst into a small blue flame and slowly grew until it turned yellow.

Mesmerized, she slowly backed toward the door until the first small flame flickered on the drape. She gave a soft gasp when she realized the fifty-dollar bill was still laying on the floor. She quickly retrieved the bill, stuffed it into her shorts and backed out through the door.

As she walked briskly away from the trailer, heart pounding and skin glistening with sweat, Mary Anne felt alive as she never had before.

Now she needed an alibi. She would go to her girlfriend's trailer who would testify that they were together for hours listening to music. Excitement surged through her young body.

But a hundred yards from the trailer, Mary Anne could not help herself. She had to watch him die. She slipped into the thick Everglades foliage adjacent to the lane and peered back toward the trailer.

A yellow glow slowly illuminated the trailer windows. Shortly thereafter she heard shouts from adjacent trailers. A crowd gathered and people started running around looking for a way into the trailer.

A man tried to open the trailer door, but yanked his hand back with a howl from the blistering heat of the doorknob. Mary Anne smiled. The faint sounds of the first sirens reached her ears and she thought they were like music.

When flames finally erupted through the roof, Mary Anne gave a satisfied sigh. She left her spot in the Everglades and walked toward her girlfriend's trailer.

That was easy, she thought.

CHAPTER THREE

LIFE WAS SLOWLY RETURNING TO SOME DEGREE of normalcy, although after my first week of three ten-hour shifts I had less energy left than I had expected. My fellow docs were kind to me. They let me work three weekday shifts and then have my first weekend off. This left me a little uneasy because payback was lurking somewhere in my future and it would undoubtedly be hell.

So, on an early-June Saturday morning, warm sun streaming in my face, I stood in my bare feet on the patio, sipping a cup of coffee, and surveyed the property. I'm a bit compulsive about some things, and given the fact that I grew up working in my father's landscaping business, one of them is having the property look fairly neat and tidy. But I had fallen way behind Mother Nature this spring, and she was reclaiming much of the farm.

Not that the farm is huge—it's thirty-five acres—but it takes most of my free time to maintain it, and the rest of my time paying for it. It's on Shepherd Road in Monkton, part of *My Lady's Manor,* as it's known, a gentrified ten-thousand-acre district of horse farms in northeastern Baltimore County, where there's no such thing as cheap. The weeds growing up around the barn and in the mulch beds were like sawdust in my eye. I couldn't wait to get rid of them.

The pasture which lay beneath the knoll of this brick house—built by a mill owner in 1823—was in pretty good shape. My neighbor Sally

Horn's two thoroughbreds who board here kept the grass down. The lushest grass was just outside the black-board-fence perimeter. The horses were very adept at turning their heads to the side and nibbling about six inches beyond the lowest board on the fence, thus eliminating the need for me to weed-whack along the fence. Very efficient.

Bittercress and chicory were beginning to arise around the edges of the little stream that meandered through the pasture, but cutting them down was low on my priority list. Most of all, right now, the grass needed cutting.

My dad had sent his crews over to mow in April and May, but once a week is not enough at this time of year and in the last several days tall clumps of emerald green blades were again rising everywhere that Maggie had peed over the winter and spring. Maggie is an affectionate golden retriever who is rather indiscriminate about where she squats, although, thankfully, that no longer includes the kitchen floor.

Since riding a John Deere lawnmower didn't require much in the way of calorie expenditure, I decided that the lawn would be my first task.

"You're not thinking about doing a lot of work, are you?" a high-pitched, raspy voice called out through the French doors behind me. "You know you're not supposed to do any work for another two weeks."

That would be Ruth, my seventy-something surrogate mother-in-residence, who started out as a once-a-week housekeeper, but who rapidly expanded her role when it became clear to her that I was in desperate need of supervision.

"I'm just going to mow the lawn. Nothing to it. Like riding on an armchair," I yelled back.

When I was discharged from the hospital, Ruth—a widow—decided that I needed constant attendance. This is a big old house with plenty of room, so she basically just moved in full-time to make sure that I was obeying doctor's orders and getting adequate nutrition. She has a knack for reading my mind.

"By the way, I won't be home for dinner tonight," I added.

"Are you seeing Penny?" she asked brightly. Ruth is constantly taking the temperature of my relationship with Penny Murray, a

Mason-Dixon ER nurse, and one of the few elements in my life of which she heartily approves. She keeps reminding me that this house needs children.

That may have something to do with the fact that Ruth had only one pregnancy as a young woman. Her beautiful little girl, Lily, whose photos I have seen, came down with acute leukemia in the days when effective chemotherapy was but a distant dream. She was three years old and only lasted a week after her diagnosis. With the exception of a sister on the West Coast, my girlfriend and I are Ruth's only family.

It was dark and the parking lot was packed by the time Penny and I reached our favorite little pizza/Mexican place in Timonium, where the beer is cold, the cheese is generous, and you can lose yourself in the crowd—a distinct advantage these days. I drove around to the back, followed by two other cars on the hunt for a coveted space, found a single empty parking spot near a big dumpster, and whipped in.

As we climbed out of the Jeep, a series of blinding flashes erupted from the blackness on the passenger side of the Wrangler and I heard Penny gasp in surprise. I knew the source instantly. Hurrying around the Jeep, I grabbed Penny and pushed her ahead toward the rear entrance, trying to keep myself between her and the cameras. The paparazzi had followed us.

"I hate this!" she said furiously, fists clenched, when we finally reached the safety of a back hallway.

We sat in the dark room on tall stools at a small table for two with a single candle. The soft light glinted off wisps of silky blond hair pulled back in a ponytail that poked through the back of a baseball cap. Gold hoop earrings flashed with each little movement of her head, framing a square face with a straight nose and generous mouth. Luminescent green eyes glittered back at me. The girl melts me every time I look at her.

"I don't know, Alex," Penny said glumly, chin in hand, "I just *hate* this. Why can't we have a normal life? I go through a line at the supermarket and there's my face, right at the checkout counter on some damned celebrity magazine. So I have to go into this long conversation with the clerk, and the people in line behind me. And they're checking out my makeup and what I'm wearing, and whether or not I have dark circles under my eyes.

"And at the hospital, people come into the ER knowing that I work there and they *look* for me. Maybe if I were at another hospital and they didn't know I worked there, I could fade into the background."

It was bad enough that Penny Murray had taken a bullet in the chest in the same ER hostage situation that left three people dead and landed me on medical leave for three months. But the bigger curse for Penny was her unanticipated celebrity status.

While a breathless national TV audience watched SWAT teams assemble and a hostage deadline approach, Penny herself had taken out the perp with her own resourcefulness and intelligence, in the process saving the lives of at least two other people, yours truly included. But that's another story. Suffice it to say that before it was over, a 9 millimeter slug had ripped through her chest, just skirting her left ventricle and nearly ending her life.

This act of selfless courage by a single mother of two had made Penny an instant public heroine who was utterly irresistible to the media. Well, that and the fact that she is drop-dead gorgeous.

Overnight, Penny's face had made the cover of virtually every tabloid in the western world. The paparazzi circled like sharks, and her voice mail was clogged with media requests. I didn't make the covers, but there were plenty of inside shots of me. Then they figured out that doctor and nurse were an item, and that really set them off, with a new twist every week on our relationship.

Worst of all for Penny were shots of her and her kids, which made her homicidal. They'd even dug up photos of Penny's dead husband, Lieutenant Patrick Murray, a SEAL team leader killed in a firefight in Afghanistan. The perfect story, right?

Perhaps normally the coverage would have faded in a couple of weeks, but Penny had steadfastly refused big-buck interview offers from

Good Morning America, People, and every other media outlet under the sun, so she remained a mysterious and fascinating enigma to the ravenous press.

I got my turn when an email from an anonymous hospital insider tipped them off that I'd been fired by a callous health care corporation—*Corporate 'Suits' Fire Hero Doctor,* screamed the headline. And then they figured out that Penny's father was Navy brass—a fighter pilot, now an admiral and superintendent of the Naval Academy—which added the nice twist of a brave and powerful military family. So the coverage dragged on forever.

In addition to recovering from our injuries, we were both doing our best to cope with this newfound celebrity status, but it was much worse for Penny than for me. Actually, I found hot girls coming on to me in the grocery store to be only a minor annoyance.

Nevertheless, now Penny was telling me that she wanted to leave the Mason-Dixon ER. At least that's what I thought she was telling me.

After a moment's reflection, I said, "Maybe you could get your old job back in the ER at Sinai."

Her body sprang bolt upright. "What?" she said. "You don't want to work with me anymore?"

"Well, of course I want to work with you. It's just—"

"What? That your life would be less complicated if I weren't around?"

Uh-oh. I should have anticipated the direction of this conversation. I'm a slow learner about some things. With women I tend to get empathy and problem solving confused.

I decided the best defense was a good offense. "Listen, Penny, what do you want me to say? I *love* you. I *want* to be with you, I was just trying to show you that whatever you need to do, I will support you. Relax a little bit." I sat back, took another sip of Corona, and stared into her eyes.

Her adorable face slowly softened and then her body slumped. She reached across the table and took my hand in both of hers.

"I'm sorry, Alex. I'm just so stressed out about this. That was uncalled for. I want to be left alone with just you and me and the kids."

19

"Give it a little more time, baby. Look, it's happening less and less often. That's the first time in what…three weeks? Our fifteen minutes of fame is almost over. They'll forget about us soon enough."

CHAPTER FOUR

Palm Beach County, Florida
Late August & September 1998

TOM BRADLEY SLIPPED UNDER THE ORANGE tape surrounding the fire scene and walked toward the burned-out trailer carcass. The door was jammed from the distortion of metal subjected to intense heat. He grabbed the knob with both hands and pulled mightily, wincing and cursing at the pain in his shoulder when it finally broke free.

Bradley had sifted through the rubble of more fatal trailer fires than he cared to remember in his career as an investigator for the Palm Beach County Bomb/Fire/Arson Unit. Nevertheless, each silent hulk had its own secrets to pry loose and its own fascinating story to tell. In truth, despite its morbid aspects, he loved his job.

He took two steps into the dank, acrid interior and stopped to allow his eyes to adjust to the light. The first room was obviously the kitchen/living area. It was clearly the site of heavy heat and smoke damage. To the right were the charred remains of a kitchen counter and sink. A small stove and refrigerator lay dead ahead. On the far wall to the left, under a window, was a vinyl sofa with metal arms.

Much of the vinyl had melted, but there was an area of preserved upholstery on the right side that corresponded, no doubt, to the location of the body that was found in the trailer. Two oblong areas of relatively clean carpet that lay below the sofa front were almost certainly the location of the dead man's feet. A small laminate-covered table on a steel pedestal sat in front of the sofa. Against the opposite wall sat a large TV, the upper plastic case of which was wavy and sagging from heat.

Bradley turned left, punched on his flashlight, and walked down a hallway. The further he traveled, the less heat and smoke damage was visible. The bath had soot deposits, but no evidence of heat damage.

Next came a tiny bedroom that was obviously the den of a teenage girl. Young male celebrity posters covered the walls. A bulletin board was plastered with mementos. Cosmetics were strewn across a tiny, scarred bureau. Clothes littered the floor.

The last room was a master bedroom, such as they are in trailers. A queen-sized bed occupied most of the room which left little space for furniture. A full-length mirror was mounted on the back wall. A TV occupied the wall facing the bed. On the narrow bureau below sat a video cassette player and stacks of porn videotapes.

Bradley returned to the kitchen/living area which was the obvious starting point of the fire. He stared again at the sofa and immediate surroundings. Fragments of a floor length window drape were still present on the left side of the sofa, but the drape behind the victim had been completely consumed. He looked to the ceiling and saw evidence of flame spread from an epicenter just above the consumed righthand drape. The fire must have started below that drape.

He dropped to one knee and checked the wall for an electrical outlet, but there was none. His eyes continued down to the carpet, relatively intact except for water and soot damage because heat and smoke rise. Below the arm of the sofa was a singed area of carpet with a nearby yellow fragment of what appeared to be the remains of a cigarette filter.

Bradley snapped a photo, dropped the fragment into a plastic bag and scratched his head. The victim had clearly been smoking, but, although singed, the carpet had obviously not burst into flame. And then he saw it: a perfectly straight line of singed carpet leading to where the bottom of the drape had lain—a highly unnatural occurrence.

District 13 Detective Sam Worley of the Palm Beach County Sherriff's Office sat with his arms folded and stared at the girl seated across from his desk. He knew Felix Alvarez, and could not believe that the tears slowly trickling down this beautiful little bitch's face were real. Something was wrong here. She should be thrilled that the bastard was dead.

"I know he drank too much. But he was good to me and he was the only father I ever had," she whimpered.

Worley had read the fire, police, and arson reports a half-dozen times, searching for clues. The line of singed carpet was the only big question mark, but analysis had revealed no evidence of a chemical accelerant leading to the drape.

The coroner's report documented that the victim had still been alive at the time of the fire—the cause of death was smoke inhalation. Likely the victim had either been drunk, or under the influence of drugs, or both, because he made no move to escape the trailer. But the toxicology reports would not be back for another week.

The girl's friend had stuck to her story that they were listening to music together at the time of the fire. But there were inconsistencies in the details. Her friend's parents had not been home, and there were no other witnesses to testify as to the Hampton girl's whereabouts at the time of the incident.

The girl's mother also had an alibi, but unfortunately for her, it led to a drug investigation that landed both the mother and five other people in jail—a nice little fringe benefit to society.

But it was also a terrible waste. He remembered the girl's mother from Belle Glade High School where she was two years ahead of him. She was a pretty girl, a senior cheerleader who had descended into drugs or whatever, and never graduated.

Worley's guts were telling him that this was not an accidental death. It had the smell of a homicide case. This girl knew something that she was not telling, but he had no clue who might be the murderer, and not a shred of evidence to hold Mary Anne Hampton.

When he finally stood, the girl pushed back her own chair, reached out her hand and shook his firmly. "Thanks, Detective. You were very nice. I feel better now, just talking about it," she said.

Ellen Smith's heart went out to the girl seated on the sofa beside her in the Youth Services interview room. *What a pity,* she thought. Rarely had she seen a more beautiful child in all her years in Youth Services.

Well, perhaps she didn't look like a child, but she was barely fifteen, with a disarming innocence. None of the attitude she saw in so many of her teenage clients. In fact, Ellen would almost label her personality as charming. How she turned out like this, against all odds, with a drug-dealing mother and boyfriend, was one of those occasional miracles of life.

And she was smart, too, although you wouldn't know it from her grades. The file said she tended toward Cs and Ds. But she was remarkably thoughtful and well-spoken. Ellen could see the flash of intelligence in those deep-set hazel eyes when Mary Anne pondered her response to questions. In the right environment this girl could be anything she wanted to be. Thank God she wasn't in that trailer at the time of the fire.

Ellen was determined to have Mary Anne Hampton placed in a good foster home, where she could grow and thrive and reach her full potential. And she had just the right family in mind.

CHAPTER FIVE

SCOTT FOREMAN HAD CLEANED OUT ALL THE night cases and had no patients to sign out to me when I walked into the ER about 4:45 Monday morning.

We used to work twelve-hour shifts that switched at 7 AM and 7 PM, but now, after being open for almost three years, the volume of patients at our little hospital had increased so dramatically that working twelve straight hours was just too much. The staff voted to go to ten-hour shifts, one of which ran from 5:00 AM to 3:00 PM.

Getting up at 4:00 AM wasn't as bad as I thought it would be, although in the spring and summer it requires going to bed before the sun goes down. Fortunately for me, I can fall asleep standing on my feet, so climbing into bed at sunset isn't a problem. For the doc getting off at 5:00 AM, the beauty is that the sun has not yet risen. You can drive home in the dark and fool your body into thinking that you actually went to bed the same night instead of the next morning.

One of the joys of being back on the Mason-Dixon payroll was that I started getting hospital emails again—thirty or forty of them a day—most of which had little or nothing to do with me.

To make matters worse, while I was fired/on medical leave, Americus had moved to a new secure email system which meant that when emails showed up in my gmail at home, I had to log into the hospital secure system in order to open them—a huge pain. Just dealing with the volume of email was taking nearly an hour of my day.

I took advantage of this little early morning lull, poured a second cup of coffee, and started wading into today's epistles. A secure email from the hospital attorney caught my eye:

Dr. Randolph:

Opposing counsel has asked for another delay in trial date in the Robert Kline case. As you know, after your medical leave we were rescheduled for June 23rd, but apparently opposing counsel now has their own medical reasons for wanting a delay until August 30th. So looks like your summer is now clear until the end of August!

Regards,

Kathleen Stefanik, Esq

Opposing counsel, having used up eight of his nine lives, was currently lying upstairs in a surgical ICU bed. Fortunately for him, *defendant* in the case was having a good day, unmarred by incompetence or negligence, when *opposing counsel* arrived in the ER. Life is full of little ironies.

"Dr. Randolph, I've *got* to make it to thirty weeks," she said softly, eyes pleading.

Beads of sweat glistened off Kaitlyn Shank's forehead. Her brown hair was pulled back off her gaunt face in a ponytail. Tiny little silver angels blowing a horn dangled from her ears.

She lay with blankets pulled to her chin, but despite the covers I could still see that her breathing was rapid and her skin was as pale as ivory. The triage nurse's summary sheet had said "fever and shortness of breath in a pregnant 23-year-old female with stage IV lymphoblastic lymphoma."

"Kaitlyn, it says here that you have a lymphoma. Is that correct?" She nodded almost imperceptibly. "And you've elected not to have treatment?"

"Not until after the baby is born. It would kill her."

"How many weeks are you now, Kaitlyn?"

"Twenty-eight. It's too early, Dr. Randolph." I looked over at Kaitlyn's young husband who sat silently in a corner chair biting his lower lip. I had the distinct impression that he had run out of things to say. Lisa Turano stood in the opposite corner, listening and taking notes.

The earliest age of viability for a fetus is roughly twenty-six weeks, but it's always a close call. At that age you can see through their skin and they have immature lungs that often fail. Even at thirty weeks, it's a long, tough haul in a *NICU* or neonatal intensive care unit for many weeks.

"OK. Tell me what's been happening in the last couple of days."

"Well, this morning I started running a fever—it was 102 at 5:00 AM. And I'm just so exhausted. I get short of breath just walking to the bathroom."

I pulled down one of Kaitlyn's lower eyelids. It looked bloodless. No doubt this malignancy of lymphocytes that was killing Kaitlyn had already suppressed her bone marrow to the extent that she was now severely anemic—no longer making red blood cells—accounting for at least part of her exhaustion, and probably most of her shortness of breath.

But the cancer was also, no doubt, suppressing Kaitlyn's white blood cells, rendering her susceptible to infection. And now she had a fever of 104. Kaitlyn was immunosuppressed. Any infection could kill her within hours.

"Any other signs of infection like cough, sore throat, abdominal pain? Does it burn when you pee?

"No."

"OK. Let's take a look at you."

I pulled the covers down over Kaitlyn's skinny body. A perfectly symmetrical, basketball-sized sphere protruded under the gown from

27

her lower belly. She shivered violently as the cool room air hit her skin. What was happening deep in her bone marrow was immediately obvious. Ugly purple bruises covered her extremities, and a myriad of tiny red dots stippled the skin of her pale legs.

Both were caused by bleeding under the skin that came from Kaitlyn not having enough platelets circulating in her blood. Platelets are little sticky cell fragments that act to plug up all the little microscopic holes in our blood vessels that arise from the micro-trauma of normal daily activity. Like red blood cells, they are manufactured in the bone marrow. Without them we bleed and die.

"Any vaginal bleeding, Kaitlyn?" I asked. She shook her head "no."

"Any blood in your stools or your urine?

"I had some blood on the tissue paper after a bowel movement yesterday," she said.

I found several large lumps under her jaw that were no doubt tumor-filled lymph nodes. Kaitlyn's lungs were clear, but her heart was pounding away at about 126 beats a minute, desperately trying to pump around enough red blood cells to meet her needs and her baby's. I could find no clear source of infection. Lisa helped me roll Kaitlyn onto her side and I did a rectal exam. Her stool was positive for blood.

Kaitlyn was walking a terrifying tightrope. To save her unborn child, she had given up her opportunity for early treatment and a fifty percent chance of being cured from the lymphoma. I wasn't at all certain that Kaitlyn—or her baby—could hold on for another two weeks until the scheduled C-section.

Lisa Turano and I walked back to the nursing station together without conversation. What do you say in the presence of a person who is consciously giving up their own life for another? Lisa finally broke the silence. "Do you think she'll make it, Alex?" she asked quietly.

"The baby, maybe. Kaitlyn, I think not."

I entered all the diagnostic orders for Kaitlyn, including two sets of blood cultures to try and track down the source of the infection that was causing her fever. I needed to start antibiotics pronto or she could be overwhelmed by happily-growing bacteria in a matter of hours. I placed the cursor over *Cefipime 1 gram IV* and clicked.

I was also sure that she would need blood transfusions and platelet infusions, but for those I would wait until the lab work had confirmed my clinical impressions.

By 9:00, the morning was picking up steam. The giant patient tracker screen above the nursing station was filling up. I pulled a miscast fish hook out of a guy's ear, which no doubt had all the fish laughing, and hustled back to the nursing station to do the paperwork. Ben Russell, today's second doc and a longtime friend from our days together at Hopkins, arrived and lowered himself into the chair at the computer beside me.

Ben is a charming and handsome black guy with a deep rumbling voice and a way with women—multiple women, to be redundant. This is a talent which, under normal circumstances, I would not have held against him except that in this instance he was taking out my sister, Anne. I harbor this very Victorian notion that I need to look out for her. I have warned Ben that Anne's brother is a very violent man with poor judgment and a short fuse.

Right off the bat he said, "Your sister and I had dinner together last night." This was a direct effort to provoke me. I ignored him.

"Not only is she a lovely woman, but she is also very good for my material well-being. My T. Rowe Price account is up six percent," he continued with a wide smile. I glared at him.

In truth, I was not sure who was taking advantage of whom in this relationship. Anne is an investment manager with T. Rowe Price. By their third date, she had Ben signed up for an account. She was now enjoying a steady stream of investment sales corresponding with Ben's biweekly paychecks.

"You know what?" I said. "I think you two deserve each other. I am washing my hands of the both of you."

"Lab work's all back on Eight, Dr. Randolph," called out Stacey Dorsey. Stacey, one of the blessings in our department, is a compulsive ward clerk who stays one step ahead of me and helps keep my mind from wandering.

I clicked on Kaitlyn Shank's name and then clicked on *LAB*. I was anxious to see how bad things looked.

It took only a second to see the answer: *terrible*. Kaitlyn's hemoglobin was only six point one grams. and her hematocrit only eighteen percent—about half of the red blood cells she needed. This first problem, however, was a relatively easy fix. A couple of blood transfusions would hold her for a few weeks.

Her white blood cell count, on the other hand, was actually pretty normal at eleven thousand. This was of no consolation, however. The cells were virtually all cancerous lymphocytes—useless in helping her to fight infection. We could only hope that her infection could be controlled with antibiotics alone. Kaitlyn's immune system would be of no help.

The bigger problem was her platelet count: only eight thousand per microliter of blood, when it should have been two hundred thousand or more. Kaitlyn could literally bleed to death at any moment. If she had a C-section at this platelet count, the bleeding would be uncontrollable. She would not survive the surgery.

Low platelets would be a continuing problem that was a much tougher issue than her anemia. We could give her massive transfusions of platelet concentrate, but there was only one little hitch. The life of transfused platelets is only three or four days. Platelets are not easy to come by. Massive platelet transfusions every three or four days would stress the supply of most of the blood banks in the region.

But that would be a problem for her oncologist. Here in the ER, I would at least get her started. I entered an order for three units of blood and six units of platelets.

Now I needed to figure out who was taking care of her and where she going to be transferred. Kaitlyn was as high a risk pregnancy as they come. We didn't have a NICU at little Mason-Dixon and we didn't do inpatient oncology. It was time to have a talk with Kaitlyn. I walked back to her room and sat on the bottom of the bed, one hand resting on her blanket-covered legs, trying to establish an emotional connection.

"Kaitlyn, we have all the blood work back now," I began. "We have three problems. First, you have a fever and probably an infection of your bloodstream. You need treatment with antibiotics for that. Second, you are very anemic and will need blood transfusions. Third your platelet count is very low and you are at a severe risk for bleeding. You will need treatment for that, too, with platelet transfusions.

"So, the bottom line is that you now need to be hospitalized, and you may need to stay there until your C-section. We'll need to transfer you, of course. Who is taking care of you for oncology and obstetrics?"

"Dr. Rothman is my oncologist and Dr. Hirsch is my OB. They're both at Hopkins. But I'm not going to go there," she said calmly.

This took me by surprise. I thought about that for a second. "You're not going to go there?"

"I'm not going to go until I'm thirty weeks. They won't listen to me down there. They keep pressuring me to have the chemo now. You can admit me to this hospital until I'm thirty weeks and then transfer me, but I'm not going now."

Wow. I had no doubt that Kaitlyn was telling the truth. In medicine, we're taught that mother comes first and baby follows—sort of a bird in the hand is worth two-in-the-bush philosophy. But this was a far more complex ethical issue. And Kaitlyn Shank vehemently disagreed with our wisdom, perhaps to her dying breath.

Stacey got the Hopkins oncologist on the line. I didn't know him from my faculty days at Hopkins. The ER at Hopkins had very little interface with oncology, and Hopkins is a very big place.

"Yeah, I know Kaitlyn," said Adam Rothman, "a remarkable girl. Look, tell her that I give her my personal word that we will respect her wishes, and I'll make sure that the residents stay off her case, too. I may give her options if she starts to go down the tubes, but there will be no pressure.

"The plan was to start her on chemo within twenty-four hours of the C-section, but I don't know if she's going to make it two more weeks. I think I'll just keep her in the hospital from now on—keep her at bedrest to minimize the risks of bleeding. And if we have to, we'll just keep transfusing her with platelets until the C-section."

I breathed a little emotional sigh of relief. Kaitlyn needed to be in a university tertiary care center if she had any chance at all of holding onto life. Maybe Rothman's promise would do the trick.

"OK, Adam. I've started her on single therapy with cefipime for the fever. We got all the cultures, and I've got blood and platelets cooking."

"That'll work."

"Let me speak to her," I said. "I'll see if I can talk her into it, and I'll get back to you.

"OK, Alex. Good luck."

Kaitlyn knew exactly what she was doing. I decided that the only way I could talk her into transfer was to convince her that it was in the best interests of her baby. And that would mean talking to Kaitlyn about her own death. I pulled a folding chair as close to the head of her bed as I could get, sat down, and leaned forward on my elbows.

"Kaitlyn," I said, "We need to discuss this transfer issue. But first of all let me tell you that I think you're the bravest person I've ever met. I am awed by your sacrifice. I don't know if I could do it.

"I think you know that you are on the verge of death. It could happen within hours or at any time in this next two weeks." I paused and let this sink in. The key point was coming. Kaitlyn lay silently, staring intently into my eyes.

"But if that happens, we have to make sure that your sacrifice is not in vain. If it was clear that you were dying, we need to make sure that we could take your baby by C-section immediately and that she would be in a place where she would have the best chance of survival at her young age. That means a university hospital."

I could see Kaitlyn's brain processing this information inside her cancer-wracked body. Her face showed no emotion. I have found this to be characteristic of people who are very close to death. Their answers to questions are short and direct. They've shed all the tears there are to shed, they've negotiated with the Almighty to a standstill, and they are very tired. It was clear that only one thing motivated Kaitlyn to continue clinging to life.

"I have talked with Dr. Rothman, and he asked me to tell you that he gives you his personal word that they will do everything possible to get you to thirty weeks and that they will not pressure you to deliver earlier. I believe him. What do you think?"

Kaitlyn considered this for a long time, her eyes never leaving mine and her breath coming in rapid, short bursts. Finally, she spoke.

"OK. I'll do it," she said simply.

CHAPTER SIX

Loxahatchee, Florida
September, 1998

D O YOU REMEMBER THE CHAOS WE HAD LAST time?" he asked his wife. "Do you remember how peaceful it was in this house when he left?"

"Yes, but he was a boy, and he had terrible psychiatric issues," she argued. "This is a girl, and Mrs. Smith says that she's a beautiful child with no attitude. Look, we've been trying to have another baby for ten years, and it's just not going to happen. I still think it's important for Charlie to have a sibling. She's fifteen. It wouldn't be for that long."

George Bryant didn't reply. He lay with one hand behind his head staring into the darkness. Amy lay in bed beside him, one arm draped over his chest. He knew how strongly she felt about this, but he had no desire to live through another year of disruption to his home.

"You had brothers and sisters," Amy continued. "You had to learn to share and compromise and adapt. Charlie needs to learn those things too."

Right now, life was pretty good, thought George. Real estate was booming in Palm Beach County. After ten years of blood and sweat and tears, his plumbing business was thriving. He had a little more free time now. Charlie was turning out to be a pretty good baseball player and George was having fun as an assistant coach. The thought of a strange kid from a screwed up home messing up his life right now was not one that he relished.

But that last thought stirred up a recurring pang of guilt. "To whom much has been given, much will be required," said Reverend Thomas of the First Baptist Church of Loxahatchee last Sunday.

"Besides, George, we've been so blessed," said Amy. "It's important that we give something back."

This damned woman can read my mind.

George sighed. Amy knew his vulnerability to this line of attack. This was obviously really important to her, or she wouldn't be pushing this button. He loved his wife. She had helped him grow into the man he was today. Maybe she was right. Maybe Charlie needed to learn that he wasn't the center of the solar system. Maybe they had an obligation to those less fortunate in this world. Maybe this girl would turn out to be a real member of the family.

Mary Anne Hampton surveyed the manicured lawn of the gray stucco house and saw opportunity. It was bigger than any house she had ever stepped foot in. She was going to live in luxury. *I deserve this,* she thought. *I killed him myself, and look where I am now. This is all my doing.* She felt powerful; invulnerable.

As the car turned into the driveway, Mary Anne's mind moved into high gear. How should she handle this family? She'd spent hours with stupid cops and social workers. They all shook her hand so hard that she thought her bones would break, And they always looked her directly in the eyes, like they were in control. Well, they weren't. They were idiots.

She had pretended that she was an actress in a movie and looked them in the eyes right back—like she was completely innocent. That seemed to work. They had completely fallen for her little performance. She'd keep doing that.

The Bryant family stood together in a semi-circle in the foyer, George Bryant towering over his wife and son, and Amy cradling Toby, her beloved cocoa-colored toy poodle. Charlie carried a remote-control dump truck with giant wheels in his right hand.

Mrs. Smith nudged Mary Anne forward through the door. Before the first word was uttered, Toby leapt from Amy's arms and with a high-pitched din of barking launched a surprise attack at the girl's ankles. Mary Anne recoiled in fright, cast a deadly look in Toby's direction, and kicked back at her attacker.

"No!" screamed Amy. "Toby! Stop!' Charlie was on him instantly and scooped up the dog who struggled mightily to get free and resume the attack.

"Charlie, take him into the kitchen," commanded Amy. "I am *so* sorry!" she gushed, as she grasped Mary Anne's arm and led her into the foyer. "Are you all right? He'll be fine as soon as he gets to know you. He's actually a very loving dog."

They all stood awkwardly for a few moments. Mrs. Smith finally regained her composure and began the introductions. It was time for Mary Anne to take the stage. She made eye contact with Amy, squeezed her hand firmly and said, "Hi, Mrs. Bryant. So nice to meet you."

As she watched Mary Anne shake hands with the rest of the family, Amy Bryant was a bit taken aback. The girl's confidence and poise surprised her. She was only fifteen. But if ever Amy could have imagined the daughter she never had, this lovely young girl with gleaming auburn hair and arresting hazel eyes would be it. She gave a little inward sigh and momentarily indulged herself in daydreams of them bonding; having intimate girl talks; braiding hair; shopping and lunching together.

George Bryant, himself, stood in shock. This was no child coming into his house. Before him stood the most seductively gorgeous young woman he had ever seen. She was flawless, with a model's face and long wavy hair cascading to perfectly rounded buttocks clad in snug jeans. A cotton top hugged her narrow waist and flared over her hips.

Yet there was something about her that was making him vaguely uncomfortable. In his business, George almost instantly sized up new vendors and customers, and his assessments were seldom wrong. He didn't know what the problem was here. In truth, he thought, it was stupid and utterly unfair to burden the girl with unfounded snap judgments. He banished the misgivings from his mind.

For his part, Charlie Bryant stood speechless at the apparition before him. In all of his twelve years he had never seen anything nearly so beautiful as this girl. When she reached out and took his hand in hers, he could feel the moistness of her skin and he thought that his knees might collapse. To his everlasting humiliation, his voice broke when he tried to mumble, "Hi."

Mary Anne looked around and marveled at the space in her new bedroom. "Mary Anne," said Amy as she helped her unpack her few possessions, "Mrs. Smith told me that you lost everything in that dreadful fire. Tomorrow is Saturday and on Monday you start 9th grade in a new school, so tomorrow we have to go shopping. We'll go to the drugstore and get you whatever shampoo and cosmetics you want, and then we're going to get you outfitted in some new clothes, and maybe have lunch together. I can't wait! It'll be such fun!"

Mary Anne was puzzled. Amy was making an offer to buy her things and Mary Anne hadn't expended an ounce of effort. She hadn't thrown a tantrum. She hadn't even asked for anything. *I wonder what she's getting out of this?*

"Wow! That will be perfect," replied Mary Anne.

Amy watched Mary Anne closely during the evening family meal. Despite her earlier poise and confidence, Mary Anne's table manners were a little rough. She helped herself from serving dishes without offering to pass them on to anyone else. Her napkin was a crumpled mass of paper lying on the tablecloth instead of in her lap, and she awkwardly held her fork in a tight fist when cutting her meat. Well, those were certainly easily correctable issues. Give me a month, thought Amy, and I'll have this girl ready for dinner at the White House.

"So, Mary Anne," said Amy, resting her chin on folded hands, "tell us what activities you were involved with at your old school."

Mary Anne put down her fork. "Well, I've been a cheerleader since seventh grade, and this year I made junior varsity, which I was very happy about," she said with animation.

"And I'll bet you were the prettiest cheerleader on the field," replied Amy.

"Maybe," said Mary Anne, flashing a brilliant smile.

"Charlie made the starting lineup in Little League this year, huh Charlie?" said George.

"Yeah," Charlie replied, looking down at his plate.

"And I also was voted best dancer in my dance class," lied Mary Anne.

"Fabulous!" exclaimed Amy. "What kind of dance?"

"Jazz dance."

"Good for you! Would you like to continue with dance lessons?"

"Uh, sure."

"I don't know if Loxahatchee High has dance classes, but we'll look for private classes if they don't," said Amy with determination.

I have to be more careful, thought Mary Anne.

Unlike her table manners, noted Amy over dinner, Mary Anne's grammar, was actually quite good. She had a native charm that was very attractive, but she looked a little bored when the conversation was not about her. *Well, we can make her a better listener, too.*

As the three Bryants carried dishes to the sink, Mary Anne sat looking aimlessly around the room.

"Mary Anne, would you mind bringing your dishes over to the sink please?" asked Amy. "We all clear the table together after dinner."

Well," said Amy, taking charge, "I think it's important that we start off with a little family meeting that gets all of us off on the right foot." The three Bryants and Mary Anne sat around the cleared oak table. Charlie pressed buttons on a Star Wars video game. George sat with his arms folded, fidgeting. Mary Anne looked bored. For the moment, Toby was locked in his crate.

"So, everyone in this family makes a contribution. Charlie, put that game down. We all have responsibilities that help us to share the workload.

"First of all, everyone is responsible for keeping their own room neat and tidy, and making their bed each morning. Everyone also helps to clear dishes and load the dishwasher at meal time." Amy paused and surveyed her audience. "Charlie, are you listening?"

"Charlie's chores include taking out the garbage, mowing the lawn, and weed-eating. Mary Anne, your chores will be cleaning the bathrooms each week and ironing your own clothes.

"Now, for assuming those responsibilities, Charlie gets a seven dollar a week allowance, and you, Mary Anne, will certainly deserve one too, but you're a little older, so your allowance will be ten dollars a week.

Charlie's eyes grew wide at this announcement, but he said nothing.

Ten dollars! thought Mary Anne. *How can I survive on ten dollars? I got at least thirty or forty every week fucking Felix.*

"OK. Next topic: homework," continued Amy. "Homework is done after school each afternoon, and no TV until homework is completed." *This is beginning to sound more and more like prison,* thought Mary Anne.

"And the last item," continued Amy, "if you are going somewhere, you must let George or me know where you are going, and what time we can expect you home. Mary Anne, you and I will discuss dating and what is a reasonable curfew later on.

"So," said Amy with a smile, "simple, clean rules that will help keep us all on track."

Who does this chubby bitch think she is? thought Mary Anne. *This is my life, not hers.* Not six hours after arrival, she began pondering plans for an exit from this boring little family and their fucking yappy dog.

CHAPTER SEVEN

I HAVE TO CONFESS THAT DATING A WOMAN with children has been an absolute revelation for yours truly. Having been celibate—well, let me rephrase that—*single* for nearly forty years, I had settled into a predictable lifestyle that was very comfortable and that I had assumed was more or less normal.

My old girlfriend, Elizabeth, besides being high maintenance, was a career woman—actually a lawyer if you can believe that—and our lives basically revolved around ourselves and her inane friends. She came from a very prominent Baltimore family, and we made appearances at all the right glittering parties. Food, entertainment, and sex—not necessarily in that order—were our major preoccupations, and they happened wherever and whenever we pleased. Actually, when Elizabeth pleased.

But a relationship with a woman with two kids—in this case Jack, just turned four, and Catherine Anne, seven—has given me a new appreciation for what the physicists call *chaos theory*. Trying to lead a reasonably organized life with two little kids is like trying to carry water in a sieve. I have no clue how Penny—truly a single parent, with a full-time job to boot—manages to hold it all together.

So now, food, entertainment, and especially sex, come in highly-appreciated little snippets. Actually, sneaking off for sex somehow makes it a little hotter. That being said, to my amazement, life has never been more meaningful and I have found myself becoming increasingly attached to Jack and Catherine, perhaps because they are an extension of Penny's flesh and blood.

Furthermore, this relationship has been good for my character. I think I fall somewhere around number three on Penny's personal priority list. This hierarchy, I try to remind myself, has nourished within me the virtue of humility, not always my strong suit.

"OK, Catherine," said Sally Horn, "don't forget, when you walk around Abigail, keep your hand on her so she knows you're there and stay very close to her." Catherine, whose purple riding helmet barely reached the bottom of Abigail's belly, extended her hand and with great deliberation slowly walked around the mare. Sally walked protectively a step behind her.

"You can go a little faster, Catherine. Great. Now we're going to check our cinch and make sure it's tight, and then we'll get on her."

Penny and I leaned on the other side of the paddock fence watching Catherine's third riding lesson. Sally effortlessly lifted all forty-five pounds of Catherine's slim figure until her foot reached a shortened stirrup. With great effort, Catherine clambered onto the saddle, squirmed around for a moment, then reached down and tried to pull her jeans out of her butt crack. Looking over at her mother, she scrunched up her face and said, "This is giving me a wedgy."

"It'll be all right, Catherine," called out Penny. "Just wriggle around a little bit."

"Here," said Sally, reaching under both of Catherine's arms and lifting her six inches off the saddle. "Straighten out your jeans." Catherine pulled at her jeans a couple of times, and Sally deposited her back into the saddle.

"Better?" Sally asked. Catherine nodded with a shy smile, revealing two missing teeth.

This was working out really well. Sally is a tall, very eligible third grade teacher who looks fabulous in a pair of jeans and who boards her two thoroughbreds here on the farm. I had at one time attempted to explore a relationship with Sally with disastrous results, but that too is another story. Fortunately, she and Penny get along famously.

Sally began to lead Abigail around the paddock while behind us Jack and Maggie engaged in ferocious battle. Maggie barked and pranced as Jack tried to grab her, but of course to no avail. Abigail ignored them. Periodically Maggie would allow Jack to catch her and they would roll together in the grass, locked in mortal combat.

As the lesson progressed, Catherine rode with a look of fierce concentration, her delicate little eyebrows furrowed, and the light from the late June sun glinting off golden hair that streamed to her shoulders. Under Sally's command, Catherine decisively pulled back on the reins and brought Abigail to a clean stop, much as her mother often does to me.

"Very good, Catherine! You made it very clear to Abigail what you wanted her to do and she did it," said Sally. A broad smile crossed Catherine's face. Very gradually she was learning to take command of a twelve-hundred pound animal.

"Good lessons in assertiveness for a six-year-old girl," I said. "She'll make a great ER nurse some day."

Penny put her hands on her hips and said, "How about doctor?"

"I wouldn't wish that on anybody."

She smiled, placed her hand on my shoulder, and leaned into me. The thought crossed my mind that I would never willingly give this up.

Now that we were both back to work, Penny and I were trying as much as possible to get ourselves scheduled off on Sundays because that was the day of Catherine's riding lessons. This meant that we both often ended up working our weekend share of shifts on Saturdays, which was OK. We could always go out together on another night, *if* a baby-sitter was available.

But in any case, dinner at the farm on Sunday evenings had become something of a mini-tradition in recent weeks, to Ruth's great delight. It was the highlight of her week. She got very chatty on Sundays, cheerfully spending all day in the kitchen making first lunch, then preparing dinner for the five of us, and always, without fail, making brownies for Jack.

It was obvious that helping to care for our little band filled some very deep need for her. Maybe once a week she would spend the night at her little clapboard house on Carroll Road, but most of the time since my injuries she lived at the farm.

With Catherine and Jack off school for the summer, Penny and the kids would also spend Sunday night at the farm on occasion, which made for some interesting sleeping arrangements. Penny refused to have the children witness us sleeping together, of course, so on those evenings Penny and the two kids slept together in my room in the king-sized bed, Ruth got her usual bed, and I slept by myself in the guest room, which falls under the category of cruel and unusual punishment.

I am gradually learning that the name of the game with two kids is efficiency. Catherine and Jack were allowed to play for an hour or so after dinner—always within sight through the kitchen window—while Penny and Ruth chatted and cleaned up the dishes. Then, about 8:30, Penny tossed both of them into the same bathtub—apparently there are no gender issues at ages four and seven. After fifteen minutes of tub play, she had them stand in turn, soaped them up, and then had them lie down to rinse off.

Jack zoomed a menacing-looking blue shark through the air as, on her knees, Penny struggled to get through waving arms to wash his chest and back. "Jack, hold still!"

Catherine was the second, and the more complicated of the two because of her long hair. The forehead is apparently off limits for shampoo, so Catherine's hair was pulled back off her face as Penny massaged the shampoo into hair that fell to the middle of Catherine's back.

"OK, Catherine, now lie down," said Penny. "Jack, scoot down and make room."

Catherine very slowly lowered her head into the water until it covered her ears. Penny placed the heel of one hand across Catherine's forehead to keep water off her eyes and with the other poured water from a plastic cup onto Catherine's soapy hairline.

"Jack! Stop making waves," Penny commanded. A drop of water trickled over one scrunched up eye and Catherine started to raise up. "It's getting in my eyes!" she cried.

Penny held her down. "Just a second, baby, we're almost finished. Just relax." One more quick cup of water, and the deed was done.

"OK," said Penny, "that's it." Catherine was up in a heartbeat.

Penny reached under Jack's arms, lifted him out of the tub and handed him to me. I stood holding the little wet body in the air away from my clothes.

"Dry him," she ordered, throwing a towel over my head and giggling.

This may all seem rather mundane, but I would not have had a clue how to do all of this.

It was one of the first hot nights of the summer, so with my little household of Ruth, Penny and the kids all in bed, I sat in the kitchen about 10:30 PM, stripped to my shorts, catching up on email. Maggie lay beside my stool at the granite kitchen counter in the darkened room, snoring quietly as I absently scratched her behind one ear with a bare foot.

I heard a creak on the sneaky staircase leading down from my bedroom and looked up to see Penny holding a finger to pursed lips at the bottom of the stairs. She smiled and tiptoed toward me in pink bikini panties with breasts gently swaying under a short lavender tank top. Hair the color of early morning sunlight cascaded over her shoulders. It was a breathtaking nocturnal vision.

She put her arms around my neck, green eyes gleaming, and whispered, "I couldn't sleep, thinking about you down here. I wanted to hold you in my arms. Do you think you could help me sleep?"

"You forget. I am skilled in the healing arts."

"Oh, no. I didn't forget," she whispered, smiling. "How could I forget?"

She lightly slid her lips back and forth over mine, nibbling at the corners of my mouth. Sweet breath hit my nostrils. My hands slid on smooth skin up and over the flare of her hips and narrow waist, reaching the silky weight of her breasts. Little nipples stiffened under my thumbs and she released a soft moan into my mouth.

Staring into my eyes, she reached under the tank top, grasped one of my hands and pulled it down between her legs, sliding it into her panties. Fireworks went off in my brain.

Penny's hips gave a little involuntary jerk, and the tip of her tongue began to dance over mine. I found her little button and began to trace tiny circles. She buried her face in my neck and whispered, "Oooh, that feels so good."

"You've been thinking about me for a while, haven't you?" I said. She nodded, her face still buried in my neck. Her hands reached for the snap on my shorts and she frantically, but unsuccessfully, tried to open them. Reluctantly, I slid my fingers from her panties and unsnapped the shorts myself.

With both hands she yanked shorts and boxers to my ankles and I sprang free to full attention. On her knees, she stared intently for a moment at the sight before her, gently running two fingers up one side and down the other. Swirling her tongue on the underside, she slowly bobbed her head several times until I was slick with her saliva, then looking up into my eyes whispered, "Are you ready yet?"

"Oh God, yes."

She stood and leaned over the granite countertop, reaching behind her with both hands and pulling her panties down over gorgeous round buttocks to mid-thigh. I knelt and pulled them to the floor. She stepped out and stood with her feet apart. Blood surged.

I gently bit one buttock, caressing the muscles of the other, then stood and grasped her hips, bobbing against her with each heartbeat. Reaching between her legs, she slowly slid me back and forth until we were both slick, then rose on her toes, guided me to her opening, and slowly lowered her hips. I sank deeply into her, a guttural moan escaping my throat.

"Shhhhh..." she said softly, pushing back against me. As we began to move together, she reached between her legs again and rotated her fingers, slowly at first and then more rapidly. This was the first time that I had seen Penny pleasure herself. That she would so freely share this intimacy with me provoked a wave of powerful emotion.

Lost in pleasure, she lay her head on her forearm. The dark room softly echoed with barely suppressed sighs as together we found both profound connection and primal release.

I lay on the leather couch with Penny leaning back in my arms, inhaling the scent of her hair; one hand caressing a breast. "I wonder if Ruth is still awake," I said. "Do you think she heard us?"

Penny giggled quietly and looked up, her eyes twinkling. "If she did," she said, "maybe it brought back some fond memories of younger days."

We were quiet for a minute. Penny broke the silence. "Do you ever wish that every night could be like this?" she asked.

"All the time," I whispered.

CHAPTER EIGHT

Loxahatchee, Florida
November 1998

MARY ANNE LEANED OVER AND GAVE THE boy a kiss he would long remember. She smiled sweetly, grabbed her beach bag and climbed out of the convertible a block and a half from the Bryant home. Tossing her hair, she waved and walked off into the setting sun with hips gently swaying, knowing that he was watching. The boy would be back, she thought with satisfaction, and now she had transportation any time she wanted it.

Better than that, it was *great* transportation, appropriate for a girl like her: a Mercedes SL500, no less. And, the boy's parents had a West Palm Beach oceanfront house to go with it. The Bryant's place was a shack. She deserved better.

"OK, well let's just eat. This food is getting cold," said Amy brusquely, carrying a dish of broccoli to the table. "She'll just have to eat a cold dinner."

Charlie had never seen his mother slam down a dish before. The three Bryants ate their evening meal in silence. Charlie could almost see the steam coming out of his father's ears. His mother absently picked at the food on her plate.

"Maybe she just lost track of time," Charlie said helpfully.

"I've been to the pool," said his father, like Charlie was an idiot. "She wasn't there. She went someplace else."

"George, maybe you should go out and look for her again," said his mother finally. "I'm starting to get really worried. She was supposed to be home by 5:00. It's 8:15."

Charlie couldn't imagine the world of trouble that Mary Anne was in. For once he was glad that he was only twelve years old. He quietly took his plate to the sink, then hunkered down in his room to await the fireworks.

George Bryant heard the kitchen door open about 8:45. He laid his reading glasses on the desk beside the computer and rubbed his eyes. He was uncertain how to handle this. A teenage girl was complex beyond his dreams. Besides which, George's blood was boiling. He was afraid that he might blow it. He decided to let Amy handle the initial confrontation and stayed in his chair, listening.

Amy was sorting the flatware from the dishwasher when Mary Anne walked briskly through the door, threw her beach bag on the kitchen island, and walked to the refrigerator where she stood holding both doors open.

Amy turned and stood silently with hands on her hips, waiting for an explanation; apology; something. When none came, she finally said, "Well?"

"Well what?" said Mary Anne.

"Where have you been? You're over three hours late. You missed dinner. I was worried sick about you."

"Don't worry about me."

"Where have you been?" repeated Amy, this time with an edge of anger.

Mary Anne sighed with exasperation and rolled her eyes. "I was at the pool."

"George went to the pool at six o'clock and you weren't there."

48

"I was at a girlfriend's house, OK?" George Bryant walked silently into the room and stood leaning against a doorframe.

"What girlfriend?" asked Amy.

"What's it matter to you?" spat Mary Anne. "You're not my mother." Toby heard the shouting, trotted up and began barking. Mary Anne shot him a deadly glance.

Amy felt control of the conversation slipping away from her. A wave of panic washed over her. She frantically searched her mind for some way to change the direction of this conversation, but came up blank. Finally she said the only thing that she could think of: "Mary Anne Hampton, as long as you are living in this house, you will abide by our rules."

"Why don't you just get off my fucking back, and leave me alone!" screamed Mary Anne. "I hate you people!" Banging shut the refrigerator doors, she stomped out of the kitchen, climbed the stairs two at a time, and slammed her bedroom door.

Holding her hand over her mouth, Amy quickly walked to the downstairs bathroom, afraid that she would be sick.

After two months of living with the Bryants, Mary Anne thought that she would go out of her mind with boredom. She was now in her second week of being grounded. At least when living with her mother she could come and go as she pleased, hook up with the boy across the trailer park when she felt like it, and spend money on pretty much whatever she wanted. Even sex with Felix had an element of danger that made her feel alive, although not nearly as much as killing him did. Life here was like living in a straight-jacket.

She had made a few friends in school, and the boy from Palm Beach was hot for her, but she couldn't hang out with any of them because that damned woman would only let her go out one night a week, even when she wasn't grounded.

Most humiliating of all, Amy insisted on driving her to wherever she was going and then picking her up again—at eleven o'clock, no less—so she could only see the Palm Beach boy when she could sneak away.

"When you turn sixteen, you'll be able to go out on a date in a boy's car as long as we have met him," Amy had said. *Well who the hell is she to pick and choose who I'll go out with?*

She lay in bra and panties, propped on a pillow in her bed, idly leafing through a *Entertainment Weekly*. *I could be in this magazine one day*, she thought. *I'm on my way up. I've got the looks and now I've got a rich boyfriend. If I could just get out of this damned house...*

She had tried to catch George Bryant's eye in hope of softening him up and getting a few more privileges, and maybe even more money, but the idiot was oblivious. She was stuck. In frustration she violently threw the magazine to the floor. "Fuck!" she screamed.

Downstairs a door slammed. Fifteen seconds later she heard Charlie's footsteps on the stairs. It was late Saturday morning. He would be coming home from mowing lawns.

George and Amy are both out, she thought. *Maybe I can have some fun with Charlie.*

She heard Charlie rummaging around his room, got up, and walked quietly down the hall to his bedroom. Charlie was pulling the lid off a coffee can on his bureau and depositing a wad of green bills into the can.

"Hi, Charlie."

Charlie wheeled around in surprise, and then stood dead still, his eyes wide and his jaw slack. Leaning against his doorframe, naked except for a bra and some string around her hips, stood a tanned goddess. Charlie's eyes followed long, bare legs to gently curving hips and then on to a flat belly ridged with muscle. Breasts peeked out above her bra and waves of shiny reddish-brown hair tumbled to her shoulders.

"I've noticed you looking at me sometimes, Charlie," Mary Anne said sweetly. "Do you like what you see?"

Dumbstruck, Charlie just stared.

"Well, do you?" she asked again. Charlie abruptly shook his head "no" and then nodded "yes."

Mary Anne did a slow runway walk to Charlie's bed and sat down, patting the bed beside her. *I'll have to go slow with this or he'll freak*, she thought.

"Sit down, Charlie."

Charlie's sneaker caught the edge of his rug, and he stumbled, falling onto the bed.

"Have you ever kissed a girl, Charlie?"

Charlie's mouth was like a desert. He couldn't form words. He shook his head "no" again.

"Would you like to try it?" she asked softly.

Struggling mightily to regain control, Charlie finally found a voice. "I…I guess so," he croaked.

Mary Anne lowered her face to his and softly brushed his lips with hers. Warm breath hit Charlie's face. He could smell her skin. Instantly, he was engulfed by a wave of fire. She raised her head.

"Did you like that?" she said smiling.

Charlie's breath was coming in short gasps now. "Yeah," he said.

"I saw you looking at my boobs, too. I'll bet you've never seen a girl's breasts before, have you Charlie? Would you like to see mine?"

Charlie now was hovering just at the verge of consciousness. He nodded once.

"OK. But this is going to be our secret, together. You and I have to make a deal. If I show you, you have to promise never, ever to tell anybody—not a friend, not a teacher, and especially not your parents. Do you understand?

Charlie nodded again.

"Say it, Charlie. Say I promise, Scout's honor, never ever to tell anyone; not a soul."

"I'll never, ever, Scout's honor, tell anyone. I promise."

Mary Anne smiled and reached behind to unhook her bra. She shook the straps off her shoulders, then cupping the bra in both hands, slowly let it fall off her breasts.

Charlie stared, mesmerized.

"Would you like to touch one, Charlie?"

Mary Anne grasped one of Charlie's hands and placed it on her breast. In a daze, he slowly ran three fingers along the side.

"They're soft, aren't they?" she asked.

"Run your finger around here, Charlie, and my nipple will get hard."

Charlie obeyed and the nipple stiffened.

"Mmmmm. That feels good, Charlie," Mary Anne sighed. "I like that. I can tell that you like what we're doing, too," she said. "You know how I can tell?" Mary Anne traced a finger along the rigid cylinder visible under Charlie's nylon trunks. "By this lump under your shorts."

She ran her hand under the leg of Charlie's red shorts and wrapped her fingers around his penis. Charlie thought that his life was ending. His mind was now completely scrambled.

"Oh, you wear boxers, Charlie. I like boxers." She rotated the palm of her hand around the head of his penis until it got slick with fluid, and then began to slide her hand up and down its length.

Exquisite sensations surged through Charlie's body. He leaned back on his hands and panted, "Don't stop! Please don't stop."

Fifteen seconds later, Charlie gasped as jets of milky-white fluid flooded Mary Anne's hand. She gradually slowed her hand, gently continuing to massage Charlie until he began to soften and his breathing began to slow.

She smiled at him, showing him her wet hand. Mary Anne felt a tingle of excitement. Charlie would now be her slave. He would do anything and everything that she ever asked. He would cover for her, lie for her, and provide her with money. He might even get her off once in a while.

~

Amy carried the basket of freshly laundered towels into her bedroom to the master bath and stopped at the bathroom door in shock. On her knees scrubbing the tub was Mary Anne.

Mary Anne looked up and smiled. Holding up a bottle of blue liquid, she said, "I'm using this all-surface cleanser I found in the cupboard on this tub. I hope that's OK."

"That'll work just fine," replied Amy. "Thanks for cleaning the bathroom."

Mary Anne rose up on her knees. "Well, I figure it's the least I can do after all that you guys have done for me. And I know that I haven't been real easy to get along with. It's just that this last couple of months have been kind of rough."

Amy silently held eye contact with Mary Anne for a long moment, battling conflicting emotions. To her great disappointment and deep hurt, she had been unable to establish emotional contact with this girl. *But what did I expect?* she asked herself. *I was looking for a daughter when what I was really getting was a troubled child who needs help.*

Perhaps Mary Anne was providing a first glimmer of change here. *She still needs my help*, thought Amy. From the information Mrs. Smith had provided, there was no doubt that this child had been through hell. *I'm not going to give up on her. I should grasp this opportunity.*

Amy's body relaxed. "Tell me, Mary Anne," she said. "Tell me about the last couple of months."

She's so stupid, thought Mary Anne. *It's so easy to push her buttons. Maybe I can get her off my back, get some more privileges, and get a new prescription for my birth control pills. A big belly with stretch marks would be the pits.*

CHAPTER NINE

I WALKED DOWN THE HALLWAY FROM THE locker room toward the ER door humming, my cheerful mood primarily a reflection of the fact that Penny and I were both scheduled to work this night shift. That would make the night go faster.

By now, almost four months after the hostage situation, everyone on the Planet Earth knew full well that Penny and I were a couple. Well, maybe there were some isolated Tibetan monks without broadband who hadn't gotten the word. Otherwise, you'd have to be blind not to at least recognize the photos of us together in the celebrity magazines.

But so far the hospital administration had chosen to ignore it. No one had challenged a physician and nurse with a personal relationship working together in the same department, perhaps because technically, nurses work for nursing administration and do not report to any physician. It's a little murky, of course, because nurses *do* take medical orders from physicians.

Of course, Penny and I work very hard not to make our relationship obviously apparent to the rest of the staff. We always retire to the housekeeping closet before making out. Just kidding.

But, in any case, I was happy that administration chose to leave the issue alone.

I passed an open office doorway with signage that said *Emergency Department Nursing Manager,* and stuck my head in the door. Julie Talbot, MSN, sat at her computer, fingernails clicking on the keys. Managers are usually daylight people. This was way past cocktail hour.

"You need to get a life," I said. "It's almost seven o'clock."

"If I didn't have to clean up after my medical director, maybe I could be at home having a glass of wine right now," she said without looking up.

"I always put my coffee cup in the sink," I said. "There's a sign there that says 'Your mother doesn't work here.'"

"Coffee cups I can handle. It's the shitload of trouble you create that keeps me up all night."

Julie loves me. She's my guardian angel and partner in running this happy little department. She keeps me out of trouble with the bureaucracy and makes my life as a department head tolerable. I trust her implicitly.

Jacquelyn Ford, our vice president of patient services and Julie's boss, hates her because Julie often thinks a little outside the box, and Jackie is firmly of the belief that her employees are not paid to think.

When I was fired back in March, I didn't believe that Julie would last. We were both in administration's crosshairs at that time. I thought that Julie would either be fired herself, or quit under Jackie's relentless assaults. But Jackie has a nose for the political winds as good as anybody's, and when the new CEO hired me back, Jackie apparently figured it was a new day and that the better part of good management was to back off and whack Julie another day.

That being said, Jackie and I have our own history. She likes me even less than Julie, and from time to time I remind myself that the current ceasefire is not necessarily a lasting peace. As General Custer said, "Keep your eyes peeled for smoke signals."

~

On the wall just outside the secure ER door, one of our inmates has hung a wooden arrow sign with a little palm tree pointing the way to *Paradise.* I passed the sign, flashed my badge, and pushed through the door. Rick Stapleton, an old classmate from Duke Medical School, was the departing day doc. He's a big, gregarious South Carolina-born boy who never learned to be ashamed of his accent from the plantation.

Rick was sitting at his computer when I walked into the nursing station. I gripped him on the shoulder and said, "Colonel Stapleton, how are you today?"

"My blood bourbon level is very low," he drawled, looking up. "It's time for me to get outta here."

We went through the sign-out slash handoff process, and I picked up three patients still in the process of being worked up. The first two would be easy quickies: an ankle sprain in x-ray, and an asthmatic kid getting a nebulizer breathing treatment. The third one caught my attention.

"Mrs. Cox is the last one," said Rick. "She's a very nice 83-year-old lady who stepped on her kitty's tail coming down the stairs. She thinks she tumbled down five or six stairs near the bottom."

"The cat or Mrs. Cox?" I asked.

"Mrs. Cox. The cat's at home nursing her tail."

"OK."

"Anyhow, she didn't hit her head, but she's complaining of pain in her right wrist, right shoulder, and right hip. So, she's getting all those x-rayed. I'm a little bit concerned because she's on Coumadin for a deep vein thrombosis in her leg a year or two ago, and she's just a little tachycardic back there. Her heart rate's around a hundred and five.

"I couldn't find anything wrong in her chest, and her abdomen's OK, too, but if her x-rays are negative maybe you ought to look her over again before you let her go. I've got a pro-time cooking."

"Gotcha," I said.

Rick logged off his computer, said "Night, y'all," and I sat down in his warm seat.

Rick was concerned—and my antennae were up—because Mrs. Cox was on warfarin, better known as Coumadin, a drug that makes your blood clot much more slowly than normal so that, in Mrs. Cox's case, she was less likely to develop blood clots in her legs again. But, like much of what we do in medicine there's a downside. If you bust yourself up, you're more likely to have serious bleeding.

You can also get too much of that stuff, and then your blood doesn't clot at all. It's difficult to control the dosage exactly right. So everyone on Coumadin has to get a blood test once a month to see how long it takes their blood to clot.

Warfarin, you will also be interested to know, is available without a prescription under a variety of brand names as rat poison. I kid you not. Rats and mice love the stuff. They eat to their heart's content, start bleeding internally, crawl into the walls of your house, and die. This leaves your house stinking for about a month and you can't figure out where the smell is coming from, I know from experience, so warfarin is off-limits at my old house, even though it serves as a resort hotel for all the local field mice on Shepherd Road.

But I digress. I looked up at the big tracker board and saw that the *XRAY* icon behind Mrs. Cox's name was still red, which meant that they hadn't yet taken her to radiology. I decided to take a look at her before I saw the first new patient.

Mrs. Cox lay on a gurney in Bed Thirteen, her swollen and bruised right wrist resting on a pillow.

I introduced myself and said, "That looks like it hurts," nodding toward her wrist.

"Well, you know, Dr. Randolph, as long as I keep it still, it hardly hurts at all," she replied briskly with a smile. "I think my cat may be in worse shape than me."

"Should I see the cat first?"

Mrs. Cox thought that was funny. I looked up at the monitor screen and noted that her heart rate was still a little over a hundred. It ought to be in the seventies or eighties, lying here at rest. But her blood pressure was still fine at one thirty-two over ninety.

"Mrs. Cox, do you have any pain in your chest or your abdomen?"

"Well, my hip hurts a little—I think I just bruised it," she said pulling up the sheet and looking for a bruise. "Well, I don't see one. But my stomach doesn't hurt and my chest is OK."

"Can I feel your belly again?" I asked. I ran my hand over all four quadrants of her abdomen, gently pressing deeply, feeling for tender spots or masses that might indicate internal bleeding. I found none. I put on my stethoscope and listened to her heart and her lungs and found nothing there either. So far, no explanation for her mild tachycardia. Maybe it was just the result of pain and anxiety.

"OK," I said. "Let's wait and see what the x-rays show."

~

By 8 PM we were cookin'. Patients were coming in faster than Scott Foreman and I could process them, and now every one of our sixteen beds was full and there were three people in the waiting room.

I picked up the chart for the new patient in Bed Three and perused the triage note as I walked down the hallway: Cody Brown; nineteen years-old; left earache for two days. This one, at least, should be quick and easy.

"Hi, Cody. I'm Dr. Randolph." Cody sat slumped on the end of the exam table in a striped tee shirt and dirty jeans, both thumbs tapping out a message on his cell phone like I wasn't there. Curving tattoos like flames streamed down both arms. I waited ten seconds, then said "Cody?"

"Yeah?" he said without looking up, the tap, tap, tap continuing.

"Do you want to be seen?" Without responding, he sullenly placed the phone on the table beside him. He still had not made eye contact.

"It says here that you've had an earache for two days. Is that right?"

"Yeah." So far, this was a very illuminating conversation. Pulling information out of Cody was going to take more time than I could afford. I had a waiting room full of sick patients to see, so I decided to move right to the examination. Picking up the otoscope from its wall mount, I grasped the top of his left earlobe just above the diamond earring to straighten out the ear canal.

Cody violently jerked away, stood, and yelled, "Ouch! That fuckin' hurts, asshole!"

Mr. Hyde emitted a brief snort, and then his eyes popped open. I hadn't heard from Mr. Hyde in over three months. He'd been slumbering peacefully throughout my enforced vacation, but he was wide awake now. I could tell from the screaming in my head. *Are you going to let that little jerk get away with this?*

Dr. Jekyll, ever the empathetic social scientist, now piped up. He never seems to sleep. *Look, he's obviously a kid from a completely dysfunctional family, he's got no social skills and he needs help. Just de-escalate him, and take care of his ear.*

Are you nuts? retorted Hyde. *How is this kid ever going to function in society if we keep teaching him that there are no consequences to behavior?* Cody had put me in a really pissy mood. I didn't have time for this. Hyde won.

"Cody, you only get to call me an asshole once. So, you're outta' here," I said, pointing to the door. Cody snatched his phone from the table and stomped out of the room. Jekyll moaned, *Oh, no! You didn't really just say that!*

I walked back to the nursing station and wrote a little note on the chart summarizing our pleasant conversation. Cody was technically what we call an *elopement*. Actually, he didn't elope. I kicked him out.

Nevertheless, elopements are frowned upon by everyone from the federal government to the Joint Commission to the Department of Health and Mental Hygiene. We're required to track them. All elopements get reviewed by the vice president of patient services, none other than Jacquelyn Ford, of course. Jackie would be thrilled. I would hear about this.

~

I saw two more patients and was sewing up a thumb on a guy who added a little fresh meat to the green peppers he was chopping, when Penny walked in the room. She said, "Dr. Randolph, the x-rays are back on Mrs. Cox and she has a radius fracture. The other films are OK."

I said, "OK, baby." Actually I didn't say that. I said, "Is the fracture displaced?"

"No."

"OK. Put an OCL wrist splint on her, and I'll be out and discharge her in a minute."

I finished up the laceration and rushed back to my computer to do the discharge instructions. Fran Williams, reading glasses dangling around her neck, walked up and said, "the asthmatic kid has finished his treatment. He's still wheezing pretty good."

"OK. I'll put another albuterol in and give him some prednisolone."

I was halfway through entering those orders when April Keller walked by and called out, "X-rays are negative on the woman in Five with the ankle sprain."

Lisa Turano touched me on the shoulder, "That lady in Eight with abdominal pain wants more pain medicine. She's already had two milligrams of Dilaudid."

I ran my fingers through my hair. This is the kind of night that makes you goofy. Sometimes for short periods it's kind of fun to multitask and feel your brain working at peak performance, but this was not likely to stop until after midnight, by which time my cerebral cortex would be scrambled.

The only way you can survive is to prioritize and then just to do one thing at a time, which means that the lower priority folks are going to have to wait. That is not good for our patient satisfaction scores. Sometimes when you've got a bunch of truly sick patients, the conflicting demands make it downright scary. You can't be in two places at once, and you keep waiting for something to fall through the cracks.

I finished the discharge instructions on the cut thumb, then pulled up Mrs. Cox's x-rays on the computer. The radius fracture of her wrist was, indeed, in good position, so she would be fine with a splint and follow-up with an orthopedic surgeon.

I finished her discharge instructions, printed out a prescription for Vicodin for pain, and ran into Bed Three to check on the kid with asthma. His lungs were definitely clearer, but we weren't quite there yet.

I slipped into Bed Five, gave Betsy Warren the good news that her ankle was not fractured and that we could treat her ankle sprain with a brace for ten days, then zipped back to the nursing station to do her discharge paperwork.

As I was typing, Penny returned to the nursing station and said, "Alex, I'm getting Mrs. Cox ready to go home, but she says she's got a little pain in her pelvis now. She's still a little tachycardic—her heart rate's one-oh-four. I don't like it. Maybe you ought to take another look at her."

I looked up at Penny's lovely face. "Uh-oh," I said. "You know, I haven't looked up her pro-time yet."

"Her INR is OK—two point one," said Penny. She had already checked the results herself. A little wave of guilt washed over me. I almost missed that.

Nevertheless, this result meant that Mrs. Cox's blood was clotting in about twice the normal time—just where it should be on Coumadin. But she was still twice as likely to bleed as you or me. I got up from my chair and walked to her room.

"Mrs. Cox, do you have some pain in your belly now?" I asked.

"It's not bad," she said smiling. "Really it's probably more pressure than pain."

I placed my hand on her belly again and when I pressed deeply just above her pubic bone she gave a little wince. I didn't like that. Penny had already taken her off the monitor for discharge, so I put my fingers to her wrist and counted her pulse myself: one hundred and ten—a little faster than it had been.

I scratched my head. "Mrs. Cox, I'm sure you're ready to get out of here, but you know, I think maybe we better do a CAT scan of your abdomen. Your heart rate is a little fast, you're on Coumadin, and now you've got a little discomfort down here," I said, patting her belly. "I'm getting a little worried that you could have some bleeding in here."

She gave a sigh and held up her wrist splint. "Well, I'm all ready to go and I think I'm OK, but if you think it's really necessary…"

"Mrs. Cox, think of it this way. You would be doing me a big favor if you'd stick around and let us get this done. I'll sleep better tomorrow morning."

I ordered the CT of her abdomen and waded back into the fray.

~

The printer whirred at the nursing station. Tina, tonight's ward clerk, picked up the printout, looked at it, and laid it in front of my computer. "Here you go," she said, "Mrs. Cox's CT."

I read the report. *There but for the grace of God go I...* No wonder Mrs. Cox was a little tachycardic. She had a huge hematoma—a collection of blood—the size of a large grapefruit hidden away in her pelvis. She'd already lost perhaps two pints of blood. If I had sent her home she may well have died before morning, bleeding to death in her bed as she slept. This is the kind of stuff that keeps you awake at night. It's why you want to hire smart nurses.

CHAPTER TEN

Loxahatchee, Florida
1999

CHARLIE LINGERED IN THE DOORWAY TO MARY Anne's room, watching as she stood ironing in a tee shirt and shorts. "What's the matter, Charlie?" she asked, as she flipped the blouse on the ironing board. "Do you need something?"

Charlie shrugged. "Nothin'," he said. "Just watching."

"What are you watching, Charlie?" Charlie shrugged again and said nothing.

"I don't think you want to learn how to iron, Charlie. I think maybe you're watching my boobs jiggle, aren't you? Or maybe you're looking at my bare legs, thinking about what's under my shorts."

Charlie's face turned fiery red.

"I think poor little Charlie's got the hots for me," she said, setting the iron on end and walking toward the doorway. Charlie's heart began to pound.

Mary Anne placed her hand between Charlie's legs and began to explore with her fingers. "Yep. That's it," she said stroking his rigid erection. "Charlie needs some attention. OK, Charlie. I'll do you a favor, but do you think you could do me a little favor, too?" she asked, looking down into his eyes. Charlie nodded.

"I really need some new bikini panties." She pulled the leg of her shorts to the side, took Charlie's hand, and rubbed his index finger along the crotch of her panties. Charlie's eyes glazed over. "See? They're kind of threadbare. Do you think you could lend me thirty dollars to get some new ones? Maybe I'll model them for you. And if you're really nice to me, maybe one day I'll let you see what's underneath them."

~ ~

Amy Bryant couldn't sleep. George lay on the other side of the bed with his back toward her, snoring softly. They hadn't made love in two weeks. He seemed perpetually angry. The house was constantly filled with tension.

After six months, Amy couldn't help thinking that she had made a dreadful mistake. Life had not been the same since Mary Anne Hampton had moved into their home. Even Charlie seemed moody and walked around in a daze half the time.

Lord knows, I have tried, she sighed. *But she just won't let me in.* Mary Anne had a wall around her that seemed to be impervious to love.

She tried to put her finger on what it was that made Mary Anne's presence so disruptive.

At least part of it was trust, she thought, the absence of which seemed to permeate and corrode the whole family. After a long period of sticking her head in the sand, Amy had finally acknowledged the fact that Mary Anne lied so fluidly and effortlessly that you could never tell truth from fiction. George didn't believe a word she said.

Whatever part of Mary Anne's brain, or soul, or whatever houses a conscience, was completely missing. She was shameless.

And thankless, too. Not a shred of gratitude. Mary Anne left you feeling used and angry. Sometimes she even seemed to have a cruel streak. Poor Charlie obviously stood in awe of her, but she was always putting him down—making him feel small. Half the time she treated him like her slave.

Amy felt horribly conflicted. On the one hand, she feared that she had failed this young girl miserably. Her inability to connect with Mary Anne had left Amy feeling guilt-ridden and incompetent. Her heart still went out to the young girl who had no control over what she had suffered as a child.

But she felt equally guilt-ridden about the suffering of her own family. They should have been her first priority. She was the one who had insisted on bringing Mary Anne into their home.

The agreement with Juvenile Services had been to care for Mary Anne for a year with an option to renew. Amy would discuss it with George, but she was slowly coming to the depressing conviction that in order to safeguard her family, Mary Anne would have to go.

~

Mary Anne flipped through a dozen channels, found nothing of interest, and angrily threw the remote to the carpeted floor. She wandered into the kitchen, picked up the wall phone and dialed her friend Monica, but got no answer. "Fuck!" she screamed, slamming down the receiver.

From his room, Charlie could hear Mary Anne wandering through the house, loudly cursing at being locked up on Friday night when everybody else in the whole world was out having fun. He quietly closed his door, knowing better than to get in her way when she was in one of these moods.

Fuming, Mary Anne absently walked back through the kitchen toward the refrigerator, and stopped dead in her tracks. Lying on the kitchen counter in front of her were the keys to George's pickup truck. A surge of excitement rippled through her.

She looked up at the wall clock: 7:15. George and Amy wouldn't be back from dinner until at least 9:30. If she left now, Mary Anne could be in West Palm Beach in fifteen minutes. Her boyfriend would be shocked when she showed up. She could spend an hour with him, maybe let him fuck her, and be back by 9:00. I could do this, she thought. I've been in driver's ed for two months.

"Charlie!" she screamed. "Come down here!"

Charlie hesitated at his door, afraid to go and afraid to stay.

"Hurry up, retard," she yelled again.

Charlie slowly descended the stairs. "What?" he asked sullenly.

Mary Anne held the truck keys up in front of his face. "You see these, Charlie? I'm taking your father's truck."

"No! You can't do that!" blurted Charlie.

"Oh yes I can, Charlie, because you're going to keep your stupid little mouth shut. I'll be back by nine and you're not going to say a word. You know why? Because if you rat on me, Charlie, I promise you, I'll never jerk off your tiny little cock again as long as I live."

Mary Anne whirled, and was out the kitchen door before Charlie's brain could process her words. An overwhelming sense of fear and dread rose through his young body, crushing his chest until he thought he couldn't breathe. He followed her and stood dumbly on the patio watching as she climbed first onto the running board and then up into the seat of the big, white F-350 backed in front of the garage.

Mary Anne turned the key and watched with glee as the dashboard lit up like a Christmas tree. Another quarter turn and the powerful diesel rumbled to life. She adjusted the seat until her feet reached the pedals, pulled the gearshift lever into drive and cautiously stepped on the gas.

The truck gradually picked up speed as she approached the end of the driveway. Leaving nothing to chance, she quickly looked both ways twice, every nerve fiber in her body gloriously alert. Two cars were parked on the other side of the street, but no traffic approached. It was clear. She rolled across the end of the driveway, stepped on the gas and started her left turn.

But the F-350 was engineered with twice the turning radius of the little Chevrolet Cavalier in her driver's ed class. Too late, Mary Anne realized that she couldn't turn the steering wheel fast enough.

Charlie watched in horror as the big F-350 failed to negotiate the turn and rolled first into the middle door post of the parked BMW and then careened into the side of the SUV parked in front. Sparks flew and Charlie held his ears against the scream of tearing metal. The truck rolled another thirty feet before he saw the brake lights go on and the truck jerk to a stop.

The door opened and Mary Anne leapt from the truck, falling onto one knee, and then running like a madwoman toward Charlie. She grabbed his tee shirt with both fists, knocking the wind out of him, and screamed, "Get over there Charlie! Get in the truck!"

He pushed her hands away and yelled, "No! Are you crazy? Get off me!"

Mary Anne grabbed Charlie's face with both hands and shook his head. "Listen to me, you stupid little shit," she hissed. "Listen very carefully. If you don't take the blame for this, I will tell your father what we've been doing, and I will tell your mother what we've been doing, and I will tell the police that you have been touching me between my legs. Do you hear me? Do you know what they'll do, Charlie? They'll send you away! They'll lock you up forever! You'll never see your parents again!" she screamed.

Charlie began to cry.

~

Mary Anne counted the last of the green bills and came up with $380. Charlie, she knew, had only $25 left in the coffee can in his bedroom. She had essentially wiped him out. There were only three weeks left until August 13th, the day of her sixteenth birthday, so the most she could probably accumulate by then was just over $400—less than she would have liked, but it would have to do. She put the money back in the shoebox at the bottom of her closet along with the birth certificate and social security card she had lifted from the files in Amy's room, and replaced the lid.

~

A wave of nausea spread over George Bryant as he stared in disbelief at the papers served by the legal firm representing the BMW owner's insurance company. The E39 had been declared a total loss. The suit filed in Palm Beach County Circuit Court demanded payment of $30,124.27 in addition to legal fees.

That amount of money represented almost all of the working capital that George had in his business to buy supplies and pay his workers while he was waiting to get paid for a job. It was unclear whether his own insurance company was going to cover the loss. They were balking at paying because Charlie was underage and under George's control. If the owner of the SUV filed a suit too, it could mean the loss of his plumbing business. At the very least it would represent a huge debt that would take him years to repay.

In a daze, he lay the thick packet of papers beside the computer and looked around the room at his and Amy's dream house. Ten years of seventy-hour weeks, no vacations, a tiny rental apartment, and tens of thousands in repaid loans had gone into building Bryant Plumbing. That his twelve-year-old son could have potentially wiped it all out in less than one minute was utterly inconceivable.

~

On her sixteenth birthday, Mary Anne double-checked the contents of her suitcase and took one last look around the room. "I am about to be released from this damned prison," she said out loud walking down the hall to Charlie's room. Pulling the lid off his coffee can, she found another fifteen dollars and smiled. *That will almost pay for the bus ticket to Miami*, she thought.

She walked to Charlie's front window and through the curtains saw the Mercedes idling at the curb, top down. Freedom was a minute away.

Pulse racing, she lugged the suitcase down the stairs and through the back kitchen door. Toby was on a twenty-foot leash inside the picket fence patio enclosure and immediately began his incessant barking.

Mary Anne looked at him for a moment, and put down the suitcase. *One last little chore*, she thought. Walking around behind the yapping dog, she picked up the leash and abruptly yanked Toby into the air by his collar. Holding the squirming dog at arm's length, she walked to the fence and looped the leash around a picket where he hung like a condemned man. *They'll think he tried to jump the fence and hanged himself*, she thought, smiling.

She watched with fascination as Toby frantically pawed the air. Strangled squeaks emitted from his open mouth and saliva dripped onto his fur. Blood oozed where his back claws desperately ripped open his neck in a futile attempt to release the collar. Very gradually the pawing slowed to a few purposeless jerks, and then the dog hung motionless.

68

Mary Anne picked up the suitcase and walked to the waiting car, humming. The boy jumped out and lifted her suitcase into the trunk. She gave him a quick kiss and climbed into the car. The Mercedes pulled away from the curb and rapidly gained speed, Mary Anne's gleaming auburn hair streaming out behind her in the wind.

CHAPTER ELEVEN

I CLOSED ALL THE VENETIAN BLINDS AS THE SKY was beginning to lighten about 5:45 AM and climbed into bed. I was out cold in about five minutes.

Usually I take an hour or two nap the afternoon before a night shift, and then sleep maybe five or six hours when I get home early the next morning. I turn a fan on year-round for white noise so I don't hear Maggie barking, horses whinnying, or Ruth doing laundry.

Ruth is accustomed to this routine. I try not to wake her when I get home shortly after 5:00 AM, and she's as silent as a cat while working later that morning until I rouse my ass out of bed.

My eyes opened to narrow streaks of brilliant sunlight pouring through the slats of the venetian blinds at close to noon. I showered, slipped on shorts and a tee shirt, and descended the sneaky staircase, as they call it, leading from my bedroom into the kitchen, the smell of coffee growing more intense with each step.

The sneaky staircase is very efficient. It probably saves me forty steps in not having to travel the upstairs hallway to the main staircase that descends into the foyer at the front of the house. This is important stuff to an efficiency freak like me.

"Good morning, sleepyhead," said a cheery voice. Ruth stood on a low stool in a flower-print cotton dress with white apron, vigorously applying furniture polish to the kitchen cabinets, her wiry gray hair in a frizz.

"Morning Ruth."

"Did you sleep well?"

"Like a baby."

"I just made the coffee, so it's fresh. Want some breakfast?"

"Too late for breakfast."

"How about lunch?"

"Too early for lunch. I think I'll just have coffee."

Ruth added more polish to her cloth and resumed rubbing the cabinets. "Were you busy last night?" she asked.

"It was crazy, Ruth. Full moon."

"Did you work with Penny?"

"I did." This was the critical piece of information for which Ruth was searching.

"Well, what's on your schedule for today? Shall I make dinner?"

"Penny's coming up about two today and we're going to try running for the first time. She'll have the kids with her. Would you mind watching them for an hour or so while we run?"

"Well, don't overdo it. She had chest surgery you know," Ruth said with authority. My preeminent priority position was falling in my own house. Ruth was of the firm conviction that this house needed children. Penny, Catherine and Jack neatly filled this need in Ruth's estimation, so I had rapidly tumbled to around number four on her list.

"Hey, you should be worried about me, not her. She usually runs me into the ground."

"And, of course I'll watch the kids," she continued. "How about dinner?"

"Actually, Ruth, I think that Penny is planning on dinner at her house."

"Oh..." said Ruth, a little crestfallen. "Well, Catherine has riding lessons on Sunday, right?"

"Right. Everybody will be here for dinner on Sunday." Ruth seemed to take solace from this.

"Well, I have to get moving," she said, carefully climbing down from her stool. "Those kids are going to be hungry. They'll need a little snack about three."

~

Penny sat in the grass, left leg extended out in front of her, gracefully stretching her hamstrings. She wore snug running shorts and a sports bra which were causing me to rethink my distaste for this form of exercise.

"Well, this will be interesting," she said, "after not running for over three months."

"You're a masochist."

"You're such a wimp, Alex. It'll be fine."

I hate running. The last time I ran with Penny, Rebecca Franklin, our ER marathoner, ran with us. We did five miles on the North Central Railroad Trail at a pace you wouldn't believe, and the two of them nearly left me a cripple. I run only because it's less tortuous than looking in the mirror and seeing my gut spill over my belt. Well, that and because staying in shape gives me a better shot at whipping John, my childhood buddy, in tennis—a major challenge given John's forehand and our lifelong history of pretty much splitting matches.

"How far do you think we should run today?" she asked, switching legs.

"A hundred yards?"

"Let's shoot for two miles and see how it goes."

In truth, I was curious myself to see how our bodies would respond to exercise after three months of lying around recuperating from our injuries. Actually, I thought that I would do OK—I had no lung injury. I was more concerned about Penny. She loves to run—she was almost as good as Rebecca—and if her lungs weren't up to it after taking a bullet through her chest, that would be hard for her.

We set off down Shepherd Road at a moderate pace, Penny in the lead. At about a half mile I began to challenge my respiratory muscles for the first time, with only mild protest coming from the intercostal muscles between my ribs.

Penny continued in the lead at a steady pace, showing no signs of tiring. At Alan Whitfield's farm, a mile out Shepherd Road, Penny slowed and said, "Not too bad, so far. I think we're at about a mile here. We should probably turn around and not push it too hard the first time."

"Great judgment," I said.

I was happy to see that about three hundred yards from the farm, Penny picked up the pace, her sculpted legs putting distance between us. *Her lungs must be doing OK,* I thought. Unfortunately for me, this constituted a direct challenge to my ego requiring a response, so I sprinted the last hundred yards. Penny sensed me rapidly coming up behind her and began to sprint herself, unwilling to let me pull ahead.

She reached the picnic table before me. I stumbled to a stop and collapsed on the table, laughing and holding my sides—very inconvenient when your lungs are desperately trying to suck air. Penny was walking around with her hands on her hips, chest heaving.

"What?" she asked.

"You weren't going to let me beat you, were you?" I gasped.

She smiled broadly, her bra drenched in the little valley between her breasts and beads of sweat trickling down her tanned face. "Not on your life," she said. "You can do some things better than me, but running's not one of them."

This was a big deal. We were far from being in shape, but despite nearly losing our lives on March 8th, we were both going to be OK.

~

As part of my ongoing domestication classes, I stood with Penny after dinner in her Padonia Road townhouse, emptying the dishwasher and stacking plates and glasses in the cabinets. Holly Broadwater, a sweet girl from Towson University and Penny's live-in baby-sitter for the summer, had the kids upstairs in the tub.

Holly had been baby-sitting for Penny for three years, even before Patrick Murray's death. To Penny's dismay, Holly had graduated from Towson a month before and would be off to California to graduate school in September. But while the kids were out of school, for this summer at least, she was still Penny's lifeline.

It was interesting to me that Holly knew Patrick, whose photos still remained scattered throughout the townhouse. He and Penny married when Patrick graduated from the Naval Academy. Ultimately he became a SEAL team leader, who died in the mountains of Afghanistan carrying a wounded buddy to safety in the midst of a firefight with the Taliban.

That Penny loved him deeply was always apparent to me. She wore his wedding ring for nearly two years after his death, and she never dated until she started seeing me.

In the early days of our relationship, I sometimes felt that there were really three of us instead of two. Without question, Patrick would be there every day forever in the faces of Catherine and Jack. I intuitively understood that this was very different circumstance from, say, dating a woman with children who were all the product of a miserable, failed relationship.

It took me a little time to come to an accommodation with Patrick Murray. Ultimately, of course, it was Penny who helped me to put him to rest. Eventually I came to view him as something of a brother, or perhaps a comrade-in-arms; someone of character for whom I had deep respect. Our bond was that we had both loved the same woman. But all of this is another story. Some day I wanted to hear more about Patrick from Holly's perspective.

"I told you that Tim is coming home from his deployment next month, right?" asked Penny, handing me another stack of plates.

"Yep."

"The *Eisenhower* is coming into port on July twenty-first, and Tim will be here for a week on the twenty-fourth. I'm so excited! It will be such fun to have him meet you and Brian and the rest of your family. Maybe we should have a party. What do you think?"

Second Lieutenant Timothy Murphy, Penny's younger brother, flies F-18's from the deck of the *USS Eisenhower*. He's Navy, of course, as is his and Penny's father, Admiral Thomas Murphy, an old F-14 pilot who is now a bigwig—superintendant of the U. S. Naval Academy. Even Patrick Murray was Navy, although a SEAL, of course, not a pilot.

My brother, Brian, a Southwest Airlines pilot, flew in the military too, but he was Air Force and was as far from a fighter jock as you can get. He flew heavy iron: KC-135s. He would clearly be outgunned by the Navy at any party with the Murphy family.

"Are you going to have the party here?" I asked.

"Of course not. We'll have it at the farm."

Wow. A Murphy family party, but at my house. Every once in a while in life you get the feeling that you've just passed a milestone.

"You know that might send out a little message to your family?"

Penny put down three glasses she had just retrieved from the dishwasher, stepped over and put her arms around my neck. "None that they haven't already received," she whispered, staring intently into my eyes. "I'm not very good at hiding how much I love you."

CHAPTER TWELVE

Miami, Florida
2003

ARY ANNE TURNED THE KEY IN THE LOCK of the second-floor apartment she shared with Vicky Rodriguez in north Miami and then briskly walked the block-and-a-half to the bus stop. The ride to the Wolfson campus of Miami Dade College downtown would take about twenty-five minutes. She had two back-to-back one-hour classes. After class she would walk the three-and-a-half blocks to Columbia Coffee on Third Avenue where she would work the 3:00 PM shift.

She dropped into a window seat, tapped her iPod, and absently watched the Twelfth Avenue streetscape rock by as Iron Maiden's *Dance of Death* blasted in her headphones. *Buses suck*, she thought. Her life in Miami was a far cry from the glamour she had anticipated when she pulled away from the curb at the Bryant's home in a Mercedes SL500 four years ago.

Exhausted after spending her first three nights on the street, she had dyed her hair black and checked into the Miami Rescue Mission under an alias. Unable to show any sort of ID, it had taken her three weeks to find her first job in a sub shop where the owner paid her under the table and was happy just to watch her ass sway around the shop all day.

But it was clear that there was no hope of a better life or better job without identification For this, her immigrant Dominican boss was helpful. After two months on the job, he finally—with great reluctance—introduced her to a man who could produce a birth certificate and a flawless Florida driver's license in a new name. The price required fucking her boss for the next six weeks until she found a new job, but it was worth it.

The next stop on Mary Anne's reality checklist was getting a GED. She averaged six hundred and sixty on the five tests, placing her solidly among college-bound students. Mary Anne was surprised after taking the test at how important that score had become to her personally—one of the first times in her life that she had had the opportunity to experience genuine achievement.

Two years ago, to her utter amazement, she had gone back to school, enrolling part-time at Miami Dade College and accumulating thirteen credit hours.

By six months after turning eighteen, she had started using her real name and Social Security card again. The authorities had never caught up with her as a runaway, but at eighteen, she knew they didn't care any more.

The name change took some explaining to Miami-Dade College, but in the end, the registrar was a socially conscious woman who was taken with the story of a beautiful young runaway-made-good.

Still, despite all that she had accomplished, Mary Anne's life was a grind.

The bus passed a black granite building and she caught a glimpse of her own reflection in the window. *I deserve so much more*, she thought. For four years she had played it straight and worked hard, and look where it had gotten her. She was a fucking barista in a coffee shop.

~

Sammy Griffith saw an empty parking space in front of Columbia Coffee and on an impulse whipped the Porsche to the curb. He checked his watch: 4:33 PM. There would be enough time to get a quick coffee and still get to the club by 5:00. Security chief or not, Sammy had seen Peter Pirelli fire senior employees on the spot for being one minute late.

He pushed through the door and took his place in line behind three other customers. Two girls were working behind the counter, both dressed in skinny black pants and black blouses with red Columbia Coffee logos. The order taker was a rather ordinary looking girl in her twenties. But the girl working the coffee machines caught his eye.

Between the people in front of him and the giant machines against the counter he could only catch occasional glimpses of her. Finally she bent over to retrieve milk from an under-the-counter refrigerator and he got a good look at her backside—narrow hips and pert buttocks atop long, slender legs. She raised up, shook her locks of shiny auburn hair out of her face, and made eye contact, flashing a brilliant smile.

Jesus Christ, thought Sammy, *this bitch is fucking spectacular. She'd be worth her weight in gold.*

He placed his order at the cash register and then waited impatiently at the end of the bar, hands jingling change in his pockets.

"Here you go, sir, a grande double espresso," she said through perfectly even teeth as she handed him the coffee. "Careful. It's hot."

"Got it," he said. "Miss, uh…if you don't mind, may I ask your name?"

"Mary Anne," she said confidently, holding his gaze.

"Well, Mary Anne, I'm sure you hear this all the time, but you are absolutely one of the most beautiful girls I've seen in Miami. Would you, by chance, be interested in considering other employment—employment that I could guarantee you would carry much higher compensation than Columbia Coffee?"

Mary Anne looked him over for a moment. She had noticed him climbing out of a Porsche. On occasion, particularly when she had just arrived in Miami and was basically destitute, she had been approached by pimps, but had no interest. Fucking wasn't the issue. It was control. Mary Anne needed to be in control. She would fuck only who she wanted, when she wanted.

But this guy didn't look sleazy. In fact, he was rather clean-cut; maybe even handsome in a way. And, he was polite. *Well, it never hurts to talk.*

"I might be," she replied.

"I'm going to hand you a card. I'm chief of security at Club Nouveau in South Beach. It's the most exclusive gentlemen's club in Miami, and everything there is completely legal and secure. Our top dancers take home close to a hundred thousand dollars a year, and *all* they do is dance.

"If you'd like to think about that, my name and phone number is on the card. Before you decide, you might even want to stop by the club with your boyfriend one evening and check it out. Then, when you're ready, give me a call and we'll set up an audition."

Sammy handed Mary Anne the card along with a five dollar tip, and walked out of Columbia Coffee.

Mary Anne turned the card over in her hand, looked up, and belatedly called out behind him, "Thanks."

~

Arms folded, she sat in her Columbia Coffee uniform on a park bench across from the brightly lit art deco façade of Club Nouveau, watching patrons come and go under lighted palm trees. A steady stream of Cadillacs, Mercedes, and BMWs pulled up to valet parking, discharging hordes of well-dressed men, sometimes accompanied by elegant women.

The longer she sat, the more convinced Mary Anne became that this was her world. This is where she belonged. She deserved to be here.

~

The audition was at 4:00 PM—to her surprise, live—in front of a group of young businessmen who had left the office early for a little divorce party.

She stood offstage in her own black bra and thong panties, waiting for the music to begin. The club was spectacular—thick carpeting; gleaming chrome and glass; accent lighting everywhere. Mary Anne looked around wide-eyed, like a child on Christmas morning.

The enormous room was divided into two sections, each with its own round, elevated stage with a center pole bathed in bluish light like a transporter from a science fiction film. Plush tables and chairs surrounded each stage, and behind them, a network of intimate spaces delineated by couches and low tables. A third stage was present behind an enormous curving bar, lined with bottles that sparkled under brilliant, focused lights.

She glanced upward and saw a mezzanine level with individual boxes looking down onto the main floor. Every square inch of the high black ceiling seemed to be occupied by spotlights or giant speakers.

A hand landed on her shoulder. Mary Anne turned and looked at Karen, the dancer standing beside her. "When you get out there, honey," said the girl, "just pretend that each one of them is your boyfriend. Make eye contact and smile at every one of them individually. And then make him so hot for you that he thinks he'll explode."

The pounding music started and Mary Anne walked purposefully to the stage. Dancing, for Mary Anne, was like breathing: effortless; natural. If there was one thing in life in which she had utter confidence, it was her own natural beauty. Men adored her.

~

Peter Pirelli smoked a cigarette as he stood behind the small crowd on an elevated portion of the floor and watched the girl walk to the stage with a confident, runway walk. She was stunning.

The girl hugged her arms to her breasts and gently swayed around the stage with her eyes closed, feeling the music. She was lithe; graceful. She lowered her head, gleaming auburn hair falling forward, and then raised her face, shook her hair and opened her eyes. A murmur went up from the crowd.

Placing her back against the pole, she grasped it with both hands above her head and slowly arched her back, pushing her hips forward and revealing ridges of abdominal muscle. Pirelli glanced at the crowd of young men. They were quiet; mesmerized.

With several twirls like a pirouetting ballerina, the girl made her way to the edge of the stage. Picking out the man of honor in the middle of the crowd, she slowly bent over, placing her hands on her knees and allowing her breasts and bra to fall from her chest until you could almost see her nipples. There was no smile. Her face was intent; passionate; in need of the man at whom she was staring. His buddies raised their arms and cheered. The man stood and pushed a twenty dollar bill into her bra.

The girl hadn't even taken off a stitch of clothing, thought Pirelli, yet already she owned the crowd completely.

The audition required the girl to stretch out her routine through the length of three songs. Ever so slowly the bra slipped from the girl's breasts only to be replaced by hands as anticipation built in the rapt audience.

Turning her back to the crowd, she lowered her arms from her breasts to her sides, and then slowly turned to face them; head bowed, like the flower of innocence revealed. With confident purpose, she raised her face. Delicately curving breasts rode high on her chest with erect nipples pointing to the sky. A rumbling, collective groan of appreciation rose from the crowd.

The panties came next, of course. Again she stood quietly with her back to the men, gently swaying; thumbs hooked into the strings of the panties at each hip that gently flared from her narrow waist. Keeping her legs straight and bending only at the waist, the panties slowly slipped over perfectly round buttocks, and then long, slender legs until they reached her ankles and her sex was revealed. The act was so intimate that each man felt that he had been privileged to enter the girl's private boudoir. Pirelli was astonished that the crowd was hushed.

By the end of the third song she stood proudly naked; feet apart, arms stretched out; head held high. Every man in the house believed that this magnificent woman had just stripped only for him. In unison, the young men leapt to their feet and roared. Money poured onto the stage.

Pirelli had never seen such elegance and grace in a stripper, and certainly never one more beautiful. There were a few rough spots that needed polishing, but she was a diamond in the rough that could make him thousands—help achieve his goal of putting Club Nouveau on the national map. He turned to the manager standing beside him. "Give her anything she wants."

CHAPTER THIRTEEN

I AWOKE WEDNESDAY MORNING SPRAWLED ON top of the sheets in sweaty boxers. The usual Bermuda high had parked for the summer off the coast of the Carolinas, and warm air was being pumped northward by the clockwise circulation on the backside of the high. It was hot.

Retrofitting this roughly one-hundred-and-sixty-year-old house with air conditioning was not in my budget. Actually, I don't like air conditioning. It may sound bizarre, but I have always thought of air conditioning as being somehow not real, and I like reality. Apart from this intellectual abstraction, I like hot weather.

Nevertheless, I had broken down and bought a window unit for Ruth's room since Ruth did not share my view of reality.

My feet had not yet hit the floor when my brain began to replay last night's conversation with Penny. Specifically, of course, that her kin would not be surprised that they would be attending a Murphy family party at the home of Alex Randolph, and more so, that Penny was an utter failure at disguising her love for me. Well, she didn't use the word *utter*, that was my interpolation. But in any case, that kind of conversation makes for very nice morning reveries.

I put my hand under the shower stream and yanked it back— freezing. A little more hot water. The truth was that I had no basis of experience for the intensity of my feelings for Penny Murray. They astonished me. I was mad for her. The little crinkles at the edge of her eyes, the curve of her hip, the shape of her smile were all indelibly etched into my brain. This was all very unscientific.

There was not a shadow of doubt, not a hint of indecision, about wanting to spend the rest of my life with this woman. I'd been thinking about this for months.

I thought that Penny was coming to a similar conclusion, but how does one ever know for sure? Was she sending me a message last night? Our times together were so incredibly easy; intimate, as if we had known each other before we were born. But in fact, we had never discussed marriage. Maybe this was all a gigantic exercise in self-deception and wishful thinking on my part.

I swiveled my jaw to one side and pulled the first stroke of the razor down my face, thinking that one of us was going to have to take the first step—just a minor emotional risk, right? And that one was probably me. But I wasn't sure how this was supposed to happen. Do you broach the subject sort of tangentially to minimize risk; give the other person an opportunity to let you down gently if they're not ready? Is it done as a committee by consensus? But then, doesn't every girl want to be asked, "Will you marry me?"

And where in the process does the ring come in? Do you decide to get married and then shop together for a ring? Or maybe you take the big romantic plunge, buy a ring, and then ask her to marry you without any preceding discussion? What if she doesn't like the ring? What if she isn't ready? What if she says no? Do I ask her father first? What if he doesn't like me and has the Navy launch a missile at me?

Ouch! I ripped off a sheet of toilet paper and pressed it against my chin, thinking maybe I should slip by a jewelry store today before my 3:00 PM shift.

CHAPTER FOURTEEN

South Beach, Miami, Florida
2007

THE CONCIERGE SAID "GOOD AFTERNOON, Miss Hampton," and pushed open the heavy brass door. Mary Anne lowered sunglasses from her hair to her eyes and stepped out of her South Beach condominium building into late afternoon sunlight. A few steps past beds of palm trees and multi-colored vincas, she reached the waiting car in the circular drive.

The valet closed the door firmly, saluted, and Mary Anne pulled the Mercedes convertible out into light traffic. It was only ten blocks to Club Nouveau—a short five-minute drive at this time of day, although later this evening, when Ocean Drive was packed, it could take a half hour.

Leaving the car to the club attendant, she made her way down several hallways to her dressing room where she changed into running shorts and a sports bra. Two doors down the hallway she entered the club exercise room and climbed onto a treadmill. Beside her, a new young dancer pounded away at running speed, her body glistening with sweat. "Hey, Mary Anne," she called out.

Mary Anne was only twenty-four, but twenty-four wasn't nineteen anymore. With top billing for almost four years at Club

Nouveau, she was determined to crush any new competition. Her face was on expressway billboards scattered all over the city and she intended to keep it that way. One hundred and thirty thousand dollars a year was powerful incentive to exercise.

Nevertheless, every year brought a crop of new young dancers, all of whom wanted the spotlight for themselves. It wasn't going to be today—Mary Anne lived very much in the present—but deep in her heart she knew that someday this would all end.

In truth, she could already feel her motivation beginning to wane—deadly for a dancer. Boredom was the problem. Stripping naked in front of a crowd of men no longer brought the same excitement; the same adrenaline rush.

Yet the spotlight, the cheers, the applause, the money pouring onto the stage, were an addiction as powerful as heroin itself—a form of self-validation that came from being adored by men willing to pay hundreds or even thousands of dollars for a few moments of her time. Mary Anne had no resolution for this conflict.

After five minutes of warm-up, she punched several buttons on the treadmill and heard the whine of the motor increase. Now running substantially faster than the girl next to her, she looked over and smiled sweetly. *Don't try to pick me off, bitch,* said the smile. *You'll never be as good as me.*

~

Mary Anne stepped out of the shower, dried, and slipped on a white, terry cloth bathrobe. Exercise always left her feeling invigorated, and sometimes in need. Today she felt like a tigress on the prowl. The cotton material of the robe rubbed against her nipples and her crotch tingled.

She slipped on a pair of flip-flops and pushed through the exercise room door headed for her dressing room. At the other end of the long hallway, Sammy Griffith walked toward her. *How convenient,* thought Mary Anne.

Sammy was the ultimate professional. Pirelli would never tolerate anything less. Employees mixing it up with the girls was strictly forbidden, and Sammy was the enforcer. But Sammy had one great weakness: Mary Anne Hampton. He was insane for her.

Mary Anne very quickly figured out that having the Club Nouveau chief of security in your back pocket was useful, especially one who was ex-military police in Iraq. Her shadowy world could get a little tricky at times. Sammy knew how to take care of people that bothered her. He was her grown-up Charlie. She gave Sammy just enough to keep him panting at her door. Today was one of his lucky days.

She stopped in front of her dressing room door and waited for him to reach her. "Hello, Princess," he said.

Mary Anne absently played with the buttons on Sammy's shirt for a moment, allowing her robe to fall open enough for him to see the all the way to her navel. "Sammy," she said looking into his eyes, "I have a little problem this afternoon that maybe you could help me with. My nipples are sending little electric currents to my puss. I've been a bad girl. I think I need to be punished."

~

The bell rang, the elevator doors slid open, and Eddie Williams walked out into the lobby of the Fontainebleau Hotel. Gathered in a small knot in the center of the lobby were his lieutenants. He did a quick head count and saw that they had all arrived in the lobby before him—good idea if they wanted to remain a part of the organization.

The lieutenants were all smiles as Eddie approached the group, threw his hands up in the air and bellowed, "OK boys, let's go have some fun!"

The men piled into two stretch limos amid much boisterous conversation and laughter, following which the valets slammed shut the doors for the short drive to Club Nouveau.

With Eddie in the lead, the men climbed the three wide cobblestone steps leading into the elegant club foyer where the *maitre d'* said brightly, "Good evening, Mr. Williams. I'm John. Thanks for being with us tonight!"

"Evening, John" said Eddie loudly, and the group followed John to two tables covered in white linen immediately adjacent to a round, elevated stage bathed in electric-blue light.

John pulled out a chair facing the stage, Eddie took his seat, and the others followed suit. To Eddie's right sat Chad Mehlon, vice president of operations, and to his left, Eddie's chief financial officer, Milton Kopec. Four senior dealership managers took the rest of the seats at Eddie's table, and the other five junior managers took the other table.

Few men in the world could claim ownership of nine new-car franchises, but Eddie Williams was among them. When Eddie traveled, it was by corporate jet. When he drank, it was Chivas Regal Royal Salute—fifty years old and ten thousand dollars a pop. And when he whored, it was with the most beautiful women in the world, although at a not-so-young sixty-two, his lieutenants all privately wondered how much whoring actually took place.

But hey, he was a widower. He could screw anybody he wanted. If he could still get it up, more power to him.

As the men ate and drank, a parade of gorgeous young women stripped naked on the stage above them, each attempting to make eye contact with the men, and especially Eddie, who each girl clearly recognized as the money behind this little gathering.

Eddie ignored them all, while some of the younger managers at the other table sat clearly entranced by the young flesh writhing on the stage above them. Eddie handed out ten dollar bills around the two tables and waved his hand. "Go ahead," he said, "give these lovely young ladies a tip."

By 10:00 PM, with the tables cleared, the head waiter appeared beside Eddie and said, "Can I get you an after-dinner drink, Mr. Williams?"

Eddie nodded briefly. "Chivas Regal," he said, and continued recounting his story to the rapt audience at his table, his voice rising and falling conspiratorially; his bloodshot eyes animated; his arms gesturing widely. When he reached the punch line, his senior lieutenants erupted in raucous laughter.

The music stopped, the lights dimmed, and a deep, polished baritone voice came over the powerful speaker system. "Ladies and gentlemen, you've seen a lot of lovely ladies here tonight, but Club

Nouveau is now proud to present to you exclusively, the young woman who has put Club Nouveau and South Beach, Miami on the national map; the woman that you've been waiting for all evening. Ladies and gentlemen, Miss Ashley Johansson."

For a brief moment, every light in the house went out, eliciting a surprised murmur from the crowd. A single powerful spotlight suddenly split the darkness, illuminating a motionless, nearly naked young woman on the stage above the Williams tables, arms at her side, head bowed, face covered by long, glimmering auburn hair. The music began and, as if awakening from sleep, the young woman slowly raised her face to reveal the most seductively beautiful woman Eddie Williams could remember seeing.

The girl's routine lasted through three songs; the audience alternately hushed and wildly cheering. Eddie Williams sat motionless throughout the dance, arms folded, his face impassive as he studied the young woman. At the conclusion of her performance, the lights extinguished momentarily, and then the spotlight returned to bathe her nude body in brilliant light as she bowed. The audience erupted in thunderous applause. Every man at the Williams tables leapt to his feet except Eddie Williams.

~

Peter Pirelli stood in the back of the house and watched the audience roar with approval as Mary Anne finished her routine. She was still as good as ever. Mary Anne had made him a ton of money, but he sensed the beginning of the end, as always happened with strippers. She was his greatest asset and his biggest liability.

Pirelli had two other girls who didn't yet have all of Mary Anne's style and elegance—who were still not quite as good at playing an audience—but they were gorgeous, and they were hot on her heels. You had to keep the pipeline full if you wanted to stay in this business.

But he was worried about losing them. He'd already lost three good girls out of his stable of about one hundred in the last two months. Strippers always came and went, but this was different—Mary

Anne Hampton was one-by-one driving away his best dancers.

She could charm the scales off a snake when it suited her purposes, but her lies were as smooth as polished marble and her bite as vicious as a cobra. Pirelli had watched her establish lesbian relationships with several awed young girls, then strip them of self-esteem and dump them, sending them sobbing from the club. None of the girls trusted her. In fact, they despised her. Mary Anne had found more than one way over the last couple of years to screw any girl that she viewed as potential competition.

Pirelli sighed. He hated to lose the revenue, but the future of his club was at stake. At some not-too-distant point, she would have to go.

~

As she danced, Mary Anne took her measure of the crowd. Where was the money? There were a handful of big spenders in the crowd tonight, but none were spending money like the two tables right below her. The older man who sat quietly watching at the table to her left was clearly the source of the gold. She made eye contact with Midas a half dozen times during her three songs and could feel the reciprocity, even though his face remained impassive. His eyes stayed with her. The real money lay in lap dances in private rooms upstairs. A single, big-tipping client could make your night. He would be her first target.

~

Mary Anne swooped into the lap of Midas, placed her arms around his neck and leaned back, lifting her legs gracefully into the air like a trapeze artist. *Why do all the rich ones have to have jowls like bloodhounds*, she wondered. He threw up his arms in loud laughter and looked around at his lieutenants as if to say, "Well, do you guys see who she chose from this crowd?" The men clapped and hooted and nodded their heads.

"What's your name, darlin'?" asked Eddie.

"Ashley. What's yours?"

"No, I mean your real name, baby."

"You haven't told me yours yet," she said smiling. Eddie liked this.

The girl had a little spunk.

"Well, I'm Eddie Williams!" he said loudly, gazing again at his entourage for acknowledgment.

"I'm Mary Anne. Last name's not for publication. I think you liked my dance," she said flatly.

Eddie raised an eyebrow. "Really? And why do you say that?"

"You never took your eyes off me." *This girl is gutsy*, thought Eddie.

With her arms still around his neck, Mary Anne pulled her lips to his ear. "I think you'd like to see more, and maybe feel more," she whispered. "I'm going to invite you to my private room."

Eddie could smell her hair; feel her breath in his ear; feel her bottom wriggle slightly against his crotch. For the first time in many years, he could sense control slipping away. He would not normally allow his lieutenants to see him exhibit personal need by leaving with a stripper—he viewed such behavior as an admission of weakness. But his pulse was pounding and the yearning almost overwhelming. The little bitch was intoxicating. Maybe he'd had too much alcohol.

Abruptly he turned and whispered into her ear, "Lead the way." Eddie didn't even negotiate a price.

~

Two nights later, the turning of heads was not lost on Eddie Williams as the *maitre d'* led he and his companion through the crowded Fontainebleau dining room. Ahead of him Mary Anne's hips swayed in a backless, formfitting black dress that flared to her ankles. Gleaming auburn hair tumbled to just below her bare shoulder blades. Eddie noted with interest that the women in the room appraised Mary Anne as intently as the men.

From somewhere across the room, a piano played. A too-handsome young waiter with black hair slicked straight back dropped off drinks.

Eddie put the glass of scotch to his lips and watched candlelight play across the liquid hazel eyes and high cheekbones of the young woman sitting across the table. He was still trying to reconcile the elegant grace of this woman with the gritty realities of strip clubs—trying to figure out who she was and from where she came.

He leaned back in his chair and folded his arms. "You look lovely tonight."

"Thank you. You are obviously a man of discriminating taste," she said smiling and holding his eyes.

"So who are you, Mary Anne Hampton?" Eddie asked with characteristic directness. "You intrigue me. You are a woman of rare beauty and grace. You're intelligent; quick; self-confident. But you choose to work in a strip club."

Mary Anne smiled and sipped her cosmo. "Does that surprise you?"

"You could be anything you wanted to be. I'm curious about the path that led you to become the most celebrated stripper in Miami."

"I started out with nothing," she began. "I've been on my own since I was sixteen. I don't know my father and, last I heard, my mother was in jail for drug dealing. When I ran away from a foster home I scratched out a living waiting tables and making coffee while I got my GED and then went to college.

"One day a guy walked into my coffee shop and offered me a job dancing. Now I live in a South Beach condo and drive a Mercedes. I did it all on my own."

This was a story that resonated with Eddie Williams. He and Mary Anne were cut from the same bolt of cloth.

"I, too, came from nothing," said Eddie. "My father was a drunk, and my mother waited tables in a diner. I started working in a garage when I was fifteen. I saved my money and when the garage owner died, I bought it from his widow.

"Ten years later I acquired my first car dealership. Now I have nine. I flew into Miami on a private jet, and I'm sitting here having dinner with you at the Fontainebleau Hotel."

"Well, then," said Mary Anne, raising her glass. "Cheers. We're the same people. Now you know who I am." She cocked her head and smiled. Candlelight flashed on dangling earrings, her eyes danced and Eddie Williams was smitten.

~

Eddie's CJ4 Citation jet touched down at Miami International Airport four more times in the fall and winter of 2007-2008; twice to pay Mary Anne a visit, once to pick her up for a long weekend getaway at his beachfront estate in the Dominican Republic, and once to fly her for dinner and the theatre in New York City. But he never again watched her dance.

CHAPTER FIFTEEN

J ULIE AND I HAD A MEETING SCHEDULED ON Friday before my 3:00 PM shift. Once a month we meet to go over stuff and make sure we're on the same page, but with me just back after a three-month absence, we were meeting weekly for a while. She was not in a good mood today.

"You must be a frigging idiot," she said, not for the first time. "Things were going nice and smooth around here, and then you hand Jacquelyn a .38 Special and say 'Please blow my head off.'"

"I think it was just an ice pick."

"Did you get the notice yet that you're going to meet with Myers?" The Cody Brown incident was moving up the chain fast. Jackie Ford must have hopped right on this one.

Technically my boss, Dr. Sheldon Myers was the young Nazi vice president of medical affairs that John Salzman had directed to fire me back on March first. Myers was brand new to the organization at the time, hired to replace the old VP who had also fallen afoul of Salzman and lost his job. My termination meeting was actually the only time I had ever met Dr. Myers, but now we'd get the chance to renew our acquaintance.

"Alex, you can't *do* this," Julie moaned. "You got hired, fired, hired again, and now you're working as hard as you can at getting fired again. Are you trying to set a world record? You are driving me nuts. You can't just throw patients out of the ER!

"Why not?"

93

Julie threw up her hands in exasperation. "You're gonna make me old before my time."

She was right, of course—from the bureaucratic standpoint. Federal law requires us to provide emergency care for everyone who presents to an ER, regardless of race, creed, socioeconomic status, payment history, smell, or obnoxious behavior. Full responsibility is placed on the ER care provider; none on the patient. There is no clause excluding assholes from the federal requirement to treat. I would have to take my lumps on this one, be appropriately remorseful for my behavior, and promise not to do it again.

~

I logged into my computer and was about to see my first patient when Roberta walked up from her reception desk and said, "There's a guy out here who wants to see you—Shank; Kenneth Shank."

"A patient?"

"No. He says you took care of his wife."

The name sounded familiar. "Oh, I bet that's the husband of the pregnant girl with lymphoma—Kaitlyn."

I walked out into the lobby and recognized the face of Kaitlyn Shank's young husband, standing with his hands in his pockets; eyes puffy and bloodshot.

"Mr. Shank?" I said sticking out my hand.

He grasped my hand and held onto it, slowly pumping for a long time—maybe searching for words.

"Doctor Randolph, I just wanted to thank you for talking Kaitlyn into going to Hopkins. I think it saved our daughter's life."

"Kaitlyn delivered?"

"They took the baby three days ago, when Kaitlyn got an infection again and went into shock. I think Olivia's gonna be OK. She's in the NICU, but she's doing fine." This didn't sound good.

"And Kaitlyn?"

Ken Shank's face contorted and he put his hand over his eyes to cover the tears that began to flow. "She didn't make it."

He paused, and took a deep breath. "They put her on a ventilator after the C-section, and she never woke up. She only lasted twenty-four hours. The NICU nurses brought Olivia into Kaitlyn's room when they turned off the ventilator, but Kaitlyn never got to see her."

I stood and wordlessly stared into Ken Shank's eyes, struggling to wrap my mind around the magnitude of Kaitlyn's sacrifice; to find words that would not diminish the enormity of her courage.

Finally I simply told him what I was thinking. "I have seen much human courage among dying patients and their families over the years, Ken, but never courage like Kaitlyn's."

~

As I tried to catch a quick slice of pizza between patients a little after 7:00 PM, a weather alert came over the Baltimore County Fire/EMS dispatch radio preceded by a series of tones. "A line of thunderstorms with heavy rain, damaging winds, and large hail is currently stretching from York, Pennsylvania to Westminster, Maryland and moving southeast. The line is expected to reach Hampstead about 7:42, Hereford about 7:58, and Jarrettsville, about 8:13 PM. A tornado warning is in effect for northern Baltimore County."

"Sounds like my pasture's finally going to get a little rain," I said to Lynn Saylor sitting beside me.

"With my luck, my nice new little VW will look like somebody pounded it with a ball-peen hammer," she replied.

"Wouldn't make any difference to my Wrangler."

Lynn is a tall, athletic brunette with a sunny disposition and a razor-sharp mind. She trained at Boston Deaconess, and she's an awesome ER doc. Her lovely face will forever be indelibly etched in my mind because it was the first face that slowly shimmered into focus as I regained consciousness after the hostage incident. I remember thinking that this must be an angel hovering over me on her knees in the chaotic room; protecting me; gently probing my broken body and asking where I hurt.

I stuffed the last wedge of pizza into my mouth, took a big gulp of Coke, and walked to the sink by the Omnicell medication dispenser to clean the tomato sauce off my hands and mouth. I would loved to have brushed my teeth too, but my little pizza break had already put me three more patients behind.

Pat Cole, a no-nonsense divorced mother of two teenage boys who I have seen turn intoxicated lions into lambs, stood at the Omnicell retrieving some meds and watching me wash up. "You need to change your scrub shirt, too," she said.

"What?"

"You missed your mouth. There's tomato sauce and cheese all over your shirt."

I flicked off the cheese into the sink, pinched up the part of the scrub top covered with tomato sauce, and leaned over the sink to try and wash just the stain without soaking my whole shirt. That didn't work. Water ran down my thumb and drenched the bottom of the shirt. I pulled out several sheets of paper towels and started to pat the shirt dry.

"Alex...for God's sake. Please. Just go to the locker room and change your shirt."

"Do you have a hair dryer?"

"Go!"

I turned to head to the locker room and bumped into Jen Wilke's generous chest.

"Oh! Sorry, Jen."

"Alex, you need to see this lady in Fifteen," she said earnestly. "I think she may need tubing."

I walked into Fifteen with Jen, shirt soaked, to see the room packed with Parkton Station's Medic 60 crew and two nurses completing the process of transferring the patient from ambulance stretcher to bed. An aged female with disheveled gray hair was sitting in the bed upright with a huge mask strapped to her face that made her look like an elderly female fighter pilot. She was obviously struggling for air.

Patty Friedman, a lanky thirty-something paramedic, was trying to readjust the mask to the old woman's face after transfer from the ambulance stretcher. Nurses were hurriedly connecting her to hospital monitors and stripping off clothes.

"Dr. Randolph, this lady developed sudden onset of shortness of breath about an hour ago," called out Patty. "She's got a history of congestive heart failure. I think she's in pulmonary edema. When I got there she had coarse rales throughout her chest and her neck veins were up. I put her on C-PAP and she's had nitro and Lasix, but she's not doing so good."

Congestive heart failure occurs when the heart—simply a biologic pump—is unable to handle the volume of blood being delivered to the left ventricle. Blood backs up behind the failing pump into the lungs under pressure and fluid begins to leak out of the blood vessels into the tiny air sacs called alveoli. When your lungs fill up with fluid, you essentially drown.

"What's her O$_2$ sat?" I asked.

"It was in the seventies on arrival. I haven't been able to get it higher than the low eighties, even with C-PAP."

C-PAP is a nifty little machine that raises the pressure on your airway through a tight-fitting mask. The pressure makes it easier to keep the little air sacs in your lungs inflated when they are filling up with fluid.

"What's her name?"

"Dillon. Rose Dillon."

Mrs. Dillon's eyes were closed and her head was lolling off to one side as her level of consciousness declined. Through the clear mask I could see white froth around her mouth from the fluid bubbling up from her lungs. Despite the C-PAP and Patty Friedman's other interventions, Rose Dillon was drowning. I made a snap decision.

"OK. Let's intubate her. Get me a seven point five tube. Pull the Glidescope over here." People started to scramble. Mrs. Dillon was so far gone—nearly unconscious—that I decided to do what we call a *crash intubation*: put an endotracheal tube into her lungs immediately without taking the time to use the usual drugs to put her to sleep and paralyze her.

I lowered the head of her bed and ripped the mask from her face. Jen handed me the video laryngoscope blade which I inserted deep into her throat, looking for the opening to her trachea. A video camera in the tip of the scope transmits the image to a monitor screen so you can see exactly where you are, but when I looked at the screen I could see nothing but frothy fluid.

"Suction!" Someone pushed a rigid suction tube into my hand. I pushed the tube deep into her pharynx, suctioned away the fluid, and suddenly the vocal cords leading into her trachea popped into view.

"Gimme the tube! What's her O_2 sat?"

"Down to sixty-eight," called out a voice. We were running out of time here.

Pushing the endotracheal tube through her mouth, I saw the tip come into view on the monitor screen. I advanced the tube, saw it slip off the tracheal opening twice, and then suddenly we were in.

"Got it." Hands attached a ventilation bag to the tube and began to pump one hundred percent oxygen into Rose Dillon's lungs.

The staff connected Mrs. Dillon to a ventilator and I watched her oxygen saturation steadily climb to one hundred percent.

~

I finished examining Mrs. Dillon, pulled up her old records on the computer to review her history, and began entering orders. A quick check of her chest x-ray revealed the fluffy white pattern of congestive heart failure, as we expected, and my endotracheal tube was in good position above the split of the mainstem bronchi.

In the background, above the steady white noise of the air conditioning, I thought I heard a faint boom.

The lights flickered for a moment and then everything was black. This would be a huge pain. All of the computers would go down and it would take forever to get the system up again. Two seconds later the lights came back on for a second, and then went out again. It was pitch black—not a glimmer of light visible.

I waited for the diesel-powered emergency generator to kick in, which usually takes just a couple of seconds. Five seconds went by, then ten. People started talking in the darkness around me. Fifteen seconds went by and no power. Scattered around the department patients began calling out from their rooms. It was suddenly clear to me that the emergency power system was not coming on.

Holy shit. Mrs. Dillon's on a ventilator! Without electric power to the ventilator we would have to disconnect it and breathe for her manually with a ventilation bag or she would die.

To my left I saw the faint light of a smartphone screen go on. *Great idea.* Reaching out my hand out into the darkness, I found my iPhone on the counter, tapped the screen several times for the flashlight app, and suddenly there was light.

"OK, who's here at the nursing station?" I called out.

"Lisa."

April."

"I'm here," said Lynn's voice.

"First priority is Mrs. Dillon in Fifteen, I said, beginning to move in that direction. "Is anybody still in her room?"

"Jen should still be in there," I heard Lisa's voice call out.

"OK, I'm going in there. Everybody else make your way from room to room and start collecting flashlights and bring them back to the nursing station. Lisa, you issue flashlights to everyone and then everybody start checking patients one-by-one."

I made my way to Fifteen as quickly as possible without falling over empty chairs at the nursing station. As I neared Fifteen I could see a faint glow of light through the doorway.

A single lighted flashlight provided ghostly illumination of Jen Wilke, standing at the head of the bed, calmly squeezing a ventilation bag attached to Mrs. Dillon's endotracheal tube.

Jen smiled, her white teeth reflecting the meager light. "Piece of cake," she said. "Just like the power going out in the milking parlor at home." An expansive and cheerful mother of four elementary school-aged kids, Jen and her dairy farmer husband milk one hundred and fifty Holstein cows twice a day, every day, beginning at somewhere around 4:00 AM.

"Like the milking parlor?"

"Yeah. Hospital or milking parlor, you gotta squeeze bags by hand when the power goes out," she said laughing.

~

Fifteen minutes into the blackout, we had gotten reasonably well organized. The department had two crash carts equipped with portable battery-powered monitors which we connected to our two sickest patients. All of the walking wounded were escorted into the lobby where windows transmitted the feeble daylight that remained in the midst of a raging thunderstorm. There we did quick screening exams and then sent them off to neighboring hospital ERs for treatment. Most of them decided to sit and wait out the storm before they went to their cars, which goes to show you how urgent are most ER visits.

Hereford Fire Department Engine 441 appeared on the scene and within twenty minutes of the blackout had snaked extension cords from their on-board generator into the ER and the ICU upstairs. One of these was used to power Mrs. Dillon's ventilator, for which Jen Wilke was very grateful. Even a dairy farmer's hands get tired.

One healthy baby was born upstairs by flashlight. The ICU was constructed in the corner of the building, with windows in all the patient rooms providing daylight, so they didn't fare too badly.

Fortunately, since it was after 7:00 PM, only one surgery was in progress up in the OR. Poor Phil Timmons was in the middle of a laparoscopic appendectomy when the power went out. You can't see through fiber optic scopes without power, so he had no choice but to pull out the catheters, keep his fingers crossed that there would be little bleeding, and zip the patient by ambulance to the closest hospital, Greater Baltimore Medical Center on Charles Street, where they took him straight to the OR.

Of course, we couldn't get any medications out of the Omnicell medication dispensers because they are electronic, but fortunately we have stocks of emergency drugs in the code carts. I've always had this insane urge to take a sledgehammer to those Omnicells, but fortunately for me, no urgent need arose for a medication that we didn't have in the code cart, or I would have received a bill from the hospital for a sixty thousand dollar machine.

Baltimore County dispatch headquarters put out a divert notice for all ambulances, sending them to other hospitals, and announcements went out over all the TV and radio stations that the ER at Mason Dixon was closed until further notice.

Interestingly, communications within the hospital were the least affected by the power outage because everyone has cell phones.

In the end, nobody died and we only had to transfer three patients out of the ER by ambulance to other hospitals. When the power came back on about 10:30, we only had three patients left in the ER.

"Wow. That was kinda fun," said Lynn. "I wonder what my car looks like?"

CHAPTER SIXTEEN

Baltimore, Maryland
2008

EDDIE WILLIAMS SAT SILENTLY ON THE EXAM table as the surgeon removed the sutures from first the wound on his upper left arm and then in his left axilla.

"There you go, Eddie. The wounds look great," said Dr. Andrew Holland, associate professor of plastic surgery at Johns Hopkins University School of Medicine. He tossed the disposable suture removal kit into a trash can, picked up a manila folder from the counter, and sat on a stool beside Eddie.

"We have the pathology report back from the lesion I removed from your arm, Eddie, and as I suspected, it is positive for a melanoma. We'll certainly hope that we got it all, but the sentinel node in your axilla did have some microscopic disease in it."

"What does that mean?" asked Eddie, more curtly than he had intended. He was not accustomed to men twenty years younger than he being in control of a conversation.

"Well, it means that some of the cancer cells had spread from your arm up to a lymph node in your armpit. But we took out about six lymph nodes and only one of them had any evidence of cancer."

"So, does that mean I'm cured?"

"It doesn't mean you're cured, but it does mean that you have a

102

reasonable *chance* of being cured." Eddie was not happy with this answer. He was accustomed to running his business by the numbers, and he sure as hell wanted some numbers attached to this statement.

"What's reasonable? Give me some numbers."

"Eddie, with a single positive lymph node, that places you in what we call Stage two B disease. The five-year survival rate runs about fifty to sixty percent, so the odds are in your favor."

"That also means that I've got a forty to fifty percent chance of dying in the next five years, right?"

"That's another way of looking at it," said Dr. Holland.

~

Eddie walked through the parking garage to his Cadillac Escalade thinking about his life. Suddenly he felt old. He was a widower, never had any kids, and now he faced a fifty percent probability of dying within the next five years—alone.

Since the death of his wife five years ago, he had partied and whored and had his fill of the single life. But when he came home at night it was to a silent, empty, ten-thousand-square-foot mansion. Maybe *mausoleum* was a better term, he thought. He might be dead in a couple of years. In truth, he had not a single close friend and could not think of a soul who would mourn his passing. For the first time in his life, Eddie felt real fear.

He shook his head violently to clear his mind. Maudlin introspection was not his thing; he was a man of action. Besides which, maybe he wouldn't die.

By the time he reached his SUV, Eddie had come to two decisions. The first was not to tell anyone about his cancer. Power and respect declined when people sensed a chink in your armor. No one would trifle with him as long as he could help it. He would not be a lame duck.

His second decision was more interesting: he was going to marry again. If it were possible that he had only a few years remaining, then by God he was going to go out in style, with a beautiful woman at his side; a woman men would envy—maybe even a woman who would be with him at the end, if it came to that.

~

On a clear night in late August, Mary Anne Williams watched the magnificent Baltimore skyline slowly drift by as Citation seven-zero-papa turned on final approach for runway two-two at BWI Marshall Airport. A palette of neon colors from the lights of dozens of tall buildings shimmered on the still waters of the Inner Harbor two thousand feet below her. The flight from Las Vegas had taken just over four hours.

Absently twirling two Tiffany rings on her left hand, she smiled. Across the aisle of the elegant jet sat Eddie Williams, kingpin of a mid-Atlantic automotive empire and her new husband. *That makes me the queen,* she thought. *And I'm on my way to the palace.*

The king was a bore, of course—nothing like her smooth-muscled Sammy. But Mary Anne was very adept at keeping the customers happy. Having sex with Eddie was a no-brainer. She could zone out anytime she wanted. Now she had money, status, a mansion, and a staff, not to mention a private jet. She could find ways of keeping a little excitement in her life.

This is my destiny. I've made all the right moves. I've got all the looks and the talent. I earned this.

~

Mary Anne descended the grand staircase in tee shirt and snug running shorts; hair still wet from her first shower at Ascot Farms on *My Lady's Manor* in Baltimore County's gentrified horse country. *Let's see... how do I get to the kitchen?*

Eddie leaned against the massive granite counter drinking his second cup of coffee when he finally heard Mary Anne's footsteps coming down the hallway. When she entered the room, he was struck again by her elegant beauty: tall and slender; radiant hazel eyes; long, wet auburn hair reflecting morning sunlight; proud breasts gently swaying under her tee shirt. *She belongs here at Ascot,* thought Eddie; *lights up the house; gives it life and youth. Just wait until I walk into Baltimore Country Club with her.*

"Good morning, sweetheart," boomed Eddie. "How did my queen sleep last night?"

Mary Anne smiled sweetly. "Like a rock, your lordship." Eddie liked that and laughed loudly.

"Well, first things first. You haven't received your wedding present yet." He turned to the young, dark-skinned woman working at the kitchen island and said, "Manuela, we'll take breakfast out on the patio."

Walking to his new bride, he first kissed her on the lips, and then placing his arm around her waist, led her out through French doors onto an expansive tiled patio.

Mary Anne gazed around in awe. Six massive white pillars supported a roof over a spacious elevated section of patio closest to the house, under which sat several elegant groupings of dark wicker furniture covered with bright chintz cushions. Immediately ahead lay a ninety-foot, crystal-clear infinity pool surrounded by blue and white chaise lounge chairs.

Beyond the far end of the pool stood a stucco pool house covered with a red-tiled roof that extended out over a long, open granite counter populated with stainless steel appliances. In the center of the counter was an open fireplace.

The entire complex was delineated by dark green hedges with shiny leaves, and clusters of pink dogwood trees rising from beds of pink and purple impatiens. Even in Miami, Mary Anne had rarely seen an estate of such elegance.

"This way, sweetheart," said Eddie. He turned left off the elevated section of patio and led Mary Anne down a stone walkway toward a parking area under a canopy of tall poplar trees. To the right sat a five-car carriage house.

"What do you think?" asked Eddie. "Fitting for a new bride?" Mary Anne's eyes grew wide. Dwarfed by Eddie's Escalade, and wrapped in a huge red ribbon, sat an obsidian black SLS Mercedes Roadster convertible. She couldn't remember all of the letters designating the particular model, but Mary Anne knew that this little beauty came in somewhere around two hundred thousand dollars.

~

"I'll take another orange juice," said Mary Anne. "And put a little ice in this one." Manuela bowed her head silently and left the patio for the kitchen. Mary Anne watched the young Salvadoran's hips sway under her knee-length dress as she walked toward the French doors.

"So out there to the left is the main barn, and a couple of outbuildings," continued Eddie, pointing with his index finger, "and then all of the fenced-in area you can see behind the pool house there is pasture." Eddie sat up and squinted at the black cattle grazing in the fields.

"You see that largest animal just to the left of that dogwood tree?"

"Which is the dogwood tree?"

"The one in that bed of pink and white flowers."

"OK. I see it. That big black cow."

"That, my darling, is not a cow. That is Sir William Ascot 049, 2009 Grand Champion of the Eastern National Livestock Show. He's worth almost as much as your new little Roadster. And he is an Angus bull. He would not be happy if he overheard you calling him a cow."

"How can you tell?"

"How can you tell what?"

"That he's a bull."

"C'mon," said Eddie, laughing as he pushed back his chair. "Let's walk over to the fence and see if you can tell that he's a bull."

The closer they got to the fence, the more Mary Anne could see that this animal was a monster. Sir William idly turned as they approached, and a pair of bull testicles swayed into view.

"Oh my God!" she gasped. "They're huge—like cannon balls!"

Eddie Williams laughed. He suddenly realized that for the first time in many years, he was having actual fun. *This was a good decision*, he thought.

~

Gerald Stine made the last pass around the field with the mower and turned the orange Kubota tractor toward the implement shed. As soon as it came into view, his eyes zeroed in on the pool. The woman was out there again. From this distance it almost looked like she was naked. Maybe she was. Or maybe she was wearing a white piece of string.

He watched her gracefully sway along the edge of the pool and then bend over to turn a lounge chair to face the sun. She plopped down into the chair and lay back with her legs wide apart. Gerry felt his cock stir.

He'd heard that the old man got married. Maybe that was his new wife. Gerry wasn't allowed near the house, so he'd never met her. *But hell*, he thought, *that girl's my age. Well, if she ever gets tired of fucking an old man, I'll give her a fucking she'll remember.*

~

"Pull!" yelled Eddie. The clay pigeon went streaking out low over the orchard grass to Eddie's right. He whipped the Browning 12-gauge around and fired off a first shot that splintered the edge of the spinning disc, followed immediately by a second blast that powdered it just before it reached the grass. Mary Anne stood holding her hands over her ears.

"Ha! What'd you think of that?" Eddie asked, turning to his buddy.

Nathan Card took a slow sip of Heineken and replied, "A waste of good ammunition. I'd have powdered it on the first shot."

"OK, darlin', your turn," said Eddie. "Come over here. I've got just the little gun for you." Nathan cast an appreciative eye on the girl as Mary Anne walked to Eddie in painted-on designer jeans and a pair of brown leather riding boots that had obviously never been worn before.

"This little baby is light and won't knock your shoulder off," said Eddie, holding up a single-shot 20-gauge. "Let's just set up a pigeon on the ground over there so you can get used to it first." Mary Anne had never had a gun in her hands before, but the idea excited her.

"I don't know if I can do that," she said demurely.

"Sure you can," boomed Eddie "Now you gotta hold this thing tight against you shoulder so it doesn't come back and slam you."

Mary Anne pulled the stock tightly into her shoulder, aimed, closed her eyes, and pulled the trigger. She was completely unprepared for the recoil which knocked her flat on her butt. The clay pigeon sat there undisturbed. Eddie and Nathan convulsed with laughter.

Mary Anne climbed to her feet, pissed. "Gimme that gun again."

The second time she fought to keep her eyes open when she pulled the trigger, and the clay pigeon vanished in a puff of powder. Eddie and Nathan cheered. Mary Anne smiled. *I like this*, she thought.

~

"What else do you have in that bag?" she asked.

"Well, let's see." Eddie rummaged around in his gun bag and pulled out a compact black pistol with a rubber grip.

"Now this little number," he said, "is just the right size for a lady—a Sig Sauer P238. Watch this." He pressed a button in front of the trigger guard and pointed the gun at his forearm. A little red dot played back and forth over his shirtsleeve.

"That's a laser. You can tell exactly where you're aiming with this thing." He ejected the clip from the grip and handed the gun to Mary Anne. She hefted the weight of the pistol, turning it over back and forth with her wrist. It felt perfect in her hand. Extending her arm, she pointed the little pistol at a distant tree.

"No," said Eddie, taking the gun, "you have to hold it like this— with two hands."

Thirty yards to the east of the skeet range was a target range. The trio walked the short distance and Eddie attached a paper target with red circles to a clip. He slammed the ammo clip back into the bottom of the grip and handed the gun to Mary Anne.

"All right, now don't point that thing at anybody. Keep it aimed out in front of you. Stand with your feet apart a little bit and hold it with two hands like I showed you. It's going to kick a little, just like that shotgun, so be ready for it."

Mary Anne steadied herself, held the gun with both arms extended, and sighted over the barrel for the little red dot on the target.

"Now, hold your breath and just squeeze the trigger slowly and steadily." Mary Anne applied pressure to the trigger and nothing happened. She applied a little more pressure and suddenly with a deafening report the gun flew up in the air.

"Whoa!" she exclaimed. "Did I hit it?"

"No. You hit that cow over there!" Eddie and Nathan laughed raucously.

"I did not! You two guys are blind," she said, joining in the laughter.

After ten more rounds, several holes appeared on the target, one very near the bull's-eye.

"I think I'm getting the hang of this," said Mary Anne. "This is fun."

CHAPTER SEVENTEEN

My Lady's Manor
May 21, 2011

EDDIE WILLIAMS STOOD BEFORE THE FULL-length mirror in the master bath and adjusted the black tie, scowling at his appearance. The collar on his shirt was too damned big. *I look like Jimmy Carter.*

The black tuxedo that drooped from his once-generous frame fit no better. He was losing weight fast. *I'll be lucky to make it another six months at this rate,* he thought grimly.

Mary Anne scurried into the bath and stood before her dressing mirror, inserting a dangling diamond earring into her right earlobe. "Where are we going tonight?" she asked again.

"To a charity fundraiser."

"What charity?"

"The St. Mark's Country Day School Annual Patron Auction."

"So, who's going to be there?"

"The parishioners of St. Marks and most everybody with real money on the Manor."

Mary Anne turned to face Eddie, looking like a cover photo from Vogue in a white one-shoulder ankle length gown. Cocking her head to one side and pouting, she said, "Do I *have* to go?"

Eddie sighed. Sometimes he felt like he was married to a teenage girl with oppositional defiance. Nevertheless, the sight of her still melted him, and an awareness that his days were probably limited had substantially mellowed the fearsome side of Eddie Williams.

"Yes, my lovely little bird, you have to go. We've donated a week at the Fort Myers beach house and a roundtrip flight on the company jet to the auction. It's probably the biggest gift that will be sold tonight."

~

All eyes were on Eddie Williams as he entered the room with a stunning auburn-haired beauty on his arm—just the way he liked it. Immediately, a tall, slender woman with graying hair briskly crossed the elegant room wearing a wide smile. Reaching out with both hands she clasped Eddie's hand in hers and said, "Eddie...how nice to see you again."

Maybe Eddie would like to have an affair with this woman, thought Mary Anne hopefully.

"Priscilla Manning, have you met my wife, Mary Anne?"

"No, I've not had the pleasure," she gushed, now grasping the young woman's hands. "Hello, Mary Anne. Oh my, you look just stunning!"

"Priscilla is the very competent headmistress of St. Mark's Country Day School," Eddie informed his wife.

"Well, Priscilla, what a wonderful job you've done here at St. Mark's," said Mary Anne. "You must be very proud"...*of your facelift.*

"You know, Mary Anne, it would be virtually impossible without generous people like you and Eddie. Thank you *so much* for your gift tonight."

Believe me, it wasn't my idea. "It's the very least that we could do, Priscilla," Mary Anne said graciously. "Our little gift pales in comparison to your hard work."

~

I'm going to puke if I shake one more sweaty hand, thought Mary Anne. "Eddie, darling," she said, patting her husband on the shoulder, "I'm going to go get us a drink. You must be dying of thirst."

Free at last of clutching hands, Mary Anne floated away to the bar to big band tunes from a seven-piece orchestra.

"What can I get you, Miss?"

"A champagne and a Chivas Regal on the rocks, please."

Bored out of her mind and in no rush to return to the inane throng surrounding her husband, Mary Anne turned and raised the champagne to her lips, her eyes rapidly scanning the room—an art that she had honed to perfection in her years on the stage at Club Nouveau.

Without conscious effort, she quickly sorted the crowd and dropped the figures on the ballroom floor into neat little bins in her mind: the deep pockets, the fawning wannabes, wealthy women on the prowl, arrogant new money, networking opportunists, insecure wives, and barely disguised predators. Nothing at all of the slightest interest.

And then she saw him. Tall, with longish dark hair and a substantial build, he was staring intently into the eyes of a petite young blonde who, Mary Anne had to admit, just might have made the first cut as a dancer at Club Nouveau—no competition for Mary Anne, of course, but certainly interesting enough to bed for a night.

He must have said something very charming, because the blonde suddenly dissolved into laughter and then socked him in the chest. The easy radiant smile that lit up his face beckoned almost irresistibly.

They were a little far away, but she couldn't spot a wedding ring on either of them. *Hmmm...he is very hot. I wonder who he is? Maybe this charity ball wasn't such an awful idea after all.*

Mary Anne jumped at the tap on her shoulder. "Enjoying the ball?" asked Eddie.

"Oh! Sorry Eddie," she said, turning and picking up the glass on the bar behind her, "you scared me. Here's your Chivas Regal. I got distracted just watching the crowd. They're so interesting!"

She followed Eddie back into the crowd, passing fifteen feet from Alex Randolph, whose intriguing face she memorized in a final glance.

CHAPTER EIGHTEEN

THURSDAY AFTERNOON I SHOWERED, PUT ON a pair of slacks and a sports jacket, and headed off to rendezvous with Penny at her Padonia Road townhouse. There we would switch to her SUV and load up the kids for the trip to Annapolis—my first visit with Admiral and Mrs. Thomas Murphy.

The memory was still foggy, but I had met Tom and Denise Murphy only once before, in the ICU when Penny and I lay recovering in side-by-side rooms soon after surgery. I remembered Denise Murphy as a dignified and gracious woman, still rather stunning in her mid-fifties, who gently thanked me for taking such good care of her daughter. I had trouble seeing the point at the time because I was still wracked with guilt that I had failed to deflect the shot that nearly ended her daughter's life.

You couldn't miss Tom Murphy, a tall, handsome man with a face of steel—at least during that stressful time—and arresting blue eyes. He quietly shook my hand, then said, "Dr. Randolph, thank you for trying to defend my daughter."

Nevertheless, despite that congenial meeting, I was mildly apprehensive about this first family dinner gathering.

~

"What if your father doesn't like me?"

"Well, of course he likes you."

"How do you know that? What if he decides to launch a covert Navy operation against me?"

"Don't be silly, Alex, he can't launch a covert operation against you."

"How do you know that? It's all in deniability. The government's good at that."

"Alex, *really*. I can't believe you're so paranoid about this dinner."

"I have a strong instinct for self-preservation."

"Are we there yet?" asked Jack.

"Of course we're not there yet, stupid," replied Catherine. "Why do you think we're still in the car?"

"Catherine, don't call your brother stupid," responded Penny.

"Well, any idiot knows we're not there yet."

"Catherine! Stop!"

We pulled up to Gate 3 of the Naval Academy and I told the guard that we were here on a secret mission.

"Penny Murray," said Penny, leaning forward in her seat and flashing her driver's license. "The superintendant is expecting us."

"We're here to see our grandfather," offered Catherine.

The guard gave us a visitor's pass, saluted, and in seconds we were inside the lion's den.

Penny punched some icons on her iPhone, dictated "We're here, Mom," and then I heard the whoosh of a text flying off into cyberspace.

"Turn right here," said Penny. I turned right onto Blake Road, passed the Chapel, and there around the corner was Buchanan House, the cozy little thirty-four-room residence of the superintendant. You could live here with your ex and never run into her.

Standing on one of the enormous verandas under a green canopy was grandmom, waving as we pulled into a parking space.

~

I shook hands with the admiral, and he said, "Alex, great to see you." I could find no guards standing around behind curtains with submachine guns, and the admiral wore no sidearm, or medals on his chest. In fact, he was wearing jeans and a plaid shirt. I was beginning to feel overdressed.

Denise Murphy was also wearing jeans and, I must say, did not look bad in them. But that's going way too far into Freudian territory.

Catherine and Jack seemed to know where they were, and zoomed off somewhere into the maze of rooms.

"Can I offer you a drink, Alex?" asked Tom.

Do you have a drink taster who can sniff out poison?

"I'll take a Grey Goose and tonic, if you have it."

Penny, Dad, and I walked out onto one of the verandas with our drinks and took a seat in a series of rocking chairs facing the magnificent chapel and John Paul Jones' burial place. Denise apparently was getting the kids squared away someplace. It was a very sweet June evening. Some of the blossoms were still on the magnolia trees.

"I can't believe it's taken this long for us to get together," said Tom.

Every second of life is precious.

"Can you believe that tonight is the only night Mom and I could find when everyone was available? We've been trying for a month," Penny said. "It's terrible."

"So how are you two doing?" asked Tom genuinely. "Do you feel close to being fully recovered?"

"Alex and I went for a run for the first time on Tuesday. We only ran two miles, but it went OK."

"She ran me into the ground," I said. "She's the runner. Usually I only run when I'm being chased by dogs."

Tom thought that was funny.

Denise appeared with some kind of ruby-colored mixed drink and joined us.

"Well, they're playing in that dress-up play room on the third floor. Catherine has Jack in a full-length purple gown and heels," she said. "Reminds me of ET. Poor Jack. She's going to have his gender identity totally confused."

"Little risk of that," said Penny. "He's a savage. I'm having trouble civilizing him. Takes after his uncle Tim."

Or maybe his grandfather.

~

After a very lovely dinner of four courses and three different wines—served by a white-jacketed waiter, I might add—Tom said, "Come on, Alex. I'll show you around the grounds. How about a little cognac?" I like cognac. Makes me brave.

Glasses in hand, we headed off around the quadrangle, past Tecumseh Court off Bancroft Hall—comfortably chatting—and then circled around back toward the chapel with its massive green-copper dome. I vaguely wondered if wandering around the Academy grounds with an open container was legal. But, I forgot. I was with the superintendant.

We climbed the broad granite steps of the chapel and sat down on the top stair.

"Denise and I were married here when I graduated thirty-four years ago," said Tom. "Incredible how fast time flies."

For a moment I was struck with unexpected melancholy. Here also, eight years previous, Penny and Ensign Patrick Murray had exited their wedding ceremony with smiles and laughter under a canopy of drawn swords. I wondered if this was the place to say what I had to say. But then again, by this time I had finished my cognac. I started in.

"Admiral Murphy, I need to tell you that I love your daughter. In fact, I am absolutely mad for her. Before I met Penny, I had no concept that I was capable of feeling the emotions that she releases in me.

"These last six months with her have been the most wonderful months in my memory. I want to spend the rest of my life with her. Knowing how much she loves you and her mother, I would hope that you would give your blessing for me to ask for her hand in marriage."

This will likely be the place where they'll try to finish me off. I waited for the crack of the sniper's rifle, but then again, I guess you never hear the crack.

Tom sat silently for a moment looking into his glass, and then bored into me with those brilliant blue eyes.

"Alex, after Patrick's death I despaired that my daughter would ever again find happiness. The truth is that I don't know you very well, Alex, although I do know something of your character. But you have brought light and joy and love back into Penny's life. I have never seen her happier, despite the tragedy of recent months. You are an incredibly lucky man because her love for you astounds me."

The admiral held out his hand. "I would be honored to call you my son-in-law."

Well...that really wasn't so bad after all. Must have been the cognac.

"Uh...could we keep this conversation private, sir? I'd really like to surprise her."

CHAPTER NINETEEN

Baltimore County, Maryland
June 14, 2011

MARY ANNE SAT IN THE WAITING ROOM OF Dr. Andrew Holland, leafing through a several-months-old copy of *People* magazine.

The cover had a photo of an attractive blond nurse who had apparently killed a Crips gang member with some sort of injection when he was holding a bunch of people hostage in an emergency room. *Oh, my God. I know that woman! Mason-Dixon? That hospital's right here in Baltimore County—Middletown Road. That's the blonde I saw with the hot guy at the charity ball two weeks ago!*

Mary Anne flipped through the several-page story. The nurse didn't interest Mary Anne, but her doctor boyfriend did. *I can't believe it. That's him!*

There were three photos of the doctor on the inside pages. One was a distant shot of him driving a blue tractor. A second was a graduation photo—maybe from college. The third photo was a candid that looked like it was taken in a hospital. He was wearing a blue scrub suit and had a stethoscope around his neck.

So he's a doctor...no wonder I couldn't peg him. My, my...I could turn his world upside down. I'm sick of old men. Maybe it won't be much longer.

118

She folded the magazine and put it inside her purse.

~

The nurse held his arm as a gaunt Eddie Williams stepped off the scales.

Eddie coughed. "What was it?"

"One hundred and thirty-five pounds, Eddie," said the nurse.

She pulled the little step out of the bottom of the exam table, then helped Eddie step up, turn around, and sit down. "Dr. Holland will be right with you."

Eddie didn't need Dr. Holland to tell him that he was dying.

The door opened and Andrew Holland walked into the small room. "Hi, Eddie." He grabbed a wheeled stool, slid it over beside the exam table and sat down.

"How are you feeling today?" he said, placing a hand on Eddie's knee.

"Terrible."

"I see you've lost a little weight."

"Only sixty-five pounds," Eddie said with irony. What's the bad news today?"

"Well, I have your PET/CT results, and I'm afraid you're right, Eddie—they don't look good. We can see some cancer lights in your brain, a couple in your lung, and two on your spine."

"Right about here?" asked Eddie putting a hand on his low back.

"That's about the right spot."

"So what's next?"

"Eddie, you know that our treatment for metastatic melanoma has limitations?"

"I know that. What you really mean to say is that it doesn't work. How about this pain? The back is the worst."

"Are you still using Percocet?"

"Yeah. It's not working."

"OK. Let's step it up to OxyContin. I'm going to give you a prescription for thirty-milligram tablets that you can take every twelve hours. We don't want you to be in pain. But remember, this is a very

119

powerful narcotic. Don't take two at a time because you think two is better than one."

"What about my brain?"

"Are you having headaches?"

"Yeah."

"Well, you may find that they will get slowly worse."

"Yeah, but is my brain going to work?"

Holland paused for a moment. "Eddie, you may find that gradually you will have greater difficulty focusing or thinking clearly. Or you may become more lethargic. If that happens we can try shrinking the swelling around the tumor with steroids. Or we could even think about radiation."

"None of that. How much longer am I going to be able to run my business?"

Andrew Holland sighed. "It may not be for much longer, Eddie."

~

On the morning of Sunday June 19, Eddie Williams announced to his wife that they were going to church. This prospect interested her not in the least.

"Eddie! How are we going to do that? You can hardly walk!"

Sitting on the edge of his bed in pajamas, Eddie looked at the floor and said nothing for several long moments. "Help me get dressed. We're going," he said with finality.

With the assistance of Mary Anne and a cane, the trip from Eddie's bedroom to the Escalade in the driveway took ten minutes. At St. Mark's, two ushers helped Eddie up the stairs to the massive double doors. He shuffled slowly down the aisle with his head held high until the ushers gently lowered him into a pew one-third of the way down the sanctuary. Mary Anne demurely took her place beside him, fuming that she had missed her Sunday morning workout at the Maryland Athletic Club.

As the organ prelude played, entering parishioners placed their hands on Eddie's shoulder and stooped to whisper well-wishes in his ear. Mary Anne watched the parade with indifference until a slender young woman with blond hair passed her peripheral vision followed by Dr. Alex Randolph wearing a summer khaki suit. Her eyes followed him to a seat four pews ahead.

At the conclusion of the service, Eddie's wife suggested that he wait until the sanctuary emptied before attempting to exit. Randolph and his companion rose from their pew, turned, and walked toward the rear of the church, passing close enough that Mary Anne could have reached out and touched him. For the first time she was able to view every detail of his face.

He was probably close to forty, with deep-set, intelligent eyes and clear skin that reflected light. Longish hair the color of dark tobacco framed a square face with a strong nose. Fine lines radiated from green eyes toward his temples where resided the first hints of gray. Actually she wasn't sure that she would call this man handsome—at least not in the South Beach sense—but she couldn't take her eyes off him.

At least in this place, he wore a serious demeanor, although she had seen his smile light up a room at the charity auction. He walked past the Williams pew with confidence, but without swagger or arrogance.

Mary Anne felt her breath catch. She was at a loss to explain it, but for some reason this man elicited a response in her that was outside her past experience.

The slow process of moving Eddie's decimated body resumed. One of the ushers graciously followed the Escalade home and helped Mary Anne get her husband back into the house. It was the last time that Eddie Williams ever left Ascot Farms alive.

~

Milton Kopec rapped briefly on the door and then walked into Eddie's bedroom. He had labored tirelessly for Eddie Williams for twenty-three years, working his way up from an accountant fresh out of Case Western Reserve University all the way to chief financial officer of the sprawling Edwards empire fourteen years ago. But the skeleton that beckoned to him from the bed was barely recognizable as the feared Eddie Williams.

"Come in Milton, come in," said a raspy voice. "Grab that stack of papers on the desk over there and pull up that armchair."

For months, Milton Kopec had lain awake at night in bed, wondering what would become of his life's work. Indeed, what would become of *him*? He figured he was about to find out.

"Milton, I've decided to appoint you executor of my estate. The Edwards empire is going to be sold, but you and Rachel and your kids will be well taken care of. In fact, apart from your work in settling the estate, which may take several years, you'll never have to work a day again in your life if you don't want to."

Milton Kopec had no idea that Eddie Williams could even remember his wife's name. He was embarrassed to feel a sudden surge of affection for this old bastard who he had privately cursed for so many years.

"Mary Anne will get the beach estate in the Dominican Republic, a million dollar life insurance payout, and more importantly, Ascot Farms. I've set up one trust fund to maintain the farm, and another for her personal use. You will be the trustee. She's got a hot temper sometimes, but in many ways she's still a child. She'll curse you up one side and down the other. Don't let her push you around, but see to it that she's well cared for.

"The bulk of the proceeds from sale of the holding company is going to Johns Hopkins University to fund a new research facility named the Williams Cancer Research Institute. Universities are sometimes a little fickle about these things—they'd rather have unrestricted funds to do with as they please—but I'm sure you'll be able to deal with the politics.

"The papers are all signed. Take 'em with you, study them, and then put them in a safe deposit box. My attorney's got signed duplicates. Come back to me if you have questions."

~

Mary Anne sat alone at the patio breakfast table in a foul mood. Since Eddie had taken to his bed, she felt as if she were living in a nursing home. Maybe she lived in a mansion, but this place had become as restrictive as living with the Bryants. She had no freedom. There was no excitement; no electricity in her life. Stripping at Club Nouveau was heaven compared to this.

Her only escape was a daily workout at the Maryland Athletic Club in Timonium. She had plenty of admirers there, but Eddie knew where she was constantly and watched the clock like a hawk. He was in control.

Mary Anne couldn't risk an affair, especially not at this stage when the old prick was almost dead and Ascot Farms would soon be hers. She hadn't been laid in months. Her fingers were getting tired from masturbating while she thought about Alex Randolph.

In Miami, Mary Anne was in control. She was the star. People did what *she* said. Pirelli gave Mary Anne her own dressing room. Sammy would kill for her if she asked him. She could manipulate the young dancers at the club like puppets. Make them cry. Make them beg. She was powerful.

In a rage, she smashed her orange juice glass on the tile floor.

Stomping out to the firing range with her P238, she fired off forty rounds at paper targets, wishing that she had a real target; imagining Eddie's wrinkled face in the bull's-eye.

A robin alighted in the grass thirty feet to her right, pecking at the ground for a morning meal. Mary Anne put the red dot over its puffy chest and slowly squeezed the trigger. A cloud of feathers exploded and the bird disappeared.

~

Mary Anne wandered into the kitchen, plucked a grape from the bowl of fruit on the kitchen island, and popped it into her mouth. At the sink in a sleeveless cotton dress, stood Manuela, rinsing off the breakfast dishes.

She's got nice little hips, thought Mary Anne. *And smooth, brown skin.*

"How old are you, Manuela?" she asked.

"Nineteen, Ma'am."

"You're from where? El Salvador?"

"Yes, El Salvador."

123

"How long have you been in the United States?" Manuela didn't like the drift of this conversation.

"Nearly two years now."

"Your English is very good. Do you send money home?"

"Yes. I send it to my mother and my brothers and sister."

"Oh, that's very sweet of you, Manuela. I'll bet they depend on you."

"Yes, Ma'am."

"And did you get your green card?" An empty pit formed in Manuela's stomach.

"Yes, Ma'am," she lied.

"Could you show it to me?" The pounding of her heart was so violent that Manuela feared Mary Anne could see her body shake with each beat.

"I...I do not have it with me today."

Mary Anne walked to the sink and stood behind the slender girl. She placed her hands on Manuela's arms above her elbows and gently rubbed up and down.

"You have nice skin, Manuela. Do you like it here—here in the United States?"

"Very much."

Mary Anne lightly ran her hands up over the girl's shoulders, under her dress and onto her chest at the base of her neck. Manuela froze. Another girl had never touched her like this.

"And do you like your job here?"

"This job is very nice."

"Well, Manuela, I don't really think you have a green card. But that's OK. That will be our secret, and I'll never tell the INS as long as you give me good service. What do you think of that?" Mary Anne's hand now ran over the girl's breasts and into her bra.

Panic stricken, Manuela hesitated, her face turning fiery red. She knew now what this woman wanted. Manuela had been with a man before, but never a woman. She thought that was unnatural. But what could she do? Her monthly checks to El Salvador kept her mother and younger siblings in food.

If she thanked May Anne for not telling the INS, she would know for sure that she didn't have a green card. *But somehow she knows! If I lie, I may lose my job and she might call the INS. I can't lose my job and I can't go back to El Salvador!*

Mary Anne's fingers were now rubbing Manuela's nipples. The girl began to tremble.

"That is very nice of you," replied Manuela.

"Do you like what I'm doing to you—to your breasts?"

"Yes," she whimpered.

"Turn around." As the girl complied, Mary Anne pulled her own tee shirt over her head, and stood naked before the girl except for her running shorts.

"On your knees, Manuela," she commanded. The girl slowly dropped to her knees and looked up at Mary Anne, tears streaming down her face. *Awesome! She's suffering. She'll do anything I want. This is really hot!* Mary Anne pinched her own nipples.

"Now pull down my shorts, Manuela."

CHAPTER TWENTY

WITH JACK AND CATHERINE OUT OF school, Denise Murphy couldn't wait to get her hands on the kids. So we left them in Annapolis for a blessed week with *Maimeó*—apparently Irish for grandmother. Blessed for Penny and me, that is, because a week without kids opened up all kinds of possibilities. I was hoping to get down to the first one on the list this evening.

"How did you and Dad do on your little trip around the quadrangle?" Penny asked on the way home.

"We got along great."

"Well, I see you're still alive."

"What did you expect?"

"Alex, four hours ago you were worried about my father bumping you off in a covert operation."

"We reached an agreement."

"What kind of agreement?"

"I promised him that I'd stop beating his daughter, if he'd take the kids for a week. You may also be interested to know that I gave Ruth the night off tonight. Actually, I gave her the whole week off."

"I just love a man who takes control," she whispered in my ear.

An hour later, we ran into the house, ripped off our clothes, and passionately took advantage of the first night of our blessed week, made all the more delicious by the fact that this would be the first night that we had slept together through the night—ever.

~

Sunlight flooded the room when I awoke about 7:30 Friday morning to the ultimate luxury of the beautiful, naked woman that I love still soundly sleeping beside me, her arm sprawled over my chest. I turned on my side and watched her sleep for a long time, taking in every detail of her delicate face, her wispy flaxen hair; the rise and fall of her breasts.

The only bummer was that I had to be at work at 9:00. Worse yet, Penny was working the Friday night shift, so I wouldn't see her again until 7:30 Saturday morning, and then she would need to sleep a good portion of that day.

Penny had a sleep deficit because she had worked Wednesday night and gotten little sleep before our trip to Annapolis Thursday. So I gently lifted her arm, quietly slipped out of bed, kissed her forehead, and headed to the bathroom.

After showering and shaving I made coffee, poured a cup for the road, and scribbled out a little note I left near the coffee machine.

Morning Baby,

I think I had a fever last night. I remember being very hot and tearing off my clothes. You may need to take my temperature tomorrow.

Coffee is ready. See you at the change of shifts tonight.

Much love,

Alex

~

With the sun to my back, I drove through the old railroad hamlet of Monkton—essentially unchanged for a hundred years—across the bridge over the Gunpowder Falls, and headed up Monkton Hill toward Hereford, thinking about my day.

Today at 3:00 PM was my little appointment with my boss, Dr. Myers, to discuss my intemperate act of throwing Cody Brown out of the ER. I wasn't too worried because he really couldn't fire me without Harvey Mays' blessing, which was unlikely to be forthcoming. Happily, this would be a major source of frustration for Dr. Myers.

I would attentively listen to his lecture regarding liability, patient risk, violation of federal rules, etc., etc., and then say, "OK, shithead, I'll be certain that this doesn't happen again."

~

About 1:00 PM, I picked up the chart for Bed Seven—*Jacob Martin, forty-year-old male, migraine headache*, the summary sheet said.

Jacob sat on the end of the exam table dressed in work boots, jeans, and a blue denim shirt, holding his forehead in one hand. The distinctive smell of a dairy farm filled the room—not offensive, but unmistakable. I introduced myself and said, "Jacob, you have a headache today?"

"Yeah," he replied, "I think it's just one of my migraines."

"You have a history of migraines?"

"Yes, since I was a kid."

"Do you take anything for them?"

"Yes, I normally take Maxalt, but I was out of them today."

"OK. So when did this headache come on?"

"About two hours ago."

"And does it feel like one of your usual migraines?"

"Kind, of. But it hurts more in the back than usual," he said, placing one hand on the back of his head. "This is one of the worst ones I've had."

"Did you have nausea or vomiting with this headache?"

"A little nausea, but I haven't thrown up."

"Any problems with your vision?"

"No."

"Have you had any fever, sore throat, cough, earache or any other symptoms of infection?

"No."

"Is your neck stiff?"

"Not really."

This was all not too remarkable so far. But I was a little bit uncomfortable with the new location in the back of his head and the intensity of this headache. The reason these little things bothered me is because headaches can come back to bite you in the ass. There are a couple of kinds of deadly headaches that are on every doc's list of *Top-Forty-Never-Miss* diagnoses.

You can't do a CAT scan on everyone who walks into the ER with a headache—we see dozens of run-of-the-mill migraines every week. The challenge is figuring out which ones are run-of-the-mill and which ones are killers.

I did a physical exam—checked his neuro status and looked for signs of infection, but came up with nothing.

"Did your headache come on rapidly, Jacob?" I asked.

"Yeah, I was lifting the mower driveshaft to put it on the tractor PTO when *BAM*, it just hit me all of a sudden.

This, I really didn't like. There's a famous little phrase—*thunderclap*—that describes how fast a headache comes on when it is associated with a nasty diagnosis called a *subarachnoid hemorrhage*—an often lethal rupture of an aneurysm in your brain. Jacob's description of the onset of his headache was too close to a thunderclap for comfort.

My eyes went to the blood pressure recorded on the summary sheet: one-seventy over one-oh-four—elevated.

"Do you have a history of high blood pressure?"

"No."

I was liking this less and less all the time. Blood pressure often rises with a subarachnoid hemorrhage.

"Jacob, a few things about this headache trouble me. I'm concerned about how fast it came on, I don't like the new location or how severe it is, and on top of that, your blood pressure is up. I think maybe we need to do a CAT scan."

"You think that's really necessary? I had one three or four years ago."

"That was then and this is now. I'll tell you what I'm worried about. When headaches come on very fast like this one, and they're the worst ones of your life, sometimes they are due to an aneurysm leaking in your brain. They can kill you and we don't want to miss one of those."

Jacob was a healthy guy, and a rather stoic farmer to boot. He wasn't buying this. "I really think it's one of my migraines. I don't think I want a CAT scan. Can't we just treat this migraine and see how it goes?"

Well, here's a tricky little situation. It doesn't really matter how worried I am. It's a free country. We're not the Gestapo. If you don't want a CAT scan, you don't get one.

"OK, Jacob, I will treat your headache and we'll see how it goes. But if things aren't going right, I am going to really lean on you to get this CAT scan."

I walked back to my computer at the nursing station and entered an order for Reglan 10 mg IV. Reglan was a safe choice in this situation because it only relieves the headache of actual migraines, but no other kinds of pain.

So if Jacob's headache was a migraine he'd get relief, but if he had a subarachnoid hemorrhage he'd get no relief. That would tell me something. I put in my pin number, hit ENTER, and crossed my fingers for Jacob.

~

Mid-afternoon I got a call from Gwen Reynolds, one of the secretaries in the administrative offices. "I just wanted to remind you that you have a meeting with Dr. Myers in five minutes," she said brightly. I glanced at the clock. *Uh-oh. I would have missed that.*

Gwen likes me. After five or six years in the administrative offices, she is a quiet master of political intrigue. This was her way of keeping a level playing field. She didn't want the deck stacked in Myers' favor by my being late.

I turned to Ben sitting beside me and said, "You're on your own for fifteen minutes. I've got a little meeting upstairs with Dr. Myers."

"Well, give the asshole my regards. You got anybody I need to worry about?"

"No. Just a guy with a headache getting Reglan."

"Is this about throwing that kid out of the ER last week?"

"Yeah."

"I'd just loved to have seen that."

~

I walked into the administrative offices reception area, hushed by plush carpeting and rich fabrics in muted colors. Recessed lights glittered overhead and lamps on end tables softly glowed. The walls were covered with large original oils of Baltimore County scenes. I wondered if I had stumbled into the corporate legal offices of Dewey, Cheatem & Howe.

From her vast mahogany reception desk, Gwen said, "Hi Dr. Randolph! Dr. Myers is in. He'll see you now. Just go right through that door."

I rapped twice on the door and walked into Dr. Myers' office—just as sterile and barren as I remembered it being during my exit interview in March. The shelves on the bookcase were empty, the coffee table was bare, and no original oils occupied the walls. This, I thought, was a fitting environment for my Nazi colleague, who probably couldn't tell an oral cavity from an asshole on a patient.

Young Doctor Myers looked up from his perfectly clean desk and said, "Have a seat, Dr. Randolph." Between the glint of his scalp shining through the crew-cut and the glare off huge black-framed glasses, I was having trouble focusing on his face. I took my place in the chair across from his desk. Apparently handshaking was out of style.

"Dr. Randolph, do you remember a patient named Cody Brown?" he began. In the background, Jekyll was already quietly but firmly admonishing me to put a clamp on my mouth.

"Yes."

He shuffled some papers on his desk. "And there's a handwritten progress note attached to the record signed by you. Is this your handwriting?"

"Yes."

"And if I'm reading your handwriting correctly, it says here that you asked Mr. Brown to leave the emergency department prior to completing your examination and treatment. Is that correct?" *Well, I didn't exactly ask him to leave. I threw him out.*

"Yes." So far, this was going really well.

"And you know, of course, that by refusing to care for Mr. Brown you committed a COBRA/EMTALA violation of federal law that could earn this hospital a fine of up to $50,000 as well as personal civil liability for yourself?"

I did stumble into the law offices of Dewey...

"Yes." *Your Honor.*

"Dr. Randolph, I am not authorized to terminate you. But effective at the end of today's shift, you will be placed on administrative leave without pay for a period of two weeks. We take this incident most seriously and will be able to confirm to the Department of Health and Human Services that we have imposed significant disciplinary action on the offending physician.

"This incident, of course, will go into your personnel file and may reflect adversely on references, or future employment within Americus Health Systems. And you better hope to hell, Dr. Randolph, that Mr. Brown does not decide to file a complaint against this hospital with HHS, or against you personally. You're dismissed."

Hyde, who had been uncharacteristically silent, could no longer hold his tongue. *I'll dismiss that worthless piece of—*

Shut up, Hyde, said Jekyll sharply. *You're doing great, Alex. Now just get up and calmly walk out...*

I cast a malevolent glare at Dr. Myers, stood, and wordlessly left the administrative offices. *Terrific job, Alex.*

I had not expected this. My docs were going to be pissed. *I* was pissed. They were going to have to step up to the plate and cover all my shifts for the next two weeks. Two weeks of pay was also my mortgage payment on the farm. I wasn't sure I had enough in the checking account to cover that.

~

"Short meeting," said Ben when I sat back down at my computer.

"Don't ask," I said.

"Did he fire you again?"

"No. Just put me on the street for two weeks without pay."

"Whoa! So I wanna know who's picking up your shifts?"

"You."

Rebecca Franklin came briskly walking toward the nursing station and called out to me from fifteen feet away. "Alex, you need to come see Jacob Martin in Seven. I think he's going down the tubes!"

Shit! I turned to Stacy at the ward clerk's station and said, "Stacey, call CT and tell 'em I want a CT without contrast on Bed Seven right now! We're going to bring him down. Ben, enter the order for me."

I hurried to catch up with Rebecca who was already headed back to Jacob's room. "Did he get his Reglan yet?"

"I just gave it to him about ten minutes ago, and when I went back into the room to recheck on him just now he wasn't responding," she said breathlessly.

Jacob lay motionless on the bed except for his breathing.

"Jacob!" I yelled. No response. I lifted up his gown and rubbed his sternum with my knuckles—only a moan and a turn of his head. Quickly lifting both eyelids, I checked his pupils. His left pupil was blown—dilated. *Jacob is going to die.*

"OK. Unlock that stretcher. Lets get him moving to CT." As we passed the nursing station, I called out, "Stacey, get me a helicopter. Diagnosis is subarachnoid hemorrhage. Receiving hospital is Hopkins."

~

"I've got the Hopkins ER on the line," said Stacey, "Dr. Carter." I knew Roger Carter from our days together as associate professors of emergency medicine before I left for Mason-Dixon.

"Roger? This is Alex."

"Hey, Alex. How you doin'?"

"I'm having a very shitty day, Roger. But listen, I've got an ER-to-ER transfer for you. This guy's a forty-year-old male with a subarachnoid hemorrhage. He's obtunded with a blown left pupil. I'm sitting here looking at his very ugly CT and he's got a big bleed on the right, probably from his posterior circulation, with a midline shift of about eight millimeters. I'll send the CT along."

"OK, Alex. I'll get neurosurgery down here. When do you think you'll have him here?"

"The chopper should be landing now. I hope we can have him in the air within maybe fifteen or twenty minutes."

"OK. Thanks for the heads-up."

"See ya, Roger."

I had a lot of work to do in the next ten or fifteen minutes.

I walked into Bed Fifteen, our resuscitation room, where Rebecca had moved Jacob after the CT.

"Rebecca, we're going to intubate him. Get me some sux and etomidate, and get respiratory therapy down here."

"I've already called them."

Cathy Rutledge, our clinical coordinator, had smelled trouble and came in the room to help. "I'll get the sux and etomidate," she announced.

Helicopters are not the best places for attempting to putting in an endotracheal tube if your patient runs into breathing problems in the air. We always try to secure the airway prior to transport.

"What's his blood pressure?"

"Two-oh-five over one-twelve." Still high.

"OK. Give him ten milligrams of labetalol." This could be a little dicey. I wanted to use labetalol to reduce his blood pressure so that the leaking aneurysm would squirt out less blood.

But the growing volume of blood that was spilling out into the closed space of Jacob's skull was raising the pressure inside his head and compressing blood vessels. If I lowered the blood pressure too much, there wouldn't be enough pressure to push blood through the compressed blood vessels. *Nobody said life would be easy.*

The intubation went smoothly without incident. Jacob's BP came down into the one-seventies—about where I wanted it. Just twelve minutes later, he was packaged and ready for transport. The flight crew from LifeNet 6-1 wheeled him out of the ER to the waiting blue and white ship for what I suspected would be the final trip of Jacob Martin's life.

"Dr. Randolph," called out Stacey, "I have Mrs. Martin on five-one-three-one. The Jacob Martin case wasn't over yet. The hardest part was now.

~

I caught a brief minute alone in the hallway with Penny who had arrived for the 7:00 PM shift before I left.

"Hi Baby. How did you sleep?" I asked.

"Oh, it was wonderful! Sweet and dreamless and long. I needed that. But it was such a bummer when I woke up and you weren't there. I want to sleep with you every night," she said looking up into my eyes. Suddenly I was feeling all warm and fuzzy.

"Baby, I'll be there every night and every morning for the next two weeks." Penny looked at me quizzically.

"Myers put me on the street for two weeks without pay. My docs are going to hate me. But the upside is that I'm going to have plenty of time to get the farm ready for the Murphy family reunion. I can be outside working every day."

~

When I got home, I slapped together a ham sandwich and sat down on a stool at the counter to type out an email to my docs:

Guys,

Sorry to report to you that the administration has seen fit to put me on administrative leave without pay for two weeks. Sorry only because that means that you guys are going to have to pick up my shifts. I know what a pain in the ass that will be for all of you.

So now I owe you big time. If you need a shift off and need somebody to cover in the future, I'm your man. I have removed my name on the Google calendar from all of my shifts for the next two weeks. Please take a look and fill in the holes where you can.

Alex

I would pay for this forever. They would never let me forget.

~

About 10:30 I headed upstairs, stripped, and brushed my teeth. A pile of fresh laundry sat folded on the bureau, and I noted that the bed was made. There, on the pillow, was a note:

I'll miss you so much tonight! I won't be home to treat your fever, but if you're still sleeping when I get home in the morning, I'll crawl into bed with you and take your temperature.

Sleep tight, my love.

Penny

CHAPTER TWENTY-ONE

MARY ANNE FINISHED THE LAST CRUNCH ON the incline bench and collapsed, head down, her chest heaving. After three years as the wife of Eddie Williams, she was in the best shape of her life.

With a workout at the Maryland Athletic Club being virtually her only escape from Eddie's sickbed, she was now working out six days a week. Her body fat was down to thirteen percent and her ab definition created sharp vertical shadows on her belly. When she walked across the club floor, every eye in the place followed her, male and female alike.

Stripping out of her sweat-soaked outfit, she walked toward the showers, pausing to survey her wet body in the full-length mirror. Other girls walked around the locker room wrapped in towels, but Mary Anne strode proudly naked wherever she went.

She swung the SLS into a parking space at a convenience store on York Road and picked up a coffee. Scanning the magazine rack in the checkout aisle, she let out a little gasp. *Oh wow! It's him again.*

Staring back at her on the cover of *Us* was Alex Randolph, standing with his blond bitch in front of a white Jeep. It was a nighttime shot, maybe in a parking lot someplace. They both looked like deer in headlights. She picked up *Us* along with two other magazines, paid, and drove home to Ascot Farms.

In her bedroom, she stripped, slathered suntan lotion on her skin, and slipped into a white bikini. She swung through the kitchen, poured an orange juice and 7 Up into a tall, insulated glass, and with her magazines in hand, settled into a poolside lounge chair.

As she studied the cover of *Us*, her frustration grew. *That should be me in this picture*, she thought. *I'm way hotter than her.*

The inside story detailed how Dr. Alex Randolph and the nurse had both recovered from their injuries in the Crips gang hostage incident and were now being spotted in public again. But there was an interesting twist.

Randolph had apparently been fired just before the incident and later was hired back again. The guy who fired him got fired himself for embezzling hospital funds or something. It was all complicated, but the doctor and the girl were both back at work.

Mary Anne sighed. More than anything, she craved adoration and worship of the masses. She deserved it. There was no woman in the magazines that sizzled more than she. Life was unfair.

Since leaving Miami, she missed seeing her larger-than-life face gazing out from billboards, and missed the roar of the crowd as she stood naked with outstretched arms at the end of her routine.

Randolph had to live close by—probably just a few miles away. He was a parishioner at St. Mark's Church. She needed to meet him. He would find Mary Anne Williams to be irresistible. When Eddie was gone, maybe Randolph could be her ticket to cover photos on *Us*. She would replace the blond bitch. What a story! The magazines would go berserk over that one.

CHAPTER TWENTY-TWO

WITH MUCH GRUMBLING AND CURSING, the docs all filled in time on the Google calendar to cover my shifts, so I was now on vacation for two weeks. I spent a part of Saturday morning doing cash flow projections in the absence of a paycheck for two weeks.

Buying property on My Lady's Manor is not cheap. The *Manor*, as it's known to locals, is an informal district east of Monkton that roughly corresponds to the little ten-thousand-acre parcel that Charles Calvert the 3rd gifted to his fourth wife Margaret. Too many more wives and he would have run out of land.

The historic heart of Maryland steeplechase country, the Manor was once an enclave almost exclusively of the very rich, although it now includes me. But, despite inexorable development, the beautiful green rolling hills of the Manor are still populated by more than a few magnificent old estates as well as some magnificent old sums of money.

I bought my little thirty-five-acre farm just before the real estate boom from Mr. and Mrs. Stuart Robinson, an elderly couple who both ended up in a nursing home. They were sort of friends of the family and decided to hold the mortgage themselves. The price was really way more than I could afford, but the Robinsons accepted a minimal down payment, and I didn't have to convince a bank to lend me the money, which never would have happened.

Nevertheless, because of their age, the mortgage runs for only fifteen years and it takes nearly every penny of my salary to keep up with the monthly payments. As I tell my friends, it is my insurance policy against descent into the ranks of the idle rich in the British Virgins.

I calculated that by the time I got my next paycheck, my rainy day account would be just about empty but there would still be about twelve hundred dollars left in my checking account. So, bottom line: not to worry. No missed mortgage payment.

With that out of the way, I was finally able to get outside and begin to catch up on getting the property in shape while Penny slept after her night shift. I didn't want to wake her up with weed-eaters or lawnmowers, so I drove down to my dad's place—Randolph Nursery & Landscaping in Sparks—used a skid steer to load up one of his trucks with mulch, and delivered it back to the farm.

This gave me the opportunity to climb on my most treasured material possession—a blue New Holland B 3040 tractor—and use the front-end loader to distribute the mulch to the beds. I still had two years of monthly payments left on the New Holland, but it was the best investment I ever made. You can't believe the number of things you can do with a front-end loader. It's like a motorized wheelbarrow that dumps without engaging your muscles.

By the time Penny appeared about 1:00 PM—hair still wet from her shower—I was drenched in sweat and covered with black mulch. I pulled the tractor over to the patio, jumped off and kissed her on the lips, trying not to touch her with any more of my black body.

"Get cleaned up, farm boy," she said. "I've got some lunch ready for you in here."

We spent a wonderful afternoon together in the dirt. Penny planted some leftover impatiens and geraniums I had found at my dad's nursery, and I spent the rest of the day weed-eating and mowing. By six o'clock we were both tired and filthy. We stripped off our mulch-laden clothes in the mudroom, climbed the stairs naked, and spent the next hour soaping each other in the shower until the raging storm of hormones had subsided.

~

Saturday was only several days past the summer solstice. After burgers and a salad, we sat quietly together on the patio, drinking Coronas, and watching the golden colors of evening turn to crimson in the west and then twilight over the pasture below. Tiny yellow lights began to flicker as the horses faded to shadows, and a symphony of tree frogs and cicadas began to play.

I held Penny's hand and marveled at the depth of intimacy that passed between us in the quiet. It was almost as if the need for speech had been transcended.

We moved to the hammock and she lay in my arms with her head on my chest as we watched the appearance of the first stars. She turned her head and kissed my neck.

"See that star over the sycamore tree in the pasture?" she whispered as she pointed. "That's ours."

~

By Tuesday, I had accomplished all the important tasks, including mowing the pasture and weed-eating along the meandering little stream, Jack and Catherine's favorite place to play. Ruth stopped by to say hello late morning, and it was apparent that she was going through withdrawal from what she now considered to be her family. So we invited her to lunch Thursday and I informed her that we would be back on a regular schedule on Sunday when we would pick up Catherine and Jack in Annapolis and bring them home for Catherine's afternoon riding lesson.

I told Penny that dinner was on me this evening and that she should plan to dress up a little, even though I was preparing dinner at home. Simple as it may seem, it had taken me days to decide to hold this little event because tonight I was going to ask her to marry me.

I had initially thought about proposing to her at the Milton Inn in Sparks, a stately old stone inn, not three miles from where I grew up, and the site of our first real date. But somehow asking her to marry me at a commercial establishment didn't seem to fit what I regarded as the solemnity of the occasion.

Penny loved the farm on Shepherd Road and it was the place where I wanted to live my life and die. So ultimately I concluded that there was no more fitting place to ask her to spend the rest of her life with me than the patio overlooking what I thought was the most beautiful pasture on earth. This was not the Sandals Resort in Antigua, but it was me.

Obviously this means that I had also made a decision regarding the way to do the ring thing. I decided to go for broke by picking out the ring myself—after all, it was a gift from me, Alex Randolph.

To that end, I did exactly that at Radcliffe Jewelers in Towson Town Center, where I chose a very simple but elegant half-carat platinum solitaire. Four unadorned, tapering prongs arose from the body of the ring and grasped the glittering stone. I guessed at the size from looking at the saleswoman's carefully manicured fingers.

This little gem set me back the price of a new John Deere mower, but, hey, this is for a lifetime, right? I bought it just before I got put on the street for two weeks without pay, which is one of the reasons why my rainy day account was now empty.

~

I was the first to shower and dress. I put on my best khaki shorts and a pink cotton button-down shirt. While Penny showered, I opened a bottle of Grayson cabernet, my favorite ten-dollar California wine, to let it breathe.

I set up the wine, glasses, and a vase of flowers on a little round glass-top table on the patio. A bottle of Grey Goose, tonic water and freshly sliced limes completed the drink offerings. To this I added a bowel of Kalamata olives and a wedge of hard Parmesan cheese on a cut-granite board. I stood back and checked the table. *Not bad, Alex.*

Under the broad green umbrella, the patio table was set for two, with linen napkins, a full complement of utensils, and an array of polished glasses.

I had picked up a filet mignon for two, fresh asparagus, and a French baguette from Graul's in Hereford. These made for a meal that was hard to screw up.

The only thing I made that was a little bit risky was twice-baked potatoes, the recipe for which I followed from the old *Joy of Cooking* that my mother had bestowed upon me when I graduated from medical school. I made the potatoes in the afternoon and had the asparagus in a steamer ready to go. The grill was on, heating up, so I was ready for an engagement dinner party.

I poured myself a Grey Goose and tonic and waited with only mild apprehension. *I think she's going to say yes*, I told myself.

Footsteps approached and I looked up to see Penny standing with a demure smile between the open French doors. A form-fitting strapless summer dress with pink flowers hugged her slender body and then flared slightly to her ankles. Golden hair cascaded to tanned shoulders, framing an elegant face with animated, wide, green eyes. A silver choker and dangling silver earrings glinted when she moved. *Oh, she is spectacular.* I stood there speechless, staring at her.

"Well, aren't you going to offer me a drink?" she asked smiling.

"Madam, I can offer you an exquisite albeit modestly-priced California cabernet, or I would be pleased to fix you a Grey Goose and tonic."

"I'll take the cabernet."

"This is very nice," she said appraising my hors d'oeuvres table. "Did you have this catered?"

"This is entirely the fruit of my own labor," I said proudly.

"For a farm boy, you are a man of many talents."

~

With the dishes cleared, we sat at the table sharing a last glass of wine as a candle burned inside a hurricane globe. It was nearing dusk and the first blinking fireflies had appeared. I set down my wine glass, stood, and held out my hand. "Come with me, baby."

We walked over to my blue, freshly power-washed New Holland tractor that I had left parked on the grass near the patio, and I climbed up into the seat. "Jump up here," I said, holding out my hand. Penny hitched up her skirt and climbed up, sitting sideways in my lap with her arms around my neck. Her scent was intoxicating.

"Take a look out there," I said pointing to the pasture on the other side of the board fence. Abigail and General Lee stood grazing near the stream that still flashed little sparkles of light. The solitary giant sycamore adjacent to the stream elegantly reached for the sky. A square mosaic of green could still be seen from the mowing patterns in the grass.

"This is where I want to spend the rest of my life," I said. "And I want to spend it with you here by my side. You have brought to me a joy that I never conceived was possible. I simply can't imagine life without you. And to me, Jack and Catherine are just little extensions of you that bring to me the same emotions that I feel for you."

I reached into the toolbox mounted beside the tractor seat, pulled out a little black box and opened it. The ring still sparkled in the fading light.

"Penny, I want nothing more in the world than for you to marry me. Will you?"

Penny sat silently for a long moment, her eyes intently searching mine. Suddenly she locked her arms around my neck in a vise grip and pushed her face to my ear.

"Oh, yes, Alex! Yes, yes, yes!"

~

We lay in bed with Penny's head on my shoulder and her arm resting on my chest.

"Oh, I'm dreading the end of this week," she said. "Who knows when I'll get to sleep with you again? I want to set the wedding date as soon as possible."

"We could leave now and go rouse some minister out of bed," I suggested. Penny giggled.

"You know, I loved it that you proposed to me on a tractor."

"The seat of my New Holland is a very serious place."

"And I loved it that you included Jack and Catherine," she said looking up.

"It's a package deal."

"Now we can make the announcement to everybody at the family party! I'm so excited! It'll be a surprise!"

"Not exactly. Not to your dad."

Penny rose up and looked down at me in shock "You told him?"

"No. I *asked* him. Sitting on the chapel steps after my last swallow of cognac."

"That's why you were so concerned about him bumping you off! What did he say?" she asked eagerly.

"He said that you were so madly in love with me that it astonished him."

"He did not!" she said, thumping my chest with her fist.

"Oh yes he did. He also said that he would be honored to call me his son-in-law."

"His judgment is deteriorating in his old age. I bet he loved that—that you asked him."

"I asked him to keep the conversation private so I could surprise you. Do you think he told your mother?"

"Oh yeah. So I'll call her tomorrow and let her know. She'll probably cry. We won't tell anyone else until the party."

CHAPTER TWENTY-THREE

PENNY WORKED THURSDAY NIGHT AND climbed into bed about 7:30 Friday morning. I tucked her in with the sun brightly shining, pulled the blinds, turned on a fan for some white noise and kissed her goodnight.

Although thoroughly enjoying a two-week suspension from my employment, I was still the chief of the department of emergency medicine and in another eight days would once again be held responsible for how well my department worked or didn't work. Anything that happened during my absence that adversely affected the department would still be my problem when I got back.

A meeting of the hospital Quality Assurance Committee was scheduled for 11:00 AM. It was an important meeting, so I unilaterally decided that being suspended without pay for two weeks did not include a prohibition against voluntary unpaid attendance at a committee meeting.

At today's QAC meeting we were going to discuss how to better meet yet another batch of regulatory requirements from Medicare. In this instance, Medicare, through its division called CMS, had issued a set of standards for antibiotic usage for pneumonia. We have to track the data, and if we fall outside of CMS standards, then they cut the money to the hospital. Who can argue with that, right?

Only problem is, CMS is a bureaucracy. It takes them years to make recommendations and then years to change them when they are outdated.

All of my docs have a little app on their iPhones called the *Johns Hopkins Antibiotic Guide* that's up-to-the-second with current best practices, so we're not eager to live up to two-year-old "standards" from the federal government. Beyond that, hospitals spend inordinate amounts of time and money collecting data and proving to them that we're doing what they tell us to do.

"OK," said Emily Field, RN, to the five people sitting around the table, "first case is Medical Record #179915. This is a fourteen-year-old male who presented to the ER with five days of flu symptoms and had bilateral pneumonia on a chest film. He got the antibiotics ceftriaxone and azithromycin, which were OK—they're on the guidelines—but the ER doc also added vancomycin, which is not on the guidelines, so this case gets reported."

"Why does vancomycin fall out?" I asked.

"Because they don't want you to use it unless you have a MRSA infection documented by cultures."

"By which time you're dead," I said. MRSA is an acronym for *methicillin resistant staph aureus*, a horrible, aggressive bacteria that is resistant to all but two or three antibiotics, one of them being vancomycin. When you have an internal MRSA infection like pneumonia, it often kills within forty-eight hours. That's long before the two-plus days that it takes to get cultures back from the lab to prove that it was MRSA.

"You know, I think I remember this case. Do you have the chart?" Emily pushed an inch-high stack of paper toward me. It took only a few seconds of leafing through the case to refresh my memory.

"Yeah, this is the one. I was here that day. It was Ben's patient. This kid was dying. He came in blue as a robin's egg, his oh-two-sat was in the sixties, and both lungs were white with pneumonia on his chest x-ray.

"Ben had to intubate him and fly him out to Hopkins. The kid was going down the tubes so fast that Ben was worried he might have MRSA, so he started him on vancomycin."

"Well, that's why the case fell out," said Emily.

"Check with Ben," I said, "but I think when he got follow-up from Hopkins, turned out he was right. The kid had MRSA. From what I heard, he barely survived. He was on a ventilator for something like five days. Ben saved his life."

"Well, then, it is what it is," said Emily. "It'll just have to fall out."

This is one of the little problems with the protocols and rules by which the regulators require us to live. Statistically they may make for good medicine. But since patients aren't familiar with the rules, they sometimes step outside the regulators' neat little algorithms. If Ben had followed the rules, we'd have one less fourteen-year-old boy alive.

~

When I returned to the farm, I quietly climbed the stairs to see if Penny was up yet. She had just stepped out of the shower and was standing on her tiptoes rummaging around in the closet, naked except for a pair of bikini panties. I stood and watched her buttock muscles flex for a moment and savored the lovely flare of her hips.

"You don't need anything from that closet," I said. "I like you just the way you are."

She turned and smiled. I walked to the closet, put my hands on her hips and softly kissed her wide mouth.

"Oooh, I'd like to wake up to that every morning," she cooed.

"How did you sleep, baby?"

"I always sleep better knowing that you're here."

She put her arm around my waist and said, "I've got to get this closet organized. I can't find anything. Do you mind if I move some of your stuff around?"

"Well, while you're in here, I should show you something interesting." I stepped into the closet, pushing aside some of the clothes hanging on a rod, and slid my index finger through a knothole on the wood-paneled back wall. A little door swung open.

"How cool is that?" I asked. "There's a little secret room in here they must have put in when they built this house a hundred and eighty or ninety years ago. But the reason I wanted to show you this is because if the kids find this room, I've got guns in here." We ducked under the little door and I flicked a light switch just inside the door.

The little room was only about three feet deep and about eight feet wide. At either end were shelves built between the two wood-paneled walls. A .222 Remington leaned against the shelves in one corner. I picked up a box lying on one of the shelves and opened it.

"I've got a pistol in this box," but I've taken the ammo clip out of it and I put the clip up on this top shelf out of reach. The .222 ammo is up here, too."

"Oh," said Penny, picking up the pistol, "you've got a Glock." She pulled back on the slide and checked the chamber, which, of course, was empty.

"You know what that gun is?"

"Of course. You think I grew up in a military family and was married to a SEAL and don't know my way around a pistol?" *Wow.*

"Well, I don't think the kids will find this room, but if they do, you know where that ammo is."

~

By Friday I was pretty caught up with work around the farm. We decided to make Friday afternoon a play day—tennis in the afternoon and then we'd go out to dinner. I made a reservation for two at the Manor Tavern, a very pleasant local watering hole, and then we put on tennis togs and drove to Hereford High School about two o'clock.

I grew up playing tennis because my dad was an ex college player and he had my brother Brian, me, and my best friend John out on the courts all the time. Brian and John both ended up playing college tennis, although I played only intramural tennis because I just felt that my college pre-med curriculum did not allow for the time away from school that tennis required.

Nevertheless, I played at a level pretty close to Brian and John, and tennis was one of the loves of my life. One of the unexpected beauties of my relationship with Penny was that she played tennis in high school—number one seed in fact—and she could wail the ball. Today we didn't play any games, but spent an hour and a half hitting and doing drills. I've never had a girlfriend who could keep up with me in a sport before, but I have to tell you, it's just wonderful. Great bonding. By 3:30 we were soaked.

I lay back on the bed on my elbows, still in my wet tee shirt and shorts, watching Penny step out of her straight tennis skirt and then pull her sports bra over her head. She walked to the bed naked, gave me a brief peck on the lips, and then headed for the shower, smiling at me over her shoulder, lovely hips swaying. *I think that's an invitation. What a marvelous way to spend Friday afternoon.*

~

About seven we pulled into the parking lot of the Manor Tavern, where grunge never made an appearance and preppy has reigned for fifty years. The outside bar on the back porch was filled with noisy customers. We asked to be seated in the garden, surrounded by greenery and beds of blossoming impatiens, under a huge tent that makes for outdoor dining all summer, regardless of weather.

I picked off a flake of blackened Ahi tuna and dipped it in wasabi sauce. "So how do you want to do this, baby—big wedding or little wedding?"

Penny took a subdued sip of her cosmo. "Oh, Alex, I've been thinking about this all week. I must have talked to my mother on the phone about this for an hour." She hesitated for a moment and slid a strand of blond hair back behind her ear. "This is my second marriage, Alex, but it's your first marriage," she said looking into my eyes. "So I think it should be the way *you* want it."

This was so typical of Penny. She was worried about my feelings; concerned that the fact that she had been happily married before to another man might be painful to me.

"Look, baby," I said, leaning forward on my forearms, "you don't ever have to tiptoe around the subject of Patrick Murray. He's with us every day in the form of those two little urchins. They need to know about their father. He was a good man, and I know you loved him deeply. Those are facts.

"I may be an arrogant son-of-a-bitch, but I'm not stupid enough

150

to believe that I'm the only man in the world that you could have fallen in love with. I feel no less love from you because you also loved him." I leaned back in my chair. "Just don't tell me that he was a better lover than me."

Penny smiled. "He wasn't."

"Right answer. So, now that we've got that over with, just tell me how you'd like to do this wedding."

Penny's eyes lit up again and she reached across the table for my hand. "OK. I want the whole world to know that I'm marrying Dr. Alex Randolph, and I want to share it with all of our friends. And I want to get married in a church. So, how about if we do it right here on the Manor at St. Marks, and then we have a reception at the farm? What do you think? I don't even care if the paparazzi show up. It'll be such fun! I can't wait!"

"Speaking of waiting, when do you want to do this deed? Please don't tell me next year."

"How about the last week in August? That's only seven weeks from now and then the kids could start right out in their new school."

I thought about that for a second. "I'm going to have to check dates with my attorney. My malpractice case with Mr. Stern is coming up sometime in August."

"Well, then maybe early September."

"Sooner the better, baby. After this week, I'll die if I have to wait too much longer to sleep with you again."

CHAPTER TWENTY-FOUR

O N FRIDAY AFTERNOON, HEATHER MITCHELL, the hospice nurse, laid out all the meds for the coming week in Eddie's seven-day pillbox. "Eddie's pain seems to be increasing," she said to Mary Anne. "I don't know if thirty milligrams of OxyContin is going to hold him much longer. If he's in a lot of pain this weekend, I'll call Dr. Holland on Monday morning and get an order to increase his pain meds."

Mary Anne hated this. She wanted nothing to do with caring for the sick and the dying. It was gross. Eddie's bedroom smelled terrible. She desperately wanted to live her life, and this was not living. She wondered how much longer she could stand it.

Heather eyed Eddie's young wife, who seemed to be paying no attention at all, and sighed. *Well, we all make our choices in life*, she thought. *Eddie decided on a trophy, and that's what he got.* She closed the pillbox and stood. "Well, I hope things go OK this weekend, Mrs. Williams. If you have any questions or big problems, you have my cell phone number. I'll be back first thing Monday morning."

Heather nodded to Melanie Cooper, Eddie's full-time caregiver, who stood nearby and said, "See you Monday, Melanie."

Melanie worked 8:00 to 4:00 each day, giving Eddie his bath and feeding him, which now amounted to next to nothing. Manuela came in later these days—about 11:00 AM—and didn't leave until after dinner, at 7:00 PM. That left Mary Anne alone with Eddie at night, each one of which she dreaded with a passion. The hospice nurse had installed one of those damned baby monitors linking Eddie's room to Mary Anne's room, and she couldn't get any sleep.

Eddie was constantly calling out for her. He seemed to be much more needy at night than during the day when all the help was here. Every hour he wanted a drink, or the urinal, or a pill, or another damned blanket. Why couldn't he just die and get it over with?

~

Mary Anne slipped deeper in the Everglades foliage and crouched in a cluster of saw palmettos, listening to Felix call out her name. "Mary Anne? Mary Anne? When I catch you I'm going to give it to you good." He laughed. "You'll know you've been fucked for a whole week. Do you hear me, Mary Anne?"

Peering through the fronds, she could catch brief glimpses of his red tee shirt as he slowly approached. Her heart was now pounding through her chest. She smiled. He thought he was the hunter, but he was really the hunted. Finally he stepped into a small clearing not fifteen feet away, and stood scanning the surrounding foliage. She carefully placed the red dot on his temple just in front of his ear, and slowly squeezed the trigger.

Awaking with a start, her body drenched in sweat, Mary Anne looked around in the dark and saw the red lights of the alarm clock in her bedroom. "Mary Anne? Mary Anne?" Eddie's raspy voice barked over the baby monitor. She wiped the sweat from her eyes, cursed, and threw back the covers, trying to remind herself once again that Ascot Farms would soon be hers.

She padded into Eddie's room, walked to the bedside and stroked his forehead. "What is it, darling? What's the matter?"

Eddie rolled his head from side to side in a kind of delirium. "The pain! The pain! I just can't stand it any more," he moaned. "The medicine's not working. Do something, please! Do something!" he commanded. Mary Anne looked at the clock: 2:35 AM. This was the third time tonight. She was exhausted.

"Eddie, do you want me to call an ambulance?"

"Whatever…yes. Take me to the hospital. I can't stand it anymore!"

Mary Anne picked up the phone and angrily punched 911. *Maybe this is a good thing. Maybe they'll keep him for a few days and then I can get some fucking rest.*

~

"OK, Ma'am," said the crew chief, clicking the last buckle on the straps that held Eddie securely to the cot. "Where would you like us to take him?"

"Hopkins," she said reflexively. But wait. An idea flashed. What if Alex Randolph was working tonight? That would certainly help to salvage a rotten night. This might be a good way to meet him. It was worth the chance. Could they take him there? What was the name of that hospital?

"Wait. Could you take him to that hospital up on Middletown Road?" she asked courteously.

"You mean Mason-Dixon?"

"Yes, that's it."

"Sure can. That's the nearest hospital anyway."

"Wonderful! All right, then. Take him to Mason-Dixon. Thank you so much." For the first time in months, Mary Anne felt a little surge of excitement. *What should I wear?* she wondered.

CHAPTER TWENTY-FIVE

FOR THE SECOND TIME IN AS MANY MONTHS I had returned to work after an unanticipated vacation. This time, unfortunately, my return was to a Saturday night shift that was part of paying back my dues to the rest of the docs for picking up my shifts. Penny was off tonight, which made it worse, because when we worked on different nights I didn't get to see as much of her.

This Saturday night was uncharacteristically slow. By the time Lauren Dorfman went home at 1:00 AM, we had the place pretty well cleaned out. I saw one or two more stragglers over the next hour-and-a-half, and sat at my computer thinking about trying to take a nap.

The only patient left in the department was a drunk girl, sleeping it off after a minor wreck, who told the investigating Baltimore County police officer that she was the "desiccated driver" of her vehicle.

Pat Cole held her chin in her hand, reading a book on her Kindle. Fran Williams was punching icons on her smart phone. "Well, ladies," I said, "since we are enjoying such a quiet night, I think I'm going to retire to my condo in Bed Twelve and try to get a little shuteye. Did you place chocolates on my pillow?"

"Don't eat 'em," said Pat, "they're laced with amphetamines."

The tones on the EMS radio went off. "25482 Hess Road in Monkton for a sick person. Hereford Ambulance 535 alerted. Time, 2:38"

"There you go, Should have kept your mouth shut," said Fran. "Now you've got an ambulance out."

"Well, maybe they'll go some place else," I said. "I'm going to lay down." On the rare occasion when I get an hour or two to take a nap on night shift, I always lie down on a stretcher in a patient room, because I can't get comfortable. If I sacked out in the doc's on-call room in a real bed, they'd never get me out of it.

~

Lying on my back on the hard stretcher, hands over my chest like a corpse, I heard the curtain rip back. "Wake up, Sunshine, you've got one," said Pat Cole none too softly. I looked at my watch with the little glowing hands: 3:12. Thirty-two minutes of bliss.

I climbed off the stretcher and trudged out to the nursing station. "You're supposed to wake me gently—with a kiss," I said to Pat, a divorced mother of two teenage boys who you would be well advised not to trifle with.

"You're lucky I didn't douse you with water."

Fran Williams slid the new chart into the rack. "Eddie Williams. I think this is the guy who owns all those car dealerships. Sixty-eight. Metastatic melanoma. He's in a hospice program. They brought him in because of pain. His wife's with him. You won't believe it."

"Won't believe what?"

"His wife."

I walked down the hall to Bed Nine and stepped through the door. A nearly bald, emaciated, elderly male lay under white sheets with his eyes closed, softly moaning almost continuously. On a chair beside his stretcher, sitting with her legs crossed in a knee-length black and white silk dress, was the most stunning, elegant young woman I had seen in a long time. I thought maybe she was on her way home from one of my ex-girlfriend's glittering parties.

I reached out my hand and said, "Hi, I'm Dr. Randolph."

The young woman briskly stood and smiled. Gripping my hand firmly she said, "Hi, Dr. Randolph. So nice to meet you. My name is

Mary Anne Williams. I'm Eddie's wife." *Wow. Maybe only thirty-five or forty year's difference.*

"Mrs. Williams, I understand that your husband has metastatic melanoma. Is that correct?"

She looked over at Eddie and sighed. "Yes, I'm afraid that's right. He was such a vigorous man and now he's a shell of his former self."

"Is he under any form of treatment, like chemotherapy or maybe radiation?"

The girl turned back and her bright hazel eyes locked into mine. "No," she said softly. "Eddie knew that treatment was almost useless, and he decided to forgo everything. He's been very, very brave about this. So now we have hospice at home. But tonight, I just haven't been able to control his pain. He's suffering terribly."

"OK. I understand. Let me take a look at him, and then we'll try to get his pain under control. Any other problems, like nausea and vomiting, or diarrhea?"

"He's basically stopped eating," she replied. "But other than that and the pain...nothing."

"Do you know where the metastases are located?"

"I think in his brain, his lung and his spine. That's the worst—his back."

I placed my right hand on the dying man's shoulder and said, Mr. Williams?" Eddie Williams opened his eyes, slowly turned his head and looked at me with still intelligent blue eyes peering out from deep within his skull.

"That's me," a raspy voice replied. He closed his eyes again. "I don't need anything from you but pain medicine. Just get rid of this pain for me."

"OK, Mr. Williams. We're going to do everything possible to get you comfortable. I'm going to have your nurse start an IV and I'm going to give you medicine through your veins until your pain is gone."

I finished my exam and walked back to the nursing station. Because the decision had been made to forgo treatment and he was already in a hospice program, I decided not to do a workup.

"Well, what'd you think?" asked Fran.

"Mr. Williams certainly has a lovely young wife," I said, "for what good that's doing the poor soul now."

"I think that little chickadee's about to come into a ton of money." Fran has evolved just a touch of cynicism after about twenty-five years in the ER.

~

An hour later, after a total of three milligrams of Dilaudid and eight of Zofran, I walked back to Eddie Williams's room. The lights were down and Eddie's wife sat reading from a Kindle.

"How are we doing in here?" I said softly.

"He's resting much more comfortably, Dr. Randolph," said Mrs. Williams. "Thank you so much."

"Well, I think he's probably going to need more pain medicine than thirty milligrams of OxyContin."

"Actually, his hospice nurse is planning on calling Dr. Holland at Hopkins tomorrow to get his medicine increased."

"Great. That will work. I won't interfere, then, with his pain management. I'm going to get his paperwork done, and the nurse will be in shortly with his discharge papers."

Mary Anne Williams stood and held out her hand. "Thank you, Dr. Randolph. You were very kind."

"Good luck, Mrs. Williams."

I walked back to the nursing station, finished Eddie Williams's paperwork and checked my watch: 4:29. Not much sense in taking a nap now. My relief would be here in twenty or thirty minutes.

CHAPTER TWENTY-SIX

DESPITE NOT GETTING TO BED UNTIL AFTER sunrise, Mary Anne was up by noon, feeling more energized than she had for months. *What a stroke of luck!* Now she had a project. And who knows? Maybe even a glimpse of her future.

For some reason, Alex Randolph pushed Mary's Anne's buttons like no man she could remember. She had now decided that he really was handsome—mature and socially skillful, too, with an aura of quiet confidence and maybe a hint of intrigue. Mary Anne found him fascinating, perhaps because he was so different from the rest of the men in her particular universe.

Somehow she thought of him as being *real*. Randolph had authentic social status. He was a doctor with a prestigious pedigree. Despite her rise to fabulous wealth, in hidden recesses of her heart she still craved the self-affirmation such a man could bring to a little girl raised in poverty in an Everglades trailer.

Lost in her daydream, she fantasized about how powerful she and Alex could be together. When Eddie was gone, she could make Alex the master of Ascot Farms and all the magazines would cover their elegant wedding on the estate. They could be celebrities together—the perfect couple—with money and status and star power.

I'm going to work on this, she decided.

Manuela appeared on the patio carrying a glass of hand-squeezed orange juice on a tray.

"Good morning, Mrs. Williams. I hope you slept well."

"Thank you, Manuela," Mary Anne said brightly. "It was a short night, but this morning I feel incredibly refreshed." The brown-skinned girl placed the juice on the table and Mary Anne watched the rhythm of her young buttocks flexing as she walked back toward the French doors.

Manuela, come here," Mary Anne commanded. With her new burst of energy, Mary Anne's tigress was on the prowl. Manuela returned and stood demurely by her employer's chair in a blue, knee-length dress that buttoned all the way down the front.

Mary Anne reached under the dress and ran her hand slowly up the inside of the girl's slender leg to the curve of her buttocks, pulling her closer. Mary Anne was now generously paying Manuela one hundred dollars a week additional salary. It was payment for sex, of course. Perhaps it wasn't necessary because Mary Anne held the trump card of a threat to call the INS. But in truth, Mary Anne loved paying for sex—just like the men. It was power and control.

She recalled hearing in an ancient history class at Miami Dade College that wealthy Romans kept bed slaves for their personal pleasure. That was Manuela. Mary Anne owned her.

"Manuela," she said softly, "you are a beautiful girl and very obedient. From now on I'm going to let you call me Miss Anne, instead of Mrs. Williams. Understand?" Manuela nodded. It was past time to get rid of the "Williams" in Mary Anne's name. She gently ran her hand under the girl's panties and squeezed a buttock.

"And later on today, you can take a little break and maybe I'll let you give me a massage. Would you like that, Manuela?"

"Yes, Miss Anne. I like to do that for you."

~

Sifting through a stack of old magazines, Mary Anne quickly found three with stories on Alex Randolph—two in *Us*, and one in *People*. She carried her magazines, iPad, and a Diet Coke to a lounge chair by the pool, where she read each article twice, quickly memorizing every scrap of detail: University of Pennsylvania undergrad; Duke medical school; a professorship at Hopkins; chair of emergency medicine at Mason-Dixon.

Obviously he had the blond girlfriend—she was in all the articles, too. But she was really of no consequence. No man on earth had ever been able to resist Mary Anne Hampton. *If she gets in the way, I'll simply destroy her. I wonder where he lives?*

She hit *Search* on the iPad screen and instantly the Google page was populated with results for "Dr. Alexander Randolph." Apart from a few orthodontists and dentists in California and Louisiana, most of the entries were for "Alexander B. Randolph, MD", residing in Maryland, with a middle name of "Blair." *Good name—sounds very aristocratic.*

Into a hardbound notebook, she copied all of the professional information and then returned to the iPad. She was able to quickly determine that Randolph lived in Monkton, Maryland. *Nice! We're neighbors. Maybe soon to be lovers… But where in Monkton?*

Mary Anne's fingers flew over the screen. There were tons of references to magazine and newspaper articles, many of them relating to the gang warfare between the Crips and MS-13 that spilled over into the Mason-Dixon ER. Most of these she had already read.

Whole Google pages referred to scholarly articles that Randolph had written while on the Hopkins faculty. These interested Mary Anne not in the least. But she did like the idea of being married to a prestigious ex-professor.

She found an Alexander Randolph on Facebook, but it was the wrong guy. *Her* Alex Randolph didn't seem to be on Facebook.

Four websites offered detailed info on Alexander B. Randolph of Monkton, Maryland, but they all required a credit card payment. Frustrated, she threw her notebook to the pool deck and stomped into the house to retrieve a credit card.

She touched the screen for *findsomebody.com*, entered her payment information, and touched *Create My Account*. The screen flashed and suddenly it was all there: "Alexander B. Randolph, 2400 Shepherd Road, Monkton, Maryland." Quickly, she opened another tab, typed the address into mapquest.com, and then touched *Satellite*. In an instant, she was hovering over a farm with a house, barn, and a pasture to the south through which ran a small stream. *Cool! That's not five miles away!*

The findsomebody website was a treasure trove of information. Everything from a list of potential relatives to birth and marriage records, to date of birth and address history—even litigation and criminal records. Impatiently, she quickly copied his birth date, four names of potential relatives, and an email address into her notebook. She couldn't wait to get moving. *I've got to go see that place.*

Snapping shut her notebook, she walked briskly into the house, threw a cover-up over her bathing suit, and jumped into the black Mercedes. She turned right out of Ascot Farms Lane onto Hess Road and drove west toward Monkton.

On the east edge of the little hamlet she turned right onto Shepherd Road, drove a quarter of a mile and then slowed. Through the trees on the right, down a one-hundred-yard stone lane, a large old brick house came into view surrounded by immaculate landscaping. An older model white Jeep Wrangler was parked by the house.

To the left of the lane, not fifty yards from the house, stood a large wooden bank barn on a stone foundation. A separate smaller outbuilding stood beside the barn, closer to the road, and appeared to be a garage or implement shed. Black board fence surrounded a pasture behind the house and ran right up to the barn.

The barn and the outbuilding were roofed in shiny red metal, and both were freshly painted in the same khaki color as the trim on the house. She slowed past the mailbox and read the numbers: 2400. *Wow. This little place is a dump compared to Ascot Farms*, thought Mary Anne. *He would love Ascot! That's where he belongs.*

~

For most of the next week Mary Anne pondered how to make the next contact with Alex, as she now called him. She could think of no other way than presenting to the ER with her own feigned illness. But that was a tricky proposition. She had no way of knowing when he would be working. She was pretty sure that at least in the middle of the night there was only one doctor on duty, but during the day there might be two or three, and then how would she know which doctor she would get even if she knew Alex was working?

She tried calling the ER and simply asking which doctors were working that day, but the receptionist replied curtly that she wasn't permitted to give out that information. Somehow she needed to find someone on the inside of the hospital, but she knew practically no locals at all, never mind someone who worked at Mason-Dixon.

After several days of wracking her brain, Mary Anne had hit a stone wall. She thought about just going into the ER and taking her chances, but decided that was too risky. The odds were too small that she'd get Alex, and then she would have blown her chance.

~

Bob Ebbitt swung his pickup truck through the massive stone pillars that guarded the entrance to Ascot Farms, and entered the quarter-mile macadam lane that led to the stone manor house. His practiced eye quickly appraised the state of the landscaping maintenance, and then he continued on past the house to the barn.

Ascot Farms was Ebbitt Property Management's biggest customer. His meeting with Milton Kopec this morning was a huge relief. He had worried for weeks that with Eddie Williams's death, EPM would lose the contract. But now he knew that Mary Anne Williams would inherit the property and that Milton Kopec would be his new boss. Milton had informed him that property maintenance was supported by a separate trust fund, and that as long as Ebbitt continued to perform, the contract was his.

He pulled up next to an old rusted Ford truck behind the barn and went searching for its owner. Gerald Stine had worked for Ebbitt for eighteen months. He could keep any piece of machinery running, and could do carpentry and electrical repairs, too. But he was Ebbitt's least favorite employee. He was coarse and shifty. Ebbitt strongly suspected that he had a drug problem—he didn't trust him. If employees weren't so hard to find, he would get rid of him.

He didn't like Stine being here at his biggest customer's farm, but for now, all he could do was keep him away from the house and hope to hell that he didn't antagonize the owners.

Management of Eddie Williams's angus herd, as well as a half dozen horses, was split off from property maintenance. That was handled by Roger Smith, a herdsman who was a direct Williams employee. Roger helped to keep an eye on Gerry, and that made Ebbitt at least a little more comfortable.

He found Gerry on his back under a brush hog rotary mower, using an electric grinder to sharpen the blades. The brush hog was raised on the three-point hitch of a tractor, and Stine had no safety prop under the mower deck.

Ebbitt kicked a foot sticking out from under the deck. The grinder went off and Stine crawled out from under the deck.

"Put a safety prop under that deck," said Ebbitt. All he needed was a huge workman's comp claim for Stine getting his skull bashed in. "If that hydraulic system fails you're sunk."

Ebbitt reviewed Stine's work list for the next two days and then stood with his hands on his hips, surveying Stine's two-day growth of beard and a pair of filthy jeans that looked like he'd worn them for a month. He didn't want this man around Mary Anne Williams, especially once Eddie died.

"When you come in tomorrow, make sure you're shaved and you have clean clothes on. And you make sure you stay away from that house looking like this."

"Yeah…whatever," said Stine.

~

At least three times a day, Mary Anne gritted her teeth and made an appearance in Eddie's room. It was torture. The room smelled like cat piss. Urinals, bedpans, and bedside commodes were all over the place. Mary Anne didn't even know these vile things existed until Eddie got sick. Stacks of medications, tissues, pads, diapers, wipes and sheets occupied every piece of furniture.

By now, Eddie looked like a cast member from a horror movie.

His eyes were sunken and flesh hung from the outlines of his skull. He was even more of a tyrant than usual—curt and demanding; refusing all conversation. But he was still alert enough to change the will if he wanted to. Everyone—most of all Eddie—needed to see how concerned, attentive, and devoted was his young wife, Mary Anne.

She looked at her watch and sighed: 3:00 PM. *I should go in there before Melanie leaves.*

Mary Anne wound her way to the enormous master bedroom where Melanie Cooper leaned over Eddie's bed, holding a straw from a glass of water to his lips. Standing in a corner with her arms folded, Mary Anne watched and waited while Melanie finished the task. A quiet middle-aged woman without much education, she seemed to have the stomach to stay in Eddie's stinking room eight hours a day. The woman noticed Mary Anne's presence and walked over to her.

"Melanie," Mary Anne whispered, "I can't tell you what a wonderful job you're doing with Eddie. He's suffering so much and I am so grateful to you. You are making the end so much easier for him." Melanie smiled and looked down at the carpet, both pleased and embarrassed by the praise.

Mary Anne continued. "Did you know that last weekend I had to take Eddie into the ER at Mason-Dixon on Saturday night? He was in agonizing pain and I couldn't help him. It was so awful!" Melanie nodded knowingly.

"Do you know that Dr. Randolph who works in the ER?" asked Mary Anne.

"I know of him. My son works there as an orderly," Melanie said with pride. *Oh my God*, thought Mary Anne.

"Oh, Melanie, he was so wonderful with Eddie," continued Mary Anne. "He was gentle and kind and by the time we left, Eddie was sleeping peacefully. I just wish that I could know when Dr. Randolph is working in case Eddie needs to go back to the ER. But they won't tell you that. It's a shame...Dr. Randolph *knows* Eddie now, you know what I mean?"

"Yes, yes," said Melanie, nodding, "I can see it would be better for him to get a doctor that knows him." Melanie was obviously relishing her role as confidant. She paused and put her thumb and forefinger to her chin.

"You know what?" she said leaning closer. "Maybe my son could get a copy of the doctor's schedule." Mary Anne almost fainted.

"He works over the whole hospital, but he has to go down to the ER a lot. Let me ask him. I…I *think* it's for a good cause." *I can't let her have too many second thoughts! She thinks maybe she spoke too soon.*

"Oh, Melanie, would you?" gushed Mary Anne. "I would be *so* grateful." She reached into her pocket, withdrew a one hundred dollar bill and pushed it into Melanie's hand. "Tell him this wouldn't be nearly thanks enough if he could bring me that peace of mind."

Melanie stared at the green bill for a long moment and then closed her fingers. She nodded her head again several times and said, "Yes…yes, I think he would help."

That's it! I can't believe it.

CHAPTER TWENTY-SEVEN

WITH THE KIDS BACK FROM ANNAPOLIS, LIFE had returned to its usual patterns and I was back to an empty bed and a quiet house, except for Sundays when Penny and the kids would be here for riding lessons and spend the night. Ruth was back, of course, after her week's vacation, and she and I had quickly settled back into our old routines.

So far, Penny and I had told no one of our engagement except her parents, holding the big news for a surprise announcement at the Murphy family party on the thirtieth, which we now called the engagement party.

Of course, because of the announcement, that party had morphed beyond the immediate Murphy family into a rather large affair that included all of my family and most of Penny's and my friends. We were careful to keep the list pared to just those who we would invite to the wedding so we didn't have to say, "Well, we invited you to this engagement party, but don't plan on coming to the wedding."

We had finally decided to set the date for Saturday, September seventeenth. Even though my trial should be over long before that, as a practical matter it was just impossible to get out invitations with adequate notice and complete wedding arrangements any sooner.

The seventeenth was a few weeks after Jack and Catherine would start at their new school, so they would have to be driven to school until after the wedding. Holly would be long gone, leaving for graduate school in August. Because Ruth would be available to help care for kids and drive them to and from school, we decided that it would work much better for Penny and the kids to just move to the farm permanently just before school started.

Penny and her mother, meanwhile, were working furiously on wedding arrangements. The gargantuan nature of the logistics involved in pulling off a wedding were a revelation to me, made all the more complex by the necessity of keeping things secret until the party on July thirtieth.

Sunday afternoon Penny and I sat in lawn chairs by the paddock fence watching Sally turn Catherine into a horsewoman.

"You know, Alex, I think we should tell your parents," said Penny. "I don't want them to feel left out. I'm sure it will be obvious to them at some point that my parents knew before the engagement party."

"Yeah, I've been thinking about that. I think you're right. I'm off on Tuesday and you're working. Maybe I'll go over there for dinner and break the news. My mother will be shocked that I've found a woman who wants to live with me."

Penny giggled. "I'm sure she'll wonder if I should see a shrink."

"What about Ruth?" I asked. "Which also brings up another question. What do we do with her after we're married? Do we want her living here? How am I going to chase you around the house naked with Ruth around."

"Alex, you won't be able to chase me around the house naked anyhow, the kids will be here."

"Right."

"But you can chase me around the bedroom."

"So, do we keep her or throw her out?"

"Alex! You can't throw her out! She's like family. And I *do* think we should tell her about the engagement."

"So you want to keep her."

"The children love her. Jack's always climbing into her lap. And she cooks and cleans. And there would always be someone here to baby-sit when we're working or if we want to go out."

"OK. I vote to keep her." Actually it was the perfect arrangement—like having a live-in nanny, only one that was completely trustworthy and loved the kids like a grandmother. Besides which, it would have killed me to tell Ruth that she couldn't live here anymore. We were her entire life. But I had needed to let Penny make the argument for keeping her.

This brought another subject to mind. "What about work? Do you want to keep working after we're married?" I asked.

"Well, since you're always on the verge of getting fired, don't you think it would be good to have some financial security in the house?"

"OK. You work and I'll watch the kids." Penny laughed.

"Actually, I *do* want to keep working," she said, "but maybe cut back to part-time. That would really be nice. What do you think?"

"That would be perfect. I don't get to see you enough when we're both working full-time."

"I like to work. If I went part-time I could keep up my skills, but still get to be with you and the kids more."

"Well," I said, "so far, we both seem to be on the same page. How are the marriage counselors around here ever going to make a living?"

"I'm sure we'll think of something to fight about. Maybe I could suggest that we sell your tractor to help pay for the wedding."

"That would not be a marital spat. That would be the nuclear option."

Out in the paddock, we heard Sally say, "Catherine. I think you're ready to take Abigail for a little trot. Would you like to try that?"

Catherine thought about that for a second and then tentatively nodded her golden head.

"OK. I'm going to be leading Abigail, and we're not going to trot too far. You can hold onto the horn of the saddle. Are you ready?" Catherine nodded again.

"OK, here we go!" Looking over her shoulder, Sally broke into a slow jog, clicking to Abigail, and the mare followed. A look of shock crossed Catherine's face and her little butt bounced up and down like the saddle was a trampoline. At no more than five seconds into Catherine's first trot, Sally brought Abigail to a stop.

Catherine's furrowed eyebrows slowly relaxed and then she broke into a broad smile, looking over a Penny and me. Thunderous applause erupted from the two spectators.

"Yay, Catherine! Way to go, baby!" cheered Penny.

The lesson continued and five minutes of silence went by. I had the vague impression that Penny was brooding about something. Finally, she spoke.

"There *is* someone else who I think we should tell, Alex," Penny said quietly. I thought I knew who that was, and it occurred to me that I should spare Penny the pain.

"Patrick's parents."

"Yes."

"Of course. It would be terribly hurtful not to tell them."

Penny leaned her head on my shoulder.

"Thank you, Alex."

Suddenly she sprang upright in her chair. "Oh my gosh! I forgot. We've got to tell Catherine and Jack!"

"Oh yeah. We can't spring it on them at the party." I thought for a moment. "What if they say 'no?'"

"Alex, they *love* you. They'll be thrilled. They're not going to say 'no.'"

"Do they have veto power?"

"Alex, you're marrying me, not the kids! They can't say no."

"OK. Just checking."

~

Tuesday at noon sharp, Ruth called me to lunch. I always respond promptly because tardiness elicits a lecture like I never heard from even my mother.

I slid onto the stool at the granite counter that separates the kitchen area from the family room beyond, and picked up the grilled cheese and bacon sandwich.

"Ouch," I said, dropping the sandwich and blowing on my fingers.

"Watch that sandwich. It's hot," said Ruth.

Blowing wasn't working, so I dipped my fingers in the iced tea.

"You have terrible table manners," she said.

"Ruth, I need to talk to you. I'm going to let you in on a little secret."

"A secret? What kind of secret?"

"Do you have a security clearance, Ruth?"

"No, I don't have any security clearance."

"Well, can I trust you with a secret?"

"Of course you can trust me with a secret," she said irritably.

"This is serious Ruth. If you tell anyone, I might have to kill you."

"Stop it, Alex. You can be so silly at times."

"You're right. Forget it."

"What's the secret?"

"I've asked a woman to marry me." Ruth dropped her jaw and her paring knife at the same time.

"Penny!" she exclaimed.

"No, I have a new girlfriend."

"Oh, Alex! You've finally gotten some sense into your head," she said, embracing me in a fierce bear hug. This was my first actual hug from Ruth.

She pushed back, and looked at me for a long moment, obviously troubled by something. Finally she said, "Alex, you just tell me when it's time for me to get out of here."

I reached out and placed one hand on a boney shoulder. "Well, Ruth. It's kind of a package deal. Penny and I would like you to stay here, too, if you're willing to do that."

~

I was raised in a white, clapboard house with a red metal roof on Sparks Road, seven miles south of Hereford. Over time, the house gained children and additions, as well as over twenty acres of nursery plantings. Randolph Nursery and Landscaping grew from this location and provided support for the family, as well as the vehicle by which my father taught my brother, Brian, and me the virtues of hard labor. At the time, Brian and I had not yet developed a great appreciation for our father's wisdom.

I pulled the Jeep around to the back of the house about 6:30, just as my dad was coming in from the nursery grounds. He was twenty-five when I was born, but at the age of sixty-four was still a substantial man who worked with his crews every day. The hair was gone, and the sun and weather had inscribed myriads of crow's-feet around his eyes, but he still had the walk of a young man, albeit perhaps a tad slower.

He opened the mudroom door and pushed me through it ahead of him. "I could have used your help today. We're putting in a new brick walk and Josh was running the skid steer. He tore up that customer's grass somethin' fierce. You've got a lighter touch."

"Finally, you appreciate my skills."

"I always appreciated your skills. There was just a time a few years ago when we needed to make sure that your head size didn't get bigger than your hat size."

My mother hugged me and kissed my cheek. "I'm glad you came tonight. I had a roast beef in the freezer that it was time to use up. Too big for just your father and me, but just right for three."

I stuffed myself on roast beef and potatoes, which were as good as I had always remembered them, and passed on dessert.

"Did you get to watch much of Wimbledon?" asked my father.

"I saw that final between Nadal and Djokovic. Amazing. Djokovic just creamed him."

"That boy is unbeatable when he's on. He covers the court like nobody's business. You watch. He's gonna be number one and he's gonna stay there for a long time. You want to put some money on the U.S. Open final?" he said smiling.

"Don't do it," said my mother.

You would be well advised not to make tennis bets against my father.

"You mean like who's going to be in it?"

"No, I mean who's going to *win* it. A hundred bucks says Djokovic."

I smiled. "You know, a hundred bucks is a lot of money."

"OK. If you can't afford it, fifty bucks."

"Well, actually, I'm saving my money."

"For what? You've already got a farm...a nice tractor. You can afford fifty bucks."

"I'm getting married."

My mother gasped. "No! You asked her?"

"Yeah. And, I'm sure you'll be surprised to hear that she said 'yes.'"

My mother got out of her chair and pulled my head to her chest. "Oh, Alex, that's wonderful! I am so happy for you! She's such a lovely girl." She paused and looked over at my father. "I do hope she's making the right decision."

My father laughed. "Well, I tell you what, Alex. You better do it fast before she changes her mind, because that girl's the best thing that will ever happen to you in your life."

~

Sunday evening the five of us held hands and said grace. At the end, Catherine said "Ah-woman," and looked up smiling.

Penny rolled her eyes. "Where did you hear that, Catherine?"

"I made it up," she said beaming.

"Very clever, Catherine," said her mother.

"I thought women's lib was an anachronism from the sixties," I said.

"It's apparently alive and well,' said Penny laughing.

"You're a smart girl, Catherine," said Ruth.

"OK, guys, I have an announcement to make," said Penny clasping her hands together.

"What's an announcement?" asked Jack.

"It's something that we want to tell everyone," said Penny.

"OK," said Catherine loudly. "What is it?"

"Well," said Penny, grasping my hand, "You will be interested to know that Dr. Alex Randolph and I are going to be married."

"Does that mean we're going to live here?" asked Jack.

"Yes, Jack. We're all going to live here at the farm together."

"That means I get to drive the Gator," said Jack emphatically.

"Cool!" said Catherine. "I can ride Abigail every day!"

"Well, maybe not every day, Catherine, but more than you do now."

Catherine wrinkled her brow in thought, and then her face lit up. "Are you going to have a baby?"

Penny looked at me. Sometimes things seem to evolve at their own pace in a relationship. This was an issue that we had not yet broached.

"Well, Catherine, I don't know. I guess we'll just have to wait and see."

Catherine smiled widely, revealing the gap where once sat a front incisor. "I would *love* that."

"I know you would, sweetheart."

Penny turned to me. "Well, so much for worries about a veto."

CHAPTER TWENTY-EIGHT

WITHIN FOUR DAYS, MELANIE HAD COME through with a Mason-Dixon ER doc's schedule for the next three months—more than Mary Anne could have hoped for. Another fifty bucks in Melanie's hand served as insurance for the next time Mary Anne needed a hospital insider.

She sat on the patio wearing running shorts and a sports bra, finishing her breakfast and now—with the ER schedule in hand—plotting her personal visit to Dr. Alex Randolph.

Smiling to herself, she shook her head in amazement. *This is unbelievable!* At any other time in her life, she would not have given a second thought as to how to approach a man she desired.

But Alex Randolph was different. Mary Anne did not feel confident that she understood his motivation, his likes and dislikes, or what were his hot buttons. Instinctively she understood that sex alone was unlikely to sell.

Indeed, she worried that what had worked with a thousand customers at Club Nouveau might doom a relationship with Alex Randolph. There had to be seduction, of course, but she suspected that it would have to be much more nuanced and subtle. No man alive was unappreciative of her beauty, but in this case it might take more. She was making her way through unfamiliar terrain.

In the end, she decided that she needed a scenario that would allow him to see the magnificence of her body, but in a way that he controlled. All very professional. Maybe some sort of female problem. Her body plus a measure of charm—which she knew she could supply in abundance—should prove irresistible.

Mary Anne could recall three or four pelvic exams in her life—all for refills of birth control pills, as far as she could remember. A need for pill refills wouldn't work for an emergency visit, but maybe she could show up with pain in her belly. She knew of lots of girls with pain who said they had ovarian cysts. He would get to see plenty if he had to do a pelvic exam. That might work.

But it was important that Alex didn't see this as a phony visit. *I need to do some research.*

She typed "ovarian cyst" into the Google search box on her iPad and clicked on the first line for *WebMD.* There were a half dozen kinds of cysts and a zillion different symptoms. *This is not so simple. Uggh! Pain with intercourse and difficulty with bowel movements…that won't work.* She jotted a few lines in her growing notebook and continued reading.

Thirty minutes later, after visiting five or six more websites, the murky waters began to clear. Some symptoms were clearly associated with only very large cysts, which of course, Alex would *not* find on either an examination or on the ultrasound studies the websites kept talking about. So those symptoms could be eliminated.

With a little more reading she finally understood that the only symptom she really needed was a complaint of lower abdominal pain, since that was the only complaint associated with a majority of the small, not-so-serious functional cysts. *Cool…this will work.* She began to feel more confident.

With a little surge of excitement, Mary Anne hid her notebook in her bedroom and went for a run around Ascot Farms. Warming up on a smooth surface, she first headed out the asphalt lane toward Hess Road, and then cut off-road to the right around the perimeter of the large east hayfield. Bob Ebbitt kept a perimeter path mowed around the entire farm specifically for Mary Anne's runs.

She crossed the asphalt parking lot to the southwest of the biggest barn and then ran outside the fence of the northern cattle pasture. Working on a gate in the barn paddock was the rough-looking guy Mary Anne often saw watching her from a distance.

She knew Bob Ebbitt and she knew Roger Smith who took care of the animals, but she had never met this guy. She wasn't even sure who employed him. But she didn't like his looks—reminded her of the kind of scum who used to hang out at Felix's trailer doing drugs at a time that to Mary Anne, now seemed to be a century ago.

CHAPTER TWENTY-NINE

THURSDAY NIGHT—TWO DAYS BEFORE THE big engagement party—Penny and I were scheduled for a night shift together, paying our scheduling dues before having a rare weekend off together for the party. We both started at 7:00 PM, but I would get off two hours ahead of Penny at 5:00 AM. Holly was taking Catherine and Jack to Annapolis Friday morning where they would stay with their grandparents until the night of the engagement party.

Nurses always arrive earlier for their shifts than do the docs, so Penny's car was already in the parking lot when I pulled in. What this means depends upon who you ask. Lisa Turano and Penny were standing nearby when I finished taking the sign-out report from Mark Showalter.

"How come nurses always come in so early?" I asked. "You get here a half-hour before your shift starts. Are you guys slow learners or something—takes you a half-hour to get report?"

Lisa put her hands on her hips and tapped her foot. Penny shot a deadly glance in my direction. "Nurses simply happen to be much more considerate than physicians," Lisa informed me curtly. "We come in early so our colleagues can go home early after a long and exhausting shift of trying to keep doctors on track. We work twelve hours. You only work ten hours. You guys are wimps."

Penny walked over and twisted my earlobe. "Slow learners... Say you're sorry," she commanded.

"You're sorry."

"No. Say, '*I'm* sorry.'"

"Ouch! *I'm* sorry."

~

The evening rush hour was in full swing this Thursday night. Typically from about 5:00 PM to midnight is the most intense period of the day. Working parents get home only to find sick kids at the baby-sitter's, or they check in on their own elderly parents and find them confused and unable to climb out of their La-Z-Boy recliners.

Other patients who have been tossing their cookies or had diarrhea all day, finally decide by bedtime that they've had it with being sick. And, of course, after dinner until dark is America's recreation time, so that's when we crash our bikes, get hit in the face with a baseball, or break a wrist falling off our trampolines.

The department was already packed when the tones went off on the county emergency communications radio at 8:32, dispatching a medic unit for an all-terrain vehicle accident on Pretty Boy Dam Road. I glanced up at the giant patient tracker screen and saw that we had only one bed open—Fourteen—one of our two trauma rooms. *Good.* We had six patients waiting for a bed to open up, but Jen Wilke, tonight's triage nurse, had the foresight to keep one bed available in case the real thing showed up.

Ten or twelve minutes later, the voice of A. J. Fortmann, lead paramedic on Parkton Station's Medic Sixty, crackled across the radio.

"Commander seven-oh-one...quick report," said an urgent voice. "I'm two minutes out with a nine-year-old male who flipped his ATV on a bank. He's conscious, but lethargic. Was wearing a helmet. He's cold and clammy with peripheral cyanosis; hypotensive, and tachycardic. His lungs are clear. Has obvious tib-fib and wrist fractures. His belly seems pretty firm. We scooped and ran. No IV access yet. You might want to get a helicopter in the air."

"Mason-Dixon copies, Medic Sixty. Trauma Bed Fourteen on arrival. Mason-Dixon out."

I turned to Fran Williams, tonight's charge nurse, an unflappable old pro who somehow keeps things moving when we get to gridlock time. She's a grandmother of three and married to the guy who runs Baltimore County's park system.

"Fran, I want three nurses in Fourteen. Get me two units of un-crossmatched O-positive blood from the blood bank and tell them to thaw a unit of fresh frozen plasma. And where's Lauren? I may need her in here."

"Stacey!" I yelled across the nursing station, "Get respiratory therapy down here to Fourteen, and get me a helicopter for a transfer to Shock Trauma."

I slipped into a surgical gown, pulled a pair of blue plastic gloves from the wall dispenser, and by the time I walked out toward the ambulance entrance could hear the back-up alarm and distinctive diesel roar of Medic Sixty.

A. J.'s brief report drew the picture of a child in shock from internal bleeding someplace. The kid was wearing a helmet and was awake, so I doubted a significant head injury. But with a bluish tint to his cold and clammy skin, and a low blood pressure and fast heart rate, it sounded like he was losing blood fast.

With red and white warning lights still flashing, the back doors of Medic Sixty popped open. A. J.'s EMT assistant jumped and hit the asphalt first. He unlocked the stretcher and began to pull it through the ambulance doors. A. J.'s stocky figure, crowned with a shock of red hair like a rooster, descended a little more slowly, using the aluminum step.

"Still no IV, Alex," he said breathlessly as we raced down the hallway. "He went up a bank and flipped the ATV. Apparently it landed on top of him. I think his chest is OK—he's got clear breath sounds bilaterally—but he's got an abrasion in his right upper quadrant and his belly seems firm to me. Maybe he got his liver."

We rolled through the open doors to trauma room Fourteen where stood a small, silent army of medical personnel in blue gloves, waiting to pull this child back from the edge of a cliff.

It took about a nanosecond for five pairs of hands to scoop the kid from the ambulance stretcher to the trauma table and then instantly the room became a blur of action, as if someone had pressed *fast forward*.

"First priority ladies, we need a line!" I said. "What's his name, A. J.?"

"Tommy—Tommy Blake."

Tommy Blake lay on the table, his black helmet still in place, conveying the appearance of an alien with a huge head. A plastic collar enveloped his neck, keeping it stable in case he had an injury to his cervical spine.

With eyes closed, Tommy softly moaned. Streaks and smudges of dirt smeared the torn clothes and exposed skin on the left side of his body, which must have hit the ground first.

His skin was cold and white, with a ghostly blue tint called *cyanosis* that indicated insufficient blood flow from his heart out to the rest of his body; no doubt because he was bleeding extensively from somewhere inside his small frame.

While scissors clipped through clothes and hands slapped sticky electrodes onto his chest, I leaned over his face and said loudly, "Tommy? Can you hear me? Tommy!"

The young boy's lids slowly raised and a pair of unfocused eyes came into view. "Look at me Tommy," I yelled. Brown eyes slowly swung in my direction.

"Where do you hurt?" Wincing with effort, Tommy slowly raised his hand to the right side his belly. "Tell me!" I yelled again. "Tell me Tommy!" I wanted him to speak.

"Here," said a small muffled voice through the oxygen mask. *Great.* This small act gave me a lot of information. Tommy was conscious. His brain was still working, his airway was intact, and he was breathing because he could speak. I put my stethoscope on either side of his chest and heard clear breath sounds.

In ten seconds I had moved through *A* and *B* of the *Trauma ABC's*—Airway, Breathing, Circulation. Circulation would be the bigger problem. From somewhere in his abdomen, Tommy was very close to bleeding to death.

"How long before the helicopter touches down?" I asked no one in particular.

"Twenty minutes," said Fran from the back of the room, quietly watching over this scenario and anticipating the resources that would be needed by the team. This is what good charge nurses do.

"OK, as soon as we get a line and blood flowing, I want a pan scan. Call CT and tell them to clear a table." We would do a CAT scan of essentially Tommy's whole body giving us a 3-D view of his chest and abdomen with a high likelihood of being able to identify the source of his bleeding.

But first we had to get him resuscitated and stabilized. That would mean pouring blood into him until his blood pressure started to rise, his color improved and his heart rate began to slow. But therein lay a big problem—so far we didn't have IV access.

By now, Tommy's slender body was stripped of clothes and lay naked before me. His swollen left wrist twisted off at a painful angle, and the middle of his left lower leg was crooked and blue from bleeding under the skin. But these obvious fractures were the least of my worries.

April Keller, a survivor of last year's hostage incident, was on her knees, freckles glowing bright orange, struggling to start an IV in Tommy's right arm which hung in mid-air off the side of the table. On the opposite side, knelt Lisa Turano also frantically searching for a vein, but to no avail. Tommy's veins were collapsed because he didn't have enough blood left in his circulatory system to fill them.

I glanced at the color monitor screen hovering above us and saw a heart rate of one hundred and forty-five. Below that, the green blood pressure icon showed a question mark. Tommy's blood pressure was so low that it was undetectable to the machine. This little boy was slipping away from us.

I heard Penny's voice behind me. "How about an EZ-IO?"

"Do it," I said. *She's always thinking.*

An *IO* is an *intraosseus needle*—a steel needle that is drilled into the cavity inside a long bone through which fluids can be run almost as fast as through an IV. It's a lifesaver when you can't find venous access.

I lay my hands on Tommy's belly. An angry red abrasion surrounded by ecchymosis—bruising—streaked across the right side of his abdomen just below his ribs, but with no associated dirt. Maybe from the handlebar of the ATV?

I palpated his abdomen, pressing gently in all four quadrants.

Tommy's moans grew louder. Normally the belly of a nine-year-old is very soft, but this abdomen was firm, a finding that often occurs when there is a massive bleeding into the abdominal cavity. The source of Tommy's shock undoubtedly lay somewhere beneath my fingers.

I heard the whir of a drill, and watched as with practiced efficiency Penny used a small battery-powered drill to insert the steel IO needle into Tommy's right tibia, just below the knee. In three seconds it was done.

"I'm in," said Penny. *Way to go, baby.*

Lauren Dorfman appeared in the doorway. "How ya doing in here, Alex? You need a real doctor in here?"

I looked around the table. Not one square inch of space around the table was unoccupied.

"I think his airway and chest are OK, Lauren, so we don't need a chest tube. He's bleeding into his belly someplace. We just need IV access. I'm OK for now, but if I need a real doctor I know where to find one."

"Do we have blood or fresh frozen plasma yet?" I called out.

"Blood is enroute," said Fran. "FFP is still thawing."

"OK. Run normal saline wide open. April and Lisa, keep working on a line."

Penny plugged an IV line into the IO needle, pressed a couple of buttons on a pump, and finally we had fluids running. It seemed an eternity, but when I looked at the wall clock, only four minutes had elapsed since Tommy Blake's arrival in the Mason-Dixon Regional Medical Center emergency department.

"Penny, as soon as it comes, hang blood in that IO."

I felt a hand touch my shoulder. "Alex, the boy's parents are here. They want to see him," Fran said quietly.

This is one of those raw moments in the practice of medicine that lays bare the personalities of everyone involved—physicians and patients alike.

Some physicians are adamant that family not be in the room at critical times. They don't want the distraction at a moment that requires intense concentration, or they worry that family will interpret things going bad as malpractice.

For some families the scene is more than they can bear, so occasionally they lose it, and their emotional outbursts interfere with care. But in my experience this is a rare event. Most families intuitively understand that the best thing for their loved one is to stay out of the way and let the team do its job.

If it were my son on death's door, I'd want to be there with him in his last moments of life.

"Let them in, but keep them in the back of the room until we get these lines established."

A moment later the wide trauma room door opened and through it tentatively stepped a mid-thirties couple. A tall, burly male with a mustache stood in camouflage pants and a tee shirt, his colorless face reflecting utter bewilderment. Beside him, a petite brunette in a ponytail held both hands to her nose in terror. Fran guided them to a corner of the packed room where they stood quietly in disbelief that the unthinkable had happened.

"A. J., help me get this helmet off."

I removed the C-spine collar around Tommy's neck and then slipped my hands underneath, holding his cervical spine stable. A. J.'s chubby hands grasped the helmet and expertly rotated it forward, slipping it off Tommy's head and unveiling a jumbled shock of blond hair.

"Let's take a look at his neck veins. Put this table in Trendelenburg. A. J., you hold his head."

We are always very careful about not letting the neck move until we have a CAT scan of the cervical spine that assures us that there are no spine fractures. A wrong move of the neck and you can convert someone who walks and talks into a lifetime paraplegic.

Someone pushed a button, a motor whirred. and the table began to tilt head-down into Trendelenburg position. With Tommy partly upside down, what little blood remained in his circulatory system would now all run down to his head, distending the veins in his neck and perhaps giving me a shot at starting an IV.

As the table continued to tilt, gradually an external jugular vein began to appear. "That's good," I said, and the table stopped moving.

"I need an 18-gauge catheter," I said, holding out my hand without taking my eyes off the vein. Someone slapped a catheter in my hand and I entered the skin with the point of the needle just above where I wanted to hit the vein.

On the first pass there was no flashback of blood into the catheter. I withdrew the needle until just the point was left in the skin, slightly redirected it, and advanced it again.

There it is! A flash of red appeared in the catheter. I slipped the catheter over the steel needle into the vein and breathed a sigh of relief. Now we had two lines, and this one was big enough to run blood fast.

"Blood's here," called out Fran. "You'll have to sign." I scribbled my name on the un-crossmatched blood release form, Penny spiked the plastic bag of blood with IV tubing, and we now had blood pouring into Tommy's circulatory system seven minutes after arrival.

"April and Lisa, keep working on another line. I want three of 'em. Get him hooked up to the portable monitor and let's get him out of here to CT."

I wanted to get this CAT scan done so I had a definitive diagnosis for Shock Trauma. With any luck they would then be able to take him directly to an operating room with no further studies. But the helicopter would be here in about ten minutes and I didn't want the CT to delay transport. Every minute was precious during this first *Golden Hour* of trauma care.

"I've got it!" called out April. *Good girl, April!* Now we had three lines—enough to massively replace lost blood if we had to.

Six months ago, carefree, gum-cracking April Keller—barely twenty-two years old and just out of nursing school— had a gun barrel held to her temple for two minutes while waiting for Penny Murray to return to the hostage room with drugs demanded by a man who had already killed two people. At the two-minute mark the trigger would be pulled.

Penny made it back with only seconds to spare, but the trauma to poor April's psyche was unimaginable. To her enormous credit, she was back on the job in a week. Despite having to deal with deep residual anxiety, she stayed with the job she loved.

185

"Hang that second unit of blood on April's line and let's get going," I said."

In a minute the portable IV pumps and monitor were mounted on the stretcher. The team shoved through the doorway, sped down the hallway to CT, and suddenly all was quiet. I looked around the empty room and saw the parents of this mortally wounded child still standing quietly in the corner.

"Mr. and Mrs. Blake...sorry, this is the first opportunity I've had to speak with you," I said extending my hand. "I'm Dr. Randolph."

As if just clearing his head after a sucker punch, the big man slowly reached out and in a low voice said, "I'm John. This my wife, Wendy." Wendy said nothing, her anguished eyes boring into mine, holding her breath as she awaited the verdict on her son's life. *Where do I start? How do I paint this picture?*

"I think it's probably clear to you," I began, "that Tommy has suffered some very serious injuries. He has obvious fractures of his wrist and leg, but those will heal. The bigger problem is that he is bleeding from someplace internally and he is very deep in shock. He's lost a lot of blood." Wendy Blake's hands went to her face again in an unsuccessful attempt to stifle a soft whimper.

"I think he has likely lacerated his liver, but I'll have a lot more information as soon as this CAT scan is finished. For sure he's going to need emergency surgery in a place that's very good with trauma. So a helicopter will be landing here in five or ten minutes to fly him to Shock Trauma where he'll get the best care possible. They'll have a whole surgical team waiting for him

"In the meantime, you saw that we were successful in getting IVs into him and getting blood started. We're going to do our very best to stabilize him before transport."

"So...will he be OK?" asked John as if I had failed to answer his question.

He asked me an honest question. I gave him an honest answer.

"I don't know. If we can keep his blood pressure up and keep him alive until they get him to the operating room, then he stands a good chance. The next hour will tell the story."

~

At twenty-one minutes into the resuscitation, the LifeNet flight crew arrived just as Tommy was returning from CT. The blue tint to his skin was gone and I could see the first hints of pink. A blood pressure was now registering on the machine: eighty over fifty-two. *Progress.*

While they worked on packaging Tommy for flight, I brought up the CT on the PACs radiology screen. It was all there in black and white: an extensive laceration running diagonally through the right lobe of the liver to the falciform ligament, and lots of free blood in the abdomen. I quickly scrolled through CTs of the head, cervical spine and chest. At least on a quick perusal, they all looked OK.

At twenty-nine minutes from arrival, the crew had transferred all the cables and IV lines to their own monitors and pumps for transport. They pushed through the sliding glass doors of the ambulance entrance out to the helipad where sat a sleek ship with turbines whining and rotors turning in hopes of beating the clock that was ticking on Tommy Blake's life.

I watched the ship's navigation lights disappear into the darkening sky and then walked back into the ER, pleased at what my staff had accomplished. In under thirty minutes we had resuscitated this child, diagnosed his injuries, and gotten him out of here enroute to a tertiary care center. *Not a bad night's work for Mason-Dixon's emergency department.*

~

By 1:30 AM when Lauren finally packed it in, we were down to just a trickle. Three patients remained in the department in various stages of workup. The phone rang and Stacey called out, "Dr. Steagel on 5111 from Shock Trauma."

"Alex Randolph."

"Alex, Hank Steagel from Shock Trauma. Are you the one that flew out Tommy Blake?"

"Yeah, that was me."

"Well, he came out of surgery about a half-hour ago. As you know, he had a liver lac, but we also found some torn mesentery. He went through a lot of blood, but he's got a decent blood pressure now. He's still on the vent of course, but with a little luck, I think he might make it."

"You know, that's really good news. Did you talk to his parents yet?"

"Yeah, they're here in his room. They're shell-shocked, of course, but they seem to be holding it together OK."

"Hank, I really appreciate your call."

"Good work up there, Alex. Goodnight."

This is why I like my job.

~

Another nocturnal straggler came in about 2:30 AM. April walked past the nursing station accompanied by a striking young woman in snug black running shorts and a turquoise tank top that conformed to every curve of her narrow waist and hips. Shining auburn hair flowed to the middle of her back. *I've seen this woman before.* I watched her athletic body walk down the hallway and disappear into Bed Eight.

A paper clip hit the right side of my neck and tumbled onto my keyboard. I looked up to see Penny glaring at me. "Don't spend too much time in that room," she warned.

I grinned. "Only that which is medically necessary, my darling."

April slid the chart into the rack. "Pelvic pain since this afternoon. Couldn't sleep. No fever, vomiting, or diarrhea."

The name on the tracker screen said "Williams, Mary Anne." Age: twenty-eight. I clicked on the EMR icon to check for old records, but there were none. I tapped my pen on my forehead. *Williams...?*

The triage summary note revealed normal vital signs, no past medical history, and only one medication: Yaz birth control pills.

I left my chair and walked into the room to find Ms. Williams seated on the edge of the bed with her legs crossed, leaning back on her arms. She looked like a model for Gold's Gym. A brilliant smile with even, white teeth immediately flashed across her face.

"Hi, Dr. Randolph. Mary Anne Williams," she said, standing and extending her hand. "I met you once before when I was in here with my husband with cancer pain. Nice to see you again."

That's how I know her. The chick who is on the verge of coming into a fortune.

Mary Anne Williams was a stunningly beautiful woman with a body to die for. But almost instantly something about her made me uneasy. Maybe she was a little obsequious. The only people who jumped up, pumped my hand, and were this happy to see me were prescription drug addicts looking for a refill. But that was unfair. Perhaps she was just very socially skillful, a trait not unexpected in a young woman of her social strata.

"Mary Anne, you're having some abdominal pain tonight?"

"Yes. I couldn't sleep and finally decided to come in."

"Can you show me where your pain is?"

Mary Anne lay back on the stretcher, pulled her top up to her ribs, and her shorts halfway down her hips.

"Right here," she said, pointing to a spot low on the right side of a tight, muscled abdomen.

"How long have you had the pain?"

"It came on fairly suddenly about two or three o'clock yesterday afternoon after I went for a run, and it's never gone away."

"And you're on birth control pills, right?"

"Yes. Yaz."

"Do you recall the first day of you last menstrual period?"

"Just about two weeks ago."

"No nausea and vomiting or diarrhea?"

"No, thank God."

"Fever or chills?"

"Nope."

"Any new sexual partners in the last month or so?"

She smiled. "That, unfortunately, is a rarity these days." *I need to leave that one alone.*

"How about urinary symptoms? Does it burn when you pee or are you urinating more frequently than usual?"

"No."

"Any vaginal discharge or spotting in the last week or two?"

"None."

"Have you ever had pain like this before?"

"I have not."

So far nothing except pain, although I wasn't too impressed with that. The location of her pain was a little too low for appendicitis, and seemed more pelvic than abdominal. This was likely an ovarian cyst, although women on birth control pills are certainly less likely to have functional cysts than women who aren't.

Pelvic inflammatory disease, or *PID* as it's called, was another possibility, but I doubted it. She apparently wasn't sexually active in recent months, and there was no complaint of vaginal discharge.

"OK, Mary Anne. I'm going to have April come and get you into a gown so we can examine you. We're also going to do a little blood work and we'll need a urine from you. Depending on what we find on the exam and the studies, we may also need to do a sonogram. Right now, I'm thinking that the most likely cause of your pain is an ovarian cyst."

~

I returned to find Mary Anne lying on her back in a patient gown to mid-thigh. A folded sheet lay on the bed beside her.

"You know, Dr. Randolph, I think I passed you in Monkton a couple of days ago. Do you drive a white Jeep?"

"I do. A rusty, beat-up '95 Wrangler."

"And did I see you at the St. Mark's charity auction in May?"

"I was there."

"I thought so. We might be neighbors. Do you live in Monkton?"

"Yeah. I have a little farm on Shepherd Road."

"I live on Hess Road—Ascot Farms." I knew Ascot Farms—a fabulous property with a huge stone manor house and acres of manicured grounds. Miles of well-maintained black board fence surrounded the estate.

"Well, I guess we *are* neighbors. Ascot Farms is a lovely place."

"Thank you. I'm afraid, it's going to be a lonely place soon," she said. I decided we needed to change the subject.

"OK, Mary Anne, let's take a look at you." I laid the unfolded sheet over her hips and then pulled up the bottom of the patient gown to expose her abdomen.

"I'm going to work my way around your belly and I want you to tell me if you're tender any place I push."

I watched her face for signs of pain as I made my way from first the left lower quadrant counterclockwise around her belly. She held my gaze and smiled. When I finally reached the area of her complaint deep in the right lower quadrant, she winced.

"That's it," she said. "That's where it hurts."

I put my stethoscope to her belly and heard normal gurgling bowel sounds.

"Let's take a listen to your heart now." I tried to slip the stethoscope up under the gown but Mary Anne immediately reached down and pulled the gown up over both breasts to give me access. *This is a woman who is comfortable with her body.* Normal heart sounds.

"OK, now sit up and we'll take a listen your lungs. Nice deep breaths—in and out." Mary Anne had a completely normal exam except for some pelvic tenderness on the right.

"Well, you've got a little tenderness in your pelvis on the right side, but everything else looks great. I think we need to do a pelvic exam and then we'll be done. An ovarian cyst is still at the top of my list. I'm going to get April, and we'll be right back."

At the nursing station, I said, "April, get her ready for a pelvic and buzz me when you're ready."

Two computers down the counter, Penny said, "Medical necessity?"

I smiled. "I'm getting close to zeroing in on the diagnosis."

~

I pushed the sheet up over her legs and said, "OK, Mary Anne, let's drop those knees wide apart."

"Nice, deep breaths," said April, holding her hand.

Mary Anne effortlessly dropped her knees almost to the horizontal. She was completely smoothly shaven as is customary in her age group. Seated on a stool, I smeared the clear plastic speculum with surgical lubricant and spread her labia with my left thumb and index finger.

"OK, Mary Anne, nice and relaxed. Just let this thing slide right past that muscle." The speculum slid smoothly to the back of her vagina and almost immediately her cervix popped into view. It looked perfectly pink and healthy, without discharge. I twirled a long cotton swab for cultures around the opening, or *os*, as we call it, and handed the swab to April.

Removing the speculum, I stood. "Great job, Mary Anne. Now if you can stay relaxed just a little longer, I'm going to feel your uterus and ovaries, and then we'll be done."

Standing at her side and reaching over a slender leg, I gently slid first one and then two fingers deep into her vagina until I could feel the cervix. I wiggled her cervix with my fingers and asked, "Does that give you any pain?" She shook her head "no." *No cervical motion tenderness.*

Placing my left hand on her abdomen and reaching toward her left ovary with the two fingers in her vagina, I pressed my hands together until my fingers met, separated only by her abdominal wall. No masses were apparent.

"Any pain?"

"Nope."

I repeated the exam over her right ovary, and again found no masses, but this time she winced. "Yes, that's it," she said.

"Well, Mary Anne, you *are* tender over that right ovary. I'm going to order a sonogram, and when that and the blood work are done, I'll be back."

I was actually a little reluctant to order the sonogram because I really didn't expect to find much of anything, but sometimes you're surprised. Because the pain was clearly in the area of her right ovary and tube, I decided not to pursue appendicitis unless her white blood cell count came back elevated.

~

By 4:30 AM Mary Anne Williams was the last patient left in the department. I was ready to go home and crawl into bed.

The fax whirred and the sonogram report from Night Hawk in Australia slowly slid out of the machine. If that sounds strange, remember that images can be transmitted anywhere in the world in seconds. The guys in Australia are awake when our radiologists are asleep. Night Hawk is generating a very nice revenue stream contracting with American radiology departments to do nighttime reports.

I read through the report. Nothing. Only a small one-centimeter follicular cyst on the right ovary, a common finding in healthy young women.

A click on the laboratory icon on the tracker screen revealed a normal white blood cell count and a clean urine. *Good.* I would be able to get this girl out of the department before my relief came in at 5:00 AM. I walked back to the room to give her the good news.

"Mary Anne, everything looks great. Your white blood cell count is not elevated, and your sonogram looks really very normal. You may have had a very small cyst rupture, but the important thing is that we have found no evidence tonight of any serious disease. I think you'll find that this pain likely just fades over the next day or two."

She smiled and said, "Well, thank you, Dr. Randolph, for your good care. I'm sorry to have disturbed you tonight for nothing. I really feel rather foolish. You were very kind."

"Don't feel foolish. That's what we're here for."

"You know," she said, smiling and holding eye contact, "since now we know we're neighbors, maybe we should get together for dinner some time and swap stories of farm life on our marvelous My Ladies Manor."

I couldn't tell if it was Jekyll or Hyde, but a little voice in my head said, *Hmmm…I'm not sure what's going on here.*

"That could be fun," I said politely.

~

By 5:30, the last stars were fading and the eastern sky was brightening as I pulled into the driveway. General Lee and Abigail whinnied as I climbed out of the Jeep. I walked over to the fence and ran my hand over both noses at the same time. "Another beautiful day coming, guys. Sorry, no treats this morning."

Abigail tossed her head at General Lee as if to say, "Hey, get out of here. He's mine."

It was still warm at dawn—maybe seventy degrees. I stripped and fell into bed with the sweet anticipation of a lovely warm body curling up to me in just two hours. Sleep came instantly.

CHAPTER THIRTY

MARY ANNE SLAMMED HER FIST ON THE steering wheel of the SLS Roadster and cursed. "That could be *fun*..." she screamed in mockery.

Never in her life had a male so flatly deflected a direct invitation from Mary Anne Hampton. "Is he thick or what?" she fumed.

Most humiliating of all, as she left the ER, Mary Anne thought she saw his blond whore sitting at the nursing station.

Stomping on the gas, she exited the gleaming Mason-Dixon Regional Medical Center, leaving a smear of expensive rubber in her wake. A flock of birds in a nearby tree took to flight.

The Mercedes roared south on York Road down the steep winding hill to the bridge crossing Gunpowder Falls. A succession of hairpin turns took Mary Anne by surprise and for an instant the low-slung car was up on two wheels.

When the two inboard wheels returned to pavement, the car veered sharply to the left onto a gravel shoulder and entered a slide. Mary Anne released the brakes, steered into the slide, and the car returned to the road. In an instant, the gleaming black Roadster had streaked across the concrete bridge, screamed around the next turn, and suddenly was slowing up the opposite hill.

Pulling to the side of the road, Mary Anne lay her forehead on the leather-wrapped wheel and sobbed. Moments later the door flew open and she emptied the contents of her stomach onto asphalt.

~

Manuela watched anxiously as her mistress threw down four Tylenol and drained the orange juice glass. "Would you care for more, Miss Anne?"

"Manuela, this headache is killing me. Yes. Get me another glass."

Ohhh, that bastard will pay, she thought. *He can't humiliate me like this.*

Still furious, she left her chair and stepped out into the sunlight of the patio. *Maybe a swim will clear my head.* Too angry to go through the motions of changing, she pulled the sports bra over her head, kicked off her shorts and dove naked into warm, blue water.

From the distant paddock, Gerry Stine couldn't believe his luck. *What a fucking woman*, he thought.

~

By late afternoon, Mary Anne's rage was subsiding along with her headache. With great effort she forced herself to review the events of the previous night again with a cooler head.

Well, he actually didn't say "no." He said it "could" be fun. Could be if what? He wants me, but something is holding him back.

Hospice nurse Heather Mitchell walked through the French doors out onto the elevated patio and down the path to the parking lot. "Good Evening, Mrs. Williams," she called out waving. Mary Anne looked at her watch: 4:00 PM. She hadn't been in to see Eddie yet.

She walked to her bedroom, changed into jeans and a tee shirt, and made her way to Eddie's room. Melanie Cooper was still there.

"Hi, Melanie. How's Eddie doing today?"

"Actually, he's done well today. He drank altogether probably eight ounces of Ensure, and he's certainly seemed more alert today. He's sleeping right now." *Great. How much longer can he hang on?*

Mary Anne walked to the bedside and stroked her husband's forehead. *Maybe you're the problem, dear. Maybe Dr. Randolph doesn't want to be involved with a married woman.*

Eddie's eyes opened. "Hi, sweetheart," he said with a raspy voice. "Where were you last night?"

Mary Anne's heart stopped. *He's going to change the will!* She recovered almost instantly.

"Oh, Eddie, I was so worried about leaving you, but you were asleep and I didn't want to wake you. I had to go into the emergency room. I had this God-awful pain in my belly and I just couldn't stand it anymore.

"They said I had a cyst rupture on my ovary and gave me some pain medicine. I'll show you the discharge papers. I slept late today, but I'm feeling much better this afternoon. I don't ever want to have to leave you like that again."

Eddie's blue eyes stared up at her from his skeleton. "I certainly hope it doesn't happen again, too—for both of us."

~

Like lava flowing from the cone of a volcano, the anxiety welled up endlessly. All of the next day Mary Anne held her breath at the sound of each vehicle approaching Ascot Farms, waiting for the arrival of the red Cadillac driven by Eddie's lawyer, Herbert Silberstein. When five o'clock came with no Silberstein and no modification of the will—at the end of the longest day of her life—her heart rate finally began to slow.

I can't live another day like this. Ascot Farms is mine. He can't take it from me!

At 5:30 she went for a run to cleanse her body of the day's demons.

~

"Where would you like to have dinner, Miss Anne?"

"I'll take it on the patio, Manuela."

At 6:30 Manuela set a plate of fried calamari and an avocado salad at the single place setting on the patio table. She returned a moment later with a bottle of cabernet.

"Wine, Miss Anne?"

"Just half a glass, Manuela."

Mary Anne picked at her plate. The swirling events of the last twenty-four hours were coming into better focus. *It's all very simple*, she thought. Her hopes and dreams revolved around two elements: Ascot Farms and Alex Randolph. They were mutually dependent. Her rise to fame could not occur without both components—fabulous wealth and a celebrity husband.

The obstacle common to both was Eddie Williams. The risk that he might change the will on his deathbed was intolerable. The "could" for Alex Randolph, she was convinced, was that Mary Anne Williams needed to be single.

Slowly she came to the conclusion that Eddie Williams needed to be taken by cancer—tonight.

~

At ten o'clock Mary Anne prepared Eddie's evening medications. There were four meds laid out in the box for 10:00 PM: a tablet of phenergan for nausea, one stool softener, one Percocet, and one OxyContin, which recently had been increased to a sixty-milligram tablet. Eddie typically took all four pills at once, washing them down with plain water.

Heather Mitchell had instructed Mary Anne that the slow-release opioid, OxyContin, was potentially dangerous, especially if the pill was cracked or chewed, resulting in immediate release of too much narcotic at once.

Tonight Eddie would get four pills, but all four would be OxyContin—a total of two hundred and forty milligrams—perhaps not enough to kill him, but certainly enough to render him defenseless.

She placed an OxyContin between her teeth and steadily applied pressure until the tablet broke in half. *Shit!* Her intent was only to crack it, not break it. Eddie might be suspicious if there were too many pills or pieces of pill in his mouth.

She spit the two halves out and tried it again, applying the pressure more gradually this time. Sensing a slight give in the tablet, she removed it from her mouth. A tiny fissure zigzagged across the tablet. *Perfect!*

Eight tablets later, she had four whole tablets remaining, each with a tiny crack.

Eddie was sleeping when Mary Anne poured a third of a glass of water and peeled the paper covering off a fresh straw. She stroked his sunken cheek until his eyes slowly opened, as if in a fog.

"Eddie, darling, it's time for your evening medications. Open up now." In short jerks like a cogwheel, Eddie's mouth tentatively opened. She dropped the four tablets into the dry, leathery cavity and lifting his head, placed the straw between his lips. "OK, Eddie, now swallow."

For several moments, Eddie's mouth fumbled with the tablets, trying to get them into position. Finally he sucked briefly on the straw, but immediately choked, spraying Mary Anne with water and expelling one of the tablets onto the coverlet below his chin. *Shit!* She retrieved the tablet and with one finger, pushed it past the rough tongue to the back of his throat.

Again she lifted his head, replaced the straw and said, "Drink, Eddie, drink!" With great effort, Eddie wrapped quivering lips around the straw, sucked, and managed three or four swallows before releasing the straw in exhaustion. Mary Anne eased his head back to the pillow. Slipping her index finger into the side of his mouth, she probed for pills, but found none.

She touched two fingers to her lips and then to Eddie's lips. "Sleep tight, my darling," she whispered.

~

Tonight Mary Anne showered in the magnificent Italian marble bath off Eddie's room—fully half the size of the master bedroom itself. Anticipation quickened her pulse and she felt marvelously alive. Eight jets of steaming water caressed her body as she soaped her skin and then closed her eyes, slipping her fingers between her legs.

She lay with her head and shoulders on the bed, her wide-spread legs holding her buttocks high in the air; her panties halfway to her knees. Beside the bed stood Alex Randolph, his rigid cock pointing to the sky. He roughly twisted her nipples and then slapped her ass sharply until tears flowed. "You think you've been fucked before, Mary Anne? I'm going to teach you what fucking's all about."

He climbed on the bed behind her, his rigid pole blindly probing, demanding access. She reached between her legs to guide him to her pulsating wetness. In a single violent thrust he buried himself to the balls, and she groaned with pleasure.

Her fingers became a blur and her legs became water. Slowly she slid down the wall of the shower and lay with legs wide apart as the punishing thrusts increased and wave after powerful wave of exquisite sensation washed over her.

~

Mary Anne sat naked with one foot on the edge of the chair in front of the elegant master bath dressing table. With long, deft strokes she applied a coat of *Pink Chablis* to the last toe.

As she waited for the polish to dry, she leaned back in the chair and watched herself in the mirror, striking elegant poses and rearranging auburn tresses around her face and breasts.

When the polish was dry, she stood and walked to the full-length mirror, slowly rotating her body; looking for signs of age—a telltale sag or a subtle droop. But there were none. Her buttocks pouted and her breasts rode high on her chest. She watched herself run her fingers across her belly and felt the ridges of hard muscle beneath her hand.

Satisfied, she turned and padded into the bedroom, her face flushed with excitement. As she approached Eddie's bed she noted the time on the grandfather clock at the far end of the room: 11:38. She wanted to remember every detail.

Naked, she climbed onto the bed and straddled Eddie on her hands and knees. As expected, he still breathed. She watched him for a moment, then lowered her weight fully onto his pelvis and sat upright. Not a muscle stirred beneath the coverlet.

"Eddie!" she said softly with reproach, "Aren't you going to take advantage of me? You used to like this position.

"You're not interested? Oh well, maybe those days are over. Maybe it's time to cash it in—life's not worth living anymore and all that stuff. What do you think?"

Mary Anne reached for the pillow next to Eddie's head and cradled it to her chest.

"I think you've suffered long enough, darling. I'm going to help you."

An electrifying thrill surged through her body as she lowered the pillow to Eddie's face, then leaned forward, pressing her full weight against the pillow.

Nothing happened for a long moment, and then there was movement beneath the coverlet. As if rising from a crypt, a pair of skeletal hands ascended from below, reaching for her arms; the hideous fingernails digging into her skin.

She screamed and rose up on her knees, pressing harder with all the might in her muscled body. The bed moved beneath her and she held on for dear life. The pawing at her arms continued for several long moments and then gradually subsided, the grasping hands slowly sliding down her arms—inch by inch—until finally they dropped harmlessly to the coverlet.

Amidst the pounding of her heart and the heaving of her chest, a wave of primal exhilaration swept over Mary Anne. She cautiously held the pillow to Eddie's face for several more minutes, then slowly released the pressure and slid the pillow to the side. Lifeless eyes stared back at her.

Sitting upright on Eddie's pelvis, Mary Anne took a deep breath, savoring the moment. She had won. She had taken Eddie Williams's life by her own hand and watched him die. Ascot Farms was hers. Soon, Alex Randolph would be hers, too.

~

The next two hours were busy. As the first order of business, Mary Anne washed the scratches on her arms with soap and water and then applied first-aid cream.

Next, she strode into Eddie's study and went through the drawers of his desk where she knew he kept cash for emergencies. After fifteen frustrating minutes, she finally found a drawer in the back of another drawer and extracted forty-three thousand dollars.

Back in the master bedroom, she opened the top drawer of Eddie's clothes bureau and pulled nine thousand dollars from his billfold. Disappointed, she pouted, sighed, and added it to the forty-three.

Now, where to put it? I know! Trotting back to her bedroom she retrieved her Alex Randolph notebook from its hiding place and tucked the cash between its pages. That was fifty-two thousand dollars less that she would ever have to beg for from Milton Kopec.

For the next forty-five minutes she sat cross-legged on the bed beside Eddie, patiently cleaning traces of blood and debris from under his fingernails. Eddie's nails never looked so good. She placed his arms back under the covers, fluffed the pillow she had used to suffocate him, and set it back where it belonged.

Standing with her hands on her hips, she surveyed the room with satisfaction. A good night's work. Everything seemed to be in its place.

In the morning, Melanie would find Eddie finally at rest, having peacefully passed away in his sleep. Mary Anne turned out the lights, walked back to her bedroom, and crawled between the sheets. Deep and restful sleep came quickly.

CHAPTER THIRTY-ONE

WITH NICE, CLEAR DIVISIONS OF DUTY, Penny and Ruth were in charge of the house and food preparation, and I was responsible for the outside. The bar was my sole responsibility on the food and beverage side, which was OK with me. The music was mine, too.

Of course, it doesn't matter what time you start getting ready for a party, it always goes right down to the wire. But, given the inviolability of that theorem, we did pretty well. By seven o'clock we were headed for the showers and by 7:30 we were dressed and ready for the fun to begin.

As the last act of preparation, I lit the tiki torches around the patio, opened a cabernet for Penny, and poured myself a Grey Goose and tonic. I offered Ruth a Jack Daniels straight up, but she opted for ginger ale.

The first car to enter the driveway was an SUV bearing military license plates. The doors flew open, discharging Jack and Catherine, who bounded out and made a beeline for Penny.

Maimeó Murphy had obviously invested in some bonding moments with her gorgeous granddaughter, who appeared with a braid and multicolor beads in her golden hair, wearing a long daffodil-yellow strapless sundress.

Jack, for his part, at least initially looked clean in a pair of khaki shorts and a red polo shirt. That lasted about five seconds until he was ambushed by Maggie enroute to giving his mother a hug.

Tim Murphy rode up from Annapolis with Tom and Denise. After a long embrace with his sister, he turned to me. I shook his hand and said, "Tim, I've heard a lot about you. Your sister seems to think her little brother has done well in life, and believes that her mentoring is responsible for your success."

Penny slapped me on the shoulder. "I never said that!"

"It's true," said Tim grinning. "All those years of being beat up by your older sister produces character."

"What can I get you to drink?"

"What do you have in the way of whiskey?"

"How about a little Jack Daniels?"

"Perfect. On the rocks."

"See?" I said turning to Penny. "No chardonnay for him. He's a fighter pilot."

"Oh, God. Everywhere I turn there's nothing but testosterone." She floated away to her parents.

"I'm envious—you're getting paid to fly," I said, handing Tim his drink. "I'd love to do that."

"It's the best job in the world."

"Too bad we have only one life, huh? There's a dozen things I'd love to try. I think being the skipper of a nuclear sub would be just a gas."

"I've got a couple of buddies who think that *that's* the best job in the world. I hear your brother flew in the Air Force."

"KC-135s. He flies left seat for Southwest, now. You'll get to meet him later on this evening."

'You have your own testosterone moments in the emergency department, I understand," Tim said, looking me in the eye.

"Well, I know you've heard the story, but you've got a sister with more courage than any ten men I know."

"I'd take her for my wingman any day," he said.

~

By the arrival of dusk and fireflies, the grounds around the house were a cacophony of music, loud conversation, and laughter. I don't know about anybody else, but I was having a wonderful time.

Penny and I stood talking with Lisa and Frank Turano. Frank's a Baltimore City homicide detective who I have known for years since my days at Hopkins, including an evening when he took a baseball bat in the face from a friendly Crips gang member and appeared in my ER in a rather disheveled state.

As for tiny Lisa, her last attempt at a boy had resulted in a third little princess, and she has now sworn off trying to produce an heir to the throne. However, Frank appears perfectly content surrounded by women. He is one of the nicest people you've ever met, although I have never had a conversation with him from the other side of his gun barrel.

"So, Frank, I may need some advice from you. Since I met Penny, I am gradually acquiring some new skills."

"Do you want to go and talk someplace privately?"

"Last week I learned how to bathe two kids at once."

"Point of clarification," said Penny laughing. "He was on observer status only."

"Well, next time I think that I can do it," I said.

"OK, Alex, I've got this down," said Frank. "I can do three of 'em at a time. Took me a while, but I think I've mastered it."

"It took him a *long* time," interjected Lisa. "I've invested hours in him."

"Well, we're men. We're are all slow learners, right?" said Frank.

"Huh!" said Lisa. "You should have heard what Alex said about nurses Thursday night. Penny had to wring his ear, didn't you Penny?"

"But he did finally apologize," Penny said, twisting my ear, "with a little encouragement."

"What did he say," asked Frank.

"He said nurses are slow learners!" Lisa said with incredulity.

Frank looked at me and winced. "Alex, you are a courageous man...I think."

~

Close to ten o'clock, Penny grabbed my arm and said, "Alex, don't you think we should make the announcement? I don't want anyone to leave before we make it, and maybe you ought to do it before too many more Grey Goose and tonics. It might not come out the way you planned," she said laughing.

"I think you're right. I could end up telling them about your voracious sexual appetite."

"I think you need your ear twisted again!"

"OK. Let's go."

I put my arm around her and we walked out into the middle of the crowd.

"Attention! Quiet! Ladies and gentlemen! Everybody else! Quiet! We have an announcement to make!" The crowd gradually subdued and somebody turned down the music.

"Tonight, we have Tim Murphy with us, home on leave from defending all of us aboard the *USS Eisenhower*, whose visit was the reason for scheduling this date. Tim, thank you for protecting us. God bless you. We're so happy to have you home." Cheers, whistles, and applause went up from the crowd. Tim waved.

"Penny and Tim's parents, Admiral Tom Murphy and his lovely wife Denise, are here tonight, too, as well as my parents, Ed and Barbara Randolph." A few catcalls and hoots arose.

"But we have another reason why we invited you here tonight. We have other news to share with you, and that is that Penny Murray, the woman I love and adore..." and here a murmur started to rise from the crowd, "...has agreed to marry me!"

A roar erupted from our gathered friends and loved ones. I picked Penny up by the waist, she fiercely wrapped her arms around my neck and legs around my waist, and I twirled her as hands reached out to us.

~

The rest of the evening was a bit of a blur. By 1:00 AM we were down to my brother, Brian, and his wife, Susan, my sister, Anne, and her date, Ben, and my childhood buddy, John, and his wife, Annick, all of whom stayed for the cleanup detail. Ruth suddenly appeared, after being incommunicado all night, and with her usual efficiency began to make short work of the serving platters, bowls, and other washables.

"Man, they sure went through the vodka," said Ben, throwing empties in a trash bag.

"Who's 'they?' asked Anne. "I think maybe you should have used the pronoun 'I'. Guess who's going to have to drive you home."

"Wine too, there must be twenty-five dead soldiers here," added Brian. "My airplanes don't generate this much trash."

"That's because you only feed 'em peanuts," I said.

"I have no clue how you're going to get everything done by September seventeenth," Susan said to Penny. "It took me six months to get everything together, and even then the last week was chaos. You have the church and the reception dinner lined up?"

"We were incredibly lucky. Both St. Mark's and the Manor Tavern were available on the sixteenth for the rehearsal and dinner," said Penny. "It'll be so convenient—they're only a few hundred yards apart. And then, St. Mark's was available on the seventeenth for the wedding, and we're having the reception here. Actually, Mom and I have already been working on this for six weeks. Anne's helping out, too."

Penny held up her fingers and counted, "July, August, September—a little more than three months to get it all done. But still, if it wasn't for my mother, it would be impossible."

"It took me over a year," said Annick.

"That's because you had to fly half of France to the United States," Susan said. "Plus you had nobody here to help you."

"Only John," said Annick smiling, "who was of limited usefulness."

John looked up from his trash bag and smiled. "Hey, if you ever get married again, you'll appreciate how helpful I was. You'll wish I was around."

"Darling, I'm sure my second husband won't mind you helping out."

That was a good one. Even John held his sides.

Annick is a little spitfire from Aix en Provence who John met when he was studying in France for a year. He adores her. They have a new little boy at home, two months old. She teaches undergraduate French at Hopkins. *And,* she plays tennis.

Actually, everybody in this group played at least high school tennis except Susan, poor girl, who had no choice but to pick up the game, like it or not. But she's taken a lesson once a week for three or four years, so she still gets in her licks in our mixed doubles games.

Susan is an OB-GYN from Hopkins who I, of course, introduced to Brian when Susan and I were both residents. She's a terrific obstetrician as well as one of those congenitally happy people who are just a pleasure to have around. No kids yet, although the clock is really ticking now on Susan.

The three guys loaded up all the trash bags on my beat-up John Deere Gator and we headed off across the lawn with one guy walking on either side to keep the enormous pile of bags from falling off. I drove—owner's prerogative.

Holly had taken the kids back to Padonia Road about eleven o'clock, so it was just Penny, me, and Ruth spending the night together. Penny and I decided that we didn't mind sleeping together with just Ruth in the house, so about 2:15 we climbed into bed together, exhausted and happy. Tomorrow, riding lessons. Life was good.

CHAPTER THIRTY-TWO

MELANIE LET HERSELF INTO THE MANOR house with her key at 7:30 Saturday morning, as was her custom. Mary Anne usually slept late. Melanie only worked a half day on Saturdays, but it was her best day because she earned overtime.

She carried a large bag filled with antiseptic wipes, giant diapers, and paper goods to Eddie's room, set it on a bureau, and began distributing the contents to their designated places. Melanie prided herself in keeping the sickroom neat and organized. It was bad enough to be dying without dying in the midst of a pigsty.

She grabbed the water pitcher, walked back to the kitchen, and filled it with ice and fresh water. Eddie's medicines were due at 8:00 AM, but first she would check his diaper and change him if need be. In the last three or four days the poor man had lost control of his bladder.

Eddie lay in almost exactly the same position in which she had left him last night, with his mouth gaping. But…his eyes were open and dull. There was no movement. She pulled back the covers and watched his chest, but it was still.

Melanie sighed. This would be her last day on the job at Ascot Farms. She was sorry it was over. It was a lovely place to come to work.

"Well, Eddie…I guess it's over. I'm glad it was peaceful for you."

Melanie pulled a piece of paper from her purse and unfolded it. Picking up the handset at Eddie's bedside, she dialed Heather Mitchell's cell phone.

"Heather Mitchell."

"Heather, this is Melanie—Melanie Cooper. I'm here at the farm. I think Eddie Williams has passed away."

"Well, I'm glad his struggle is finally over. It was time. Is Mary Anne Williams up yet? Does she know?"

"No, I think she's still sleeping."

"Well, you better wake her."

"OK."

"I'll be over and pronounce him in a little while, and then I'll notify the undertaker and have Dr. Holland sign the death certificate. Why don't you go ahead and start cleaning up. But don't leave Mrs. Williams alone until I get there. OK?"

"OK, Heather."

Melanie walked down a wide hallway covered with an oriental runner and adorned on the left by continuous bookshelves, then turned right down another hallway to Mary Anne Williams's bedroom.

She hesitated for a moment, and then rapped briefly on the door. She waited thirty seconds, but there was no answer and she could hear no stirring inside. She rapped briefly again and called out, "Mrs. Williams?"

"Just a minute."

Fifteen seconds later the door opened and Mary Anne Williams's tousled head appeared in the doorway.

"Oh…hi, Melanie."

"Mary Anne, I just came in, and…well…I think Eddie has passed away."

Mary Anne looked at Melanie silently for several seconds, and then a tear rolled down her cheek.

"I'm sorry, Mary Anne," said Melanie.

"It's OK, Melanie. I knew he was going to die. It's just that he suffered so much…"

~

By noon, Eddie had been pronounced dead and his body taken from the manor house at Ascot Farms. All of the sickroom supplies were removed, the room was cleaned, and the bed remade with clean linens.

At exactly 1:30 PM, Milton Kopec's Cadillac drove down Ascot Farms Lane and parked beside Eddie's SUV. Milton's work had begun.

Mary Anne was eating cereal in the kitchen when he rapped on the door. When she put her arms around him and whispered, "Oh, Milton, Eddie's gone," he was shocked and stood awkwardly holding his arms out from his rotund torso.

Five minutes later, a second Cadillac entered the lane bearing Herbert Silberstein. The accountant and the lawyer were immaculately dressed in nearly identical pinstriped suits. Each removed stacks of paper from their briefcases and carefully laid them on the kitchen table with perfect symmetry.

Herb Silberstein intoned, "Mrs. Williams, I'm sure this has been a horribly difficult day for you, but Milton and I are here hopefully to help ease your burden.

"Eddie laid out with great precision exactly how he wanted things to happen with regard to the days immediately following his death and with regard to the funeral. You will find that virtually all of the arrangements have been made."

Jeez, I'm glad there's air conditioning in here, thought Mary Anne. *These two are sweating like pigs. They're going to stink the place up.*

"Before his death, Eddie transferred the title to the beach estate in the Dominican Republic to your name only. Since it is titled in your name, it will not have to go through probate."

Milton slid a document across the table. "Here is the title. You may keep it yourself in a safe place—I would suggest a safe deposit box—or I will gladly hold onto it for you.

"In addition, you are named the beneficiary of a one-million-dollar life insurance policy, the proceeds of which will be disbursed to you as soon as the company receives a certified death certificate.

One million dollars and the beach property? That's it?

"As you know, you have also inherited Ascot Farms, the

maintenance of which will be supported by a trust fund administered by Milton. You will never have to worry about the expense of keeping up this wonderful property. But, of course, the will must go through probate, so that will take a little time. Milton is the executor of the estate. I am leaving a copy of the will here for your reference.

"Eddie also established a trust fund for your personal support, and that is already operative. Milton will explain that to you."

Milton cleared his throat. "Mrs. Williams, so that you could be certain to have access to cash before the estate goes to probate, this trust fund became active upon Eddie's death.

"As directed, I have opened a checking account in your name that only requires several signatures from you to activate, and I have placed in it an initial deposit of twenty-five thousand dollars."

Milton slid several papers across the table to Mary Anne and handed her a pen. "More, of course, will be deposited as the need arises."

Oh, my God! That's chump change!

"Oh, Milton, thank you so much. May I ask how we determine when the need arises?" asked Mary Anne sweetly.

"Your monthly allowance under the trust is twenty thousand dollars, which will be deposited automatically on the first Monday of each month. Of course you will incur no housing expense—which, by the way, includes one maid—so except for discretionary items like food, travel, and entertainment, you will have no substantive personal expense.

"Should the need arise for an occasional capital expenditure, such as a new vehicle, that can be discussed."

Milton reached into his pocket and pulled out an envelope. "In addition, I am providing you with ten thousand dollars cash to cover any short-term needs."

Mary Anne was furious. She did a quick mental calculation and guessed that after taxes she would probably only have a little over one hundred and sixty dollars a year to spend from this trust. *Where does he get off leaving me practically penniless like this?*

Milton pushed another stack of papers across the table. "Here is a copy of the trust for your records. Please let me know if you have questions."

"Well, you two have been just so kind," said Mary Anne. "I am at such a loss right now that I wouldn't know where to begin if it weren't for you. This is all very complicated, of course, so I'm sure when we get past this coming week and my mind clears, I'll have some questions. But we can get together in a week or two and discuss this in more detail."

"Most importantly in the short run," continued Milton, "all of the public announcements, funeral arrangements, and other necessary tasks have been completed and won't intrude on your grief.

"I have taken the liberty of giving your cell phone number to the funeral director so that he is able to keep you abreast of developments, and check to see if you have specific wishes.

The two gentlemen rose from their seats. "I'm so sorry for your loss, Mrs. Williams," said Herb Silberstein, extending his hand. "Please let me know if there is anything I can do for you."

"Mrs. Williams," said Milton handing Mary Anne his business card, "I'm here to help in any way I can. Feel free to contact me anytime you need me. My cell phone number is on the card. I'll be in touch."

The two men exited the kitchen and Mary Anne breathed a sigh of relief. Eddie had been pronounced dead and his body was probably being embalmed at this very moment. There would be no autopsy and no investigation.

Despite her disappointment with the financial arrangements, Mary Anne could feel only exultation as she watched the two Cadillacs recede down the lane toward Hess Road.

The first of her two major tasks was complete. She had pulled it off without a hitch. Eddie was dead and she was now a glamorous widow with a fabulous estate.

Perhaps the next challenge would be a little trickier, but ultimately, Alex Randolph would succumb to her charms. Their journey together as the ultimate power couple could then begin. As far as the money went, if she and Alex wanted to buy a winter place on St.

Maarten…well, maybe Mary Anne's photo shoot and media interview fees could cover that without dipping into her capital accounts.

CHAPTER THIRTY-THREE

THE EULOGIES FOR EDDIE WILLIAMS OCCUPIED the better part of the service on Wednesday, painting the picture of a leading thinker and philanthropist of his day. The Vice Chancellor of Johns Hopkins University described the enormous advances in our understanding of cancer that could be anticipated in coming decades from the new Williams Cancer Research Institute, and the executive directors of several other Maryland charities receiving lesser amounts, waxed eloquent on the direct impact of Eddie's gifts on thousands of lives in the Baltimore area. Eddie's name would live on forever.

Mary Anne sat in the second row of the cathedral, properly attired in elegant black mourning clothes, accented by a designer hat and veil, all of which she could not wait to strip from her body. As the service droned on, her mind wandered to Alex Randolph. As was apparent to all the world, she was now a single woman, freeing Alex to pursue her. But despite the extensive local media coverage of Eddie's bequest to the university, it was entirely possible that his death might not appear on Alex's radar screen.

That might be a fairly easy problem to solve. A brief note to Dr. Randolph, thanking him for his compassionate care and informing him of Eddie's death, was a nice little low-risk way to let Alex know that it was now open season on Eddie's gorgeous widow.

But what Mary Anne needed most of all was time with Alex. *All I need is one date!* How to arrange that was a problem whose solution still eluded her.

"We commend you, Eddie Williams," intoned the reverend, "to God's healing and mercy, to God's forgiveness and love. Blessed be God the Father who makes the light of Christ shine on us all."

The candles were extinguished, the organ dirge mourned, and Eddie Williams made his way down the long aisle, his mahogany casket borne on each side by members of his old corporate entourage.

As the grim procession passed Mary Anne's pew, one of the pallbearers caught her eye and winked, the first public acknowledgment, thought Mary Anne with satisfaction, that she was now a single woman—albeit a very rich one—and fair game.

Following the casket, Mary Anne was the first mourner to be escorted from the enormous cathedral. She entered a black limousine in the company of Milton Kopec whose corpulent mass occupied most of the seat beside her. They drove in silence, Mary Anne quietly sniffling into a tissue and Milton daubing his dripping face continuously with a white handkerchief.

At the graveside, the sun beat down mercilessly, Mary Anne's black dress soaking up the heat until she could feel beads of sweat trickling down her thighs. *It's like the damn Everglades out here.* She tossed a single red rose on the coffin, wiped the tears from her eyes, blew a final kiss to Eddie, and now sobbing uncontrollably, climbed back into the limo.

After an endless afternoon at the elegant post-funeral reception, accepting condolences and thinly veiled passes from legions of Eddie's business associates, the long black car finally turned into Ascot Farms Lane about 5:30. Throwing her hat to the patio floor and kicking off the designer dress, she dove into the pool naked.

When she surfaced, her elegant face raised to the late afternoon sun and her auburn hair streaming out of the water behind her, Manuela was picking up the widow's discarded mourning clothes from the patio tiles. This afternoon Mary Anne was possessed of an exceptionally generous mood.

216

"Manuela, you may have those clothes if you wish. I will never wear them again."

"On no, Miss Anne, I couldn't."

"No, they're yours. I insist. Take them."

She bowed. "Thank you, Miss Anne."

The brown-skinned girl hugged the dress to her chest and carried the expensive clothes into the house. Mary Anne would never give up Manuela, who knew every little crevice and sensitive spot of Mary Anne's body. But Mary Anne was desperate for a man—someone to inflict pain and punishment; someone who could make her feel alive.

~

Shortly after 8:45 PM, Mary Anne blotted her lipstick, pulled on a silky, loose-fitting top with silver thread, and stepped into a black miniskirt. At the full-length mirror, she gave her gleaming hair a final brush, slipped platinum hoops into her ears and then walked out of the manor house in high heels to her SLS.

Traffic on I-83 was light on this Wednesday night as she took the Jones Falls Expressway south toward the Inner Harbor.

She was not quite certain where she was headed, but with this funeral finally over, Mary Anne could not wait another day to claim her freedom and do exactly as she pleased. At the very least, she was going to drink and dance to her heart's content. And if she found a hot-looking guy who appealed to her, maybe tonight she would get laid for the first time in months.

She was vaguely familiar with the Inner Harbor from many visits with Eddie, mostly to the plush corporate boxes of Camden Yards or M&T Stadium, but she had never driven downtown herself.

I know I'm getting close. Maybe I better take this exit. Mary Anne negotiated the turn onto East Fayette Street, but almost immediately realized that she was at least several blocks north of the waterfront. She took the first available left at North Holiday Street and proceeded south. At the first stop sign she looked both ways for traffic and to the left saw a flashing neon sign with a naked woman in high heels. The cross-street sign read *Baltimore Street.*

Ahhh...this has to be the "Block." Mary Anne had heard of Baltimore's strip club neighborhood, but had never seen it. On both sides of the street to her left, neon announced the presence of naked women.

She could see nothing, of course, that approached the elegance of Club Nouveau—most of the clubs looked pretty seedy—but near the center of the block was a larger strip club that at least looked newer and more appealing than its competitors. The marquee over the extended canopy read, "Wednesday-Amateur Night."

The black SLS crossed Baltimore Street and a half block further suddenly swerved with a squeal into an empty parking space. Mary Anne sat with the engine running. It had been a long time since she had moved her body to the pulsating music and heard the wild cheers of men; a long time since under the heat of the spotlights the electricity had surged through her.

She climbed out of the SLS, slipped her credit card into the parking meter and walked back toward Baltimore Street. A man stood outside the side door of a club and said, "Hey doll, it's free in here for you." She stopped, pulled a twenty dollar bill out of her purse and handed it to the man.

"If that Mercedes is still here without a scratch when I get back, there'll be another twenty for you."

She walked around the corner and into the King's Court Cabaret.

At the admissions counter the girl said, "Hi. You here to meet somebody?"

"No. I'm by myself."

The girl looked Mary Anne up and down. "You danced before?"

"No."

"Well, it's amateur night. With a body like that you ought to give it a try. Five hundred dollars to the winner. Think about it. No cover for you, honey."

~

A waitress in a G-string made her way up to the second tier of tables above the stage, assessing the stunning woman who sat alone.

218

"Hi, sweetie. Can I get you something? You look fabulous. Love your outfit. You drinking, dancing, or both?"

"Drinking and watching," said Mary Anne smiling. "I'll take a dirty martini. And do me a favor," she said slipping the girl a twenty, "keep the guys away from me for now." The girl looked at the twenty and said, "You've got privacy, sweetie."

She sipped her martini and studied the layout of the room, the lighting, and the men in the crowd. Often, she knew, the men enjoyed good amateurs as much as the regular girls, perhaps because they sometimes had more the feel of the girl next door than a professional performer, which made it all just a little more forbidden and exciting.

She watched the parade of girls come and go. Most of them were kids with big grins on their faces, getting a jolt from taking their clothes off in front of a room full of men for the first time. Half of them had ten or fifteen pounds of extra puppy fat. Several were slender with decent bodies and a natural seductiveness. But none would make the first cut at Club Nouveau.

Mary Anne's waitress reappeared. "How're we doin'? Ready for a refill?"

"I think I'll take just a tonic water and lime. And tell the manager I'd like to see him." The girl glanced at Mary Anne with a hint of suspicion and said, "Sure."

~

A big man wearing a headset atop a shaven scalp made his way up the tiers to Mary Anne's table. He couldn't get a good look at her body because she was sitting with her legs crossed, leaning forward in her chair. But any idiot with eyes could see that she was gorgeous. He'd never seen an undercover Baltimore cop that looked like this.

He stuck out his hand. "Hi. Name's Aaron. I'm the manager. How can I help you?"

"I'm Ashley Johannson. I'll dance for you tonight, Aaron, but I'll be the last one. I'll show you a photo ID with an age, but you won't see the name on the ID, and I won't provide any contact information." Aaron did not like this. Amateurs didn't dictate terms. Something about this did not make sense.

"Sorry, ma'am. I've gotta see that whole ID."

Mary Anne smiled. "Well, I'm sorry we can't do business together." She unfolded her legs and stood. Aaron appraised the definition of the long legs extending from the short skirt, the flat belly, the narrow hips; the elegance of her face. This was the most beautiful woman who had ever walked into King's Court.

What was this girl's agenda? He weighed the risks and decided that they were minor.

"OK," said Aaron with misgivings. "You've got a deal. You'll be number eleven."

"One more thing," said Mary Anne. "No lap dances. When I'm done, I walk out of here." Aaron nodded.

"What are you going to wear?" he asked.

"My street clothes," said Mary Anne smiling sweetly. "Don't you like them?"

"You look hot, Ashley. We'll see if you can dance. Just be sure to be back in the dressing room by the end of number nine's dance."

~

Mary Anne handed the DJ a twenty dollar bill.

"This is the song I want when I come out. Got it?"

"You bet, sugar."

"Who controls the lighting?"

"Me."

Mary Anne handed him another ten. "I want the spots out when I take the stage. You bring the lights up the moment the song starts. Then they go off for ten seconds on the beat at the end of the song."

The DJ smiled revealing a gold tooth. "Got you covered, baby."

Mary Anne sipped her tonic water and lime as numbers eight and nine finished their dance. Tonight she would have to do some improvisation—although mostly at the beginning until the skirt and top were off. Then she could pretty well cruise through an established routine.

~

Startled, Aaron Nicolescu glanced around the room. The lights had never gone off before. He barked into his headset. "What happened to the lights?"

"Comin' back up, boss," came back the DJ's voice.

On the first beat of the music, brilliant light bathed the stage, revealing Ashley Johansson standing motionless, fully dressed in a miniskirt and silver top, eyes closed and chin on her chest. Her knees touched, but her ankles were splayed wide apart like a little girl. Her arms hung straight at her side, palms facing backwards. She looked for all the world like a beautiful sleeping puppet on a string.

As the incessant beat continued, the puppet awoke, gazing around the room wide-eyed as if arousing from a dream. She yawned and stretched, the miniskirt rising to reveal just a hint of green panties. A glimpse of breast came into view through the wide sleeves of the loose-fitting top.

Aaron Nicolescu watched with fascination. The men in the room, he noted, were quiet, leaning forward; every eye—even the waitresses—intently watching this pantomime unfold.

The puppet began to move; at first jerkily, then with increasing fluidity and grace. The belt of the miniskirt came off first, and then the skirt buttons opened; the crowd's anticipation rising.

Slowly the skirt descended over perfectly rounded buttocks with a little hollow at the hip, and then down shapely thighs until, with legs straight and the puppet flexed completely at the waist, the skirt reached her ankles. A puffy swatch of panties protruded beneath her buttocks between closed legs.

Crossing her arms, the puppet grasped the bottom of the silvery top and began to raise it inch by inch revealing ridges of muscle on a sculpted abdomen, until the soft lower curves of each breast appeared. She slipped first her left arm inside the sleeve, unveiling glimpses of a rigid nipple pointed toward the sky, and then the right. Finally the top came over her head, and with a shake of her hair, the puppet stood naked except for the green thong that disappeared between her firm buttocks.

The crowd finally found voice and began to wildly cheer. Electricity flowed through Mary Anne's nervous system as the adoration washed over her.

Innocently, as if alone in her bedroom, she played with the leg band of her panties, gently ran her fingers over the crotch, then slipped a hand inside the green material. Lifting her head and closing her eyes she slowly began to rotate her hand. Men rose to their feet. The din of cheers grew.

When the panties finally came off and she was naked, Mary Anne raised one knee to the side, placed her toes on the opposite leg, and pirouetted like a ballerina, allowing her audience full view of her glorious sex. The crowd roared, adrenaline surged, her heart pounded, and standing with legs wide apart and arms raised, she reveled in her nakedness. The lights snapped off on the last beat of the song.

~

By the end of her second cosmo at The Get Down in Fells Point, Mary Anne had already blown off a half dozen guys who had the guts to approach her. But the seventh held promise. A dental student at University of Maryland, he didn't qualify as an idiot, had a nice head of blond hair, a ruggedly handsome face, and was still sober enough to get a hard-on.

After ten minutes of conversation and two dances, she decided that he met the criteria for a couple of hours of sweaty, pounding sex.

He whistled when he saw the black SLS and sat staring at her when he climbed into the car, like, *where did you come from?*

With five hundred dollars prize money in her purse, Mary Anne paid cash for a room on the top floor of the Hyatt Regency, opened the curtains with a view of the harbor, and ordered him to strip.

~

Savoring the still-fresh memories of her first night of freedom, Mary Anne wriggled her sore bottom around on the chaise lounge, trying to find a position that didn't sting. She stood, doubled-folded a towel for her buttocks, and sat down again, iPad and notebook resting on the table beside her. Since checking out of the Hyatt, she had thought of nothing else but her next contact with Alex Randolph.

Clearly another trip to the ER was out of the question. Alex was going to be far too guarded and professional for Mary Anne to make any progress. Not only that, but with another trip to the ER, he might begin to conclude that she was a little nuts.

There had to be a way for them to meet in a non-professional place. Maybe a flat tire in front of his farm? Way too obvious. Someplace like a gym or a grocery store would be perfect, but Mary Anne had no clue where Alex hung out when not in the hospital.

She was coming to the conclusion that, time-consuming as it was, there was probably no choice but to follow Alex Randolph for a while until she could figure out the next best place to approach him.

At least she had his hospital schedule, so she'd know what days and what times he left work. She would have to be careful about this. The Mercedes SLS stood out like a girl in a gay bar. She needed another car that would blend in with the traffic and not be so noticeable. Maybe it was time to go shopping…but not at a Williams dealership.

In a rare moment of introspection, Mary Anne paused in her plotting and lay the notebook down on her lap. It suddenly struck her that she was obsessed with Alex Randolph. She had never wanted a man this much before. Why was that? She understood all the obvious reasons. But somehow there seemed to be more. *Could this be love?*

CHAPTER THIRTY-FOUR

WEDNESDAY EVENING WE SAT AT THE kitchen table in Penny's Padonia Road townhouse, trying to finish up the guest list for the wedding so invitations could go out. Distant shouts and squeals emanated from the upstairs bathroom where Holly bathed the kids before bed.

"I know it would be so horribly painful for them, and maybe—probably—they won't come, I don't know, but I think I have to send an invitation to Patrick's parents. They're still Jack and Catherine's grandparents." Penny said.

"I think the right thing to do is to send them an invitation and it will be their choice whether to attend or not. I hope they do. It would be a good sign."

"You know, maybe they'll come. They're great people, and when I called Patrick's mother she said, 'Penny, I'm so glad that you have found someone to love. You're young. You deserve happiness, and those children need a father.'"

I raised my eyebrows. "Wow, what a gracious woman, Catherine and Jack are their DNA. The kids are their only remaining contact with their son. I should work on building a relationship with them, as painful as that might be for them in the beginning."

Penny picked up my hand and held it to her cheek. "Thank you, Alex, for making this so easy for me."

Twenty minutes of bedtime stories intervened. Jack sat on my lap and slammed back the pages as he finished looking at the pictures, ignoring the text. This is rough on story continuity.

Catherine insisted on reading her own story to Penny, looking at the pictures for a clue when she couldn't figure out a word, which was not often. I have discovered that at the age of seven, the rate of progress is astonishing. Even I could see Catherine's reading vocabulary burgeoning monthly.

To Catherine's great annoyance, Jack intervened with shouted guesses whenever Catherine hesitated over a word.

"Quiet, Jack! How can a person concentrate with you around? Mommy can you make him stop?"

"Jack, don't interrupt Catherine when she's reading," admonished Penny. "That's not polite."

With a second and third goodnight kiss from Penny, and a "no" to a glass of water request, the bedtime ritual was over. We returned to paring a list of about a hundred and fourteen back to an even one hundred. This is a process laden with guilt—or glee—as names are ruthlessly stricken from the list.

~

Friday morning about 8:45 I changed into scrubs, grabbed the mail out of my box and made my way to the nursing station. I glanced at the patient tracker screen and saw only three patients on the board in various stages of workup. With no new patients to be seen, I started sorting through the mail.

Most of the mail went straight into the plastic trash receptacle I had pulled up beside my chair. Two items caught my attention. The first was a notice from the Credentialing Verification Office of Americus Health Systems:

Dear Dr. Randolph:

The item listed below is an issue you need to address in order to keep your credentials file in compliance with regulatory agencies.

Outstanding Mandatory Item

Hand Hygiene Competency

Must complete Hand Hygiene Computer Based Training. Access by logging into www.americushealth.org. Click on the "Medical Staff Services" link, then click the link for "Hand Hygiene CBT" and watch the CBT. Then click the link for "Hand Hygiene Posttest" and complete the posttest.

Sincerely,

Deborah Johnson
Medical Staff Services

What the hell is a posttest?

I turned to Ben. "Did you see this lunacy?"

"Yeah. I've already completed that," he said proudly. "I studied for a whole evening before I took the test. I still remember it. You want me to tell you what you have to know? It's a little complex. You may want to take notes.

"There's five key steps that you have to remember," Ben continued. "First, wet your hands. Next apply soap, third, rub hands together vigorously, fourth is rinse carefully, and five, dry thoroughly."

He smiled. "Got that? Want me to run that by you again?"

"The sad thing is that we're paying somebody a hundred and fifty thousand dollars a year to sit around and think this stuff up. Then what do you think they spent rolling out the program and monitoring compliance?"

I decided to get this chore over with and spent the next fifteen minutes online watching the video and taking my test.

"Ughh...that was painful."

The last item left in my mail pile was a personally addressed envelope to me. I ripped it open and found a handwritten notecard inside:

Dear Dr. Randolph:

Because you were so kind to my husband during our visit several weeks ago, I thought you would want to know that my husband, Eddie Williams, left this world this Saturday past. Sadly, we buried him on Wednesday.

He suffered so in the last days, but your compassionate care made the end easier for him. It's nice to know in this impersonal world that there are still caring people out there.

I hope to see you again someday under less trying circumstances. Thank you.

Sincerely,

Mary Anne Williams

Sometimes the people you do the least for are the most grateful. It was kind of her to write. I tossed the note in the trash can and picked up my first new patient chart of the day.

CHAPTER THIRTY-FIVE

FRIDAY MORNING, MARY ANNE FINISHED AN early morning workout at the Maryland Athletic Club, showered and drove the short distance east on Timonium Road to Mid-Maryland Lexus.

From his desk, Chad Morgan watched the exquisite SLS Roadster arrive and thought *this might be my lucky day*. The driver climbed out and Chad's eyes widened. He swiveled his head to see if another sales person had noticed the car's arrival, and leapt out of his chair.

Holding open the showroom door for the most gorgeous woman in memory, Chad smiled, sucked in his gut, and said, "Morning, ma'am."

Mary Anne stopped short of the door. "I don't think we need to go in there."

Chad looked into the showroom and back at Mary Anne. "OK. Sure. How can I help you?"

"I want to look at the cheapest used car on your lot."

Chad blinked. This was not what he had expected. It took a moment to switch gears.

"Hello. Do you sell cars?"

"Yes…of course. The cheapest car on the lot?"

"Would you like me to write it out for you?"

Chad felt a burning in his lower esophagus and reached into his pocket for a Tums. "Uhh…could you wait here just a second, ma'am? Let me run in and check the inventory sheet."

Two minutes later, Chad reappeared carrying a set of keys. His confidence had returned. "OK, ma'am, if you'll just follow me, I think I've got the car you're looking for."

Mary Anne followed Chad around the west corner of the building toward the back of the huge lot, enduring a steady stream of chatter as they walked.

"You know, every pre-owned vehicle on our lot has undergone a rigorous thirty-six-point inspection to ensure that it's up to Mid-Maryland's standards of excellence. It's our commitment to our customers that they're getting real value for their dollar."

Red helium balloons zoomed in the breeze above cars of special value. Finally the pair stopped at the back row in front of a little gray car with no balloons.

"Here it is," said Chad extending his arm. "A 2003 Saturn ION 2 in nearly mint condition"

Perfect, thought Mary Anne. *Small, non-descript, and a neutral color. He'll never notice me.*

She peered inside the dashboard. "How many miles?"

"Seventy-three thousand."

"How much?"

"Seventy-three thousand."

Mary Anne looked at the ground and shook her head. "*Money*…how much *monneey?*"

"Sorry…six thousand, nine hundred and seventy dollars."

"What's your best price for cash?"

"I'll have to check with my manager, but if it's cash, we could probably do it for sixty-eight hundred."

"If you want to sell a car in the next five minutes, I'll give you sixty-three hundred, and that's it. Otherwise, I've got some shopping to do."

Twenty minutes later, the paperwork was completed and Mary Anne handed over sixty-three hundred plus tax and fees in hundred dollar bills.

"Have the car ready by 2:00 PM and I'll be back for it." Alex, she knew, would leave work today about 7:00 PM. She didn't want to miss this first opportunity to tail him.

"Yes, ma'am. We'll have it ready to go."

~

Mary Anne found Manuela washing windows in the kitchen.

"Manuela, do you have a driver's license?"

"No, Miss Anne."

Shit! Mary Anne needed someone to take her to Mid-Maryland to pick up the car. But who?

Milton was certainly out of the question. She wanted to keep this purchase off his radar screen—too many questions. Mary Anne was acquainted with some of the women who were dames of the great estates close by Ascot, but none of them would be caught dead picking up a used car.

With no other options, Mary Anne could think of only one remaining candidate.

~

Drenched in the unrelenting August sun, Gerry Stine peeled off his tee shirt and wiped the sweat from his eyes. As was his habit every minute or two, he glanced toward the manor house just in time to see the girl take off out the lane for her run.

This was the highlight of most of his days at Ascot Farms. The little cunt would be passing by the barn in about ten minutes and he would be treated to a nice close-up of her tight little ass. He unscrewed the plug on the oil pan of the Kubota and watched the oil steadily flow into a bucket.

At the sound of shoes pounding on asphalt, he looked up and watched the girl approach across the barn parking area. To his amazement, she ran directly toward him, smiled, and slowed.

She stopped beside the Kubota, hands on her hips; puffing for air. Sweat drenched the sports bra in the hollow between her breasts. Low-riding spandex running shorts left her belly bare and cupped every curve of her little hips and round butt. Jerry felt his cock stir.

"Hi," she said, holding out her hand. "I'm Mary Anne Williams. I've seen you out here, but I've never met you."

Gerry was unaccustomed to shaking hands with women. He looked at his hand, wiped it on his jeans, and wordlessly reached out.

"What's your name?" she asked.

"Stine. Gerry Stine." *What does this woman want? Maybe she's decided it's time for a good hard cock.*

Mary Anne had grown up around trash like Stine. It took her but a nanosecond to spot the linear track marks over his forearms—tiny little blemishes over veins that signified repeated needle sticks. He was a heroin user.

"Who do you work for, Gerry?"

"Ebbitt Property Management," he said, glancing at her crotch.

"Well, since Ebbitt works for me, I guess that means that you work for me, too. I need a little help with something. Do you think you could help me?" she asked sweetly.

He eyed her suspiciously. "What do you need?"

"I need you to take an hour out and go with me to pick up a car. Could you could do that for me, Gerry?"

Stine stared at her, dumbfounded. Ebbitt told him to stay away from this woman, but Gerry knew instantly that he could never resist this invitation. *Fuck Ebbitt.* If Gerry refused, the girl might have him fired anyhow. Besides, the little cunt actually wanted him.

"Yeah, I can do that." He smiled. "Whatever you say, baby. You're the boss."

Gritting her teeth, Mary Anne struggled to restrain herself from launching a foot at his balls.

~

Stine edged the Saturn up to one of the carriage house garage doors next to Mary Anne's SLS and climbed out. Fishing a twenty dollar bill from her purse, Mary Anne handed it to Stine, then, holding her breath, hugged him. You never knew when scum like Stine might be useful.

"Gerry, thank you so much! I don't know how I would have

gotten that car home without you. It's good to have a man around here," she said, beaming with gratitude.

As Stine disappeared back to the barn, Mary Anne pulled the Saturn into one of the carriage house bays. It was best to keep that car out of sight.

~

At 6:30 PM, a gray Saturn slowly cruised the east parking lot on the emergency entrance side of Mason-Dixon Regional Medical Center. Mary Anne soon found Alex's white Jeep Wrangler. She selected a parking spot a discrete distance from the Wrangler, lowered the sunglasses from her baseball cap, and waited.

Less than a minute later, a white Honda SUV swung into a parking space three cars from the Saturn. Mary Anne watched a slender blonde in a blue scrub suit climb out of the vehicle, then reach through the open door to retrieve a bag.

"Bitch," swore Mary Anne softly. Penny Murray slung the bag over her shoulder and briskly walked to the ER entrance. Surveying the parking lot and seeing no one, Mary Anne slipped out of the Saturn, walked to the white SUV, and copied the license plate number into her notebook.

CHAPTER THIRTY-SIX

AT 6:20 PM I GRABBED THE CHART OF THE LAST patient that I would have time to see before the end of my Friday shift.

Seven-month-old Emma Stewart lay on the table in Bed Three wearing nothing but a diaper and a huge smile. Wriggling like a fish on dry land, her arms and legs were going so fast that I was getting tired just watching.

"I can't remember ever having that much energy," I said to Emma's mom, a thirty-something woman in bermudas and a bright yellow shift doing little to disguise a baby bump.

"I wish I could bottle it and take a hit about two o'clock each afternoon," she said laughing. "I'm Patty Stewart."

"Hi Patty. I'm Alex Randolph."

Patty stood with one hand on Emma's chest, restraining the infant's best efforts to flop off the table. With the other hand, she reached into a diaper bag and pulled out a fresh diaper which she expertly unfolded with one hand. Women with two kids and one on the way are good at multitasking.

"Well, I must say that Emma doesn't look horribly ill."

"She's not. She just has a little bead up her nose, courtesy of her brother, John" said Mom. At the sound of his name, a towheaded three-year-old boy playing on the floor with a starship looked up to assess how much trouble he was in.

"It's blue. You can just barely see it. I tried to get it out, but all I accomplished, I'm afraid, was to push it further back."

I looked at the little blur of motion on the table. "Well. Patty, I don't think I stand a prayer of getting that out with this little wriggle worm awake. It wouldn't be a problem if we could get her to hold still, but I doubt that Emma is too good at following directions at this age."

"Hopeless," said Patty.

"I think we may have to sedate her."

"I figured that," she said matter-of-factly. "We had to put John to sleep to get an eraser out of his ear. He loves stuffing things in holes."

"OK, well, we need to take Emma to another room where we can do this, and we'll be giving her a shot of a drug called Ketamine. It'll put her into a kind of twilight sleep."

"That's what they gave John."

"Good, then you know what this is all about."

"Yep."

Ketamine is the stuff they shoot into wild animals that inadvertently stray into the middle of the city—maybe on a shopping expedition, or something. It works great on kids, too, only we don't shoot them with darts. Well…not exactly.

I looked at my watch: 6:30. This was going to take a while. I wouldn't be out of here by 7:00, but then again, I rarely am.

~

I finished reviewing the informed consent with Patty Stewart and walked into Bed Fifteen. Rebecca Franklin, Emma's nurse, and Jill Brown, this shift's respiratory therapist, were about finished setting up for the procedure. Emma lay in a web of wires, cables, and tubes.

"Oh, she's so adorable!" cooed Rebecca, sitting on the edge of the table and holding Emma's hands to keep her from ripping off the cables. She leaned close to Emma's face. "I'd love to have a little one like you someday."

Maybe that wouldn't be too far away for Rebecca. A wedding date

234

was set for the fall with Peter Reed—a recent law school graduate who clearly worships the ground upon which Rebecca walks, or I should say, runs, since she logs about thirty miles a week. With professional objectivity, I can tell you that Rebecca has a very healthy body to show for her efforts. She and Penny run together sometimes.

Rebecca is one of my favorite people, so over the period of time that I got to know Peter, I was happy to conclude that he's a very good guy. I like him despite his choice of careers.

"OK ladies, everybody ready? How much ketamine do you have there, Rebecca?" I asked.

She checked the syringe. "Thirty-two milligrams."

I recalculated the dosage in my head. Emma weighed eight kilos, so at four milligrams of ketamine per kilo, thirty-two was right.

"Jill? Yankauer suction and BVM ready?"

"All set."

Everybody has very specific assignments when we put people to sleep in the ER—a process called *procedural sedation*. We do it every day, but I never approach this casually. It's a little bit like flying an airliner: very safe, but very serious. You have to pay attention. We continuously train and prepare for the worst so that the worst never comes.

Jill's sole responsibility was maintaining Emma's airway and monitoring her oxygenation and ventilation. Rebecca was responsible for medication administration and monitoring Emma's other vital signs. I, on the other hand, as my attorney friends will gladly tell you, was responsible for everything.

"OK. Let's go."

While Jill cuddled Emma in her arms, Rebecca squeezed up a large wedge of Emma's chubby thigh between her fingers. Holding the syringe like a dart, she plunged it deep into muscle. In a flash, thirty-two milligrams of ketamine were injected and almost immediately the chemical was being absorbed into the baby's bloodstream.

Emma's eyes grew wide for a moment, and then the pitiful wailing began, as if she had just been betrayed by a trusted friend. It was short-lived. Not more than a minute later, the wailing began to rapidly subside and Emma's face slowly transitioned through bewilderment and then incomprehension. By the three-minute mark, she lay motionless and expressionless, her eyes staring off into space. The stuff works incredibly fast.

We have just the gadget for retrieving blue beads from nostrils. With Emma zoned out, I was able to easily slip the tip of a tiny four-inch catheter past the little blue ball residing deep in her nasal cavity. Attaching a syringe, I pushed about one cubic centimeter of air into the catheter, inflating a tiny balloon at the tip.

With the balloon now inflated behind the bead, I gently tugged on the catheter and *voila*, a shiny, metallic-blue bead popped out of Emma Stewart's dainty little nostril.

"There it is," I said. "My first delivery of the day." With Emma blessedly asleep, the extrication procedure itself took all of fifteen seconds.

Getting the bead out was no big deal. Putting Emma to sleep and bringing her safely back to her mamma was a very big deal.

~

I didn't finish my paperwork and the process of signing out two patients to Lauren Dorfman until 7:25. Emma was substantially recovered from her procedural sedation by then, but Rebecca would observe her for another half hour before discharging her.

Penny had come in about 6:30 for the night shift. I was scheduled to work another nine-to-seven shift tomorrow so I really wouldn't get to see her until the next night, when she and the kids would spend Saturday night at the farm.

We met up in the ambulance entrance just before I walked out the door. Every time I don't see her for a day or two, I am always shocked by the emotion the sight of her releases in me.

I've thought about this a lot. It's very interesting because although Penny is incredibly lovely, my old girlfriend, Elizabeth, was just as physically alluring and I don't have the slightest urge to see her.

That's not to deny the overwhelming physical attraction I feel for Penny, and why would I want to? But the emotion she stirs in me when

I see her is more complex than simply visual, it's a melding of the seen and the unseen.

All wrapped up in the arch of her eyebrows, the wisps of flaxen hair and the seductive curve of her hip are an easy, sunny laugh; a wisdom in the way that she mothers her kids; a directness bordering on innocence utterly devoid of pretense. Her authenticity astonishes me.

Behind the delicate curves of her breasts beats a huge and courageous heart, and behind that a spine of steel. In those luminescent green eyes, surrounded by tiny crow's-feet, I see intelligence and humor; love and anger; joy and sadness. I am unable to separate her physicality from all of these unseen characteristics, and no doubt it's folly to try.

This is all by way of trying to explain to myself why the sight of her stirs my heart, when the sight of another beautiful woman doesn't. My musings are the pursuit of an idiot—a useless line of inquiry.

"Do you have your list?" she asked.

"Got it," I said, patting the back pocket of my shorts.

"Don't forget. Ask the butcher to cut the sirloin one-and-a-half inches thick."

"One-and-a-half inches."

She rose on tiptoes and kissed me briefly, her soft lips brushing mine. "I can't wait 'til tomorrow night," she whispered, her green eyes boring into mine.

CHAPTER THIRTY-SEVEN

MARY ANNE IMPATIENTLY LOOKED AGAIN AT her watch: 7:28 PM. Could she have missed him? Of course not, his Jeep was still there. He must be working late.

Two minutes later the sliding glass doors of the ambulance entrance slid open and Alex Randolph walked out in shorts and a tee shirt. Standing just inside the entrance behind him was his blond whore, who watched him walk away for a long moment before she turned and disappeared. *Enjoy it, sweetie. It won't last much longer.*

As Alex drew closer, the detail of his square face, bare arms and tanned legs came into clear focus. Mary Anne's pulse quickened and a *frisson* of excitement rippled through her breast.

He climbed into the Jeep, drove out the hospital access road to the stop sign, turning right onto Middletown Road. Mary Anne reached the stop sign herself just in time to see the white Wrangler turn left onto the southbound entrance ramp of I-83. By the time she merged onto the interstate, the Jeep was a quarter-mile ahead. *This is fun! I wonder where we're headed?*

Three miles south, the right turn signal blinked and the Wrangler took the long Hereford exit onto Mt. Carmel Road. Randolph drove east a quarter of a mile and turned left into a small shopping center adjacent to the interstate, where he parked and entered Graul's Market.

Pulling the Saturn into an empty space on the other side of the lot in the low sun, Mary Anne sat thinking. A supermarket was the perfect place to approach Alex, but somehow it had not occurred to her that the contact might be today. She suddenly felt unprepared. She'd given no thought as to how she would dress, what she would say, or what kind of invitation she would extend.

Biting her lower lip, she looked down at her clothes: white cotton shorts and a loose, brick-red tank top—could be worse. Perfectly appropriate for grocery shopping, yet still a little sexy. After her run today, she had washed her hair, so that was OK. She wore no makeup, but actually, she thought, that might appeal to Randolph.

Perhaps this would be a rare opportunity. If she didn't make contact today, Lord knows how many weeks she would have to spend tailing this man before another such opportunity arose.

Oh, well. I'm just going to have to improvise. I'm good at that. I can do this. Glancing at herself in the rearview mirror, she summoned her courage, climbed out of the Saturn and walked through the supermarket doors to find Alex Randolph, and perhaps, her destiny.

~

Alex bantered for a time over the counter with John Martin, Graul's famously exuberant meat cutter, and placed his order for a three-pound sirloin, precisely one-and-one-half inches thick.

"Ya gotta help me out here, John. I received very clear instructions about the dimensions of this steak. I'd hate to tell you about the consequences of failure to comply."

"No worries, Doc, I've got you covered. These things, I understand. We're going to keep you in the little lady's good graces."

Alex reviewed his list, pushed the cart another twenty feet to a refrigerated cheese display and scanned the choices. The list read "cheese," but didn't specify what kind. Alex quickly decided that this oversight was a compliment—Ms. Murray obviously had confidence in his culinary instincts.

He picked up a wedge from the blue cheese section and examined the label.

"If you like blue cheese, that's a scrumptious Stilton," said a vaguely familiar voice. Randolph turned and looked into the eyes of the petite young widow from Ascot Farms. *What was her name? Mary…Mary Anne. Mary Anne Williams.*

"Goes fabulously with a nice Bordeaux," she said, a radiant smile gracing her elegant face.

"Well," said Alex, extending his hand and returning the smile, "we finally run into each other outside the hospital."

Mary Anne grasped his hand and continued. "The only thing you have to be careful about is to make sure that your date is munching on it, too," she said laughing.

"You're right about that," he said, pointing at her with his index finger and sharing in the laughter.

"Doing your weekly shopping, Dr. Randolph?"

"Alex. Please call me Alex."

"All right, Alex," she said, maintaining eye contact.

"Uhh…actually just picking up a few things for the weekend. I have a housekeeper who usually does the weekly shopping."

"Me, too," she said brightly. "But you miss out on all the great little impulse buys if you don't shop yourself sometimes, like…Oreo cookies," she said holding up a package from her cart and giggling. "But, really, there's not much shopping to do since Eddie died. It's just Manuela and me in that huge house."

"I got your very kind note. I'm sorry about your loss."

"Well, I try to look at it as a blessing. He suffered so. I'm just glad he's finally at peace now." A moment of silence ensued.

"Do you like wine, Alex?" she asked.

"I love wine, as long as it's not over ten dollars a bottle. Occasionally I'll splurge and go up to fifteen."

"Red or white?"

"Red—with everything."

"Same for me. Eddie liked reds too, so now I have this wine cellar filled with two-hundred-dollar bottles of Bordeaux and old vine zinfandels, and nobody to drink them," she said holding up both palms.

"Terrible waste."

"Well, maybe we could do our part to make sure that those grapes didn't die in vain," she said, laughing and touching his arm. "How would you like to stop over for dinner one evening, and we could have our own little wine tasting on the patio by the pool?" *That was good,* thought Mary Anne with satisfaction.

Alex stared at her for a moment, then smiled and scratched his head in bemusement. In another lifetime he would have snapped up an invitation to spend an evening with this gorgeous and charming woman in a heartbeat. The marvel was that at this time in his life, he had not the slightest interest.

"Mary Anne, I am smiling because I can't believe I'm about to turn down your lovely invitation. You're an incredibly beautiful and charming woman. But the truth is that I am in love with someone else. In fact, I am marrying her in just about six weeks on September seventeenth."

Mary Anne smiled and cocked her head to one side, hazel eyes glittering amidst a tumble of shining strawberry hair backlit by the late evening sun streaming through the store windows. "Are you very sure, Alex? This could be our little secret—just between the two of us. Maybe you could think of it as a little prenuptial bachelor party."

Wow. This woman is tenacious. And this invite is for more than dinner, thought Alex. *I think I need to be clear and then I need to get the hell out of here.*

"Not going to happen, Mary Anne," he said softly.

They stood silently holding eye contact for several long moments. Mary Anne turned and without another word briskly pushed her cart toward baked goods. Alex watched the muscles flex in her long tanned legs until she disappeared around a corner.

CHAPTER THIRTY-EIGHT

OR THE BETTER PART OF THREE HOURS, MARY Anne drove aimlessly, finding no outlet for the fury that consumed her—unable to find escape, comfort, or solace from the searing humiliation. Had Manuela been at Ascot, Mary Anne would have beaten her until her buttocks were purple, but the manor house was empty.

She cringed to think that she had practically begged Alex Randolph to fuck her. Never had she made herself so vulnerable or shown a man that much love. In return, he had totally blown her off, purposefully throwing his little bitch in her face.

The Saturn zoomed up behind a slow-moving green Honda whose brake lights illuminated unexpectedly around a gentle curve. Mary Anne slammed on the brakes, cursing and blowing her horn. She passed on the curve, holding up a finger to the frightened elderly woman behind the wheel.

For the first hour of her rage, she had seriously considered killing Alex. It would be as easy as killing Felix had been in her dream. With great satisfaction, she pictured herself placing the little red dot between his eyes, watching the color drain from his face at the realization of his imminent death, and then squeezing the trigger.

But the fantasy would not come to life. In the end, Mary Anne was not willing to give up Alex, who had captured her heart and in whom she had invested so many hopes and dreams. She could envision no other viable options for her future.

Most infuriating, she knew that the smug little nurse thought that Alex was all hers. She was feeling cozy and secure with her little diamond and her little wedding dress, scurrying around to florists and photographers; buying honeymoon lingerie to please her famous doctor husband-to-be. Well she could forget all of that.

Mary Anne knew that Alex wanted her—she could tell by his smile; by the way he looked at her; by his acknowledgement of her beauty and charm. But the fool didn't have the balls to tell the blonde to kiss off. *Well I'm going to help him with that.*

A yellow light flashed on the dashboard, indicating low fuel. In a daze, Mary Anne looked around and realized that she was downtown. For an instant she considered driving to King's Court Cabaret and dancing. Like heroin, the adulation of the crowd would provide escape, wiping away the humiliation, the depression and the pain. But she quickly realized that on this night she was utterly incapable of even dancing—an activity that for her was as natural as breathing.

She fought to clear her mind. Instinctively she understood that further approaches to Alex at this time would be futile. Until the blonde was gone, he would not be moved.

What would killing a woman be like? she wondered. Her mind wandered back to Felix and Eddie—even the Bryant dog. She remembered the thrill of danger; the electrifying sense of power; the primal exhilaration of triumph. Never had she felt more alive than in those moments.

But killing the Murray girl would be different. She wanted to see this woman suffer—maybe on her knees with her hands tied behind her back and tears streaming down her face, begging for her life. Mary Anne gritted her teeth. She could almost feel the long knife in her hand plunging through tissue and gristle beneath the girl's left breast. Her heart beat faster as she envisioned watching the life slowly drain from the girl's surprised face.

Over the course of several hours, only this one recurring vision brought Mary Anne any measure of solace and calmed the raging storm churning within her. By the time the headlights of the Saturn swept through the darkened entrance gate to Ascot Farms, her fury, like molten steel, had begun to cool and harden into resolve. She knew what had to be done. With a first glimmer of peace and a trace of excitement, Mary Anne began to plot the death of Penny Murray.

CHAPTER THIRTY-NINE

THE NINE-TO-SEVEN SHIFT ON SATURDAY wasn't so bad. By midsummer there are no snotty noses, sore throats, or coughs to clog up the ER, so particularly on nice days, you occasionally luck into an easy shift. I turned into the gravel lane of the farm about 7:20 on Saturday evening, starved and looking forward to the rest of the weekend, shortened as it was. Penny's SUV sat in the parking area beside Ruth's ancient Buick whose oxidized maroon paint looked as if someone had sifted white chalk dust over the entire car.

Jack drove his little electric Jeep down the brick sidewalk toward my own Jeep. Catherine was standing on the bottom board of the paddock fence leaning over and trying to brush Abigail's mane. Abigail had enough sense to stay just out of reach. Both kids came running up to the Wrangler as I climbed out.

Jack threw his arms around my leg and I picked him up. Catherine, who stood with hands on her hips looking for all the world like a little Penny, said with annoyance, "Abigail won't hold still so I can brush her mane."

"She's just like you," I said. "She doesn't like to have her hair brushed either."

It's impossible, of course, to hold off dinner until 7:30 for a four-year-old and a seven-year old, so Penny, Ruth, and the kids had already

245

eaten. When I walked through the mudroom into the kitchen, Penny was pulling a plate of spaghetti out of the microwave with oven gloves. I kissed her as she passed by on her way to the table. Ruth pulled a plate of salad out of the refrigerator, placed a small baguette of French bread on a bread plate, and dinner was ready.

I popped open a bottle of Grayson Cabernet and poured two glasses for Penny and myself. "Ruth, do you want a glass of wine?"

"Of course not. You know I don't drink that stuff."

"Might make you more mellow, Ruth."

"That's nonsense, Alex," she said with annoyance.

Penny pulled up a chair beside me, put her chin in her hand and said, "So how was the Mason-Dixon ER today?"

"Easy. Didn't see a truly sick patient all day. Did you sleep, baby?"

"Like a rock. Slept until two. Holly packed sandwiches and took the kids to the playground, so it was quiet."

"Do you remember that girl who came into the ER last week with pelvic pain?"

"What girl?"

"The one in the middle of the night who caused you to become violent and throw a paper clip at me."

"What about her?"

"I ran into her at Graul's last night."

"And...?"

"She invited me to dinner at her house."

Penny frowned. "And you said...?"

"I told her that I was in love with another hot woman, but if she was into sharing, we might be able to work something out." Penny punched me in the chest.

"You better be lying!"

"Actually, I think the invite was for more than dinner. When I told her I was getting married, she said the dinner could be a secret just between the two of us. She suggested that I think of it as a little prenuptial bachelor party."

"Now I know you're lying."

I started laughing. "I'm serious!"

Penny jumped out of her chair and put me in a headlock. "If I ever catch you around that woman, I'll scratch your eyes out. Do you hear me?"

Now I was helpless with laughter. "OK, OK. I'll call her and tell her that you're not interested in sharing."

"Ooohh, why do I put up with you?" she screamed, delivering another blow to my chest.

~

With the kids finally tucked in, Penny and I sat together at the kitchen table about 9:30. Ruth had discreetly disappeared, and I was eagerly anticipating a little time alone with my sexy fiancé. Without acknowledging such, we both sat there marking time until we could be relatively certain that everyone else was asleep.

From a cloth shopping bag, Penny dumped several days of mail on the table and started opening envelopes. I was in the market for a used manure spreader, so I sat at my laptop combing through Craig's List, looking for the best deal—on a manure spreader.

A soft whimper broke the silence. I looked up to see Penny holding a letter with tears streaming down her face. Slowly, as she lost control, the whimpers grew louder until they merged into anguished sobs.

"What, baby?" I stood and pulled her up to me. "What is it?"

Penny held out the letter, as she sobbed inconsolably. I grasped the heavy ivory stationery and at the top saw the seal of the White House:

THE WHITE HOUSE
WASHINGTON

August 2, 2012

Dear Mrs. Murray:

As Commander In Chief of the Armed Forces of the United States of America, and on behalf of the United States Congress, it is with both great sadness and profound honor that I inform you that your late husband, Navy Lieutenant Patrick James Murray, has been selected to receive our nation's highest award, the Medal of Honor, for his heroic actions in the service of his country.

As you know, your husband commanded a SEAL team in the mountains of Afghanistan in 2008. After a prolonged and intense firefight during which he personally killed three combatants, Lieutenant Murray lost his life carrying a wounded team member to cover in complete disregard for his own safety. The full text of the nomination detailing his courageous actions is enclosed.

The award ceremonies will take place at the White House at 2:00 PM on Thursday, October 18th. An aide will be in touch with you shortly regarding details.

I am pleased to inform you that as the result of this award, yours and Lieutenant Murray's children will be eligible for admission to the United States military academies without regard to nomination or quota requirements.

You and your children will, of course, be the guests of highest honor at this ceremony. It will be a deep privilege for me to meet you and present you with this award.

Sincerely,

Barack Obama

~

We lay on the leather family room sofa in darkness, Penny curled up in my arms. Neither of us had spoken for fifteen minutes.

"I'm so sorry, Alex," she whispered. "It was too much—all just so overwhelming, and so very sad. I was crying for Patrick, and his parents, and Catherine and Jack, and you and me—for all of us. I know what you must be thinking, but it's not that at all." She raised her head and looked into my eyes. "I love you so very much. I don't want to relive the past. I want nothing more in life than to be with you. I...I don't know if you can understand..."

I placed my index finger on her lips. "Shhhh...why wouldn't you cry? What could be sadder? Life is like this. Great joy and great sadness."

~

I awoke in the early morning hours to the soft brush of Penny's lips over mine, her golden hair tumbling around my face in a curtain of intimacy; her breasts pressed to my chest. As she showered my face with kisses, she held my head with both hands and whispered, "Oh, I love you so much."

Parting her lips slightly, she tentatively reached out, touching the tip of her tongue to mine. My hand slipped under her tank top to find bare skin, caressing the muscles of her neck and back, then slipping beneath her shorts to her buttocks.

As passion slowly awoke, she stood, slipping out of her clothes and pulling off my shorts, then quickly climbed back onto the sofa, straddling my pelvis.

Locked together as one, we breathed each other's air, our bodies moving languorously; our souls trying to merge. Gradually the movements became more urgent as powerful waves began to build. Finally the waves crested in a rush of consummate pleasure, desperate emotional release, and affirmation of life.

CHAPTER FORTY

L ATE MONDAY MORNING, PENNY SAT AT THE kitchen table, searching her calendar for a date to do pre-school clothes shopping for Jack and Catherine. She was looking forward to that little excursion, but this close to the wedding, the calendar was packed. *Bummer! Today is the only open day I see. But I work tonight.*

Sitting with her chin in her hand, she pondered her options. There were no other choices. *Oh well, I slept Saturday and Sunday nights. I can make it through tonight without a nap if I have to.*

"Holly, I've *got* to get some clothes for these kids before school starts. I think I'm going to take them shopping this afternoon. There's just no other day. It's eleven-thirty. Let's get the kids fed and we'll try to get on the road by twelve-thirty. Maybe if I'm lucky, I can still squeeze in an hour nap before work."

~

With a car full of raucous kids, Penny swung into the right lane on East Joppa Road and turned into Towson Marketplace, winding her way around the east side of the mall to Marshalls department store. Five cars behind, the driver of a gray Saturn followed, watching as two young women and two small children exited the white SUV and all holding hands, walked across the street into the store.

~

"What do you think of this, Holly?" Penny asked, holding up a little red-plaid flannel shirt.

"Oh, that's adorable! You could match it up with a pair of beige corduroys."

"Jack, come here," called out Penny. Jack, following Catherine on the run, zoomed into a nearby rack of pants, and disappeared.

Thirty seconds later Penny and Holly had cornered Jack and nabbed him. Penny knelt in front of him.

"Jack, listen to me!" she said sternly, holding both of his arms. "A department store is not a playground. Do you understand? You cannot be running through this store like a wild man. Now you stay right here by me until we get your clothes picked out."

Holding the shirt up to Jack's chest, she said, "That's about the right size. He might even get two years out of this." She checked the price tag on the sleeve. "Ooohh, nice! Only four ninety-five!"

With Jack the center of attention, Catherine slipped through a rack of dresses, across an aisle, and into a maze of women's fall coats. Jack would never find her in there.

~

"Can't we go? I don't want to shop any more," Jack whined.

Penny gathered up the sweaters, shirts, and pants into some sort of order and filled the small shopping cart. "Holly, go get another cart and we'll get started on Catherine. At least she'll be easier than Jack— she likes to shop."

Penny glanced at the adjacent aisles, but Catherine was out of sight. "Catherine," she called, "where are you?" With no answer, Penny began to walk down a main aisle, checking left and right for her missing daughter.

At age seven, Catherine was conflicted. Completely invisible in the middle of a circular coat rack, she didn't want to leave this exquisite hiding place. But there was a trace of worry in her mother's voice. If she stayed in hiding much longer, she would be in big trouble for sure.

Decision made, she zoomed through the coats on the circular rack. To her astonishment, she ran headlong into a pair of bare legs in shorts. Hands touched her shoulders and she looked up to see a pretty woman with a ponytail just like her mommy, only her hair was reddish-brown.

"Whoa!" the woman said with a broad smile. "Are you lost?"

"No, I just have to find my mom. She's been calling me."

"That's a super hiding place."

"I know! Jack would never find me in there!"

"Is Jack your brother?"

"Yes. He's only four."

"What's your name?"

"Catherine," she said shyly.

Placing both hands on her knees, the woman bent at the waist to the young girl's eye level. "Well, Catherine, you're a very lucky girl to have such beautiful blond hair and gorgeous blue eyes. Would you like me to help you find your mommy?"

Catherine hesitated, remembering her mother's lectures about strangers. But it was safe here—inside a store—and this woman was very nice.

Penny Murray glanced down an aisle and spotted Catherine. A woman stood bent at the waist, talking to her daughter.

"Catherine!" Penny snapped.

The young woman stood upright, turned to Penny and smiled. "I think this gorgeous little girl is looking for her mommy," she said warmly. "And there's certainly no question about who her mom is. She's a carbon copy of you."

Penny's shoulders slowly relaxed. There was something vaguely familiar about this attractive woman.

"Catherine, you need to stay by me or we'll never get this shopping done."

Penny turned to the woman. "Sorry, but I flip out sometimes when the children disappear."

Making eye contact, the woman said, "Don't even think about it. It's a scary world out there. You can never be too careful these days."

Mary Anne stood at the checkout counter and through the store windows watched the Murray woman and her young companion load the kids and packages into the SUV. *Awesome. I looked her directly in the eyes. What a rush! One day soon when she's dying, she'll remember my face.*

CHAPTER FORTY-ONE

PENNY CLOSED THE DOOR OF THE DISHWASHER and punched the button for *Quick Cycle*. "Holly, I'm going to jump in the shower now," she yelled. "Catherine, you come with me and we'll get you showered, too."

"Why do we have to get fitted?" asked Catherine.

"Well...so the dress fits."

"Why do you buy a dress that doesn't fit?"

"You don't. You buy the size that comes closest to fitting you perfectly, and then you make little alterations so that it *does* fit perfectly."

"Will this take long?"

"It's going to take a little while, honey. I want you to pick out two books to take along in case you get bored."

"Is Maimeó going to be there?"

"Yes, baby. She's meeting us at the dress shop, and then we're all going to have lunch together. Won't that be fun?" Catherine looked unconvinced.

"Is she getting fitted too?"

"No. She's not in the wedding like you and me. She's going to wear one of her own dresses."

~

At 9:30, Penny and Catherine walked out the front door of the townhouse to the white SUV sitting in the driveway, the little girl with

254

long flaxen hair climbing into the back seat under her own power. One hundred yards to the north, Mary Anne watched from her Saturn as Penny reached through a rear door to check the girl's buckles, then climbed behind the wheel and drove south out of the development toward Padonia Road.

~

Amanda Stern watched her husband pour a last cup of coffee into an insulated travel mug.

"Frank, why don't we just take a week off and go to the shore? It's been such a stressful summer. You have to need a vacation as much as I do."

"Can't. Too much to do," he said curtly, adding Half & Half to the coffee mug.

"Why couldn't we go the last week of August? That would give you two weeks to clear out your schedule. Maybe even if just for three or four days."

Frank slung his suit jacket over his shoulder. "Amanda, how many times do we have to have this discussion? I've got this Randolph trial on August thirtieth. It's already been postponed for three months. The court won't let me delay it again."

"Randolph?"

"Yeah."

"He's a doctor?"

"You think he's a plumber?" asked Frank with irritation. "What business am I in?"

"What's his first name?"

"Alexander."

"What hospital?"

"Good God, Amanda, why the third degree? Mason-Dixon. What difference does it make?" Frank picked up his briefcase and headed for the door.

"I think that's the doctor who saved your life." Amanda said quietly.

Frank stopped at the door and stared at her for a long moment.

"So?"

"He came out to the counseling room to talk to me. He said he didn't know if they would be able to save you, but they were going to try like hell."

"What's your problem, Amanda?"

Amanda shrugged her shoulders. "Nothing, I guess. I don't know. It just seems a little strange to be attacking a person who saved your life. Doesn't that make you feel a little uncomfortable?"

"Why should it? He screwed up with my client. They deserve compensation. You like driving that Mercedes?" He turned, and disappeared through the door to the garage.

~

Penny backed to the end of the driveway and looked both ways. A small gray car was parked at the curb a few houses away, but there was no other traffic. She continued backing out, put the SUV in drive and pulled away for the fifteen-minute trip to Betsy Robinson's Bridal on Reisterstown Road.

A mile to the east, she checked her rearview mirror before merging right onto the I-83 entrance ramp. Traffic was light, and the only vehicle she could see in the mirror around Catherine's head was a gray car in the distance behind her. She absently wondered if it was the same car she had seen parked in her development, and then concentrated on merging into the southbound traffic on Interstate 83.

After several miles of uncharacteristic quiet, Penny searched for Catherine in the mirror, whose profile could be seen staring out a side window. A moment later her daughter spoke.

"Mommy?"

"What, honey?"

"When you married Daddy, did you buy your wedding dress from the same store?"

A lump formed in Penny's throat. "No, baby. I bought that one at another store."

"Do you still have it?"

"Yes, Catherine, I do."

"Why don't you wear that one?"

Against her will, a tear rolled down Penny's cheek. She wiped it quickly, afraid that her daughter might be watching in the mirror.

"Catherine…when I married your daddy that was *his* dress. It was for him, and for nobody else. That dress will always be his."

Catherine looked up at the mirror and saw tears flowing from her mother's eyes.

"After he was gone, I thought that I would never love a man again. And then I met Alex. I don't know if you can understand this, baby, but I love him just like I loved your daddy. And when we get married, this wedding dress that we buy today will be his dress. It will be for Alex and nobody else."

"Of course I understand. I'm not a baby, you know. You don't have to cry. Is it a white dress?"

"Yes, my dear Catherine, it's white."

"And what color is my dress?"

"Your dress is purple."

"Awesome. I love purple."

~

From the Baltimore beltway, Penny took the Reisterstown Road exit, drove north for about four blocks, and eased into the left-hand turn lane at the Castleon Avenue traffic light.

"Here we are, Catherine," she said looking in the rearview mirror. Three cars behind her she noticed a gray compact pull into the left-hand turn lane. "Betsy Robinson's bridal is right over there," she said pointing to the left.

I wonder if that's the same car? The paparazzi had not bothered her since when—June? Photos of her and Catherine entering a bridal shop would certainly command a price, but how could they know that today she was shopping for a bridal gown?

The left-hand turn arrow flashed to green. Penny turned left, then made an immediate right turn into Betsy Robinson's and found an empty parking space. She looked around before exiting the SUV, but could see no sign of the gray car. Maimeó's Accord was parked three spaces away. *I must be getting paranoid in my old age.*

~

A block ahead, Mary Anne watched the white SUV swing into the left turn lane at Castleon Avenue and cursed. This was going to put her too close. She slowed, hoping for other cars to pull into the left turn lane before she reached the SUV.

By the time she changed lanes, Mary Anne was the third car behind the Murray woman—still way too close. She was going to have to be more careful.

The SUV turned left onto Castleon and then made an immediate right into a bridal shop parking lot. Mary Anne zoomed by the entrance, hoping not to be noticed, and drove three more blocks before turning around.

She retraced her route and turned right into Emeritus at Pikesville, an assisted living home across Castleon Avenue from the bridal shop, where she found a parking space from which she could safely view the white SUV.

Today was obviously wedding dress day, a dead end for Mary Anne. This was the fourth day of following Penny Murray, observing her movements and looking for patterns of behavior that could be useful. This dress shop trip was of no value at all—not predictably repetitive.

Mary Anne was doing little but sleeping and shadowing Murray. When on the move, it was fun, but most of the time it was just hours of stupefying boredom.

In the five days since Randolph had stupidly brushed her off, Mary Anne was getting to know Penny Murray. The bitch was boring. She lived in a little townhouse development—unfortunately surrounded by neighbors—had the gargantuan baggage of two kids, and obviously was just a working-class woman in a low-paying job. What Alex Randolph or the media saw in her was beyond Mary Anne's comprehension. Maybe she gave good head.

Mary Anne presumed that the college-aged girl living with Murray was a relative, or maybe an *au pair*. So far, the only time Murray had left her home was to buy clothes at Marshalls on Monday afternoon, to work at Mason-Dixon on Monday night, for grocery shopping with the kids and the baby-sitter on Tuesday afternoon, and for a run around her development on the same day in the late afternoon.

Saturday and Sunday she had spent the night at Randolph's little farm. Mary Anne wondered if that would turn out to be a pattern. At least the farmhouse was isolated, but Randolph seemed to always be there.

On Tuesday evening about 7:45, Randolph came to Murray's townhouse for dinner and left about 10:00 PM. Too bad she hadn't decided to kill him instead of his bitch. He would have been an easier target.

Figuring out a way to eliminate Murray was a more difficult task than she had first imagined. There were few times that Murray was alone or in an isolated spot—essentially only when running or driving to work—and the time of day she would run was so far unpredictable. Even if Mary Anne could get close to her, how would she do it and not get caught?

The method was all important. A blatant murder would provoke an investigation, and most surely an intensive one, given Murray's celebrity status. It would be national news. The police would be under enormous pressure. Mary Anne sighed in frustration. There had to be another way.

~

Correen Royer had Penny Murray turn around twice in the simple, formfitting ivory silk gown with spaghetti straps by Monique Lhuillier. She whistled softly to herself. Not many girls could wear that gown, but this girl looked spectacular. "Oh my, you are gonna turn some heads with this dress, girl."

"What do you think, Mom?" asked Penny.

"You look like a blond version of Pippa Middleton," said the girl's mother laughing. "It's fabulous."

Bummer, thought Correen. *If this hadn't been a sample sale, my commission would have been triple what it's going to be at this price.* She pinched an inch at the waist. "I think we take this in just a half inch on each side, shorten the hem by an inch, and we're in good shape."

Penny smoothed the dress in the full-length mirror and sighed. "Well, I guess that's it. I hope he likes it."

"Well if he doesn't, there'll be a dozen other guys in the sanctuary who will marry you on the spot," said Denise Murphy. "I think your major problem will be keeping the testosterone under control."

"What's testosterone?" asked Catherine.

CHAPTER FORTY-TWO

KATHLEEN STEFANIK STRAIGHTENED THE stacks of papers arranged in a semicircle on the table in front of her, brushed a wisp of graying hair from her intelligent face, and said, "OK, Dr. Randolph, I know this is your day off, so we're going to try to make this as short and painless as possible." This, I thought, was an auspicious start.

To the left of my defender in shining armor sat Joel Russo, her fresh-scrubbed young associate who I assumed was a child prodigy since he looked under drinking age. I sat at the head of the table in Conference Room B, and to my right sat Mason-Dixon's Vice President of Patient Safety Barbara Knoble, RN, whose job it is to see to it that we don't kill too many people in the ER.

"I want to remind you, Dr. Randolph, that this case is going to trial because we believe it is defensible, and that your actions were in concert with the community standard of care." *A ringing endorsement of my competence.* "This is important for you to understand because we want you to be a relaxed and confident witness on the stand."

"A pretrial Grey Goose and tonic might work," I said. Joel thought that was funny and stifled a little guffaw.

Kathleen smiled indulgently. "We'd all like one of those, Dr. Randolph, but the court unfortunately frowns upon pretrial libations.

Perhaps I can buy you one after the trial." *Good idea. I'm sure you'll be able to afford it.*

"One of the things you'll want to keep in mind during your testimony is that opposing counsel has secured an expert witness from the department of surgery at the University of Pennsylvania who will testify that: a) you should have obtained a CAT scan, and, b) that you should have obtained a surgical consultation." *Wonderful. My college alma mater is supplying the bullets for my execution.* "So you may want to make points during your early testimony that will preemptively address those issues.

"I personally think that you will make a very good witness, so I want you to just relax on the stand, and tell your story." *She's a bit repetitive, but I'm beginning to like this woman.*

"Of course, I'll be leading you through the case in small bites, question by question, but the most critical questions will involve your analysis of the case and the medical judgment you used in arriving at your decisions. You will have access to the medical record when answering questions.

"But for purposes of refreshing your memory as well as ours, let's just have you briefly summarize the patient encounter for us without all the questions."

I picked up a copy of the medical record, quickly perused it to refresh my memory, and began.

"It was not a complex case," I said. "Robert Kline was an eight-year-old male who was brought to the ER by his parents with a chief complaint of abdominal pain and vomiting.

"I saw Robert about 9:58 PM. The school nurse related to the family that Robert had first vomited about 2:00 PM, which constituted the onset of his symptoms, so the total duration of his illness at the time I saw him was about eight hours.

"At some point after his father picked him up from school, he apparently began to complain of vague abdominal pain, saying that his belly hurt. His parents were unable to provide any information regarding a specific location of the pain. During the course of the evening, he vomited two more times, prompting his parents to bring him to the ER.

He had virtually no other symptoms, including no diarrhea, no respiratory symptoms, no urinary symptoms, and no fever or chills.

"Robert's vital signs at presentation to the ER were all normal, including body temperature and heart rate. His entire physical examination was normal with the exception of some mild scattered tenderness around his belly. I examined his abdomen a second time, to see if the locations of the areas of tenderness would be consistent, but they were not.

"He did not grimace and I could find no point tenderness in his abdomen, nor any evidence of guarding or rebound tenderness, which are signs of a surgical problem. Specifically, he was not tender over McBurney's point, the location of the appendix. His bowel sounds were normal.

"I ordered a CBC—a complete blood count—blood chemistries, and a urinalysis all of which were normal.

"At this point I had a discussion with his parents regarding the differential diagnosis of Robert's pain. I told them that my suspicion for appendicitis was low at this point, and that although I couldn't be certain, I thought it most likely that his abdominal discomfort was from spasm of the bowel associated with a virus in his GI tract that was producing vomiting.

"I further indicated that although a CAT scan would provide more information, I did not feel that the level of suspicion for appendicitis was high enough at this time to warrant the radiation associated with a CAT scan. I explained that the radiation dose was roughly equivalent to four hundred chest x-rays. Children are especially sensitive to radiation because their cells are dividing—kids are growing, of course—and radiation produces the greatest damage to dividing cells. There is a small, but real risk of a future cancer resulting from radiation exposure.

"By this time, it was close to midnight. I suggested that a reasonable approach might be to re-examine Robert in eight hours, at which time we would also repeat a white blood cell count. The white blood cell count usually rises with appendicitis. If his belly became more tender, or we saw a rise in his white blood cell count in the morning, we could always do a CAT scan at that time.

"I asked the family to keep his oral intake limited to clear liquids, and to return at 8:00 AM. But, as we all know, he did not return in the morning and subsequently presented to another hospital two days later with a ruptured appendix. And that is the story in its entirety."

"Very well done, Dr. Randolph," said Joan of Arc, "that was succinct, clear, and to the point. Don't you agree?" she asked, turning to Joel and Barbara who in unison nodded their heads in vigorous assent.

"You addressed the CAT scan issue in your summary, but didn't address the issue of a surgical consult. You might want to include that during your testimony. But if you forget, I will ask you.

"Just so you know that you won't be out there all alone, we have, of course, retained an expert witness in emergency medicine who will testify that your approach to this case was reasonable and prudent. *She's really worried about my feelings.* And we have also obtained an expert witness in surgery who will testify that had the family followed your instructions, the plaintiff would likely not have suffered a ruptured appendix."

This is what it usually comes down to in malpractice litigation—*he said, she said.* Lacking the technical expertise to make their own judgment, twelve of our lay peers often find themselves deciding a case based on which of the witnesses they trust the most—or maybe even like the most.

But I thought that perhaps in this case, the real question would be one with which the jury would be more comfortable: who was responsible for the delay in diagnosis—the doctor or the family? Where does the doctor's responsibility end and the patient or family's responsibility begin?

Of course, at the end of the day there's an easy way to avoid all of these life-changing trials and tribulations. You simply order a CAT scan on every abdominal pain that walks through the door—a defense which no small number of my colleagues have adopted. CAT scans in children have risen five hundred percent since 1995.

~

"Well, how was the pretrial conference?" asked Penny. We sat together dressed in shorts at the bar on the porch of the Manor Tavern on a rare night out together. It was a very sweet August evening.

"Not so bad. Stefanik is OK, although very concerned about my self-confidence."

"You? You're kidding."

"No. She wants me to come across on the stand as confident in the way that I handled the case."

"She obviously has no idea what an egotistic, commanding son-of-a-bitch you can be," she said smiling.

"I'll take that as a compliment. How was your day?"

"Today was fitting day at Betsy Robinson's. It was tough. Catherine wanted to know why I didn't just wear the dress from my wedding with Patrick."

"Ooohh. How did you handle that one?"

"First, I cried. Then I told her that that dress was just for her daddy, and nobody else. Then I told her that I loved you just like her daddy, and that this dress was for you, and nobody else. I said, 'I don't know if you can understand these things.'"

"And what did she say?"

"She said, 'Of course I understand. I'm not a baby, you know, and you don't have to cry.'"

I smiled. "The girl's got it together."

Penny took a sip from her cosmo and ran her fingers through her golden hair. "So, where do you want to go on our honeymoon?" she said brightly, her tanned skin glowing in the soft light. "We haven't made any reservations or anything. I am bone-tired. I can't wait."

"I don't know that it's likely to be restful. My plan is to wear you out."

"Funny. That was my plan for you," she said, placing her hand on my knee. "I might be able to outlast you." Her green eyes glittered with mirth.

"Don't count on it, baby. Maybe all we need to do is book a room for a week at the airport Sheraton."

I thought for a moment. "You know where I'd love to go?"

"Where?"

"Italy. I want to hear you speak Italian, and I want to hang out in one those little fishing villages on the coast, like Portofino. And I haven't been to Rome yet, either."

"Wow. I haven't been back to Italy since Dad got reassigned when I was fifteen. But I like that idea! That would be such fun!"

"Maybe we could fly into Rome, rent a car, and each morning just get up and say, 'Well, where do you feel like going today?'"

"Perfect. Relaxed. No itinerary or schedule."

"How long do we have off?"

"Well, I was able to get two weeks, including two days before the wedding, so that would leave maybe ten days for the honeymoon and two days after we get back to see the kids and get organized."

"Yeah, I got two weeks, too. Your mom's keeping the kids, right?"

"Yes. Holly's long gone by then. She leaves for graduate school August fifteenth. But the kids start school at the end of August, so Mom will stay at the farm with them and Ruth until after the honeymoon. Actually, she's picking them up on the fifteenth when Holly leaves and taking them back to Annapolis to stay with her and Dad for a week."

I pulled up the calendar on my iPhone. "OK. I'll hop on the web and get airline tickets tomorrow for departure on September eighteenth and return on the twenty seventh."

Penny leaned forward on her stool and kissed me softly on the lips. I could smell her sweetness. "I can't wait," she whispered.

CHAPTER FORTY-THREE

SHORTLY AFTER 10:30 PM, MARY ANNE PULLED the Mercedes into the same parking spot a half block south of Baltimore Street that she had used the night of her amateur audition at King's Court.

Fifty feet away, at the side door to a club, stood the same guy who she had paid to watch her car the last time. He saw Mary Anne approach and said, "Hey baby, looks like you might need someone to watch over those sweet little wheels again."

Mary Anne reached into her purse and pulled out two fifty dollar bills. "No. Actually, I came to see you. I'm new in town. I need a little help," she said, pushing the bills into his hand.

The man smiled, neon lights glinting off a gold tooth. "Your wish is my command."

"Listen carefully, because you'll only get one shot at this. I need five bags of smack—regular street cut."

The smile vanished from his face. "That's not my gig, doll."

"But you know someone whose gig it is, and when I come back, if you've put me in touch with the right reliable dealer, you'll be holding six more of those little greenbacks in your hand."

The man fidgeted and looked down at the crisp bills. Four hundred dollars in total. That was a lot of money. But what if this woman was a cop? Couldn't be. Cops didn't tool around in Mercedes, and they didn't dance at clubs. He'd heard about this girl's dance at King's Court.

"There's more," said Mary Anne. "I also need three bags of purified heroin—uncut. The best money can buy."

The man whistled softly. "That's gonna cost you, girl."

"Not an issue," said Mary Anne.

The man hesitated. Maybe he wouldn't have to make the actual transfer. Maybe he could just be a middleman and stay in the shadows. Finally he spoke. "This'll take a little time."

"You've got three days. I'll be back Saturday night around the same time." She opened her purse and pulled out two more fifty dollar bills. As the man watched, light glinted off metal inside the purse. *Christ*, he thought, *that's a gun!*

Mary Anne stuffed another hundred dollars into his hand. "Don't screw with me," she said. "I know how to use that pistol." She turned, climbed back into the SLS, and drove away.

~

Thursday night, the alarm on Mary Anne's iPhone went off at 1:30 AM. Struggling to bring herself to wakefulness, she cursed, rolled over, and silenced the alarm. She padded to the bathroom, peed, splashed hot water over her face, then slipped into jeans and a tee shirt.

Thirty minutes later, she pulled the gray Saturn into the 7-Eleven convenience store in Hereford and bought a small coffee. She would not have the opportunity to pee again for several hours, so a large coffee was out of the question.

The store was empty except for a male clerk behind the counter who whistled softly to himself in admiration when he saw the slender young woman in skintight jeans enter the store. She flashed him a brilliant smile as he made change. *What's a gorgeous little thing like you doing out by yourself at this hour of the night*, he wondered.

Mary Anne pulled into an employee parking space outside the emergency entrance of Mason-Dixon Regional Medical Center about fifty feet from a light pole, and turned off the engine. The Murray woman's white SUV was in its usual parking space. She slipped on her headphones, hit the icon for Iron Maiden on her iPhone, and leaned back against the headrest.

~

John Mitchell snapped his radio into the belt clip and left his security office at 3:00 AM for his hourly rounds. He carried a small wireless device that would read and record the time at which he reached each of twenty boxes mounted in various locations around the grounds, ensuring that every inch of the hospital campus was patrolled each hour, and not incidentally, ensuring that there would be no nap.

The whole process took about thirty-five minutes. It was mindless work, but a hospital job came with health insurance, paid time off, and job security. For that, he could put up with boredom. He had a wife and young daughter to feed.

The only saving grace was that he and his partner at the ER security station switched off every hour. At least the ER was more interesting, and every once in a while you got a little action—mostly combative drunks who settled down once they saw some muscles in a security uniform.

But occasionally there was real action. Last year three people has been killed in a hostage situation, but that would probably never happen again in a lifetime. He hoped not, because he was unarmed. The only weapon that hospital policy allowed was a Taser, which was holstered on his belt. That was good enough at close quarters, but beyond ten or fifteen feet the Taser was useless.

The motion sensor on the sliding glass doors of the ambulance entrance picked up his approach and the doors slid open. He crossed the entrance drive into the parking lot and walked toward a light pole one hundred and fifty feet into the lot—his first stop. His eyes scanned the parking lot as he walked, but recorded no motion. At 3:04 he flashed his reader at the box mounted on the pole, heard a beep, and walked west toward box number two.

~

Mary Anne watched the second security guard walk south toward the next light pole and checked her watch: 4:05—within one minute on the hour of the appearance of the first guard. Over the two-and-a-half hours that she observed the lot, the only other activity had been several new patients who had arrived in the patient parking area one hundred feet closer to the ER, and three employees who had walked to their cars to smoke. Satisfied, she waited ten more minutes, then started the Saturn and drove home.

CHAPTER FORTY-FOUR

S HE SMILED AND WAVED TO GERRY STINE AS she jogged past the barn. He turned off the circular saw and watched her ass flex under snug running shorts as she ran east toward the sun along the pasture fence behind the manor house.

It was almost as if she were naked, he thought. As she disappeared, he licked his lips, and angrily turned back to cutting boards for repair of a rotted window sill. He couldn't get the fucking girl out of his mind. Most nights as he was falling asleep, the image of that ass was his last conscious thought.

After her shower, Mary Anne slipped into a bikini and took breakfast on the patio. Manuela delivered a croissant and fruit, but Mary Anne didn't even look up from the little book in which she was constantly making notes. Manuela wordlessly walked back into the kitchen and eyed her mistress anxiously from a window. Something was wrong.

Miss Anne had taken to sleeping until close to noon every day. Most of the time she seemed to be walking around in a daze. Manuela couldn't even remember their last real conversation, and it had been more than a week since her mistress had demanded sex. *What could I have done wrong?* she wondered.

Licking her fingers after the last morsel of croissant, Mary Anne drained her glass of orange juice, grabbed her magazine, and walked toward the pool. In the distance she could see Gerry Stine's head turned in her direction. In a few moments, she would have his blood boiling.

Standing in the sun beside the lounge chair, she stretched languorously, then reaching behind her, untied the bikini top and allowed it to slip off her breasts. Topless, she settled into the chair and picked up the magazine. On the left side of the cover of this week's copy of *Us*, a small headline read, *Hero Doctor Faces Lawsuit*. Beside the headline was the chiseled face of Alex Randolph.

She flipped through the pages until she found the article. On the lower right corner of the page was a photo of a young boy flanked on either side by unsmiling parents, their arms draped protectively around the boy's shoulders. From the top of the page, Alex stared back at her, his brow furrowed and his jaw grimly set. *Soon you'll have more than a lawsuit to be worried about, my dear Alex.*

She skimmed the article, uninterested in the details of the malpractice case—apparently involving appendicitis—but very interested in the venue. The trial would begin in Towson, Maryland later this month. No doubt, his little blond whore would plan on being there at the side of her man. But with any luck at all, it would be only Mary Anne Williams sitting in the courtroom providing support and comfort to the beleaguered celebrity doctor. There might even be a few photos of a gorgeous auburn-haired woman at his side exiting the courthouse.

~

Still topless, Mary Anne climbed out of the pool and without drying, pulled a tee shirt over her wet body. She stepped into flip-flops and padded into the kitchen, where she poured iced tea into a plastic glass and dropped in a slice of lemon. From the patio breakfast table, she grabbed a black nylon fanny pack, and then set out through the yard, taking a shortcut to the barn.

~

Stine's pulse quickened as he watched the girl climb out of the pool, slowly slip a tee shirt over her nearly naked body, and then walk into the house. *She knows I'm watching her*, he thought. To his astonishment, moments later she reappeared and began to walk toward the barn.

At first, from a distance, he could only see the gentle sway of her breasts with each step, but as she drew closer, the curves and the nubbins of her nipples became as clear under the wet shirt as if she wore nothing. She had to know that the shirt was nearly transparent. His cock grew rigid. There could be no doubt. He knew now that she had come because she wanted him.

"I brought you a little refreshment," the girl said, handing Stine the iced tea. "It's hot out here today. You must be dying."

Gerry took a gulp and grinned. "Dying for you, baby."

You dumb shit, thought Mary Anne, *you are clueless.* She reached into her fanny pack and pulled out a waxy envelope the size of a postage stamp. "I brought you a little present to thank you for helping me pick up that car the other week," she said, handing him the little packet.

The color drained from Stine's face. He stared dumbfounded at the envelope of heroin in his hand, then looked up at the girl with hard eyes. "What's this?" he asked curtly.

"You know what that is, Gerry. It's good stuff. Enjoy it. That'll save you a little hard-earned money this week."

Stine's mind was reeling. Indirectly, at least, this woman was his employer. *How did she know? Did she do dope herself?* He glanced at her arms, but they were clean. *What the hell was she up to?*

"You look surprised. I saw the track marks on your arms. My stepfather was a dealer. I grew up around this stuff. I don't use it every day, just when I'm in a party mood—like having dessert, or a cigarette after a good meal, you know? Or sometimes when I'm horny," she said with a fetching smile.

Bewildered, Stine eyed her suspiciously, afraid to make any comment. This woman was intimidating—sapped him of his confidence. Somehow, no matter what he tried, she always made him feel like she was in control.

The girl reached out and lightly touched his jeans on the inside of his thigh, then turned and walked back toward the manor house.

Throwing her hair over her shoulder, she looked back and smiled. "Enjoy!"

Shit! cursed Stine under his breath as he watched the girl walk away. *She was there for the taking, and you blew it!*

~

Tara Carpenter lit another cigarette and paced the tiny kitchen, bouncing the crying six-month-old on her hip. She glanced at the wall clock: 4:02 PM. Gerry would be home in another couple of minutes. He couldn't stand crying babies.

She walked into the living room and spotted a pacifier lying on the stained carpet. Holding the cigarette between her lips, she balanced the baby on her hip, picked up the pacifier and stuffed it into his mouth. But there was no consoling the red-faced boy. With the next open-mouthed wail, the pacifier fell once again to the floor.

For the last two weeks Stine had been even more intolerable and contemptuous than usual, like he was some fucking rock star or something, and she was roadside trash. He was rougher, too.

She lived in fear of him, but even more so for the baby. Sometimes she couldn't control Jason's crying, and Gerry would go into a rage, especially if he'd been drinking. It wasn't his baby, which only made her more fearful.

Last week when the baby was crying, he picked up the infant seat and shook it like a dog shaking a groundhog. She screamed at him and he backhanded her across the face, sending her flying against the wall, but at least he put down the infant seat. Her jaw still hurt when she chewed and the purple bruise in front of her ear was just now turning to yellow.

The only time she felt safe was when Gerry shot up. Sometimes he would fall asleep for the rest of the night and there would be peace until he came home from work the next afternoon.

She pulled a bottle of formula out of the refrigerator and pushed the nipple into Jason's mouth, but he wasn't interested. The din from the wailing child only increased. The screen door slammed and Jerry walked into the kitchen.

"Doesn't that fucking kid do anything but cry?" he snarled, opening the refrigerator door and pulling out a beer.

"It's OK, Gerry. He'll stop in a minute. I'll take him outside." Quickly she carried the baby through the screen door and out onto the concrete porch.

Raising the can to his lips, Stine looked around the room at the dishes piled in the sink; at the table cluttered with cereal boxes, empty baby food jars, and a full ashtray. "What a fucking fat slob you are. This place looks like a pigsty," he yelled after her. "What do you do all day, watch TV?"

Tara walked out into the driveway further away from the house, rocking the screaming child from side to side.

~

By 8:00 PM, four empty cans of Rolling Rock lay scattered around the living room. From the wide-screen TV, a half dozen AK-47s rattled while explosions rocked an oil refinery. Draining the last of his fifth beer, Stine angrily crushed the aluminum can in his fist and threw it at the empty baby seat in the corner of the room.

Never again would he let a woman intimidate him. Next time he would take control with the Williams girl and the little bitch would get what she wanted. She'd be back on her knees begging for more after Jerry Stine was done with her.

He looked through the open wall into the kitchen at the silhouette of Tara Carpenter, standing at the sink in shorts and a halter top. *There's another woman who needs to be on her knees*, he thought.

~

Slowly and gently Tara lay the sweaty infant down on the plastic cover of the crib mattress, praying that the child would stay asleep. As she slid her hands out from under him, the baby gave a little jerk, then stilled, his breathing gradually becoming deep and steady.

Holding her breath, she tiptoed from the bedroom and then quietly passed through the living room into the kitchen, hoping to avoid Stine's notice. He'd already had a lot to drink—the living room was littered with beer cans. She prayed to God that he hadn't run out of heroin. Maybe he would soon shoot up and doze off on the couch.

At the sink, she opened the faucet and began to scrub dried food from two days worth of dishes. The explosions emanating from the TV rattled her frayed nerves. She was only twenty-two years old, but felt like she was forty-five.

Some days she thought that she just couldn't go on any longer. It was as if the pit in which she was trapped had smooth walls, and no matter how hard she tried, she was unable to climb out. This morning she had stood in the bathroom staring at twenty Percocet in her hand for a full ten minutes before the baby cried and she finally put them back into the container.

From the living room, Stine's voice rang out and she froze. "Hey bitch, how can I hear the TV with you rattling all those dishes? Come in here." Heart pounding, she turned off the faucet, dried her hands with paper towels, and walked into the living room toward the man sprawled on the couch. She stopped six feet from him and stood with her arms folded over her breasts.

"You need to take better care of the man who keeps you. Cigarettes and diapers and baby food—they're expensive, you know? Don't you think that would be a good idea?"

"Sure, Gerry."

"So I'm thinking maybe you want to show a little gratitude. Like getting down on your knees here. You like sucking cock, don't you Tara?"

"I love it, Gerry. Especially your cock."

"Get naked," he commanded.

Tara bit her lip. *I need to make this good.* Acutely aware of the effects of recent childbirth on her body and deathly afraid that she would burst into tears, Tara did her best to do a striptease, slowly removing each item of clothing until she stood naked before him, arms hanging awkwardly at her side.

Stine sensed the girl's discomfort and his cock hardened. She was powerless, obeying his every command without resistance. He stood and dropped his shorts.

"Now, on your knees, Tara."

She knelt before him, tentatively took him into her mouth, and slowly began to bob back and forth. Stine seized her ponytail and violently jerked back her head, sending pain zinging through her cervical spine. "Look at me when you suck, woman," he bellowed.

Eyes wide, she struggled to look up, gagging as he held the back of her head and powerfully pumped his hips.

Above her, like a hovering demon, Stine's eyes burned with malicious glee. Her throat ached and her breath came in short gasps through her nose.

Just as her vision became dim and she feared that she might black out, his eyelids closed and his narrow face contorted. Loud grunts echoed through the room as her throat suddenly filled with fluid until she thought she might drown. Desperately she tried to swallow, over and over, until finally he slowed the pace, she gained on the fluid, and suddenly she could breathe again.

~

Stine fingered the waxy little envelope from Mary Anne Williams and decided to try it. Why not? She knew that he was a user. He'd already accepted the gift. And there was no reason to think that this little envelope didn't contain good shit.

He mixed the white powder with several milliliters of water in a spoon, heated it with a lighter until the powder was completely dissolved, and then sucked it into the syringe through the cotton from the end of a Q-tip.

Better do this carefully, he thought. *I don't know how strong this stuff is.* He pushed just a milliliter of the solution into his vein and waited until the first hints of a rush hit his brain. *Ahhh...nice. This is good stuff.* His thumb pushed on the plunger and the remainder of the solution streamed into his circulatory system.

As euphoria washed over him, Stine's body relaxed and sank deep into the couch. He sighed with satisfaction. It was a good evening.

CHAPTER FORTY-FIVE

I WALKED PAST THE "THIS WAY TO PARADISE" sign and buzzed myself through the secure ER door at 6:45 Monday evening. Lisa Turano brushed past me and said, "Welcome to hell, Alex. We've been expecting you."

The nursing station was packed with people. Day shift was signing out to night shift, and four harried attending physicians were admitting those patients sick enough to get a ticket into our very expensive hotel. On the other side of the station, I spotted Penny taking report from Fran and jotting a few notes on a slip of paper. Tonight would score higher than usual on the job satisfaction scale.

But the best part about tonight was that Penny would be coming home to sleep with me at the end of her shift. Today in an emotional parting she had bid farewell to Holly, and her mother had picked up the kids for a week with grandmom and granddad. That meant a week of bliss dead ahead.

I glanced up at the patient tracker board which confirmed the worst in my immediate future, however: fifteen beds full and another eight patients with the acronym *RECEP* behind their names, which meant that they were in the reception area waiting for a bed to open up.

I managed to find a place to stand at the counter beside Lynn Saylor's computer station. She blew a wisp of hair off her face as her fingers flew across the keyboard. "You may as well start seeing new patients, Alex. I won't be ready to sign out to you for another fifteen or twenty minutes. Here," she said, holding up an electronic tablet, "use my iPad."

I logged Lynn out of the software and logged back into the iPad under my user name and password. For months, we had been preparing for the transition to an all-electronic patient record. One week ago today was D-day—affectionately known to the staff as *Disaster Day*: no more paper charts.

Moving to an all-electronic medical record—better known as an *EMR*—was a mandate of the federal government. Actually, that's not true. The government doesn't force you to make the conversion. Medicare just won't pay you if you don't.

You might think that switching from paper to computers would be a godsend—make everything faster and easier. That's true for some tasks, like retrieving lab and x-ray data, or pulling up old records. But for recording the story of a patient's visit, trying to do that on a computer is really pushing the technology envelope.

Creating software that can quickly and efficiently capture the infinite variability of each patient in digital form is far more complex than the calculations for sending a man to the moon. The result is software with so many menus and subroutines that it takes forever to record a single patient's history and physical exam.

Some day the technology will advance to the degree that the computer beats paper, but not yet. This week, the productivity of my docs was down thirty percent. That's like having two fewer physicians on my staff. Our door-to-doctor times and length of stay in the department had soared.

I anticipated that this horrendous decrease in productivity would improve modestly over the next several months, but, in truth, most institutions making the conversion experience a permanent twenty percent decrease in productivity that just won't go away.

I touched the icon for Bed Three: *Regina Burczyk, 52, Female*. This icon contains helpful gender information. Sometimes when you walk into a room it is not clear by visual inspection whether the person sitting in front of you should be addressed as Mr. or Ms.

Conveniently posted beside the icon was the patient's photo—in this case, a middle-aged woman with dark circles under her eyes and frizzy gray hair that looked like she had just placed her hands on a static electricity generator.

The triage nurse's note read: "Claims 16 weeks pregnant with twins. Having abdominal cramps. History of schizophrenia."

Hyde, ever the skeptic, immediately piped up. *Get ready for a long visit, Alex, my boy. This chick is whacked out.*

Jekyll, naturally, took offense to this grossly discriminatory characterization. *Alex, you know, of course, that women over fifty can get pregnant. It is patently unfair to write this woman off because she is fifty-two and has a history of mental illness.*

I took the counsel of these two under advisement, and walked into Bed Three. Ms. Burczyk leaned forward on a chair in the corner of the room, her chin in her hand and her elbow resting on crossed legs.

"Hi, Ms. Burczyk, I'm Dr. Randolph."

Never moving her chin from her hand, she reached out with her other arm and wordlessly shook my hand.

"Tell me what the problem is today."

"That's what I was hoping you'd tell me."

"Well, what symptoms prompted you to come to the ER?"

"Cramps."

"Where are you having cramps?"

"In my stomach, where else?"

Patting the exam table with my hand, I said, "Why don't you hop up here on the table, Ms. Burczyk, and you can lay back and show me where you're having these cramps."

She lay down on the exam table and pulled the patient gown up above her Bermuda shorts. A wiry woman, her stomach was as flat as an ironing board—no basketball visible.

"OK, now, show me where you're having these cramps." She ran both hands over the lower quadrants of her abdomen below her belly button.

"And are these cramps constant, or do they come and go?"

"Come and go," she said. "I think it's from the twins."

"The twins?"

"Yeah. There's two of them in there."

"So, you think you're pregnant?"

"Yep."

"Ms. Burczyk—"

"Just call me Regina."

"OK. Regina. Have you ever been pregnant before?"

"Nope."

"Have you seen an OB-GYN yet?"

"Nope."

"Did you do a home pregnancy test?"

"Nope."

"Well…how can you be sure you're pregnant?"

"My period's late. I can just tell. I know they're in there."

"Regina, do you recall the first day of your last menstrual period?"

"Nope."

"Well, about how long ago was it?"

Regina shrugged her shoulders. "Couple of years."

"Are you sexually active?"

"No, but the guy upstairs is."

"The guy upstairs?"

"Yeah. He comes down every night."

"So, you live in an apartment?"

"Yeah."

"And the guy comes down, and you have sex?"

"Sometimes."

I ran my fingers through my hair. "OK, Regina. Well, I think maybe we ought to do a pregnancy test just to be sure."

"If you want to."

I asked Regina a few more questions and examined her flat belly, which was completely non-tender and without any mass suggestive of an enlarging uterus.

"Regina, your nurse is going to be back shortly and she'll give you a little cup so we can get a urine specimen. Then, after I get your pregnancy test results back, I'll be back. OK?"

281

"Whatever," said Regina.

It took me a while to get this interesting little story into a digital format that would make the computer happy. Some parts of the story were certainly rather unique to Ms. Burczyk, and for those parts I used the dictation software resident on the iPad.

To record an historical element like, *First day of last menstrual period*, I had to use a dropdown calendar and make up a date, since it did not occur to the software developers that "a couple of years ago" should be an option. But, with only two or three expletives unfit for publication, I finally got the job done.

I came away from my encounter with Regina unconvinced of the presence of either physical disease or conception. That made entering orders easy. The only study that I wanted was a urine pregnancy test. Unfortunately there's no blood test available for *certifiably nuts*.

~

It's interesting to me how mood can affect one's productivity, even if you're a fairly compulsive and consistent workaholic. Maybe working with Penny provoked a surge of endorphins in me, because even tonight's crush of patients couldn't sway my upbeat mood. My afterburners were generating blue light. By 7:45 PM I had seen four patients and the nurses were having trouble keeping up with me.

"Rebecca, did you get that urine for me yet on the kid in Bed Two?"

Rebecca put her hands on her hips and stared at me with incredulity. "OK, Alex, you just make up your mind. You tell me what you want first: the urine on Two, the Dilaudid for Mrs. Cook, the Zithromax in Seven, or set up the pelvic exam in Three."

"Well, what have you been doing for the last forty-five minutes?" I asked smiling. "I thought nurses were more efficient than doctors."

Rebecca growled and threw her hands up in the air. "You are a pathetic, hopeless misogynist, Alex."

I started laughing. "I don't know what that means. Spell it for me."

Rebecca opened her mouth but never got her next word out. From the triage area, loud voices interrupted our little sparring match. I waited. Several moments later Fran's commanding voice rang out: "I need a doc in Fifteen!" Scott Foreman was some place in a patient room, so that would be me.

I arrived in the room at the same time as Fran, who was followed by a man carrying a young girl of perhaps seven years of age in his arms, his face contorted with terror. Long, golden hair flowed around the girl's tanned face, spilling over his arm. Instantly I thought of Catherine.

The girl was obviously awake and there were no tears, but her petite oval face displayed complete bewilderment, as if she had just awakened at the rabbit hole in *Alice In Wonderland*. Around her right arm was wrapped a bloodied green towel.

"Help her, please! Oh, God, please help her!" the man pleaded. Fran guided the man's arms to the bed and he released the girl, his body trembling violently. Penny entered the room, along with John O'Malley, the only other male on tonight's shift, so now I had three nurses.

John is six-three, two hundred and twenty-five pounds, and definitely doesn't look like an angel when he's hovering over your stretcher—more like an NFL linebacker who just crushed you. The female nurses like it when he's working—makes them feel more secure.

"What's her name?" I asked.

"Sarah...Sarah," the man replied.

"What happened?"

"Lawn mower...I ran over her arm with the lawn mower," he cried pitifully, covering his face with his hands. "I...she fell off the swing as I was going by with the mower, and...oh, God, I can't believe it!"

"Sarah, I'm Dr. Randolph, and we're going to help you. I'm going to gently unwrap your arm here, so we can take a look. I'm going to be very careful not to hurt you."

As the folds of the towel opened I could see that the pass of the first blade had cleanly sliced off the thumb at the bottom joint, while the second blade had entered her arm between the index and middle fingers, filleting open her hand and forearm straight up between the radius and ulna almost to the elbow. It was now as if she had two right arms. The engine must have stalled when the blade filleted her forearm.

I swallowed hard. Usually, I am nearly emotionless in the heat of battle, but this little girl was too close to being Catherine.

Remarkably, there was little bleeding, but the open halves of her split hand and forearm were stippled with blades of embedded grass. In a way, the pass of the blade up her forearm was a stroke of luck. All the blood vessels, nerves, muscles and tendons run longitudinally down the arm, so the blade had gone between them all, and few were cut. After many hours in the OR, it might be possible to save her hand and arm, although she would clearly be minus a thumb.

The nurses had swung into motion. John began attaching Sarah to monitoring equipment. I saw Penny bend down and softly kiss the girl's forehead, then whisper in her ear. She straightened Sarah's good arm and began gently probing with her fingers for a vein.

Sarah's young father stood six feet from the bed wringing his hands in anguish. It was a pitiful sight. For the rest of his life he would be relentlessly haunted by the sound of the blade thudding into his daughter's arm—the little human being who looked to him for protection—and the engine suddenly jerking to a stop. There would be no personal forgiveness—ever.

"Penny when you get that line, I want a gram of Ancef, and let's give her fifty of fentanyl. John, for now, let's just cover her wounds with wet saline dressings. Get her ready for transport. I'm going to get Union Memorial on the line."

A broad spectrum antibiotic, Ancef would give us a head start on preventing infection. Fentanyl is a powerful short-acting narcotic that would cover Sarah's pain and hopefully make her sleep. But I had no drugs that could ever relieve Sarah's father's pain.

I walked to the corner of the room where he stood, and placed one hand on his shoulder. "Mr...."

"Carbaugh...Steven Carbaugh."

"Is Sarah's mother here?"

"We're separated. She doesn't know yet. Oh, God!" His hands went to his face again in a convulsion of agony.

"Mr. Carbaugh, this is a horrendous injury. For sure, Sarah's thumb is gone. But there might be more hope for a reasonably good outcome than you might imagine." I waited until he removed his hands from his face and looked at me again.

"First, all of the blood vessels, nerves, and tendons run longitudinally down the arm," I said, demonstrating on my own arm, "so very few of them were cut. The blade went between them, not across them. That means that the blood supply is still good all the way down to her fingertips. Do you understand?"

He nodded his head, his eyes now focused on mine.

"Second, we are lucky to have in Baltimore, the largest hand center in the nation—and probably the best—at Union Memorial Hospital. If there are surgeons anywhere in the world who can put this arm and hand back together, it's at Union. Sarah's going to get absolutely the best care possible.

"I'm going to get them on the line now, and we're going to have her on the road very shortly."

I walked back to the nursing station thinking about the serendipity of life. This is the way it always is with accidents.

Sarah had to fall off the swing at precisely the right moment, and her father's lawnmower had to be at exactly the right position during his pass around the yard for this horrifying accident to occur. Had the timing been off by a mere second, Sarah would have had some scrapes and bruises, or perhaps a burn from a hot muffler, but life would have gone on as usual.

As it was, this accident would now change the lives of the Carbaugh family forever. Surgery, years of rehabilitation, and some degree of lifelong disability lay ahead of Sarah, and perhaps lifelong anxiety and depression, too.

Her relationship with her father would be profoundly altered. Like Atlas with the world on his shoulders, Steven Carbaugh would awake every morning for the rest of his life with an overwhelming burden of guilt. His work performance and job security would suffer from absenteeism and a lack of focus. Medical catastrophes are the single largest cause of financial ruin and personal bankruptcy in the United States.

Any opportunity for reconciliation between Steven and his wife was probably gone. A raging custody battle had now become a high probability, ironically making the impact of divorce on poor Sarah's psyche that much greater.

"Stacey, I need a hand surgeon from Union on the line. She's going to need ALS transport, too." Sarah's life itself was not in danger, so we would use ground transport rather than a helicopter. With lights and siren, they could reach Union in a little more than thirty minutes, and the long and painful process of trying to put Sarah's life back together would begin.

~

I sat down on the wheeled stool and slid closer to Regina Burczyk, trying to establish some personal connection for news that I was certain she would not welcome.

"Regina, I'm sorry this has taken so long. I had a severely injured patient come in that I had to take care of. But I have the results of your urinalysis and pregnancy test back now. Your urine was clean, and your pregnancy test was negative." I waited for the response.

Regina looked at me and shrugged her shoulders. "You know, one of them's a girl and the other's a boy. I couldn't decide whether to paint the nursery pink or blue, so I finally decided on both. The top half of the wall is pink, and the bottom half is blue," she said with an enthusiastic smile. "Good solution, huh?"

~

By 3:00 AM the department had quieted. I had only two patients remaining in various stages of workup. I looked over at Penny who sat at a computer two chairs away, staring off into space.

"A penny for your thoughts," I said, pun intended.

She turned and looked at me wordlessly for a moment.

"When I was working on poor little Sarah tonight, all I could think about was Catherine."

"Me too."

"I'm so glad I'm coming home to sleep with you this morning. I need you to hold me."

CHAPTER FORTY-SIX

STINE WATCHED AS MARY ANNE WALKED around with hands on her hips catching her breath. *She's back.*

He watched the little rivulets of sweat trickle down over the smooth, tanned skin of her abdomen and marveled. She was like a dream—like the huge poster of a girl working out that he had once seen in the front window of a gym.

"Whew! It's hot today," she said.

"Not as hot as you," Stine replied with a grin revealing decay near the gum line of his left front incisor and canine.

Mary Anne smiled. "Do you like what you see, Gerry?"

"Maybe as much as you like what *you* see," he said with growing confidence. After all, she was coming back to see *him.*

"Maybe," she said, brushing her hair back behind her ear. She sauntered closer to him and touched his belly button with her index finger. "Did you get a chance to try my little present?" she asked, looking up and cocking her head to the side.

Stine instantly felt a rush of blood to his groin. "That was some sweet shit."

He reached for her arms, but she stepped quickly back and did a graceful pirouette, her auburn hair swirling. "Maybe later," she said smiling.

"How long you gonna make me wait?" Stine blurted out in anger, his confidence suddenly faltering again.

"I don't know you very well yet. A girl has to be careful about these things." She smiled sweetly. "But I need another little favor, Gerry, and if you can help me with that, maybe we really can get to know each other better."

Every damned woman comes with a fucking price. The price he paid with Tara was room and board, and that screaming kid. But he'd pay a big price to get into this one's pants."

"There's a guy that's been bothering me—won't leave me alone— and you're the only person I know who's man enough to help me." Off balance again, Stine's confidence did another wild swing, zooming upward at this reference to his manhood.

Rotating a nylon fanny pack around her waist, Mary Anne unzipped it and pulled out a thick fold of cash. Stine watched in amazement as she peeled off twenty-five one-hundred-dollar bills and held them out in her hand.

"There. This is a little down payment for your help. There'll be twenty-five more of these when you're done. And, oh, I almost forgot," she said, her hazel eyes glittering gleefully as she pulled a tiny waxy envelope from the pack, "here's another little thank you!"

~

From a dead sleep, Tara Carpenter sat straight up in bed at the blaring sound of a claxon. Heart pounding, she swiveled her head rapidly in both directions, searching for the source of the sound, before finally realizing with relief that it came from the alarm clock on the nightstand.

My God, that will wake the baby! Bolting out of bed, she slammed the snooze button and held her breath, waiting for the first sound of a cry. But it never came. She looked at the clock: *2:00 AM.*

Stine sat up, rubbed his eyes, and then slowly climbed out of bed. Tara watched him pick up the jeans lying on the floor, lose his balance, and hop around on one foot, trying to get the other into a pant leg.

"Where you going?" she asked with apprehension.

"No place that you need to know about," he growled.

She crawled back in the bed, not daring to question him further, and after hearing the screen door slam, drifted off again to sleep.

~

On time, as was his habit, at precisely 3:04 AM, John Mitchell held his reader up to the box on the first pole in the emergency entrance parking lot and heard the beep acknowledging connection of the two instruments.

A trickle of sweat ran down his neck. He reached inside the tee shirt he wore under the blue uniform and tried to wipe away the sweat with the back of his fingers.

It was deathly quiet. Not a breath of air was moving. The only sound was the distant warble of tree frogs from a hedgerow at the eastern perimeter of hospital property.

This second week of August had seen three days at nearly one-hundred, and even now, in the middle of the night, the temperature was still eighty-five, not to mention humidity so high it felt like you were breathing water.

Still, it beat walking rounds in January, with the wind whipping and the air so cold that he couldn't feel his fingertips under thick sheepskin gloves.

He gave the parking lot a cursory look, saw no movement, and continued on to pole number two. Within fifteen minutes he had reached pole number thirteen on the west side of the building.

~

Unnoticed, a rusted Ford pickup truck entered the emergency entrance parking lot—designated the *Orange* lot—of Mason-Dixon Regional Medical Center at precisely 3:19 AM. Gerald Stine pulled into an empty parking space and quickly doused the lights. He sipped on coffee as he surveyed the lot for signs of activity, but nothing was moving.

Sweating under a dark navy-blue nylon jacket and cursing softly at the oppressive heat, he began a systematic search of the lot on foot and quickly found a white Honda Pilot. From his jeans, he pulled a crumpled piece of paper bearing a scribbled license number and compared it to the Honda: a match. This was the car.

Pulling a pair of thin rubber gloves from his pocket, Stine took a long last look around the parking lot, slipped on the gloves, and dropped to his knees.

~

At 6:50 AM Penny Murray stood in front of her locker in the staff dressing room, tapped some icons on her phone and brought up her list of things to do for the day. Keeping an electronic list of tasks was a new feature of her life in recent weeks as her wedding day approached and she juggled caring for kids, keeping the refrigerator stocked with food, and tracking a myriad of wedding details.

Alex had gotten off two hours earlier, and she couldn't wait to get to the farm and crawl in bed with him for the first time in several weeks now. But she wanted to make dinner for Alex and Ruth tonight, so first she would make a quick stop at Graul's and pick up a pack of arugula salad mix and fresh tilapia.

This afternoon at 3:00 she had an appointment with Terry Lombardi at Manor Tavern to review menus for the rehearsal dinner and wedding, and she needed to call the photographer. With a little luck, she would get five hours of sleep before her afternoon appointment.

Even at this early hour of the morning, the August heat and humidity were so high that the cool glass of the sliding doors at the ambulance entrance was opaque with condensation. Shading her eyes from the blinding sun that had risen just over the horizon, she walked through the doors into a virtual sauna.

She pulled the Honda Pilot straight ahead through an empty parking space and drove out the hospital access road, taking the right exit ramp that merged onto Middletown Road. As she slowed for the left turn onto the I-83 southbound entrance ramp for the short trip to Hereford, it occurred to her that the brake pedal felt slightly different— maybe spongy—but the car slowed as expected and she continued onto the entrance ramp. *Maybe it's my imagination*, she thought.

Three minutes later she swung onto the long one-quarter-mile exit ramp for Mt. Carmel Road at seventy-five miles per hour and eased off the gas. Three hundred feet from the stop sign, she began to apply the brakes.

On the underside of the vehicle, a powerful jet of brake fluid erupted from two locations in the brake lines at more than one-thousand psi of hydraulic pressure.

Still traveling at sixty-five miles per hour, the SUV slowed perceptively for a moment and then the brake pedal went to the floor. Panic-stricken, Murray pumped the brake pedal furiously, but there was no response from the Pilot.

As the SUV zoomed toward the end of the ramp she frantically pulled the shift lever down into drive one and the transmission whined like a jet engine in protest. The vehicle began to slow, but she was now merely sixty feet from the end of the ramp and still traveling at fifty miles per hour. In desperation she stomped on the parking brake. The car slowed further, but it was now clear that it was too late.

Murray's brain began to process two split-second choices. Straight ahead lay a stop sign through which she could roar across Mt. Carmel Road and down into a steep ravine on the opposite side. The second option was a curving ramp to the right that merged onto Mt. Carmel westbound.

To her right, moving eastbound on Mt. Carmel, was a blue pickup truck. In an instant her brain had assessed the relative velocities of the two vehicles, predicted likely impact just beyond the stop sign, and selected the option of trying to negotiate the curving ramp at a high rate of speed.

In her last thought, milliseconds before the two vehicles met, the faces of Jack and Catherine Murray flashed in slow motion before the young mother's eyes.

~

As he approached Hereford, driving east on Mt. Carmel Road into the morning sun, twenty-two-year-old Jeffrey Ackers squinted and adjusted his sun visor. He looked at his watch: 7:01—enough time to pick up a coffee at the 7-Eleven on York Road and still be on the construction site by 7:20.

He smiled grimly. Lord only knows why he'd want hot coffee when the temperature was already in the high eighties. Of all days to pour concrete, it would have to be today when the forecast was one hundred degrees for the fourth straight day.

Around a curve, he crested a hill and accelerated toward the I-83 interchange a quarter of a mile below him. As he neared the southbound exit ramp his eye caught a flash of movement to his left. In an instant a white vehicle on two wheels had filled his windshield. Before his foot reached the brake pedal, his body was violently slammed by an airbag, and the screaming sound of tortured metal filled his ears.

The world revolved in slow motion as his truck skidded through three hundred and ninety degrees of rotation before the rear bed of the truck crashed into the abutment of the bridge crossing I-83 and an eerie quiet ensued.

Stunned, he slowly looked around in a daze until his eyes alighted on a crumpled white SUV lying on its roof in the middle of the road seventy-five feet to the west, light gray smoke rising from the wreckage. It wasn't until moments later that he began to feel searing pain in his right hip. He took no notice of the gray Saturn that slowly drove down the exit ramp, paused for a moment at the stop sign, then turned left.

CHAPTER FORTY-SEVEN

MARY ANNE DROVE EAST ON MONKTON Road with elation. Over and over she replayed in her mind the image of the demolished SUV on its roof, gray smoke peacefully drifting from the stillness of the carnage. She smiled with satisfaction. If you were thinking about fucking with Mary Anne Williams, you needed to think twice.

It had taken all the will she could muster, but Mary Anne had forced herself to drive away from the scene of the accident. It would have been risky to hang around. It might be a day or two before she knew the ultimate outcome, but if Alex's whore wasn't killed, at the very least she had to have been severely injured.

Weeks of careful planning and sleepless nights had paid off. Only one element of the plan still required execution, but it was perhaps the most dangerous element, and her heart raced with anticipation and excitement at the thought.

~

Manuela walked through the house calling for her mistress, but the mansion was silent. She knocked, then opened the door to the master bedroom where Miss Anne had taken up residence since Mr. Eddie's death, but although the bed had been slept in, the room was empty.

Mary Anne Williams was a complete enigma to her servant. She kept incredibly strange hours and often would be gone when Manuela arrived in the morning, and then upon her return, would sleep all day. Manuela had no clue as to where she disappeared at night. Maybe she had a boyfriend, or worse, what if she had a pretty new girlfriend? Manuela was surprised to feel a pang of jealousy and anxiety at the thought.

Miss Anne's moods were completely unpredictable. Manuela prided herself on anticipating her mistress's needs, but often these days Mary Anne Williams was oblivious to Manuela's presence. Some days when Manuela was ignored, anger would well up within her. *I've given her everything—even my body*, she would think, *and what do I get back? Nothing!*

She returned to the kitchen and almost immediately heard footsteps on the patio. Mary Anne bounded through the French doors. "Good morning, Manuela!" she said brightly.

"Good morning, Miss Anne." This was the most upbeat Manuela had seen her in weeks. Her heart immediately softened. "Would you like some breakfast?"

"I would *love* some breakfast, Manuela, but a little bit later— maybe in forty-five minutes." Mary Anne walked briskly down the hallway and a moment later Manuela heard the bedroom door close.

From a secret compartment in the floor of an ivory-inlaid jewelry box, Mary Anne pulled three small waxy envelopes, two of which were marked with a "P" in black felt pen ink.

Donning a pair of thin rubber gloves, she pulled two syringes sealed in paper packets from the jewelry box and opened the two envelopes marked "P" containing highly purified heroin. In the marble-tiled master bath she sprinkled the powder from the two envelopes into a teaspoon, "cooked" it under a lighter, and sucked the resulting deadly solution into the first syringe. She held the syringe up to the light. *That ought to do the trick.*

Satisfied, she carefully placed the syringe in the top compartment of her fanny pack, together with a rubber tourniquet and several packets of alcohol swabs.

Using only one-third of the powder from the remaining unmarked envelope of street-grade heroin, she cooked another batch and sucked it into the second syringe. This second syringe of diluted heroin was her safety net in case things went wrong. She placed it in the bottom compartment of her fanny pack and zipped it shut.

~

Gerald Stine was moving slowly this morning. He had not been able to sleep after arriving back home at 4:10, and to make matters worse, the thermometer tacked onto a barn beam was already hovering at ninety.

He didn't give a shit about whoever the guy was that was bothering Mary Anne, but he had seen two child car seats in the back of the white Honda last night, and somehow that was bothering him. But not nearly so much as his worry about fingerprints.

Mary Anne had been adamant that he had to keep the latex gloves on when cutting the brake lines, but in the end that had proved to be impossible. The cuts had to be made on the top of the brake lines and just barely through the line so that all of the fluid didn't leak out until heavy pressure was applied to the brake pedal.

Both front and back lines in the Honda Pilot were rubber hydraulic hose. In each instance, he had to feel with his fingers for the first trace of brake fluid in order to know that the depth of the cut was proper, which he couldn't do with gloves on.

He had wiped both lines with a greasy cloth from the toolbox in his truck, but there was no way that he could be certain that he had wiped away all the prints. Being picked up by the cops for a narcotics charge was trifling. Attempted manslaughter—or maybe even murder—was a different story.

Why did I let that little cunt talk me into this shit? he wondered with growing anger. *She better fucking put out or I'll strangle the bitch.*

Gerry wiped the sweat from his eyes and reached for his water jug. His increasingly rapid pulse pounded in his temples. Last night was the first night in weeks that he hadn't shot up because he had to get up at 2:00 AM. He licked his lips and looked around with aimless anxiety, knowing that as the day wore on his withdrawal symptoms would worsen. He couldn't wait for this day to be over.

~

Mary Anne pulled a loose fitting, white cotton top with narrow shoulder straps off the shelf of her dressing room—not terribly practical for running, but, then again, she wouldn't be running that far this morning.

Slipping the top over her naked body in front of the full-length mirror, she first turned to the side and raised her arm, then bent forward to check the view from the front. In both instances generous amounts of breast fell seductively into view.

Instead of snug running tights, she reached for a pair of short denim cut-offs one size too big that fell low below her hip bones to where her public hair would have started, if she had any. Not too subtle, perhaps, but subtlety was not Gerry Stine's bag and it was too damned hard to gracefully wriggle out of running tights.

Satisfied with her look, she laced up her running shoes and headed to the patio for a leisurely breakfast.

~

Stine laid the paintbrush across the top of the can, placed the can in the shade of the gatepost and with trembling hands, lit another cigarette.

It seemed as though time was standing still. For the umpteenth time, he looked at his watch: 10:30. It would be five and a half more hours before he could get home and shoot up.

Angrily, he cast his gaze toward the mansion house. Where was that bitch? It was her fault he was in this condition. She owed him twenty-five hundred dollars, and a lot more.

As if in answer to his question, he saw the distant figure of Mary Anne Williams walk from the patio to the driveway and start off on her daily run. He watched her run out the driveway, around the front hayfield, and then turn north toward the barn.

As she approached, she spotted him and broke into a smile. Today she wasn't wearing her sports bra and running shorts. Instead, he could see her breasts bobbing freely under a short, loose white top, and she wore a pair of jeans cut off up to her ass cheeks. For a moment, he forgot about heroin.

She stopped ten feet from him and bent over with her hands on her knees, puffing away; sweat trickling off her finely chiseled nose. The top fell away from her chest and two rounded white breasts capped with little nipples came fully into view. Stine stared intently. Even in his distracted state of withdrawal he was mesmerized by her astounding beauty.

She looked up at him and smiled. "Well, there's my hero."

Stine's heart unexpectedly leapt. He had never been anybody's hero.

"You put yourself out for me last night—stood up for me. It took a lot of courage. I think I owe you." She walked to him and placed both hands on his bare chest. Stine felt his cock go instantly rigid.

Inclining her head to the side, she slowly leaned into him. He could feel her breath on his face and smell her pungent yet intoxicating odor. Her lips softly touched his and then she pulled away.

"First things first," she said. Reaching into her pocket, she pulled out a thick wad of cash. "Count it. Make sure it's all there."

Stine opened the roll of one-hundred-dollar bills—damp with her sweat—counted them, and looked up in surprise. "Thirty?" he asked.

Mary Anne smiled. "A little bonus for a job well done. Put them away. It's time for another bonus." Grasping both of his hands and placing them on her breasts, she leaned in for a second kiss. But this time her mouth was open and her tongue darted in and out, sending little lightening bolts to Stine's brain.

Restraining her urge to gag, Mary Anne ran her tongue over the side of Stine's face to his ear. "Did you ever watch a girl strip while you shot up on heroin, and then fuck her afterwards?" she whispered. "Double the pleasure. This is your lucky day." Stine's tongue caught a thick glob of saliva just before it rolled out of his open mouth.

Pulling her black nylon fanny pack to the front, Mary Anne unzipped the top compartment, displaying its contents to Stine. He stared hungrily at the clear plastic syringe. From a place deep in the recesses of his mind that wasn't completely obsessed with a fix, an alarm sounded.

Stine had never before shot heroin he hadn't cooked himself, or at least directly watched someone else prepare. What if she wanted to kill him?

Feebly he asked, "What about you?"

Mary Anne smiled and unzipped the lower compartment of the fanny pack, displaying a second syringe. This was the critical moment. She had been smart to anticipate this response. She prayed that Stine couldn't see her chest heaving a mile a minute. What if her face turned red?

"This one's mine, but it's only got one-third of an envelope of powder. If I use more, I'll be out cold for a week." Her hand went to his crotch and slowly measured the length of his erection. "Ooooh. My God, that's nice! I want to be awake to feel every inch of you. You can shoot me up after you fuck me. But, if you want to, you can use mine," she said, offering Stine the second syringe."

For a moment, two regions of Stine's mind did feeble battle, but the craving was irresistible. It was no use. Almost immediately he caved completely. He reached for the first syringe with one hand, and pulled out the tourniquet and alcohol swipes with the other. Mary Anne breathed a deep sigh of relief.

"Sit over here," she said, patting a vertical wooden beam out of view just inside the barn loafing area. "Don't worry about Ebbitt. If he comes, I'll distract him and take him up to the house. Just sit back and enjoy. I want to make you want me."

Stine sat and quickly whipped the rubber tourniquet around his left arm, pulling the end tight with his teeth. In a few rushed seconds he had cleaned his forearm with alcohol and found a vein. He pulled back on the plunger and a little gush of red entered the syringe, confirming that the needle had entered the vein. Releasing the tourniquet, he leaned back against the post and smiled. "It's your show, baby."

Mary Anne's heart pounded with excitement as her confidence soared. She was now firmly in control. The rest of it was second nature to her.

Her eyes never leaving his, Mary Anne's right hand began to slowly raise the bottom of the white top until Stine could just see the under curve of her left breast. As her hips began a slow, rhythmic sway, the other hand slid demurely and tentatively down over her belly as if she had never before touched herself in front of a man. Ever so slightly, her fingertips dipped into the top of her shorts and she smiled.

The hand rose, gently caressing her skin as it made its way upward and under the billowing top to reach her breasts. She grimaced as she pinched a nipple, closing her eyes and tilting back her head in ecstasy. Stine pushed the plunger a quarter of the way into the syringe.

As the first waves of euphoria hit his brain, the top slipped over her head and she shook out her gleaming hair, revealing petite white breasts sitting high on her chest, with rigid little nipples that cried out for fondling.

Her hands went to her shorts again, but this time she brazenly rubbed a palm up and down over her crotch, crouching slightly with legs wide apart, her eyes burning with pleasure.

As hooked thumbs pulled down the front of her shorts revealing the first glimpses of her sex, Stine groaned with pleasure and pushed the plunger home. It was his last earthly act.

~

She stood cautiously three feet from the slumped body as if Stine were a dangerous wounded animal, watching intently for movement of his bare chest, but there was none. His right hand had fallen away from the syringe, but the needle remained in his arm. *Cool,* she thought, *they'll find him that way.*

"Well, how was it, Gerry?" she asked aloud, kicking his foot with the toe of her sneaker. "Great way to go, huh?" Stine didn't answer.

She pulled on her top, then sat down on the concrete floor at the foot of the motionless body, arms wrapped around her knees and chin on her kneecaps. As she watched with fascination, her victim's skin slowly changed colors, the hues transitioning from pink to a hint of baby blue, and then moving on to deep purple. Saliva slowly dripped in strings from the corner of his open mouth.

After ten minutes, she felt safe in placing her ear against his chest, but she could hear no heartbeat. She brushed off her knees and rose, staring at the lifeless body of Gerald Stine with hands on her hips as the addictive euphoria of power and victory washed over her tiny frame.

This is better than an orgasm. Every element of her plan had gone off without a hitch. Stine was the only loose end that could tie her to a plot to kill Penny Murray, and now he wouldn't be talking to anybody.

Tomorrow, Ebbitt—or somebody—would find Stine's body with a syringe still in his arm, and that would be it. Case closed. Perfect.

Taking great care not to disturb the position of his arm, she reached into Stine's jeans pocket and retrieved three thousand dollars. That refund meant that Penny Murray's little accident had only cost her twenty-five hundred dollars—not a bad deal.

Just in case she had somehow left her fingerprints on the alcohol wipe packets, she next retrieved them and stuffed them into her pocket. She had watched enough episodes of CSI to know that it was important to leave as little evidence at the scene of the crime as possible.

Her eyes alighted on the rubber tourniquet. Had she left fingerprints on that? She thought not, but perhaps it was too big a risk to leave it at the scene. But then a smart cop might notice that there was no tourniquet by the body and wonder what was up with that. This was a problem she hadn't thought about.

She could pull his belt from his jeans—which she had seen many addicts use for tourniquets—and lay it by his arm, but she had no rubber gloves and could not risk leaving fingerprints on the belt. Looking around the barn, she spotted a nail from which hung multiple strings of hay binder twine. Perfect!

She stuffed the rubber tourniquet into her pocket, retrieved a length of twine, and carefully slid it under Stine's lifeless arm.

What else? Footprints! The floor in this part of the barn was concrete, but it was dusty and there could still be an impression of her sneakers somewhere. Five minutes into a systematic search of the floor she found it: an impression of the forefoot of her right sneaker in a pile of hay dust. On her knees, she blew on the dust pile and the sneaker impression vanished.

Whew! That was close, she thought. Mary Anne spent another five minutes putting herself into the mind of a cop or forensic pathologist, but could think of nothing that she had missed. Finally, she cast one more glance at Stine's purple body, and said brightly, "See ya, Gerry."

Pulling her iPod from her fanny pack, she loaded up Iron Maiden and began to walk back toward the mansion house, hips swaying to the incessant pounding beat of *The Number of the Beast*. Life was good.

~

Twenty-five minutes after Miss Anne had entered the barn, Manuela saw her mistress emerge into sunlight and walk back toward the mansion house. Quickly she moved away from the kitchen window and returned to polishing silver.

What could she be doing down there all this time? Certainly she couldn't be flirting with the man with rotten teeth. She was such a mystery.

Five minutes later Mary Anne bounced into the kitchen and for the first time in weeks began to unbutton Manuela's dress. Manuela flushed with pleasure.

CHAPTER FORTY-EIGHT

PENNY MURRAY FELT LIQUID TRICKLE UP HER cheek and into her right eye. She wiped her eye and looked at her fingers: blood. Why was it running uphill? In a fog, she absently looked around and saw a concrete bridge, and up a hill, on the other side of the bridge, a bank, and there was a gray car slowly driving away from her. But they were all upside down.

Suspended in mid-air by her seat belt harness, her mind struggled to make sense of this upside down world. Suddenly it all came flooding back. *My God, I'm still alive!*

Instinctively she began to assess her injuries; tried to move her arms and her legs. To her enormous relief, they were responding normally to the commands from her brain. *Do I have pain?* Maybe some aching in her chest, but no part of her body seemed to be sending out signals of major distress at this point. Her fingers pushed against her belly, but it was soft and there was no discomfort.

Where was the blood coming from? She touched the tip of her nose and looked again at her fingers: more fresh blood. *I can live with a bloody nose,* she thought grimly.

There was another vehicle—a truck! Penny bit her lip. Frantically she swiveled her head and to her right spotted a crushed blue pickup truck resting against the abutment of the bridge. She could see no movement amidst the wreckage. *Oh my God, please let him be OK!*

A wisp of smoke drifted past her eyes, the pungent smell reaching her nostrils. But there was another odor, too. *Gasoline!*

Placing one hand on the roof below to break her fall and flexing her neck forward until her chin touched her chest, she reached for the seat belt clip above her and pushed on the release bar. Nothing happened. There was too much weight pulling on the clip.

With her one hand on the roof she pushed with all her might, trying to reduce the weight on the harness. Suddenly there was a click, and instantly, her body fell to the roof below. She winced as she landed on her shoulders, then struggled to right her body in the confined space until she was on her knees on the interior roof of the inverted SUV.

Another thicker wisp of smoke drifted past. She reached for the door handle and pushed against the deformed door with her shoulder, but it wouldn't budge. Cursing, she looked for another door, but the SUV must have landed on the back of its roof when it flipped because the roof was smashed down against the back seats and there was no way she could crawl to a back door, nor were they likely to open anyhow.

She turned back to the driver's window—splintered with cracks like a spider's web—and pounded violently until the heel of her hand was bloodied, but the window remained intact.

In a panic she crawled on her belly to the front passenger door, but it was more deformed than the driver's door. There was no prayer that it would open.

She inched her way backwards toward the driver's door, coughing violently as the acrid smoke became denser. Her eyes watered and now her nose and throat burned like fire. She placed her hand over her nose and mouth as the smoke tore at her lungs. Outside she could hear voices, and in the distance, a faint siren.

~

Charles Bailey swung wide as he made the left turn from York Road onto Mt. Carmel Road, watching in his outside mirror to make certain that the trailer carrying a skid steer behind him cleared the first car in line at the stoplight. As he accelerated the F-350 up the hill past

First Baptist Church, the wail of the massive siren on the roof of Hereford Volunteer Fire Company reached his ears.

Fire or accident? he wondered. Since resigning as a volunteer captain in the fire department five years ago when his business picked up, he had missed the action—the electricity of responding to a call, never knowing what you would find. *Oh well, there's a time in life for everything, and now isn't that time.*

Dressed in his usual workday uniform of baseball cap, plaid shirt—sleeves cut off at the shoulder—and jeans, he drove out the flat past the pharmacy, and crested the curving hill leading down to I-83. Below on the far side of the bridge a collection of vehicles sat dead still.

Bailey drove a little further and squinted his eyes. *Son-of-a-gun. That must be the accident.* A crumpled white vehicle lay on its roof, and close by, a barely recognizable blue pickup rested against the bridge abutment as if it had been crushed by the hand of a giant and tossed aside.

As he drew closer he could see smoke rising from the rolled car. *I hope there's no one still in there!* A small crowd milled around the vehicle, arms gesticulating, as if unsure what to do. He stepped on the gas and the F-350 surged forward.

The trailer wheels locked with a squeal as he slid to a stop as close to the scene as he could safely approach. With practiced ease, in one smooth motion his six-foot-four-frame slid from the truck seat, leaving the door wide open behind him. Reaching into a large, full-width toolbox in the truck bed, he extracted a short crowbar, then broke into a run for the smoking SUV.

"She's in there! There's a girl in there!" screamed a white-haired woman, pointing at the cracked but still intact driver's side window. Bailey's nose immediately detected the smell of gasoline, setting off a deafening claxon in his brain. He roared at the crowd, his massive arm brandishing the crowbar like the hammer of Thor, "Back! Everybody back! There's gasoline all over the place!" The crowd scattered like rabbits before a bloodhound.

He knelt on one knee, and immediately felt wetness soak into his jeans. Around his knee trickled a little stream of gasoline. *Shit!* Heart racing as he fought to contain his fear, he peered into the window, struggling to identify the location of the occupant through the spidered window and smoke. The vague form of a small bluish figure—perhaps on her knees bending forward—wavered in and out of view through the dense smoke. But she was definitely alive—he could hear violent spells of coughing.

The proper way to extricate this girl would be to lay down a blanket of foam over the entire car as well as any gasoline that pooled on the road. The faint siren of the first approaching engine was audible. But they might arrive too late, both from the standpoint of smoke inhalation as well as, God forbid, an eruption of fire and brimstone.

Extricating her would be risky. In this pool of gasoline, a spark from metal on metal would provide a rapid exit from this life that he didn't want to think about.

Bailey made a decision. He knew what had to be done, but it had to be done very carefully. Gripping the crowbar with both hands, he gently swung the tip of the bar through an arc to gauge where it would hit his target: the lower right-hand corner of the cracked window. A properly placed blow in this location should shatter the whole window. If he missed and hit the metal frame…God help him.

Holding his breath, the muscles in his arms tensed and he delivered a powerful blow to the window. As if by magic, the entire window transformed into a thousand little jigsaw pieces of glass and fell away.

Tossing the crowbar onto a nearby patch of grass, Bailey groped blindly through the open window, found the girl's armpits and unceremoniously dragged her body through the window. He knew her neck should have been stabilized with a collar and her spine protected with a backboard, but there was no time for that. *What will be, will be*, he thought.

Effortlessly, he lifted the young woman in a blue scrub suit like a rag doll, threw her over his left shoulder and ran like hell toward the first arriving Hereford engine from which a crew was pulling foam lines.

Fifty feet from the smoking SUV, shock waves from a powerful *whump* thumped his body and ears, followed by searing heat on the

306

back of his neck as the pooled gasoline ignited. It was the closest Bailey had ever come to death in all his years as a volunteer in the fire department.

~

Officer Calvin Bacon of the Baltimore County Police Department stood respectfully in the corner of the room, gripping his clipboard and waiting his turn for access to the young woman who lay with her eyes closed on the trauma table. She wore an oxygen mask, and he absently noted that with each exhalation, fog would form on the inside of the clear plastic.

The young woman was known to him: Penny Murray. Well, after all the publicity, who *didn't* know her? But Officer Bacon knew her directly, not only from the M-15 gang wars, but also because he saw her in the ER frequently when he came to interview drivers involved in accidents.

She was beautiful, and sweet. Not at all taken with herself, despite her celebrity status after killing the bastard that held everyone hostage in the ER and killed his good friend, Jack Schmidt. But between being shot and this accident, she had certainly had a rough year or so.

"OK, Penny, that's it," said Rebecca Franklin, applying Bacitracin to the last of the airbag abrasions on Murray's face. "You must have nine lives. *Please* don't use up any more of them."

Murray opened her eyes and with a groan, sat up. "What about the other guy, Rebecca? I want to *see* him," she pleaded.

Rebecca put her hands on her hips in exasperation. "You *can't*, Penny. He's in the OR," she said sternly. "He's going to be OK. He has a dislocated hip and a fractured femur, but everything else looks good. We don't have the CT back on your chest yet, so you need to *stay put!*"

She gripped her friend's hand tightly and then spoke more softly. "Just relax, Penny, *please!* Calvin Bacon's here, and he needs to talk to you. Alex is on his way and he should be here any minute."

~

Mary Anne punched buttons on the remote, flipping back and forth between the local Baltimore channels during the evening news hour like a child obsessed with a video game. Nothing. No news about this morning's accident in Hereford.

Five minutes before the end of the news hour she heard it.

"When we come back, a local hero rescues a Maryland celebrity from certain death in a fiery crash this morning in Hereford."

~

John Locke put the key in the door to his auto repair business in Hereford early Friday morning at 6:45. Today he was anxious to get started. He wanted to figure out what the hell happened to Penny Murray's Pilot.

He didn't know Penny very well—well enough to know that she was gorgeous, of course—but he did know her fiancé, Alex Randolph, and he liked him—they were casual friends. It was one of the nice things about living in a small town.

Alex's rusted Jeep was held together by chewing gum and rubber bands, but the doc wouldn't give it up. He only brought it in to the shop when the Wrangler was *in extremis*.

When John had arrived with his tow truck at the bridge over I-83 yesterday, he couldn't believe the girl had lived. The crushed SUV was a burned-out hulk. Late in the afternoon, Calvin Bacon had stopped by and impounded the wreckage. Murray had claimed that the brakes failed completely. That didn't happen very often.

John turned on the shop lights and put three little cups of Chock full o' Nuts into the grimy coffee maker. When the carafe was full, he poured a first cup, pulled on a pair of coveralls and headed outside to take a look at the crushed Honda Pilot.

Although he worked on cars, Locke had the mind of an engineer. He understood the complexities of late-model ABS braking systems as if he had designed them himself. If anyone could extract the story of system failure from this corpse of a vehicle, it was Locke.

He groaned as he lowered himself onto the creeper—this wasn't getting any easier with age—then rolled under the distorted mass of metal. The acrid smell of burned rubber and plastic was still so strong that it burned his nose, but fortunately the fire department had poured foam on the vehicle almost immediately after the pooled gasoline had ignited, so less of the vehicle had burned than he might have expected.

After much cursing, he found the brake fluid drain plug amidst twisted, displaced components, and was able to get a wrench on it.

As he turned the last few threads with his fingers, he slid his creeper to the side and pulled a short plastic tub into place below the drain plug. But he could have saved himself the effort. Several drops of fluid slowly dripped from the open drain hole, and then it was done—no fluid in the system.

Well, there's the reason for the failure. But why? Where did all the brake fluid go? The major interest of the police in cases of brake failure, of course, was to make sure that the lines weren't purposely cut, which he couldn't imagine in this case. But inspecting the lines would nevertheless be his next task. Although many contemporary vehicles had metal brake lines, the 2010 Honda Pilot had reinforced high-pressure rubber lines.

He pulled on a pair of thin latex gloves and began with the high-pressure rubber line to the left front brake caliper, working his way back. Portions of the line were rough from burning, but the line looked intact—at least the bottom. He started back at the caliper and ran his fingers across the unseen top of the line. Almost immediately he thought he felt a fine disruption in the continuity of the rubber, but he couldn't be sure. He ran his fingers lightly back and forth. *Yes.* It was subtle, but it was there. By feel, it was a very fine, straight line.

Reaching for the his flashlight, he twisted the line until the top came into view, and there it was: a clean slice across just the top of the line. He bent the line to open the cut and could see that it just barely entered the lumen of the rubber tube. Locke whistled. Whoever made this cut knew what he were doing.

His job was now simple. If the brakes had failed completely, there had to have been a second cut in the separate fluid circuit in the rear brake lines, otherwise Penny Murray would still have had some stopping power, although diminished.

It made sense that the second cut would be on the same side of the car at the most accessible point. He slid his creeper to the rear of the vehicle and quickly surveyed the bottom of the rear line with his flashlight. There was more evidence of flame and heat damage here at the rear of the SUV, but the reinforced high-pressure line still appeared to be intact. When he ran his fingers across the top of the line he found it again almost immediately: a second cut that he was certain also barely entered the lumen of the tube so that the brake fluid would not be lost until subjected to high pressure when attempting to stop at high speed.

Wow. Somebody really has it in for Penny Murray. He slid out from under the vehicle, washed his hands in the shop sink, and dialed Calvin Bacon's cell phone number.

CHAPTER FORTY-NINE

PENNY STAYED WITH ME AT THE FARM ON Thursday night after her release from the hospital, while the kids were in Annapolis. Ben was kind enough to work my three-to-one shift so that I could be with her. Penny's mom was beside herself, but stayed in Annapolis because of the kids.

After hours of tears and asking, "what if the children had been in the car?" and, "what about that poor guy I hit?", she finally drifted off and passed a restless night, moaning and whimpering in her sleep. I rubbed her back and held her tightly while she slept, hoping to allow her some small sense of safety and security after such a terrifying experience.

After fitful sleep myself, I finally climbed out of bed at 7:30 and showered while Penny slept. I smelled coffee as I descended the sneaky staircase into the kitchen, along with a tantalizing aroma of something baking.

"What have you been up to this morning, Ruth? It smells like Atwater's Bakery in here."

"Sticky buns. They'll be out in five minutes. Did you get any sleep?"

"Penny tossed and turned all night long, poor thing, crying like a five-year-old in her sleep. I think she was dreaming all night. She seems to be quieter now. I hope she sleeps 'til noon."

I stood pouring coffee and adding sugar with my back to Ruth.

"I saw it on TV last night," Ruth announced. "Somebody videoed it with their phone—that guy pulling her out of the car and then the fire. I couldn't sleep last night either. She almost died, Alex!"

I turned and looked at my taciturn housekeeper who quickly turned her back, wiping her eyes on her apron. I put my hands on both boney shoulders.

"But she didn't, Ruth," I said softly. "And she's not going to."

~

Sometime shortly after 9:30 AM my cell phone rang—a local number that I didn't recognize.

"Dr. Randolph, this is Calvin Bacon from Baltimore County." I knew Calvin well. He was in the ER constantly, interviewing drivers involved in accidents.

"How ya doin', Calvin."

"I'm calling you, Doc, because Penny gave me your cell phone number yesterday. I hope that's OK. She lost hers in the crash."

"Of course it's OK, Calvin."

"Is she up yet?"

"No. She's still sleeping, thank God."

"Doc, uh...John Locke did an inspection for us on the brake system this morning, and...well, somebody cut Penny's brake lines."

I said nothing for a moment while the significance of this announcement settled in.

"You're sure?"

"Somebody knew exactly what they were doing. Cut the lines just enough that they wouldn't lose pressure entirely until trying to stop at high speed. A fine cut—probably with a utility knife, on both the front and back system. They're independent, so you had to cut two lines to lose the brakes completely."

"Wow."

"I'm sorry. I'm sure Penny must be a wreck after all that yesterday, but I'm going to need to stop by after she's up and talk to her about this."

"I understand, Calvin."

"Maybe you could give me a buzz when she's ready to talk."

"OK. I'll do that Calvin. Your number came up on caller ID. I'll get back to you."

~

Penny appeared in the kitchen just before noon in a pair of my boxer shorts and a tee shirt, hair still wet from the shower.

"Ooooh, I feel like I've been run over by a truck."

She leaned into my chest and I held her tightly for a long moment then pushed her back. "Let's see your face."

Smiling, she looked up and said, "Am I beautiful?"

"You're absolutely gorgeous, but we need to get a fresh coat of Neosporin on those abrasions. I pulled a tube out of the sparse first aid section of one of my kitchen cabinets and began applying ointment to the tip of her nose and wide areas on both sides of her forehead that looked like someone had taken a piece of coarse sandpaper to her face.

"My nose must still work," she said, gently touching the tip with her index finger. "It smells wonderful down here."

Ruth slid a cup of coffee and a plate with a sticky bun onto the granite counter and said, "Sit down. Eat. They're fresh. Just baked them this morning."

Penny ate a few bites and sighed. "Oh my, I didn't have time for this. I need to find that guy today who rescued me. And I guess now I've got to go shopping for a new car. My cell phone's gone. And what about my purse? I wonder if it's still in the car. It's got my drivers license, and credit cards."

"I know where your car is—at least what's left of it. It's at John Locke's garage in Hereford. We'll stop by today. There's something else we need to talk about. Let's go out and sit on the patio."

Penny grabbed my arm and whipped me around. "That guy didn't die did he?" she asked, her face suddenly filled with anguish.

"No...no. He's fine. They fixed his hip and he's doing OK. He's going to be fine. Just grab your coffee cup and come with me."

I led her by the hand through the open French doors and we sat under the noon sun in metal chairs beneath the patio table umbrella.

"What is it?" she asked. "Tell me."

I looked into her pleading eyes, swollen and bruised from the air bag. "Penny, that accident wasn't your fault. There's nothing more that you could have done to prevent it. Somebody cut your brake lines."

Somebody...what...?" She stared at me with incomprehension, then slowly and pitifully began to sob.

~

"Penny, I can imagine how difficult this is for you, but I need to ask who you can think of who would have the remotest possible reason to want to hurt you," said Calvin Bacon gently.

Penny placed her elbow on the patio table and put her forehead in her hand. "I can't believe this. I've been thinking about that for the last hour, Calvin, and I can't think of a soul—at least anybody I know. I'm...I just can't think of anyone. It's so...bizarre."

"Well, the Crips are obvious candidates, or a relative of Ronnie Reynolds," said Calvin. "Has there been any hint of contact from the gangs?" This made sense to me since revenge had been Ronnie Reynolds' motive in the botched assassination in our ER last year that was ended by Penny's intelligence and courage.

"Absolutely no contact," replied Penny. "And to the best of my knowledge, I don't think any of them have ever come back to our ER."

"I wonder if Ronnie has any other relatives in the Crips?" I asked.

"I don't know the answer to that question," replied Calvin, "but we're going to work on that. Captain Louis says we've got contacts in the Baltimore City Police Department who can work that angle for us." I raised my eyebrows. Louis was the precinct commander for Cockeysville. I was surprised that the case had already made it to that level.

Calvin continued with his questions. "Any patients or co-workers that you've had a run-in with? Anybody who's been after you romantically?"

Penny shook her head, then turned to me and smiled broadly. "Just Alex. He's always after me." A faint blush crossed Officer Bacon's face. "No Calvin, I can't think of any patients, and no men have really hit on me." Penny was slowly regaining her composure.

"How about you, Doc? Anybody come to mind?"

"I don't think Penny's got an enemy in the world, Calvin—at least among people that she knows. Maybe there's a stalker out there—somebody who's seen her in the media and imagines that she has rejected him or something."

"That would be very tough to track down." Calvin continued along this line of inquiry. "Any emails or other contacts from fans or anybody else that seems odd or remotely threatening?"

"I don't get much of that, Calvin. People don't know how to contact me. I keep my email address and telephone number very private. The few that get through are usually magazine editors or TV producers, or something."

"Maybe you could be the target," Calvin said turning to me. "Anybody out there who has it in for you, who thinks they could hurt you through Penny?"

I hadn't thought about that. There were always patients who were pissed off at me when, for one reason or another, they didn't get what they wanted, but no one stood out. It would also have to be someone who had intimate knowledge of Penny's and my relationship, but maybe that was everyone.

Mary Anne Williams flitted across my mind for an instant, but that wasn't fair. She certainly wasn't the violent type and she had plenty to lose in fooling around with a crime like this.

"Calvin, I'll have to think about that and get back to you. That's an interesting thought, but nobody comes immediately to mind."

Calvin closed his notebook and stood. "OK. We're having the forensics lab take a look at those brake lines—see if they can pick up any fingerprints, although I think it's unlikely after that fire. But you never know. The fire department was there when it lit off. They got it out pretty fast. I'll keep you posted if anything comes up."

We all shook hands and Calvin climbed back into his cruiser. It struck me that Baltimore County was putting a lot of effort into this case, and I wondered why. Maybe because Penny was so high-profile. I had no doubt we'd see more of her on the newsstands in the coming week.

CHAPTER FIFTY

MARY ANNE AWOKE EARLY ON FRIDAY morning with eager anticipation, knowing that at some point that day, somebody was going to find the body of Gerald Stine, heroin addict and victim of his own self-abuse. Most likely it would be Bob Ebbitt when he did his end-of-the-week inspection of Stine's work.

Of course, the police would be called immediately and they would interview everyone regarding the events on the day of Stine's death, including the mistress of Ascot Farms.

That would be exciting; challenging; part of the fun. Cops were always so stupid. And all the while that they asked their questions they wouldn't be able to take their eyes off the mistress.

Nevertheless, she shouldn't take their stupidity for granted. The safest way to deal with their questions was to tell the truth about everything except that thirty-minute period yesterday. That way you didn't have to remember lies. Actually, she needed to be careful not to let slip that she knew he died yesterday.

For half the morning, Mary Anne put herself in the shoes of a detective and practiced answering her own questions about events. The other half of the morning she pondered her next move—Murray had survived.

In retrospect, it was naïve to think that cutting brake lines would result in the bitch's death. Mary Anne chided herself. That had been wishful thinking. There was no room for that.

But the overall plan had worked—in fact, it was beautiful—and the only person who could implicate her as the accomplished mastermind was dead. The police interview, if, in fact, there was one, would be a piece of cake. The cops were no match for Mary Anne's mind.

As for the blonde, she had gained only a few more anxious days on this earth. Next time she would face Mary Anne Williams directly. Nothing would be left to chance.

Manuela watched her mistress pace around the immaculate mansion grounds talking to herself—oblivious to the rest of the world—and wondered what was going through her mind.

~

Sergeant Dan Fry looked down at Gerry Stine's body sprawled against the barn beam and without conscious thought began to process the scene. Standing uncomfortably beside him, shifting his weight from foot to foot, was Robert Ebbitt, apparently the man's employer, who had found the body shortly after lunch and called 911. It was obvious to the arriving medics that the man was long dead, and they had called the police.

The only sound in the empty barn was the constant buzzing of flies who were having a field day around the eyes, nose and mouth of the deceased.

Off to the right—a safe distance away from the disgusting body— a gorgeous young woman with flowing auburn hair quietly stood in shorts and a pink tee shirt, her arms folded and her face distraught.

This, apparently, was the lucky little widow who owned Ascot Farms. Actually, she almost didn't look old enough to have been married. But some people always manage to be in the right place at the right time.

The obvious clue to the cause of death was a syringe, the needle of which was still buried in the deceased's left forearm. Fry thought he may actually know this man from his days on a northern county drug task force. He'd have to check the records.

The right arm had fallen away into the dead man's lap. Under the left arm was a doubled string of binder twine which apparently had been used as a tourniquet. This struck Fry as a little odd. The twine was thin and would likely cut into the skin and produce pain when tied tight enough to occlude the veins. Why didn't he use his belt?

The position of the body appeared natural for an overdose. Fry doubted that it had been moved. The dead man was shirtless, so it probably happened in the heat of the day, but not likely today, he thought.

Fry squatted on his haunches and placed his hand on the man's skin. It was cold. Body temperature drops roughly three quarters of a degree per hour, so he'd been dead for quite some time.

He pulled up one leg of the man's jeans and noted a line of purplish color all along the bottom of the leg. This was lividity, the result of blood pooling over time by gravity, a process that took at least several hours.

He tried bending the dead man's leg, but it was stiff as a mannequin—*rigor mortis*, also requiring hours. Fry guessed that the man had died yesterday rather than this morning, but he'd leave an accurate time of death up to the medical examiner.

"When was the last time somebody saw this guy alive?" asked Fry.

"This is the first time I've been here in three days," replied Ebbitt.

The young woman spoke up for the first time. "I saw him around the barn yesterday late morning when I went for a run."

If indeed he had died yesterday, someone would have missed him last night. That should be easy to track down.

"Did you notice his truck still here last night after the end of his work day?" Fry asked the woman.

"No, I didn't notice. It's hard to see the truck from the house with all the trees."

"Anybody else been around who might have seen him?"

"Just my housekeeper," replied the girl, "but she never goes out of the house."

"Did you know this guy—ever talk to him?"

Mary Anne shrugged. "Hardly at all. I've only spoken to him a couple of times—usually when I was out for a run."

"He had strict instructions to stay away from the house," Ebbitt offered.

"Did he ever appear to be under the influence of drugs on the job?"

"I can't say yes to that," said Ebbitt. "He was a low life for sure. I had my suspicions about him, but I have to say honestly that I never saw him intoxicated, or high, or whatever you call it, on the job."

Fry stood. "OK. Well, the forensic investigator should be here shortly. We'll see what she wants to do."

So far, so good, thought Mary Anne. *That was almost too easy. I'm sort of disappointed.*

~

Tara Carpenter's hand trembled as she shoved another spoon of pureed carrots into the baby's mouth. Her nerves were shot. Not only had Stine gone out at 2:00 AM on Wednesday night, but yesterday he had never come home from work. She hadn't slept all night. Now it was 4:20 PM and he wasn't home yet.

Normally the only time she felt relative peace was when Stine was gone, but today her anxiety level was over the top. What if something had happened to Gerry? What if he had another girlfriend? Where would she live? How would she feed the baby? How would she get around without his truck? Already she was low on cigarettes—only three remained in her pack.

Her body jerked at the loud rap on the flimsy screen door. Nobody ever came here. This couldn't be good. She lay the spoon on the baby food jar cap and cautiously walked toward the door, peering around the wall that obscured the doorway. *Oh my God, it's a cop!*

"Are you Mrs. Stine?" asked the cop.

"No. I'm his girlfriend, Tara Carpenter."

"I'm Sergeant Fry, Miss Carpenter. May I come in?"

Tara lifted the latch and pushed open the screen door. "What is it?" she blurted. "Has something happened to Gerry?"

Fry removed his cap and stepped through the door into a kitchen that looked like the scene of a bomb detonation. A single bare lightbulb glared over a table covered with a green plastic cloth, over which was strewn days-worth of dirty dishes, cereal boxes, empty baby food jars, toys and ashtrays.

In a highchair at the table sat a infant clad in only a diaper, orange baby food blending in with the smudges of dirt streaked across his face.

"Miss Carpenter," said the officer, "I'm afraid I have some bad news for you. Gerry Stine is dead."

~

Tara paced the floor, smoking a cigarette and bouncing the baby on her hip as the questions continued.

"Did you notice any unusual behavior in Stine in recent days?"

"Gerry was always irritable, and rough with me and the baby, but the last week he was worse than usual, like he was somebody big and we were fucking trash," she said bitterly.

"Then on Wednesday night the alarm went off at 2:00 AM. Scared me to death. I was afraid it would wake the baby so I jumped out of bed and turned it off.

"Anyhow, he got up and got dressed and left. He wouldn't tell me where he was going. I heard him come in at four or five o'clock, but he never came back to bed. Then last night he never came home."

"How much heroin do you think Gerry used?"

"I don't know, but he shot up every night. It was a relief. He'd go to sleep and leave me alone."

"Did he shoot up on Wednesday night?"

Tara stopped pacing and thought about that. "You know, I don't think he did. In fact, I'm sure he didn't. He wasn't himself—he left me and the baby alone—and then he came to bed early. I couldn't figure out what was going on."

Fry struggled to put the pieces of the puzzle together. Maybe Stine went out to get a resupply of heroin early Wednesday morning, then shot up at work the next day because he was going through withdrawal. Almost certainly he died yesterday.

There was little hope of figuring out where Stine went on Wednesday night, but maybe, in truth, it really didn't matter. Fry's backlog of cases was big enough. He closed his notebook—little point in spending an inordinate amount of time on the victim of another heroin overdose when he had real crimes that needed work.

~

Mary Anne took a leisurely shower, dressed in casual clothes, and hopped into the Mercedes at 6:35 PM. At Walmart in Cockeysville, she selected a high-end anonymous pre-paid smart phone with a ninety-day unlimited card, for which she paid cash.

Fifteen minutes later, she slipped into a booth at Paolo's Ristorante in Towson. As she dipped hard-crusted bread in olive oil, and sipped cabernet, she placed a call to Florida.

Upon her return to Ascot Farms, much of the evening she spent with Google, typing "immigration," "extradition," and "off-shore banking" into the search engine. If something went wrong it was important to have Plan B already in place.

Her final searches were for "Crips gang", "Crips gang signs", and "Crips gang symbols". She knew that Penny Murray had killed a Crip—a key factor in the plan which was gelling in her brain.

In her notebook, she sketched several Crip hand signs used to identify gang members, and made notes regarding tattoos and clothing, placing a star in the margin beside "blue bandanas."

By the time she finally powered down her iPad at 2:00 AM, there was little left to learn about the Crips that she didn't already know.

CHAPTER FIFTY-ONE

A LLISON PETRY SLIPPED INTO A GOWN AND gloves in an autopsy room of the gleaming new Office of the Chief Medical Examiner building on West Baltimore Street shortly after 8:00 AM Saturday morning.

Being two steps below the chief and one step below the deputy chief, Allison was one of a dozen or so assistant examiners to whom weekend call fell. And the rabble on the streets were screwing up her weekend royally.

Four bodies awaited her attention this morning. Each was the product of man's search for nirvana, dominance, and revenge in the last eighteen hours. That would pretty well shoot her Saturday, not to mention the veins in her legs.

Of course, those bodies were collected from all over the state since Maryland was one of the few states to have its coroner services organized on a statewide basis rather than by county and city.

Thank God the room was cool. August was not a good month during which to be thirty-six weeks pregnant. Most days she felt like she was in a bake oven.

Struggling to tie the strings of the gown behind her, she finally gave up and said with annoyance, "Jackson, tie this gown for me."

Jackson Hilliard, her thirty-something autopsy assistant gathered the paper ties from the gown on either side of her generous belly and whistled. "I'm not sure these are gonna be long enough, Doc."

"Shut up, Jackson."

Allison reviewed the forensic examiner's report on the first case. *Gerald Stine, thirty-two years old. Known heroin addict found dead at his workplace on a farm with a syringe still in his arm. The presumed injection of heroin was unwitnessed.*

Body was found late morning Friday. No one had seen the victim since the previous morning. He did not return home after work on Thursday night. Estimated time of death between noon and two on Thursday.

Body found leaning against a wooden post in the barn, shirtless, clad in jeans and boots. A string of binder twine was found under the left arm and was apparently used as a tourniquet. No other drug paraphernalia was discovered on the body or at the scene.

Elements in question: a) binder twine is an unusual tourniquet in view of narrowness of the string and potential infliction of pain, and b) absence of drug packaging or paraphernalia, indicating that heroin was likely pre-prepared in another location and subsequently brought to the scene; or that paraphernalia had been removed from the scene prior to police arrival.

Allison began her inspection of the external body, dictating notes into a microphone headpiece as she progressed. She noted tattoos, distinctive marks, and the evidence of track marks in the arms, including one prominent mark in the left arm that had probably been the location of the syringe in place at the time of death. The corneas were cloudy, indicating a time of death of greater than twenty-four hours. No external evidence of trauma was apparent. The distribution of *livor mortis* was consistent with the position in which the body was found.

Using a magnifying lens, she carefully inspected the left arm above the elbow for evidence of use of the binder twine string, but could see no marks, fragments of string, or petechiae—tiny punctuate bleeding spots—indicating use of the twine. That was, perhaps, puzzling.

As she poised the scalpel above the dead man's sternum to begin examination of the internal organs, Jackson spoke out. "You might want to check out that long hair on his chest before you make that cut."

At Jackson's prompt, Allison spotted it immediately. Entwined in the short hairs on the man's chest was a single long hair of a different color. *Why didn't I see that before?* she murmured to herself irritably.

She lifted the hair and held it up to the light. "Auburn, I think. Well cared for. He's been messing with a chick with auburn hair who takes care of herself. Seems unlikely, don't you think?" Jackson held a plastic bag open and Petry dropped it in.

"You've got eagle eyes, Jackson."

~

Someone making more money and getting more vacation time than Calvin Bacon made the decision not to send a forensics team to go over the Murray car. Calvin was not happy with this decision. Given Murray's high public profile, he argued, at the very least we should examine the brake lines themselves for prints, which could be detached from the vehicle and brought to the forensics lab with minimal time, effort, and expense. Bacon himself could also attempt to lift prints from the car body in the vicinity of the wheel wells.

To this proposal he received grudging consent, aided by the public relations officer who complained that his phone was ringing off the hook with inquiries from the media as to the state of the Murray investigation.

At 8:30 Saturday morning, Calvin pulled his cruiser into John Locke's garage on York Road. It took John about ten minutes to cut the two short lengths of hydraulic hose from the vehicle. Using disposable blue plastic gloves, Calvin inserted the two hoses into a clear plastic evidence bag which he would transfer to the forensics lab after report on Monday morning.

From a zippered bag he pulled a bottle of dark gray powder and a brush and began to lightly dust the white paint that remained between the crumpled front wheel well and what was left of the headlight assembly. Flame had burned away the paint from the front door post all the way to rear of the vehicle, so this small patch of remaining paint was his only hope. Maybe his bosses were right.

As the brush worked its way clockwise around the wheel well, the pads of four finger tips slowly appeared as if by magic on the front side of the well. The print of the ring finger was distorted by a crimp in the metal, but the other three prints were pristine and perfect.

Calvin whistled. He was betting that this set of prints belonged to the guy who had nearly ended Penny Murray's life. Most criminals weren't too bright. If this set of prints belonged to the perpetrator, he may as well have left a business card taped to the front fender.

He photographed the prints, lifted them with tape, and with a satisfied sigh, pressed the tape onto a white card. That little card might bring Penny Murray's nightmare to an end. Happily, this find was not likely to be missed by his superiors either.

One task remained. He had to stop by the farm and get a set of elimination prints from Penny, the car's owner. If the prints from the wheel well were Penny's, they were back to square one.

~

Mary Anne stood with legs apart and both arms extended as she steadily increased pressure on the trigger. The Sig Sauer P238 barked and a fifth hole appeared within the inner circle of the target.

Satisfied after thirty rounds that she hadn't lost her touch, she walked back to the mansion, cleaned her gun, and zipped it along with a box of twenty rounds into a leather case.

Just before noon, she withdrew nine thousand dollars in cash from her Sovereign Bank account at the Hereford branch—one thousand under the cash withdrawal amount that triggers a government report.

The remainder of Saturday afternoon was passed poolside on her iPad, researching travel options.

CHAPTER FIFTY-TWO

BY SATURDAY MORNING, THE RED GLOW OF the abrasions on Penny's forehead and nose had faded and rows of tiny scabs had replaced raw, open tissue. The swelling around her eyes was pretty well gone, although purplish areas of bruising were still visible. After sleeping untold hours, her body must have caught up with its needs, because she was up this morning before me, and I awoke to hear the shower running.

The shower enclosure is glass, of course, and I was unable to resist the opportunity to watch her scrub through the glass, semi-opaque as it was with steam. I leaned back against the vanity counter brushing my teeth as she went head to toe with a soapy sponge. It was a lovely sight.

When she opened the door and saw me she smiled. "What are you doing?"

"Watching you."

"You should be ashamed—spying on a girl in the shower when she doesn't know you're there."

"I've wanted to do that since seventh grade," I said smiling.

"I was right. You're a pervert."

I pulled her wet body against mine and kissed her, the smells of soap, shampoo, and toothpaste all mixed together. It was intoxicating.

When we broke the kiss, she looked up with fire in her green eyes. "I just *love* waking up this way."

"Feeling better this morning?"

Placing her hands in the small of her back, she smiled and stretched, pushing those lovely little breasts skyward. "Still a few kinks, but all in all, much better."

"Maybe we can try to get those kinks out later on this morning," I said staring with appreciation.

"Do you know how to do that?," she asked, putting her arms around my waist.

"That's only one of my many talents."

I pulled her to me again and held her wet head against my bare chest, kissing her forehead. "And how is your head this morning, baby? Not your face, but your head." For a moment she was silent. I felt her arms tighten around my waist.

"I'm scared, Alex. Somebody tried to kill me and I don't know who, or why, or when they're going to try again. I don't want to live like this. What if the police never catch them? Mom's got the children now, but...what if there's no resolution? How can I ever have Catherine and Jack around me again when..."

Her last sentence trailed off into little choked sobs, and the water trickling down my chest from her hair mixed with tears. I had no answer to her questions.

~

Penny spent the morning talking to her mother on the phone and furiously digging into remaining tasks for wedding arrangements. I thought that this was good therapy.

Shortly before noon, Calvin Bacon's cruiser pulled into the driveway, gravel dust billowing up behind him like a rooster tail. I was mowing grass—bare-chested in a pair of shorts—when he arrived, so I drove over to his cruiser and shut down the engine on the little John Deere mower. Three seconds later it gave a deafening report like a 30-30 rifle shot going off beside your ear. Calvin's hand went for his gun.

"Morning, Calvin. Sorry. She always backfires like that when you shut her down."

Calvin grinned sheepishly and visibly relaxed. "You oughta get that thing fixed, It's gonna blow your engine apart."

327

"Tried. Nothing works. Mechanic says it's pretty specific to that year and model. You working on a Saturday?"

"We gotta cover the streets 24/7, just like you guys," he said smiling. Calvin seemed more lighthearted than the last time we saw him. Maybe that was a good sign.

"What's happening today?"

"Well, it might turn out to be a good day. It's possible that we have a break in this case. Is Penny around?"

"OK, come with me. Let's go get her."

The three of us sat around the patio table and Calvin related the finding of fingerprints on the Honda wheel well.

"Does that mean that you'll find him?" Penny asked with barely suppressed excitement.

"Two caveats," said Calvin holding up both hands to signal *slow down*. The first thing we have to determine is that the prints are really those of the perpetrator, and not yours or your car mechanic's. So I need to get your fingerprints while I'm here today for comparison.

"The second is that if these are the perpetrator's prints, he has to be in the database in order for us to find him. If he is, we'll find him because the prints are perfect. If not…well, they could at least help us if we were to identify any suspects."

CHAPTER FIFTY-THREE

MARY ANNE STOOD IN FRONT OF THE FULL-length mirror in the master bath trying to choose between brunette and blond. In her early days on the streets of Miami as a runaway, she had been a brunette. In fact, she couldn't remember, but she may have still been a brunette when she first enrolled at Miami Dade College. She needed to check on that.

Returning to the bedroom, she pulled her old college ID from a top drawer containing mementos. *Yep. Brunette.* She stared at the beautiful young face in the photo ID while walking slowly back into the master bath. The card bore the name *Allison Cooper*. Mary Anne laughed hysterically. Alice Cooper had been playing in her headphones when they asked her name at the Miami Rescue Mission her third night on the streets at the age of sixteen. For the next two-and-a-half years she answered to the name Allison until after she had turned eighteen and the authorities were no longer interested in her.

How old was I in that photo? She looked at the date: September 2001—eighteen. What was today? She checked the date on her iPad: Sunday, August 21. *Oh my God! I forgot my birthday last week. I'm twenty-eight!*

Her eyes returned to the mirror. The girl staring back at her was still beautiful and, if anything, more elegant, with flawless skin and not a trace of a wrinkle, but she was somehow older. Good enough, though, she thought. Where she was going, no one was going to take too close a look at that old ID.

By early afternoon, brunette Allison Cooper was back. The difference was astonishing, but someone might still recognize her face from a photo. She would wear aviator sunglasses and her hair down on either side of her face in a frizz so you couldn't see the cut of her jaw. Or maybe she should wear a baseball cap. But then they wouldn't be able to see all that black hair.

From the garage she retrieved an old moss green backpack. Into the bottom she placed seventy-two thousand dollars in cash, carefully grouped into packets of ten thousand. On the rear of the pack was a zipped compartment into which she slipped the P238 in its leather case. The remainder of the bag was filled with toiletries and clothes, and a blue bandana.

~

Most of her coworkers thought that the night shift at the Haines Street Greyhound Station in downtown Baltimore was the pits. But Nikki Cole liked it. It was quiet. No bosses around to make your life miserable. More importantly, she could see her two kids off to school in the morning and spend the evening with them before work.

Like every night shift worker, she was chronically short on sleep. But, hey, you gotta put food on the table. She felt lucky to have a decent paying job with health insurance for her and her kids.

A slender college-aged girl wearing camo cargo pants and a black Iron Maiden tee shirt approached the counter.

"Where're you headed, honey?" Nikki asked.

The girl pulled headphones from her ears, the white plastic headpiece promptly disappearing into a jumble of frizzy black hair.

"Sorry. What?"

"Where're you headed?"

"Florida—Miami."

"Going to find your fortune?"

The girl smiled shyly. "Maybe," she said reaching into the cargo pants and pulling out a wallet.

330

"You got a ticket or a reservation?"

"No. I need to buy a ticket."

"What's your name, honey?"

"Cooper. Allison Cooper."

"You got an ID, Allison?"

The girl reached into her wallet and pulled out a card, holding it up in front of the clerk. "This is it. I don't have a driver's license."

Nikki glanced briefly at the college ID the girl held up and went back to pecking at her keyboard. The girl was covering a portion of the ID with a finger—probably an issue date—and she was also wearing sunglasses here in the brilliance of midnight at the bus station, so you really couldn't compare her face to the photo on the ID. Nikki decided that this girl had something to hide, as did so many who rode the buses at night.

But it really didn't matter. There were no terrorist lists to compare names to, no metal detectors, no searches of carry-on items and no shoes removed.

"You're lucky. There's one seat left on the 12:50 AM bus. Gets into Miami at 4:20 Tuesday morning. You got any luggage?"

"Just my backpack."

Nikki eyed the worn green backpack which was likely stuffed with this young girl's every worldly possession. It would fit under the seat.

"OK, that'll be a hundred and ninety dollars."

Unsurprisingly, the girl began to pull cash out of her wallet. This would not be a credit card transaction.

Nikki handed her the ticket. "Here you go, hon. You'll be boarding at Gate Four in about thirty minutes. Have a nice trip. Good luck with finding your fortune."

"Thank you," the girl said quietly. Nikki watched her walk away, wondering if the fortune she found at her destination would be a life on the streets.

~

Early Monday afternoon, Baltimore County forensic scientist Neil Saliker examined the two brake hoses, grimaced, and shook his head.

331

Why did they brings these damned things in here? he wondered. To the naked eye, at least, it appeared that there was enough fire damage to the surface of the front hose that retrieving prints was unlikely. For sure, the rear hose had too much flame and heat damage to identify anything at all. Over the next forty-five minutes he tried several different methods of identifying prints on the front hose, but quickly gave up.

The prints taken from the paint in front of the wheel well however, were quite good. These, he entered into the computer and accessed his local database to begin a search for a match. If no match popped up, he would then access the AFIS system maintained by the FBI and do a national search.

While his computer churned, he returned to his lab bench and began work on another case.

CHAPTER FIFTY-FOUR

THE STREETS OF NORTH MIAMI WERE deserted as the Greyhound motored south along NW 6th Avenue in the early morning hours. Mary Anne watched the familiar skyline pass and caught her own reflection in the window. How long had it been since she had ridden a bus every day to Columbia Coffee and school? That must have been...what, 2003? Eight years that seemed an eternity ago in a parallel universe.

How ironic that here she was again, riding a bus through the streets of Miami. Except this time she was no pauper. She was the mistress of Ascot Farms, soon to be wed to the celebrated Dr. Alex Randolph, although she vaguely realized that Randolph mattered less and less to her these days.

What mattered—what was deeply satisfying—was that skinny little Mary Anne Hampton from a trailer park in the swamps had metamorphosed into a brilliant, rich, and deadly foe—a beautiful butterfly with a deadly sting. Now it was the thrill of the chase, the matching of wits, and the wielding of the power of life and death that was electrifying. Like cocaine, it had become all she lived for.

She smiled and the face of the strange girl in the window smiled back. This little façade was fun. The police, if she ever needed to flee, would find not a trace of Mary Anne Williams, nor of her August trip to Miami.

The bus pulled into the station on NW 27th Street, near the airport, ten minutes late at 4:20 AM. Despite sleeping in only intermittent catnaps, she felt energized; ready to start the day. It was good to be back in Miami again. Already she could feel the energy of the city. She hadn't fully realized how boring was her existence during the last three years at Ascot Farms. *Oh, well. It was an investment—a very good investment, actually.*

There were only a couple of people that Mary Anne needed to see on this trip. In fact, it was important that she keep a low profile. She would not be able to see any of her old friends except one—too great a risk that someone could identify her as having been in Miami this month.

But she was surprised to feel her body throb at the thought of the one. It had been a long time since she had had a man, and this one had always more than satisfied her. But that would come later.

The terminus of her twenty-seven-hour bus trip was on the west side of town near the airport. She needed a place with free WiFi to work for several hours until the business day began. On a whim she decided that Columbia Coffee would be perfect. The staff had long ago turned over, and no one there would recognize her.

A twenty-minute-cab-ride later she ordered a latte, pulled her iPad from the backpack, and settled into a cozy leather couch. Opening her notepad, she reviewed the day's tasks and spent another hour revising the life history of Allison Becker. Unexpectedly, she felt a little twinge of melancholy that innocent young Allison Cooper had passed from the scene.

~

The handsome, tanned desk clerk at the Fontainebleau Hotel on Collins Avenue looked the scruffy brunette in camouflage pants up and down and sniffed, "No reservation? I'm terribly sorry, but the hotel is booked."

The Fontainebleau was the perfect base for Mary Anne's work this week. With fifteen hundred rooms, she could get lost in the crowd. Moreover, it was an address that would not raise questions in the minds of the people who would be forwarding her international Federal Express packages.

Laying two one-hundred dollar bills on the counter, she said, "Find a room." Pretty boy looked at the money then stared blankly at Mary Anne. "A suite—with an ocean view," she added.

"Let me check the cancellation list, Miss…"

"Becker. Allison Becker."

He punched a few keys and waited for the screen to change.

"Whoa!" he said with surprise. "Miss Becker, today is your lucky day. I have a Sorrento junior suite on the seventh floor with a furnished balcony that just opened up twenty minutes ago. It's a stunning room —fabulous ocean view."

"I'll take it."

"Wonderful. Which credit card would you like to use?"

"Cash."

"Cash?"

"Please don't tell me that the Fontainebleau doesn't like cash."

"Uh…yes. OK. If you will please just fill out this little card, Miss Becker, with your name and address, cash will work just fine."

~

After a run on the beach and a shower, Mary Anne sat with her feet on the ottoman in the morning sun finishing her bowel of granola and a plate of fresh fruit. Seven stories below her balcony, throngs of rich New Englanders, Mid-Westerners, and Canadians roamed the hotel grounds and beach, along with a smattering of South Americans escaping winter.

Wiping her lips with a linen napkin, she picked up her pre-paid phone and placed an international call to the independent island of Dominica in the Lesser Antilles. It would be a short call.

After a long evening of research on the internet, Mary Anne knew exactly what she wanted. Within five minutes, the agent on the other end of the line had taken her order for a prepackaged offshore financial entity whose structure would make tracing ownership and movement of money nearly impossible. The goal, of course, was to make tracking down Mary Anne Williams nearly impossible.

The package included formation of an offshore trust in the Bahamas which would be the owner of an empty but already incorporated "off-the-shelf" company available for immediate purchase on the island of Nevis.

The nominee directors of both entities and the nominee shareholder of the corporation would be supplied by the agent and these would be the only names that would ever appear on a document. But each would sign a power of attorney to the beneficial owner, Allison Corbett Becker.

The corporation could own real estate, vehicles and any other real property desired. A corporate account would be established at a bank on Antigua which would issue a debit card and checks in the name of the shelf company.

Mary Anne could not have cared less about the magnificent beach-front estate in the Dominican Republic. It could be sold and the proceeds used to fund the offshore trust and corporation. If she discounted it for quick sale, she could probably still generate two million in cash. Getting the cash out of the U.S. from the life insurance policy without it being traceable would be trickier.

The address of record for the corporation would be a forwarding address in Belize. Should the beneficial owner desire to invest money in securities, that would be accomplished through a corporate brokerage account in Panama.

By paying the "rush" price, the entire transaction could be accomplished in four business days by overnight international courier. Allison Becker gave Suite 7204 at the Fontainebleau as the address to which the documents would be delivered by FedEx for signatures.

Several additional documents would have to be attached to the signed package prior to return to the agent, including a copy of a photo ID—in this case a driver's license—and verification of a residential address in the form of a utility bill. Those she hoped to have available in two days.

Remarkably, the cost of the entire package was under five thousand dollars which she would pay via cash enclosed in the return package—slightly illegal, of course, but an acceptable risk and untraceable.

Mary Anne punched the *END* icon on her phone screen and leaning back in her lounge chair, sighed with satisfaction. It was not yet noon of her first day in Miami and already a great deal had been accomplished.

~

"Go slowly down this street," she ordered. The driver slowed and Mary Anne studied the single story ranchers along NW 3rd Street in West Little Havana, most of which posted no street number. It had been twelve years since she had been on this street as a sixteen-year-old runaway.

The cab passed a white stucco house with barred windows and a fence around the perimeter. Tropical vegetation nearly obscured the low structure. *This is it.* She remembered the faded pink pelican yard ornament beside the front fence gate.

She had the cabbie drive a block further and then pull to the curb. "Wait here," she said, handing the driver a twenty dollar bill.

Pulling on her backpack, she walked to the house and rapped on the screen door. A minute passed without an answer. *No signs of life except a window air conditioner running. But I bet he's in there.*

Opening the screen door, she rapped sharply again on the main door and a minute later began to bang repeatedly with her fist loud enough to wake Gerry Stine.

The door opened in mid-swing of her fist, which glanced off the door and hit a restraining chain, eliciting a cry of pain.

"What do you want?" an accented male voice angrily asked from the darkness beyond the door opening.

"I came to see you," replied the girl as she sucked on skinned knuckles. "You helped me twelve years ago and I need your help again."

"I don't know you, or what you're talking about." The door began to close.

"Wait! I can show you your work!," she blurted, reaching into the pocket of her camouflage pants and holding up a driver's license.

"Here. You made this for me. And I've got a birth certificate, too. Allison Cooper. Martinez from the pizza shop sent me to you."

After a long period of silence, the door opened.

~

"This will take some time," he said, "especially the passport. And I'm not sure you've got the money. I want it all up front—ten thousand dollars."

Mary Anne pulled a thick wad of cash from a zippered pocket of her backpack and counted out seven packets of hundred dollar bills.

"One thousand dollars per packet," she said. "Seven thousand upfront is all you'll get. If you're finished by Friday, there will be an extra thousand."

The man looked up in surprise. "All right. Friday at 4:00 PM. You'll bring four thousand dollars more."

"2:00 PM," she replied. "I've got a courier deadline to meet."

CHAPTER FIFTY-FIVE

CALVIN BACON LOOKED AT THE ID ON HIS cell phone and answered immediately. "Bacon here."

"Morning Officer Bacon. Neil Saliker at the crime lab. I've got a match for you on those prints you lifted from the Murray woman's car. We had a set on file from an old assault charge."

"Very cool. I'm in my car. Let me get a piece of paper." Bacon edged his cruiser to the shoulder of the road and pulled out his notebook. "OK. Shoot."

"Gerald Leonard Stine. Age thirty-four. Last known address 3105 Harris Mill Road, Parkton. But let me save you some time. Don't bother going looking for him. He's not there."

"How do you know that?"

"Because another set of prints was pulled on him Saturday down on West Baltimore Street."

Calvin thought about that. "No! Medical examiner's office?"

"Yep. Gerald Stine's not with us anymore."

Calvin whistled. "You know what, Saliker? This is getting really interesting. Thanks. I'll chase that down."

~

Calvin returned to the precinct station at lunchtime and pulled the Stine file. Dan Fry had worked that case, but it didn't look like much

339

---

was happening. Over a Subway Black Forest Ham with green peppers and jalapeños, he quickly perused the sparse file.

Stine's girlfriend reported his departure at 2:00 AM the morning of Murray's accident, and a return just before sunrise. That would fit perfectly with a trip to cut Penny's brake lines.

Incredibly, Stine died of a heroin overdose the same day. That was a pretty big coincidence. Bacon picked a green pepper off the report. Stine died on the job, no less, at some big estate on Hess Road.

And what the hell was his connection with Penny Murray? Did she piss Stine off when he was a patient in the ER? Was he some sort of a spurned suitor?

Or maybe his death wasn't accidental. Maybe he was working for someone else who wanted him dead after his work on Murray's brake lines, although the preliminary autopsy report supported a heroin overdose as the mechanism of death and nothing in the investigative report suggested foul play.

Calvin looked around the office. *Where the hell is Fry? We need to talk.*

He tossed the remains of his sub in the trash, slipped a Rolaid into his mouth to counter the green peppers and jalapeños, and headed out to his cruiser. He needed to talk to Penny Murray about this character. He also needed to let her know that ironically, the guy who tried to kill her was now himself gone from this world.

~

Calvin could see cautious relief wash over Penny Murray's face combined with puzzlement.

"I just don't understand Calvin. I don't have a clue who this guy was or why he'd want to kill me. I've never seen him before in my life," she said staring at Stine's picture. "I'm glad he's dead, but if I knew why, I'd feel a lot better. What if there was someone else behind this?"

"We'd all feel better if we had a motive," said Calvin. "I think I'll swing by the hospital and show these photos to Alex—see if they trigger anything in his mind."

"I don't recognize him Calvin," said Alex Randolph. "Let me do a quick search and see if he's ever been here." Alex accessed the patient search function on his computer and typed in the name.

"Nope. Never been in the ER. There's a half dozen Stines that come up, but none with his name and birthdate." He leaned back in his chair with his arms folded. "So he died the same day as Penny's crash—at work— of a heroin overdose?"

"Yeah. He was a farmhand. They found him dead in a barn on one of those big estates on Hess Road."

Alex sat up in his chair. "Hess Road?"

"Yeah. Why?"

"What was the name of the owners?"

"I think it's owned by the widow of that big car dealer—Williams." Calvin saw Alex's face turn white.

"Oh my God, Calvin. That woman's been after me."

CHAPTER FIFTY-SIX

S AMMY GRIFFITH LEFT CLUB NOUVEAU AT 2:15 AM Thursday morning—earlier than usual, but he was highly motivated to get out of there. Sammy knew literally hundreds of beautiful women and could have almost any of them any time he wanted. But none of them had ever moved him like Mary Anne Hampton. It had been three years since he'd last seen her.

He walked under palm fronds and umbrellas through the sidewalk tables at News Café on Ocean Drive, but there was no trace of the auburn beauty who appeared so frequently in his dreams.

"Sammy." He stopped at the sound of his name and turned. A gorgeous brunette in a long, white cotton dress with buttons all the way down the front sat with her legs crossed and arms folded, smiling at him.

"My God! Mary Anne. You're a brunette."

He walked to her and kissed her on the cheek. Mary Anne grasped his head with both hands and kissed him softly on the lips. "You're still as handsome as ever, Sammy," she breathed. The exotic scent of her breath hit the security chief's brain and his head began to spin.

Sammy swung into a chair. A waiter appeared instantly. "Cognac, please."

"I'd forgotten how beautiful you are. You're a stunning brunette," he said.

"I like natural auburn better, but right now, brunette will do."

"You look like life's been kind to you."

Mary Anne shrugged. "I was in the right place at the right time. My husband died of prostate cancer. I'm pretty well fixed for life. And you, Sammy?"

"How could I leave Club Nouveau? Pirelli pays me well. But no girl has appeared in the stable like Ashley Johansson. I dream about her."

Mary Anne smiled. "And no man has moved me like Sammy Griffith. You know me so well."

~

Mary Anne stretched her naked body—glistening with sweat—on the king-sized bed and sighed. "God, that was good. I needed that." Turning on her right side, she snuggled into Sammy's shoulder.

After a moment of silence, she said softly, "Sammy, I need your help."

"You know there is nothing that I could refuse you."

"There's someone who has been making my life miserable…really miserable—won't leave me alone. Every day is torture. I can't stand it any longer."

"You want me to take care of that?"

"No. I don't want you involved, Sammy. But I know that you know someone who could help me with a permanent solution. Money's no object."

Sammy rose up on his elbow and stared at the liquid hazel eyes. "You're serious, aren't you?"

"I've never been in this kind of situation before, Sammy, and I don't know who else to turn to."

"Tell me about it. Maybe I can help."

"I can't, Sammy. I don't want any possibility that you could be hurt by this. And if you know nothing, no one can hurt you. That's why no one but you can know that I've been in Miami this week, and why I can't see you again until this is over."

Sammy carefully considered her words and exhaled. "Wow. That's a big order."

"Please, Sammy. I'll be grateful to you the rest of my life."

"You know, Mary Anne, even for you I have to think about this. The people that I think you are talking about are not nice people. I've never been involved in anything like this before."

"But that's just the point, Sammy. I don't want you involved. I care about you too much. I just want a contact."

~

Bacon and his superior, Fry, met Thursday over coffee and a box of donut holes from Dunkin' Donuts at the Cockeysville precinct station after morning report.

"How many boxes of those do you eat a day?" Fry asked his corpulent colleague.

"Hey, I brought this box to share. How 'bout a little gratitude?"

"You gonna pass the next physical?"

Bacon patted his belly. "There's an enormous amount of energy stored in here—enough to carry me for miles."

"OK. So let's hear it, Calvin."

"OK, we agree that it's too big a coincidence that Stine died the day after he cut the brake lines," said Bacon. "His employer just *happened* to be Mary Anne Williams, who just *happened* to be putting the make on Alex Randolph big time."

"So Randolph says she asked him to cheat on his fiancé?"

"Yeah. Then she turned bitchy, got angry and stomped off when he said 'no'. This little chick is used to getting what she wants. Penny Murray is in her way."

Fry took a sip of black coffee. "Have you seen her?"

"No."

"Well, when you do, you might conclude that you would not lightly turn down an invitation to screw, although this is looking more and more like you might be screwing a black widow with a bite."

"Did you see that little bit in the autopsy report about finding a long hair on Stine's chest that was reddish-brown in color?" Bacon asked. "Is her hair reddish-brown?"

Fry looked at him silently for a moment. "Yes it is, and yeah I saw that."

"If we could get a sample of her DNA, we could see if the hair came from her."

"And what if her attorney says, 'Yeah, of course that's her hair. She was standing right beside the body when you did your investigation, idiot. Come back to us when you have some real evidence.'

"There's another little problem, Calvin, and that is that we have no evidence of a murder. What do you think the state's attorney will say about that? How did she do it? The medical examiner has ruled the case an accidental death.

"And in any case," continued Fry, "everybody knows everybody up there on the Manor, and they're all screwing each other. There's nothing illegal about putting the make on somebody just because they're engaged.

"So far, we've got nothing except a lot of speculation and some titillating gossip. But, Calvin, my friend, this is the closest we've come to having a motive, and for the moment, I am buying your speculation. Let's go talk to our hot little black widow."

Calvin threw his black-brimmed cap over the cowlick that covered most of the left side of his head, and the two officers climbed into Fry's car for the trip to Ascot Farms.

~

By Thursday morning, Manuela was beside herself. She had not seen or heard from her mistress since the end of her workday on Friday after that man's body was found in the barn. Mary Anne had disappeared for a day or two many times before, but never this long.

Earlier in the week Manuela had been angry. Did it mean nothing to Mary Anne that Manuela was her lover? How could she leave and not tell Manuela where she was going? It was so inconsiderate.

But by Thursday Manuela was physically ill with worry. What if something had happened to her? What if she never came back? Should she tell someone that her employer was missing? And who should she tell? Or what if Mary Anne was in trouble and Manuela had done nothing to help her?

Over and over again Manuela had replayed in her mind the image of Mary Anne walking back from the barn to the house on Thursday afternoon. The next day they had found the man dead. What did that mean? Mary Anne seemed very happy when she returned from the barn. She had even stripped her and made love to her for the first time in weeks.

Was it possible that her mistress had killed him? Manuela shook her head as if to rid herself of such an evil thought. It was not possible.

~

The girl's English was not so good. Fry was getting frustrated. "So what day did you see her last?" he asked again slowly and loudly.

"I see her Friday," the girl replied biting her lower lip.

"And you have not heard from her since?"

"No Señor."

"And you don't know where she went?"

"No Señor."

"She didn't tell you when she was coming back?" The girl shook her head.

"Did you know she was leaving?" Another shake of the head.

Fry looked at Bacon. He wasn't sure whether the girl simply knew absolutely nothing or whether she was hiding something behind the apparent language barrier.

She was as nervous as a cat, but she was probably an illegal alien terrified of authorities and deportation.

"Do you know where Mrs. Williams lived before she married Mr. Williams?"

"I think she live in Miami."

"Have you tried calling her cell phone?" Fry asked.

"No Señor, I no know the…number."

"Are you worried about Mrs. Williams, Manuela?"

"Oh yes! I am worried."

"Mrs. Williams has never been gone this long without telling you, has she?"

"No. Never."

"What if something has happened to her? What if she's in trouble? She's a very rich woman. What if she's been kidnapped?"

The young woman bit her lower lip. She was familiar with kidnappings.

"Manuela, Mrs. Williams may need our help." Fry said earnestly, leaning forward in his chair. Manuela nodded.

"We can help find her and make sure that she's OK, but to do that we need your help. Do you want to help find her?"

"Yes," said the housekeeper, a single tear trickling down her cheek.

"It will be very easy for you to help us, Manuela. We will write up a missing person report, and all you have to do is sign it. Would you do that?"

Manuela was consumed by fear—fear for Mary Anne, and fear that if she signed papers she would be discovered and deported. But what if Mary Anne really was in trouble? What if the policeman was right and she had been kidnapped? Manuela couldn't bear the thought.

"Yes," she said, tears now streaming down her face. "I will sign."

~

The two officers walked outside to the cruiser carrying photos of Mary Anne Williams collected from the mansion, one of her hair brushes, and other assorted evidence. Incredibly, there had been no computer in the house, although there was a wireless network. Calvin spoke first. "It pains me to say this, Fry, but that was brilliant."

"We don't have a snowball's chance in hell of convincing a state's attorney or judge that there's enough probable cause to get search warrants or subpoenas to go looking for Mary Anne Williams," said Fry. "But if we have a missing person report, we are obligated under the law to do everything we can to find her, aren't we?"

Bacon smiled. "That's why you make the big bucks, Sergeant."

"Calvin I'm taking you off all other duties effective tomorrow morning. I want you to find this woman. Get her into the NCIC missing persons database. Check her credit cards, phone records, airline reservations, ping her cell phone—everything—but find her."

CHAPTER FIFTY-SEVEN

MARY ANNE CAREFULLY EXAMINED THE documents bearing the name of Allison Corbett Becker: a Florida driver's license, U.S. passport, and a Florida Power & Light utility bill. The address utilized in the documents was a non-existent address in a high-end section of South Beach that Mary Anne herself had provided, along with a birthplace and date extracted from her fictional outline of Allison Becker's life.

Sitting in the dark room with shades drawn, she flipped through the fresh pages of the passport with mounting excitement. She loved this game. The forgeries were of exquisite quality—at least to Mary Anne, they appeared completely authentic.

How did he do it? Were the driver's license and passport stolen blanks? In any case, the documents opened up a whole new world of possibilities—including untraceable escape should the need arise—and they were now in her possession.

She placed her hands in her lap and sighed with pleasure. "You've done an extraordinary job, and you had it done by 2:00 PM today—Friday. So...four thousand dollars more," she said, passing the stone-faced man a pack of cash restrained by rubber bands, "plus an extra thousand on retainer in case I ever need you in a hurry."

Without counting the cash, the man grunted, rose, and unceremoniously showed her to the door.

~

To the papers she had already signed, Mary Anne added a photocopy of Allison Becker's driver's license and the utility bill from Florida Power & Light. She slipped the papers into a FedEx Pak, followed by a separate envelope containing four thousand eight hundred and fifty dollars in cash. She completed filling out the international air waybill to an address in Dominica, entering a dollar value of five dollars in the customs box, and listing the contents as brochures.

By 3:00 PM she had passed the FedEx package to a Fontainebleau desk clerk and wandered out to the pool. Twenty laps later, she stretched her long legs out on a cabana bed, ordered a frozen margarita, and lifted a private toast to Ali Becker.

~

With a profound sense of foreboding, Sammy eased the Porsche into an empty parking space one-half block south of Columbia Coffee at 4:28 PM.

The kind of contact for which Mary Anne had begged him was not easy to come by. There were three degrees of separation between Sammy and the telephone number written on the piece of paper in his pocket. Getting that number had begun with a whispered word to a regular customer at Club Nouveau to whom Sammy would rather not have owed anything. But once he had made that contact, he was committed. There was no turning back. He feared that in return, someday the customer would call in a favor of a kind that he could not refuse.

Working as security chief at Club Nouveau required him to occasionally overlook a few things that the law actually considered to be criminal acts. But in Sammy's judgment, they were all victimless crimes. Without difficulty he was able to preserve his self-image as a patriotic, law-abiding citizen and veteran of the United States Army.

This was different. Sammy had killed many men—how many, he wasn't sure—but they were all enemy combatants who, given the chance, would have gleefully slit his throat. Never before had he participated in a venture that he knew would lead to murder, even if at someone else's hand.

He did his best to justify his involvement. Mary Anne could take care of herself, so whoever this guy was, he must be a real prick, and Mary Anne must feel herself in danger with no other options. He made the contact for her, he finally realized, because he loved her.

And why? She was as free as a bird in flight. He had not seen or heard from her for three years, and quite likely might never see her again after today. What was it about her that so intoxicated him and so clouded his judgment?

He looked at his watch. Mary Anne had insisted that there be no telephone or texting communication between them and that all information be exchanged in person. When Sammy figured that there were only seconds left until precisely 4:00 PM, he exited the Porsche and walked toward Columbia Coffee.

Halfway to the entrance he glimpsed a slender young woman walking toward him through the crowd in a gray tank top and camouflage cargo pants. Her eyes were shaded by a baseball cap and black sunglasses, but there was no mistaking her elegant, confident walk. As she strode past him, her arm swung out and in one smooth motion Sammy deposited a piece of paper in her palm. It was the last time he would ever touch his lover's skin.

~

Calvin Bacon was at his desk first thing Friday morning to begin the arduous task of tracking down Mary Anne Williams. After entering everything he knew about Mary Anne Williams into the National Crime Information Center missing persons database, came the painful task of working the phones. Without knowing any of the woman's commercial relationships, his first call went to Sovereign Bank in Hereford, figuring that she would have an account at a local bank.

With a lot of cajoling, he was able to talk the local manager into confirming that Mary Anne Williams had an account at Sovereign. Fifteen minutes later he had faxed a search warrant to the bank's security officer and within another half hour quickly learned that payments were made monthly to AT&T and CapitalOne.

Sovereign further confirmed that Mary Anne Williams had made a cash withdrawal of nine thousand dollars on Saturday morning, August twentieth at 11:50 AM. There had been little other activity in the last month.

This was to be the highlight of Calvin's day. The rest of his day turned out to be a fruitless exercise in frustration. By 3:00 PM his mood had turned foul. Despite the air conditioning, he was mopping sweat from his forehead with a white handkerchief and mumbling curses.

Mary Anne Williams had literally vanished into thin air. Her cell phone hadn't been used since the day before Stine's death, and her wireless carrier was unable to locate a signal from her phone. Incredibly, Bacon couldn't even find a trace of her in on-line social media.

Her last credit card charge was ten days ago at a local gas station. Although Calvin had only had time to contact about a third of the airlines serving BWI airport, his painstaking check with the air carriers revealed no reservations or passengers in Williams' name in the period since Friday, August nineteenth, the last day that she had been seen.

A DMV search turned up two vehicles registered in her name: one a new Mercedes Roadster that must have cost more than two years of Calvin's salary, and the other—rather inexplicably—a 2003 Saturn. Calvin remembered seeing the black Mercedes gleaming in the Williams's driveway, but could not remember seeing the Saturn.

His desk phone rang.

"Bacon here."

"What have you got so far, Calvin?" asked Fry.

"She's gone, Sergeant—vanished. There's not a trace of her out there. But she's got plenty of cash—she withdrew nine thousand bucks in cash on Saturday from Sovereign. And she owns a 2003 Saturn that I didn't see at the farm. We need to check on that."

"I'll stop by the farm on the way home. What's another late dinner? If the Saturn's missing I'll have you add it to the NCIC report."

CHAPTER FIFTY-EIGHT

PENNY WORKED HER FIRST SHIFT BACK IN THE ER schedule on Thursday night, seven days after the accident—or should I say after the attempted murder—and then she doubled back again on Friday night. She had an affection for her trashed Honda Pilot which she felt had protected the driver's compartment and saved her life, so she drove a brand new 2011 white Honda Pilot—just like her old one—which we had purchased on Tuesday.

Long ago she had scheduled vacation days for Saturday through Wednesday, corresponding with the anticipated three-day duration of my malpractice trial, which was scheduled to commence bright and early Monday morning, assuming that Franklin Stern didn't blow out his aorta again.

My last shift prior to the trial was Saturday day shift, so Penny and I managed to keep to our usual tradition of being off together on Sunday—riding lesson day.

For the past week, my colleagues had graciously insisted that I work only day shifts so that I could be with Penny at night as she was recuperating—a process much more psychological than physical. As I lay awake much of the night watching her fitful sleep, my own emotions swung from heartbreak for Penny to burning hatred for whoever had done this. At this point in time, incredible as it seemed to me, Mary Anne Williams occupied the top spot on the list—actually the only spot on the list. But it seemed incomprehensible that such a woman could be a conscienceless sociopath.

Penny had appeared slightly more relaxed since the death of Gerry Stine, but all was still not clear and she was not yet back to her old self. Although perhaps we had a motive—me, to my great discomfort—it was still all conjecture and it was hard to figure out why according to the police that Williams had disappeared.

Even assuming that she was behind both Stine's cutting of the brake lines as well as his death, Williams had no way of knowing that the police had found Stine's fingerprints on the Honda and had thereby tied Stine to the attempted murder. So it didn't make sense that she would be on the run from the police. She was obviously still out there someplace though, and no one had a clue where she was, what was going through her mind, or what were her intentions.

Perhaps the cruelest impact of this disaster was Penny's fear of having her children near her. She missed them terribly. On Sunday and Tuesday, we had driven to Annapolis so she could be with them. We had all decided that no useful purpose would be served by telling the children of the event that nearly killed their mother, so they were blissfully unaware that anything was amiss, and thrilled to be spending a week with Maimeó and Pop, as the admiral preferred to be called.

I was furious that Penny, at the time of her approaching wedding, had to fear for her own life and that of her kids. She deserved some peace and happiness. Between Patrick Murray's death, her shooting in the ER, and now an attempt on her life, the events of the last three years would have made an utter basket case of any other man or woman I knew.

As for the last two weeks, life was chaotic with an approaching wedding, malpractice trial, attempted murder investigation, and the start of a new school year at a new school for the kids. This is the stuff out of which movies are made.

I had cautiously offered to delay the wedding as a means of reducing the pressure, but Penny had steadfastly refused, saying that she would allow no one to control her life, including whoever it was that wanted her dead. Besides which, she would feel safer being at the farm with Ruth and me. Her best reason, however, was that she wanted nothing more in life than to be married to me, which I had to admit was very sound reasoning.

Tom and Denise brought the kids back to the farm for Catherine's riding lesson. There was now little choice about the kids returning to Monkton, whether Williams had been found or not. Classes at nearby St. Mark's Country Day School started the next day, Monday, August twenty-ninth.

Sunday was beautiful—cool and crystal-clear with the first hints of the approaching fall. We all sat on lawn chairs with drinks in hand mid-afternoon watching as Sally patiently taught Catherine how to assert her will over Abigail.

"Penny, you know I could stay here next week to help with getting these little urchins off to school while Alex is in trial," her mother suggested. "I know you want to be at the courthouse."

Penny giggled. "Mom, do you realize that with you and me, and Ruth and Alex, the adult supervisors would outnumber the kids two-to-one? And by now, I'd think you'd be looking for escape from those two."

"My grandchildren are angels," Denise replied.

"Really, Mom, it's going to be OK. I'm going to drive the kids to school in the morning before the trial, and if I'm late getting home, Ruth's going to pick them up. It's only three miles from here.

"You've done enough with keeping the kids this week. I was a nervous wreck, but I felt safe knowing that the U.S. Navy was watching over them," Penny said, smiling and gazing at her dad. "With Stine dead and Williams missing, I'm feeling a lot more comfortable. Ruth will be here every night, and Alex, almost every night."

"Ruth and Maggie are our first line of defense," I said. "I'm just the reserves."

CHAPTER FIFTY-NINE

MONDAY, ON BOTH DAY ONE OF MY TRIAL
and the start of school, Penny drove the kids to their
first day at St. Mark's Country Day School in the heart
of My Lady's Manor, and I headed off to Towson to the courthouse.

In the category of silver linings in clouds, I was aware enough of
my own emotions to note that I carried remarkably little anxiety about
this trial. An attempted murder of a member of your family has a way
of focusing your mind on what's important.

I was certainly not pleased about having my name raked through
the mud for the next three days, but the outcome of this trial was way
down on my list of concerns. The relative peace that I enjoyed was
probably also related to the fact that I was personally convinced that I
had done the right thing for Robert Kline—the same thing that I
would have done for Catherine, or Jack.

I was a little bummed not to have the opportunity to see Catherine
and Jack's reaction to the little school where they would likely spend
the next eight years, but to the American system of justice that was not
a valid excuse for delaying a civil trial. It mattered little today if Penny
was late because today was jury selection, which, unless your own ass
was on the line, was perhaps a less interesting exercise than watching
the trial itself.

Nevertheless, since my own ass was indeed on the line, I watched with interest as Franklin Stern and Kathleen Stefanik engaged in their first skirmishes with peremptory challenges of prospective jurors, a process known in attorney-speak as *voir dire*. I don't blame them for having their own little secret professional language, as I daily speak to patients in Latin-based terms that may as well be derived from a native language of Venus or Mars as far as the patients are concerned.

Frank did not hesitate, of course, to strike a juror whose sister was a pediatrician, and Kathleen was not enthusiastic about a woman whose brother had received substantial sums in settlement from Exxon from a famous ground pollution case in Harford County resulting from a leaking service station gasoline tank.

Being the completely objective scientist that I am, it was interesting to me to watch my own reactions to prospective jurors. I found myself looking into their faces and trying to discern character, the definition of which was whether they would likely vote me not guilty of gross negligence.

As the process droned on, Judge Theresa Bower looked to me to grow a little bit fidgety. Finally about 10:15, she called for a ten-minute recess. I absently wondered if perhaps she had to wee-wee, but if so, that was OK with me because I needed to dump a load of coffee myself.

When I rose and turned to head out to the men's room, I spotted Penny two-thirds of the way back the courtroom, which was now packed to the gills. She smiled, and I felt gratitude that there was at least one person here who loved Alex Randolph because I was about to come under attack in full view of a national audience.

To our great dismay, Penny was back in the national news again, first for the fiery accident and then again after someone leaked the news that the accident was attempted murder to the media. Her travails contributed to also getting *me* back in the news. The double jeopardy of a murder attempt and a malpractice trial for the celebrity couple was like throwing a bucket of chum into a pool of sharks. The courtroom was packed with media.

Fortunately—or unfortunately—Penny's cell phone was lost in the crash, so she had a new phone with an unpublished number that had not yet been discovered by probing journalists, producers, and publishers. But we were beginning to see paparazzi again slowly driving past the farm, who occasionally were lucky enough to catch one of us leaving the farm in our car and follow in pursuit.

This was my first malpractice case, and since all my other friends had already been sued, I had always enjoyed basking in the illusion that there was something special about me. But, I guess not. There is something quite shattering about reading the description of yourself as being grossly negligent and incompetent; as being someone who has inflicted harm on a patient who naïvely entrusted you with their life.

To the opposing attorneys who laugh and share drinks together after work, it's just business—another day in the office. But to those of us who are sued; who see our names in the newspapers, and in my case in the celebrity media; who run into patients in the grocery store who now look at us and wonder, it's an emotionally wrenching experience. For us, the lawsuits call into question the very core of our self image—of who we thought we were.

~

Shortly after 1:00 PM, the war began. This was a very important case for Franklin Stern—his first shot at national media coverage and all the fame and riches that might bring. With twelve jurors and three alternates now seated, he rose from his chair to his full height and delivered his lengthy opening salvo.

In a hushed voice, Frank told the story of a concerned family's arrival in an ER late at night, bearing their ill eight-year-old son, conscientiously seeking skilled and careful care for their only child.

But as fate would have it, the physician to whom they entrusted their son's life was Dr. Alex Randolph, who without adequate testing cavalierly blew off their son as merely having a virus and sent him home.

Two days later, a physician at another hospital immediately diagnosed Robert as having a life-threatening ruptured appendix and rushed him to the operating room, wondering why the family hadn't sought treatment sooner. Of course they had, but the physician they were forced to see at Mason-Dixon Regional Medical Center was completely negligent, failing to order the studies which are the recognized gold standard of care for diagnosing appendicitis.

By this time, life-threatening infection was running rampant within the small boy's abdomen and infiltrating his bloodstream. His temperature soared to one hundred and four and pus oozed from drains that had to be inserted into his abdomen. His pulse rose and his blood pressure fell as he slipped into shock. In the intensive care unit, his doctors fought back with powerful antibiotics, and poured liters of fluid into his bloodstream to combat the shock.

It took ten days and the best efforts of an enormously skilled team of physicians to save Robert's life. During that time Robert suffered greatly. Today he bears multiple scars on his abdomen in testimony to the grossly inadequate care at Mason-Dixon hospital that precipitated this nightmare.

As for Robert's poor parents, they didn't sleep for ten anguished days as they prayed to God that their only child would survive. Neither parent, of course, would leave the bedside of their son. Both lost two weeks of pay, and ultimately, Susan Straley would lose her job as a result of making her son's recovery her first priority.

As Frank revealed the horrifying story of Robert Kline's ordeal, waving his arms with flourishes of indignation, eight women and four men who would be called upon to pass judgment looked at the fresh-scrubbed, now eleven-year-old boy sitting at the plaintiff's table with wonderment that he had survived.

"In the next several days, good ladies and gentlemen of the jury," continued Frank, "we will demonstrate to you beyond a shadow of a doubt that the needless anguish and suffering of Robert Straley and his caring parents was the direct result of the gross negligence of Dr. Alexander Randolph."

I vowed to myself not to read, watch, or listen to any of the media coverage.

CHAPTER SIXTY

MY DEFENDER, KATHLEEN STEFANIK, ROSE and slowly walked to the front of the jury box. A tall, slender woman with swept-back gray hair, immaculately dressed in a linen jacket and skirt that fell just below the knee, she was the picture of dignity and elegance.

She stopped six feet from the jury box, bowing her head in thought for a moment, then raised her head and silently searched the eyes of the men and women before her, whose rapt attention she now commanded.

"Ladies and gentlemen of the jury," she began in a clear voice, "what happened to Robert Straley—now three years ago—was a dreadful thing. It is hard to imagine the anguish of his parents as they watched their only son valiantly fight for his life, aided by a caring team of doctors and nurses. For ten days they hardly slept, fearing the loss of their most precious treasure. Hearts broken, they shed tears at every needle stick, and every dressing change as they saw their child's face contort with pain. We will dispute neither this family's suffering, nor the conclusion that much of it was probably needless.

"What we *will* dispute, is the notion that Dr. Alexander Randolph was in any way responsible for that suffering, or in any way negligent in the performance of his duties. Indeed, we will vigorously assert that Dr.

Randolph—based on the evolution of Robert's illness at that time—utilized completely appropriate clinical judgment that was fully compatible with the community standard of care. Moreover, we will show that Dr. Randolph's approach to the diagnosis of Robert's condition reflected uncommon knowledge of the most current concerns in the medical literature regarding the diagnosis of appendicitis in children.

"We will learn during the course of this trial that appendicitis is a disease with an insidious onset that frequently cannot be diagnosed in its earliest stages, but when suspected, *can* be safely diagnosed in a timely fashion by careful follow-up and observation.

"Finally, you will learn that Dr. Randolph made specific recommendations at the time of Robert's discharge that—had they been followed—would likely have prevented this young boy's suffering."

With the conclusion of the second opening statement, my trial began in earnest.

~

"Your honor," intoned Frank, "I would like to call Dr. Irwin Laffer to the stand for purposes of qualifying him as an expert witness." Frank was calling out his big gun as the very first witness.

Tall and gangly with a gigantic Adam's apple and imperious bushy eyebrows, my fellow University of Pennsylvania undergraduate alumnus rose and took the stand. Perhaps the size of his larynx accounted for the reason that he wore a shirt with a collar two sizes too big, but that would fall under the category of petty sniping, which is unbecoming. I decided to call him Ichabod.

Frank ran the forty-something associate professor of surgery through his sterling credentials, including an undergraduate degree from Penn. He looked familiar to me. But that was likely my imagination. He was probably five or six years ahead of me.

I figured they must not be paying him enough at Penn, since here he was in Baltimore, taking a day off of work to put the screws to one of his fellow alumni. Of course, his wife could also have caught him in bed with another woman, or maybe he had two kids about to go off to college, both events demanding inordinate amounts of cash.

Judge Bower qualified Laffer as an expert witness, and Frank moved on.

"Dr. Laffer, can you tell us exactly what you do in the course of your duties as an associate professor of surgery at the University of Pennsylvania School of Medicine?"

"I am an attending surgeon responsible for the surgical care of patients admitted to University Hospital under my service. In addition, I am responsible for teaching and supervising resident surgeons in training, as well as medical students rotating through the department of general surgery."

"Do cases of appendicitis fall under the department of general surgery, Doctor?"

"Yes. Appendicitis is one of our most common diagnoses."

"Can you tell us about the depth of your experience in caring for patients with acute appendicitis?"

Ichabod lowered his head in humility. "Let's just say extensive—" he said, "hundreds of cases."

"Am I correct, Doctor, that you have written a number of articles on appendicitis that have been published in national medical journals?"

"Yes, that is correct."

"And really, you are considered an expert on appendicitis among your peers in the medical community, isn't that so?"

Ichabod smiled modestly. "Well, I *did* write the chapter on appendicitis in *Carson's Textbook of Surgery*."

"Well, thank you for taking time from your busy schedule to be with us today. I think we can all benefit from your expertise and analysis in this tragic case." *Oh, please Frank. You've only paid Ichabod ten or twelve thousand bucks to be here.*

"You've had an opportunity to carefully study all of the medical records pertaining to the case of Robert Straley?"

"Yes, I have."

"Can you tell us please, Doctor Laffer, what happened to young

Robert after he presented to the emergency department of Greater Baltimore Medical Center?"

Ichabod immediately went into professorial mode, speaking loudly and clearly with utter authority.

"Certainly. The triage nurse at GBMC was highly suspicious of appendicitis in Robert. She was so concerned that she pushed him to the front of the line and brought him immediately into the emergency department where he was promptly seen by the staff emergency physician. She, too, suspected appendicitis and had the good judgment to immediately order a CAT scan—the gold standard imaging study for diagnosing appendicitis. The nurse and the ER physician were both right.

Very nice touch, Ichabod. Even a lowly nurse could diagnose this case.

"Can you tell us—in layman's terms—what that CAT scan showed?"

"The CAT scan, unfortunately, showed not only evidence of a ruptured appendix, but also suggested the spread of infection from the appendix throughout Robert's abdominal cavity, a life-threatening condition called *peritonitis.*

"You see," Ichabod said, turning to the jury, "an infected appendix not only contains pus, but also intestinal contents, or feces, which contain billions of bacteria. When the appendix ruptures its contents are released into the abdominal cavity." A female juror made a yuck face.

"And can you rely on this x-ray study, Dr. Laffer? How accurate is a CAT scan in diagnosing appendicitis?"

"A CAT scan, or CT as we call it, has been the absolute gold standard for diagnosing appendicitis for nearly two decades," Ichabod repeated. "In multiple studies in the medical literature, the diagnostic accuracy ranges between ninety-five to ninety-eight percent."

"So a CAT scan is very accurate. Does it take a long time to do this test?"

"It's very fast. The actual study itself can be performed in less than ten minutes."

"I see," said Frank, like this was amazing news, "so this rapid, highly accurate test was ordered immediately by the second physician who saw Robert Straley?"

"That is correct. It was in the first set of orders entered by the emergency physician at GBMC."

"So very quickly, this ER physician at Greater Baltimore Medical Center established an accurate diagnosis. What happened next?"

"Robert was very quickly seen in consultation by an attending surgeon who rushed him to the operating room within two hours of Robert's arrival. He, of course, removed Robert's appendix, and did his best to *irrigate*—or wash out—the feces and infection that had now spread throughout Robert's abdomen. The surgeon even made an additional incision to insert a small tube to help drain pus and fluid from the abdominal cavity, but it was nearly too late."

"Why was it nearly too late, Doctor?"

"Because during the course of the surgery, Robert went into shock from *sepsis*—meaning that the infection had now entered his bloodstream. His blood pressure fell dangerously low into the sixties, and his heart rate dramatically rose into the one-forties."

"Other complications occurred too, didn't they?"

"Yes. This gets rather technical, so bear with me for a moment and I'll try to explain what happened next," Ichabod said condescendingly.

"Very shortly after surgery—in the intensive care unit—Robert also developed multiple organ dysfunction syndrome, or MODS, as we call it. This is when multiple organs in the body start to fail because of the shock.

"In Robert's case, he developed acute respiratory distress syndrome where his lungs filled up with fluid, requiring him to remain on a ventilator after surgery. The oxygen content of his blood fell dangerously low."

"Do patients usually have to be on a ventilator after surgery for appendicitis, Doctor Laffer?"

"No indeed. In fact, they usually don't need a ventilator at all, and sometimes go home from the hospital the same day of the surgery.

"OK, so when you are on a ventilator, you have a tube going through your mouth and throat into your lungs, and a machine breathing for you, is that correct?"

"Yes, that's correct. You can't talk or completely close your mouth, so your mouth and tongue get dry." *Now we're building the suffering part.*

"How long did Robert have to be on a ventilator?"

"For four days."

"And were there any other complications?

"Yes. Robert's kidneys also began to fail. His urine output dropped to almost nothing for a day before it began to pick back up again."

"So all these complications of a simple appendicitis—which sometimes requires only same-day surgery—occurred in Robert Straley. And were these complications dangerous, Doctor?"

"Highly dangerous. Robert almost died. He was lucky. The mortality rate for septic shock with multiple organ dysfunction syndrome in many studies approaches fifty percent."

"Is it your opinion, Dr. Laffer, that these horrible complications that nearly ended Robert's life; that this suffering and expense could have been avoided if Robert's appendicitis had been diagnosed earlier?"

"Yes, most certainly."

"Dr. Laffer, let's go back for a moment to Robert's first visit to an ER, two days before he was seen at Greater Baltimore Medical Center. Have you reviewed those medical records carefully?"

"Yes, I have."

"And on that first visit, do the records show that Robert was seen by Dr. Alex Randolph at Mason-Dixon Regional Medical Center?"

"Yes, they do."

"With what symptoms did Robert present at that first visit?"

"He presented with approximately eight hours of abdominal pain and three episodes of vomiting."

"Are these symptoms that would cause a reasonable and careful physician to be concerned about appendicitis?"

"Absolutely. Appendicitis is the most common surgical disease encountered in an emergency department. It often starts with vague abdominal pain that is poorly localized, and vomiting is quite common."

"Would the fact that Robert's pain had not yet localized to the right lower quadrant of his abdomen and that he was not yet tender over his appendix lessen your concern that Robert might have appendicitis?"

"Absolutely not," said Ichabod with conviction. "Localization of pain to the right lower quadrant coupled with vomiting is present in only fifty percent of cases. If you didn't investigate patients with Robert's poorly localized symptoms further, you would miss fifty percent of all patients with acute appendicitis—a totally unacceptable miss rate."

"So, what's a doctor to do in this circumstance? What could Dr. Randolph have done to avoid missing this diagnosis?"

"It's very simple," intoned Ichabod, "even a medical student knows that the way to avoid missing this life-threatening diagnosis is by doing a CAT scan."

"Is there anything else that Dr. Randolph should have done that would have prevented this tragedy?"

"Certainly if he had obtained consultation from a qualified surgeon, it is highly unlikely that this diagnosis would have been missed."

"Anything else?"

"Well, he could also have ordered an ultrasound study of the appendix. They are not as good as CTs, but they're still pretty good. In the right hands, they catch as many as eighty to ninety percent of cases."

"So if I may summarize, Dr. Randolph failed to make this diagnosis in two ways: first by failing to order a CAT scan, or even an ultrasound study, and second, by failing to obtain expert surgical consultation that could have spared Robert and his family this terrible ordeal. Is that correct?"

"You are correct."

"A key issue, Dr. Laffer. Do you believe that this failure on the part of Dr. Randolph constituted negligence?"

"I believe that Dr. Randolph was grossly negligent in the performance of his duties," replied Ichabod, looking directly at the twelve grim faces in the jury box.

Kathleen Stefanik was entirely silent during the lengthy testimony of Dr. Irwin Laffer, raising not a single objection.

CHAPTER SIXTY-ONE

MIGUEL HERNANDEZ WATCHED THE GIRL dressed in cargo pants, a frayed black tank top and aviator sunglasses climb into his cab. On the seat beside her she threw a worn, green backpack. A long black ponytail flowed out the back of a white Miami Heat baseball cap. This was not his usual Fontainebleau fare.

But despite the unglamorous attire, the girl carried herself with confident authority. Miguel couldn't see her eyes, but her face had elegant lines with high-cut cheekbones. No doubt she was a college student born to the rich and the beautiful, who carried in her pocket an unlimited credit card.

One of the little games that made the day pass faster for Miguel was to guess where his clients were headed, and in this case his guess was somewhere on South Beach along the ocean. Where else would a rich young girl go in Miami carrying a backpack?

The doorman slammed shut the door and Miguel pulled away from the curb. "*Buenos dias*, Miss. Where to?"

Without comment, the girl provided an address off 84th Street in Hialeah. Miguel frowned and involuntarily his foot came off the gas pedal. That was not a section of town through which he wanted to drive.

"Are you sure of that address, Miss? That is not a nice

neighborhood. It's very dangerous over there for a pretty young girl." Amid blowing horns, Miguel pulled the cab to the curb.

Mary Anne checked the dashboard ID photo and found the driver's name. "I'm very certain, Miguel." Reaching into the front seat, she held out a hundred dollar bill. "Not only do I want you to take me there, but I want you to wait for me while I see someone. And when I come back out, there will be another one hundred dollars for you, plus your fare."

~

With a kick, Mary Anne sent the plastic Pepsi bottle sailing out of her path, climbed the single concrete step, and pushed open the scarred wooden door. As her eyes adjusted to the light in the quiet, dark room, she was able to make out a bar along the left wall, behind which stood a barkeeper silently drying a glass. Two patrons sat on red-cushioned chrome stools and stared at her over half empty glasses of beer, cigarette smoke slowly rising in perfect helixes above their heads.

Empty, dark booths lined the right wall. At the rear of the long narrow building, two men in white tank shirts stood just outside a cone of dim light from a single lamp above a pool table. Bending at the waist, the shorter man pumped a cue stick, sending two sharp cracks echoing around the silent room. *One of those two is my contact*, she thought.

Pulse pounding, she briskly walked to the rear of the room, heels clicking loudly so they would know that she was coming and was unafraid. She stopped four feet from the table and silently stared at the two light-skinned young Latinos with shaved heads and thin mustaches. The short one broke the silence. "You like pool?" he asked.

"No."

He smiled, maintaining eye contact. "Then maybe I can buy you a drink."

"Maybe I can buy *you* a drink," replied Mary Anne.

Now he laughed out loud. "Sit down," he said, pointing to the nearest booth. "I pay for the drinks. Roberto, a round of tequila," he yelled to the barkeeper. Mary Anne slipped off her backpack and slid into the booth.

Pleasantries over, the man placed his forearms on the table and leaned in toward Mary Anne. "Do not waste my time, woman," he said in a low voice. "What do you want?"

"I want your name first. I don't do business with people without a name."

The man leaned back and folded his arms. "Call me Raoul."

"Tell your friend to get lost, Raoul," she said looking the taller man directly in the eyes."

Raoul laughed again. "You have a lot of balls for a little white whore."

"My business is very private."

"This is Facundo, my bother. He stays."

Mary Anne looked at the folded arms, the right of which displayed a crude tattoo of a pentagon. On Raoul's left forearm was tattooed the characters "MSXIII". She had wondered who would be the hit man, and now she knew. Raoul was a member of *Mara Salvatruca*, or *MS-13*, a Latin gang with Salvadoran roots known for drug distribution, child prostitution, and utter brutality. *Perfect.*

"Your name?" he said, snapping his fingers.

"Alice Cooper. I've been told that you could provide me with services."

"What, you need a good fuck, Alice?" Raoul said, turning to his brother and erupting with laughter. The bartender slid three shot glasses of tequila onto the table.

"Your dick's not big enough."

The laughter ceased and Raoul's eyes narrowed. "You like living on the edge, don't you, bitch? I can only guarantee your safety for thirty more seconds, and then you'd best be out that door."

"I need someone eliminated. They're in another state. But it's a woman, and I'm not sure you've got the stomach for it."

Raoul hesitated and stared at her. "How do I know you're not wearing a wire?"

Mary Anne slid out of the booth and stood. Unbuttoning her cargo pants, she let them fall over her narrow hips to the floor,

368

revealing a pink thong with a puffy crotch. Next, she pulled her tank top up above bare breasts.

"Satisfied?" she asked, standing before the two gawking men. She quickly dressed and slid back into the booth.

Raoul sat in thought for a few moments, and then upended his shot glass. "You don't have that kind of money."

"Name your price."

Raoul wiped his mouth with the back of his hand. "Fifty thousand dollars…plus expenses."

The girl reached into her backpack, pulling out five wads of cash and placing them on the table.

"Twenty-five thousand down, and twenty-five thousand when the job is finished. We leave for Maryland on Wednesday. I go along on the operation."

Raoul stared at her incredulously. "You're out of your mind, bitch. No woman goes on no operation."

Mary Anne reached out, pulling back the twenty-five thousand and stuffing it into her backpack. She slid off the end of the booth seat, turned, and wordlessly walked briskly for the door, heart pounding; heels clicking loudly. She wasn't certain that they would cave to her bluff. Moreover, now she was at risk for simply being murdered and the two fuckers making off with the cash.

"Wait!"

Mary Anne stopped in her tracks, but didn't turn.

"OK, cunt. You're on."

CHAPTER SIXTY-TWO

JUDGE BOWER LOOKED AT HER WATCH AT THE conclusion of Ichabod's testimony and grimaced. "Ladies and gentlemen, it's getting late in the day and I'm afraid that we are going to run over in testimony this afternoon.

"Dr. Laffer can only be present today, and we will have to allow the defense adequate time for cross-examination. I apologize ahead of time for the lateness of the hour. So let's take a brief fifteen-minute recess, and I want everyone to be back and ready to go by 4:30."

Kathleen and I huddled for five minutes reviewing the potential holes in Ichabod's testimony before I made my way toward the rear door of the courtroom, meeting Penny in the aisle. No sooner had we exited the courtroom doors into the hallway, when flashbulbs started to go off and microphones were shoved in our faces. We pushed our way through the crowd to the restrooms without comment or conversation.

~

"Dr. Laffer," began Kathleen Stefanik on cross-examination, "you've been taking out appendices for a long time, right?"

Quite a few years," he said with pride.

"How long have you been performing appendectomies?"

He thought for a moment. "Sixteen years, not counting residency."

"How many cases do you think you might have done?"

"Oh, I don't know. Probably over eight-hundred," he said with a modest smile."

"Good for you. That's a lot. I would certainly think that qualifies you as an expert, do you agree?"

A hint of confusion crossed Laffer's face. He wasn't sure where this line of questioning was leading. Finally he responded, "Yes, I believe that has already been established by the court."

"Actually, we have heard that you have written quite a few papers on appendicitis that were published in highly respected journals, correct?"

"Yes, I have," he responded cautiously.

"Have you ever taken out an appendix without first doing a CAT scan?"

"Well, yes, of course. CAT scans have only been around for maybe fifteen years or so."

"How did you decide to take out an appendix before CAT scans?"

"On a clinical basis. You looked to see if the patient had fever, you examined the belly to see if they had tenderness over the appendix, and you evaluated the white blood cell count."

"Did you ever get sued for missing an appendicitis, Dr. Laffer?"

"No, I never did."

"How many cases of acute appendicitis did you miss based on your clinical evaluation?"

Franklin Stern jumped to his feet. "Objection, your honor. My witness is not on trial here."

"Your honor," said Kathleen, "I am attempting to make a very important point here about the role of clinical judgment in diagnosing appendicitis. The witness has presented himself as an expert in the diagnosis and treatment of appendicitis and an analysis of his experience with cases of appendicitis is pertinent to this trial."

"Objection overruled. Please continue Ms. Stefanik. Dr. Laffer, please answer the question. Would you like to hear the question again?"

"Yes ma'am," answered Ichabod.

"How many cases of acute appendicitis did you miss based on your clinical evaluation?" repeated Stefanik.

Ichabod smiled conspiratorially at the jury as if it was transparent to everyone that this was an idiotic question. "Well, by definition it's hard to know how many you may have missed."

"How many do you know of that you missed?"

"Well, I don't know of any that I missed for certain."

"And this was before CAT scans, right?"

"Yes."

"So maybe clinical evaluation without a CAT scan isn't so bad, is that a fair statement?"

"Well, it certainly has its limitations…"

"But the truth is that you can't remember a single case of appendicitis that you missed before CAT scans, isn't that so?"

"Yes."

I looked at Frank who was staring down at the yellow legal pad on his table, his face red.

"Did you ever watch a patient for say, eight hours, before deciding that they really had an acute appendicitis and *then* take them to the operating room?" Kathleen continued.

Ichabod squirmed in his seat. "Well, I don't know if it was exactly eight hours…"

"But you have observed a patient clinically for a number of hours before you decided that you should take them to the operating room. Is that correct?"

"Yes, I probably have on occasion."

"How many occasions, Dr. Laffer?"

Ichabod looked down at his lap. "Quite a few perhaps," he said quietly.

"Was it ever longer than eight hours—say, as long as twelve hours?"

"I don't know the exact times."

"Do you think you have ever observed a patient who turned out to have appendicitis for as long as twelve hours?"

"Objection," interjected Frank. "My witness obviously does not keep records regarding how long he has observed patients."

"Overruled," said Judge Bowers. "Please answer the question Dr. Laffer."

"Perhaps. I'm not certain," Ichabod said weakly.

"Dr. Laffer, since you are an expert in the diagnosis of appendicitis, you are probably also an expert in interpreting CAT scans of the abdomen. Is that a fair statement?"

This, Ichabod was unable to resist. Another opportunity to have his ego stroked. "Yes, I think that's probably fair."

"Can you please tell the jury how many millisieverts of radiation are delivered to a patient during a CAT scan of the abdomen, Dr. Laffer?"

Frank leapt to his feet again. "Objection, your Honor! My witness has not been qualified as an expert in radiology."

"Ms. Stefanik?" said the judge, looking at Kathleen.

"Your Honor, the issue of Dr. Randolph attempting to spare Robert Straley the high doses of radiation associated with a CAT scan is going to be highly germane to this case. It is appropriate for me to question the plaintiff's expert witness, who, by his own admission, considers himself an authority on CAT scans in appendicitis, regarding the doses of radiation associated with a CAT scan."

"Objection overruled. Proceed Ms. Stefanik. Please ask the question again."

I breathed a sigh of relief. Technically, Laffer had admitted to being an expert in the *interpretation* of CAT scans, not the *physics* of CAT scans. Kathleen got away with that one.

"Dr. Laffer, will you please tell the jury how many millisieverts of radiation are delivered to a patient during a CAT scan of the abdomen?"

"I...I'm not sure exactly how many millisieverts, but we do thousands of CAT scans on children every year."

"Dr. Laffer, are you aware of the current recommendations of the American College of Radiology regarding imaging studies in children for appendicitis?"

"Objection, your Honor. This case took place three years ago, and current recommendations that were not in effect at the time of the incident have no place in this trial."

"Objection sustained," said Judge Bowers.

Bummer. The current recommendations would have been helpful to our case. We'd have to try to bring them out later.

Kathleen continued unfazed. "Dr. Laffer, we have heard that your many duties as an associate professor of surgery include seeing patients as an attending surgeon, as well as teaching and supervising surgical residents and medical students. Am I correct in this?"

"Yes."

"Do those duties include seeing patients in the emergency department with abdominal pain?"

"Certainly."

"Do you see *all* patients who present to the ER with abdominal pain?"

"No, just those patients that I am called to examine in consultation."

"Can you tell us please, Dr. Laffer, how those patients are selected?"

Ichabod paused for a moment, as if sensing a trap and chose his words carefully.

"Well, most of them have been worked up by an emergency physician who is concerned that they may have a surgical problem."

"So the patients you see in consultation have already been screened and preselected by other physicians, and therefore have a higher probability of having a surgical problem than the patients that an emergency physician must see for the first time. Is that a fair statement?"

"That's probably accurate," said Ichabod, folding his arms.

"Do you know what percentage of patients who present to your hospital's emergency department with abdominal pain you are called to see?"

"No, I don't know the answer to that question."

"Is it most of them?"

"No, I wouldn't think so."

"So would it be fair, then, to say that many patients with abdominal pain who are seen in an ER are sent home without a surgical consultation?"

Ichabod's facial color transitioned to a faint shade of pink. "I suppose so," he said.

"Do most patients with abdominal pain who are sent home from your hospital's emergency department receive a CAT scan?"

"I am unable to answer that question."

"Do *all* patients who present to your hospital's ER with abdominal pain receive a CAT scan?"

Ichabod paused again before he answered. "I'm not qualified to answer that question." I glanced at the jury in time to see a woman fold her arms and raise her eyebrows.

"Thank you, your Honor," said Kathleen. "I have no further questions for this witness."

CHAPTER SIXTY-THREE

I FOLLOWED PENNY'S NEW WHITE HONDA BACK to the farm to make certain that there were no issues with paparazzi, carjackings, armed assaults, or roadside bombs. The trip home was uneventful.

Penny had taken care to introduce Ruth to the St. Mark's Country Day School staff a week before school started and authorize her to pick up kids, so Ruth had already retrieved Jack and Catherine earlier in the afternoon. Neither Penny nor I could wait to see the children's reaction to their first day at a new school—Catherine in second grade and Jack in a rigorous prekindergarten program preparing him for entrance to Harvard.

Catherine leapt into Penny's arms and wrapped her legs around Penny's waist as soon as we were in the door.

"Hey, Baby! Well, how was it?" Penny asked excitedly.

"This kid—Tommy—got in trouble today," Catherine said in a hushed voice, as if this was news not fit for public consumption. "He already got his first yellow card."

"His first card?"

"Yeah, if you're bad, you get a yellow card, and if you get three cards you have to sit up front, right in front of the teacher's desk!"

"Wow. What did he do?"

"He was talking when he should have been listening," Catherine said with disapproval, "right when Mrs. Martin was explaining how to carry over in subtraction."

"Ahhh. And what do you think of Mrs. Martin?"

"She's nice," Catherine said with a winning missing-tooth-smile. "But Mr. Thompson is mean!"

"Who's Mr. Thompson?"

"He was in the cafeteria. He makes everybody clean up messes and he taps you on the shoulder if you're making too much noise."

"Well, somebody has to do that, huh? Did you get tapped on the shoulder?"

Catherine smiled again with embarrassment. "Yeah."

"Why am I not surprised?"

Peggy hugged Catherine and lowered her to the floor. Jack was nearby, loudly running a bulldozer over the armrest of the family room sofa. She scooped him up and said, "And you, young man, how was your first day of school?"

Too busy making motor sounds to answer, Jack directed the dozer across Penny's shoulder and up her neck, catching a hoop earring with the blade. Penny yelped. "Ouch, ouch, ouch! Jack, you've got my earring!"

Jack backed up, freeing the earring, then changed directions slightly and motored up the back of Penny's head, entwining long locks of blond hair in the rubber treads.

"Jack! For heavens sakes!" I decided it was time to intervene. I wrapped my hand around both Jack's hand and the dozer, holding it close to Penny's head while she slowly lowered Jack to the floor. Disentanglement took about a minute.

Undeterred, Penny scooped up Jack again, and now with his full attention said, "OK, you little terror, did you like your new school?"

Jack shrugged.

"Well, what did you do today?"

Jack's face brightened. "I built a fort!"

Penny looked puzzled. "How did you do that?"

"With...with pieces of wood that fit together," Jack said, gesturing with his hands while Penny leaned back to support his weight.

"Did you do this inside or outside?" asked Penny.

"Inside."

"Ah, Lincoln Logs, no doubt. Little logs of wood about this long?" I asked, measuring with my thumb and forefinger.

Jack smiled and nodded his head.

"I used to build forts with those myself, Jack. So, who was inside the fort?"

"Soldiers."

"And who was outside?"

"Indians." This did not sound right for a sensitive, multicultural, and ethnically diverse institution like St. Mark's Country Day School.

"Did you have soldiers and Indians?"

"Jack shook his head. "Just horses."

"I thought so."

~

As the stars rose in a blue-black sky, Penny and I sat quietly in the dark on a wicker love seat on the patio, my arm around her and Penny leaning into my shoulder.

Actually, it wasn't really all that quiet. An orchestra of a thousand tree frogs and cicadas played an ancient lullaby that rose and fell, but despite the racket, it was as peaceful a moment as life offers. After a summer of enormous stress, I felt like our souls were plugged into a recharger of immutable, limitless energy.

Penny finally broke the silence. "This is the most calm I have felt in weeks." She leaned in and put one arm around my chest. Looking up, she said, "I thank God every day for you."

I kissed her forehead with a pang of guilt. I wasn't sure she should be thanking me. I was the one who had brought terror into her life in the form of Mary Anne Williams. I hoped to God that the police would soon find her and that Penny's ordeal would be over once and for all.

"I haven't even asked you yet what you thought of the trial today," she said.

"The trial is the least of my worries. I am very comfortable with the way that I handled Robert Straley's case, and the jury's opinion won't change that.

"Frank did a very good job," I continued. "I suspect the jury thought it was an open-and-shut case after he was through. But I think Kathleen made some progress in raising some question marks after she was done with Laffer. She's very good—understands the real issues in the case."

"I hope he can't sleep tonight," said Penny.

CHAPTER SIXTY-FOUR

BY TUESDAY MORNING, CALVIN BACON'S RIGHT ear was phone-battered and painful. Bizarrely, the face of Barry Newhouse popped into his head, the fifth-grade bully on his elementary school bus who used to continually flick his ear from the seat behind. He switched the phone to his left ear and continued to listen to endless promotions while waiting for yet another airline to say, "No. No Mary Anne Williams in the last two weeks."

On the desk beside his work papers, Bacon's cell phone rang. He put it to his painful ear. "Bacon here."

"Officer Bacon, Neil Salaker here again. We've got DNA results for you on that hair you provided us from the missing person, Mary Anne Williams. It's a match with the hair found on Gerald Stine's chest at autopsy."

Bacon slapped his thigh. "I knew it! Salaker, you've been a helpful lad this week. I owe you a pizza. And hey, listen, just call me Calvin. Thanks a million."

"No problem, Calvin."

That hair match wouldn't convict Mary Anne Williams of any crime, Calvin knew. She was standing at the scene beside the body with Fry. But it was another little piece of circumstantial evidence that kept Bacon believing that they were headed in the right direction. He pulled up Fry's number and tapped the *Call* icon.

~

Allison C. Becker slid into seat 3-A of American Airlines Flight 1907 departing Miami at 10:55 AM. The young brunette—elegantly dressed in a white and blue floral print dress with pearl accessories—carried nothing but a tasteful navy blue leather purse.

Having no luggage, she was in a cab fifteen minutes after the Boeing 737-800 touched down at V. C. Bird International Airport on the island of Antigua. A short five-minute-drive later, she pushed through the heavy brass door of The Arrington Bank, Ltd.

A receptionist at the quiet bank led her down three hallways to a large corner office overlooking azure waters.

Mr. Averill Jamison jumped up from his mahogany desk and said, "Ah, Miss Becker, we've been expecting you! If I could trouble you to show me some identification, I have your account fully prepared, including an Arrington Bank CardOne debit card against your account with overdraft privileges. I understand you are on a tight schedule, and I think we can have these matters accomplished in just a few minutes."

"You are very kind, Mr. Jamison," replied his new client. "I appreciate the outstanding service." Jamison remained standing with hands clasped behind his back as Miss Becker signed the paperwork, his eyes never leaving the magnificent cleavage of his stunning new client.

"Oh, one more thing. I almost forgot," said Miss Becker reaching into her purse. "Would you mind terribly depositing this nine thousand dollars into my account? I really hate to carry that kind of cash around with me." Mr. Jamison accepted the funds and hastily scribbled a receipt.

Four minutes later Miss Becker exited the bank to her waiting cab and was back at the airport in time to catch the 3:15 nonstop back to the U.S.

As the aircraft accelerated down the runway, Mary Anne Williams sighed with satisfaction. Every element of her carefully designed plan was now in place, including a fully functional escape plan, should that be necessary. She could now access funds and travel at will, but her movements would be virtually untraceable.

Hopefully, if this operation went right, all of her careful escape arrangements would have been unnecessary. The police would find evidence at the crime scene indicating that the grisly murder of Penny Murray was carried out by the Crips gang in revenge for her killing of Crips member, Ronnie Reynolds. Alex Randolph would then blessedly find both comfort and excitement in the arms of Mary Anne Williams at Ascot Farms.

She laughed softly. The poor Crips would never know what hit them. The cops would be all over their asses.

It was a productive week. Mary Anne was having a blast. But the most exciting part was yet to come. In a few days Dr. Alex Randolph would be free of the blond albatross around his neck.

CHAPTER SIXTY-FIVE

FRANKLIN STERN CONTINUED THE PLAINTIFF'S assault Tuesday morning, having put some serious money at risk by obtaining the testimony of a second expert witness, in this case an ER doc who was an associate professor at NYU.

The most difficult decisions physicians are called upon to make involve not life or death—those are almost always easy. The hard decisions are the balancing of risk versus cost, and in many situations, the risk of missing a diagnosis versus the risks to the patient associated with the testing itself, which are often not inconsiderable. If you live in a risk-aversive society, the penalties for missing a diagnosis are formidable, which means that all of the incentives are to order every test imaginable, regardless of cost or potential harm to the patient. That's us in the U.S. of A.

Sociologically speaking, as with any large group, physicians come in many different personality types which define their personal risk tolerance. Besides being a whore to the litigation industry, Joseph Ascencio was a zero-risk, black and white, this-is-the-way-you-do-it, I-always-cover-my-ass kind of guy, not to mention an arrogant asshole.

He went right for my jugular, essentially repeating Irwin Laffer's testimony, but this time from the perspective of an emergency physician. Ascencio was not present for Laffer's testimony, so Kathleen patiently took him down a similar path, slowly poking holes in his confident black-and-white assertions until he left the stand somewhat crestfallen, but ten grand richer.

All through the trial we had wondered whether or not Frank would call a member of the Straley family, and finally he did. Frank knew that this case would hinge on the conversation between myself and the Straleys regarding Robert's illness, and most importantly, the instructions that were provided to the family. It was a calculated risk, but Frank decided to make a preemptive strike on what he knew would be our testimony regarding the final moments of the Straley visit.

Using both arms, Robert Straley, Sr. lifted his generous body from his seat and slowly walked to the stand, where he swore to tell the whole truth—at least as he saw it. Frank slowly led him through the undisputed facts of the visit, giving him time to relax and gain confidence in front of the jury.

Finally we reached the *he said, she said* portion of Mr. Straley's testimony, the credibility of which we knew would be the deciding factor in whether or not this jury of twelve of my peers would find me guilty of gross negligence.

"Mr. Straley, did Dr. Randolph tell you the results of Robert's testing?" asked Frank.

"Yes, he said they were all normal."

"Can you tell us specifically what tests were normal?"

"No, that stuff's all Greek to me," said Mr. Straley, looking toward the jury and laughing good-naturedly.

"But the important thing is that you trusted that Dr. Randolph had done all the right tests and that they were normal. Is that correct."

"Yeah. He's the doctor, not me."

"Mr. Straley, what did Dr. Randolph tell you was wrong with your son?"

"He said he had a virus."

"And did that diagnosis alarm you?"

"Nah. Everybody gets a virus," he said, waving his arm and chuckling again to the jury.

"So when you left the Mason-Dixon emergency department, you felt reassured that your son was OK?"

"Sure. That's what you take your kid to the doctor for."

"Did Dr. Randolph make any suggestions?"

"I think he said we could bring him back to the ER in the morning if things weren't going too good."

"And did you bring him back?"

"Noooo. The doctor said he was OK. That's what you pay 'em for, right? The kid was about the same the next morning as the night before. The doctor said that a virus can last a week."

"Did Dr. Randolph mention appendicitis?"

"Yeah, but he said he didn't think he had it," said Robert, shaking his head.

"Did you receive any written instructions?

"They gave us a whole raft of papers. Must have been this thick," he said measuring about an inch with his thumb and forefinger. "Who's got time to read all that gobblygook? We already talked to the doctor. Can't understand most of it anyhow. Reads like a lawyer wrote it, you know?" he said laughing again and pointing at Frank.

Frank made a good decision. Robert Straley was a likable and credible witness. He effectively minimized the impact of written instructions on the mind of the jury, and his description of our conversation was believable and not contrary to the facts. He simply omitted a few key elements.

"Ms. Stefanik," said Judge Bower, "would you care to cross-examine the witness?"

"No, your Honor."

I wasn't sure that this was such a good idea, but Kathleen felt strongly that attacking Robert Straley's family would be counterproductive. And so the plaintiff's case was finally concluded.

CHAPTER SIXTY-SIX

THE FIRST BREAK IN TRACKING DOWN MARY Anne Williams came at 2:45 PM Tuesday afternoon. A Baltimore City patrol car spotted a gray Saturn in the parking lot of the Greyhound terminal at 2110 Haines Street that had been sitting for several days and ran it through the NCIC database.

Calvin Bacon took the phone call, then immediately dialed Fry's cell phone. "We got a break, Sergeant. Baltimore City found Williams' Saturn at the Greyhound bus terminal on Haines Street."

"The bus terminal?"

"That's what the man said."

"What the hell? I wonder if she took a bus to Miami?"

"Don't know. It's puzzling. With all her money, why would she take a bus anywhere?"

"OK, Calvin. Go check it out."

Grateful for an excuse to finally leave his desk, Calvin walked out of the precinct station to his patrol car baking in the August sun. By the time the air conditioning finally started blowing cold air, his shirt was drenched.

Mary Anne Williams' disappearance was an utter puzzle. Even if she had hired Gerry Stine to kill the Murray girl, why would she disappear? There was no reason to run. She had no way of knowing that the police had found Stine's fingerprints on Penny Murray's vehicle or that Alex Randolph had informed the police of Williams' amorous advances.

Maybe, in fact, she was completely innocent. Maybe Stine had some other reason for trying to kill Penny Murray. Maybe Williams had just up and decided to go on a love boat cruise someplace for the hell of it.

But then why would there be no credit card expenditures, and why would she leave her car at a damned Greyhound terminal and take a bus when she could fly anywhere in the world that she wanted? None of it made any sense.

Calvin turned right into the small bus terminal parking lot and immediately spotted the Saturn. The gray car was locked and empty. He held his hand to his eyes, shielding the sun as he looked into the vehicle, but the seats and dashboard contained no papers, tickets, or other items apparent to a visual inspection.

Using a plastic wedge inserted into the door frame, and a strip tool, Calvin had the Saturn door open in less than a minute. A search of the glove compartment and other interior spaces revealed only insurance cards and a tube of Chapstick. He popped the trunk, but it was completely empty too.

Relocking the car, he entered the terminal and interviewed every employee with customer contact, showing them photos of the missing woman, but struck out completely. No one could remember seeing the girl in the photo, or anyone arrive in the Saturn.

I should come back tonight and question the night shift, he thought. But there were only so many hours in a day.

He thought about asking the captain's permission to do a stakeout on the Saturn, but knew there was no chance in hell that the captain would commit those kinds of resources to a case where there was no case. The coroner had ruled that Stine's death was due to an accidental overdose. There was no law against asking a single man out to dinner, and American citizens were free to take a trip and disappear without checking in with someone anytime they wanted.

Without some new piece of hard evidence, this case was going to wind down fast. Calvin felt sorry for Penny Murray.

~

Flight 1019 arrived from Antigua at Miami International Airport on time at 6:15 PM. With a winsome smile, Allison Becker flashed her passport at the admiring young agent and sailed through passport control. By 6:30 PM she had hailed a cab and exited the airport for the short ten-minute ride west to Dolphin Mall on NW 12th Street.

The well-dressed young woman handed the driver a twenty-dollar bill to wait, and through mall entry number one, walked into the huge Bass Pro Shop anchoring one corner of the mall.

Having already researched online the products for which she was looking, it took only five minutes to reach the checkout counter with three pairs of Pulsar Edge night vision goggles. She handed the bemused clerk her CardOne debit card, pulled out her Florida driver's license for identification, and the nearly twenty-three-hundred-dollar purchase was completed within a total of ten minutes.

Exiting Bass Pro Shop on the interior mall side of the store, she briskly walked a hundred yards past Old Navy and into Sports Authority where she purchased three black one-piece running suits, guessing at the appropriate size for her two accomplices.

With her shopping complete, she found her cabbie and provided directions. As the taxi rolled along the Dolphin Expressway back to Fontainebleau Hotel, she reviewed every detail of the coming operation, her pulse rising with excitement. She would have preferred to do this alone. The plan was hers, but she needed the operational expertise and brutality of the two goons she had hired in case something went wrong. This time she was leaving nothing to chance.

There were definitely risks involved, not the least of which were that Raoul and Facundo might simply try to kill her in Maryland and make off with the cash. But she had an insurance policy for that too. In addition, they had no idea that she carried a Sig Sauer P238 with which she was very skilled.

CHAPTER SIXTY-SEVEN

MID-AFTERNOON ON TUESDAY, KATHLEEN rose and began the presentation of the defense. I was the first witness called to the stand. In an effort to persuade the jury that I was perhaps not as stupid as Drs. Laffer and Ascencio may have indicated, the first item of business was to establish my credentials.

So for the next fifteen minutes we talked about medical school at Duke and residency at Hopkins, and then my days on the university faculty, and all the research papers I had published, blah, blah, blah, until I'm sure the jury was stupefied.

It was all rather embarrassing, as Kathleen made me out to be the next incarnation of Sir William Osler—flattering, perhaps, but to my mind a little over the top. It would have been much more direct to simply hand the jury a copy of my curriculum vitae, but that's not how they do things in a trial.

Finally we got around to the actual case. Kathleen led me through all the basic facts as documented in the medical record: eight hours of vomiting and vague abdominal pain, no fever or tachycardia, and only mild scattered tenderness on the plaintiff's abdominal exam, specifically with no tenderness over the appendix.

Robert's complete blood count was normal, as were all of his chemistries, including kidney and liver function studies. A urinalysis

389

was completely normal. None of these facts were in dispute.

Kathleen had earned my respect over the course of the trial. I liked her. I had decided that she knew what she was doing, so I tried to answer her questions directly and not do too much in the way of elaboration. I knew that she was building her case in a logical fashion and would get to all of the important issues in due time.

She next directed me to the section of the medical record that was crucial to the case. Handing me a sheaf of papers, she said, "Please note for the record that I am providing the witness with a copy of the medical record labeled 'Exhibit A'. Dr. Randolph can you please read for us what you wrote on the evening of Robert Straley's visit under the section entitled "Medical Decision Making?""

"At present, symptoms most consistent with a viral illness. Doubt appendicitis, but needs to be watched. Radiation from CT not justified at this time. Recheck in eight hours."

"Can you please elaborate for us, Dr. Randolph, on exactly what you meant by the phrase 'at present'?"

"Almost all illnesses that involve infectious disease, be they viral or bacterial, have an insidious onset, meaning that they start out very gradually with minimal symptoms. In the early stages, the symptoms are often non-specific, meaning that they can be seen with a wide variety of different illnesses and therefore a diagnosis cannot be reliably made until the illness progresses and clearer symptoms develop."

"Is this true also with appendicitis?"

"Certainly. The appendix is a little hollow tube with a blind end that projects out from the first part of the large bowel called the *cecum*. Appendicitis occurs when an infection develops inside this tube. Just like a boil on your skin, when the infection first starts you hardly notice it. It may take several days before it progresses enough that it produces symptoms and a diagnosis can be made."

"So by using the phrase 'at present' you were indicating that things might change and become more clear, or specific, at a later time."

"That is correct."

"And what did you mean by 'symptoms most consistent with a viral illness'?"

"We see many, many children with vomiting and vague abdominal pain, most of whom do not have appendicitis, but rather have a virus of their gastrointestinal tract that produces vomiting along with the discomfort."

"Those are essentially the same symptoms with which Robert Straley presented, are they not?"

"That is correct."

"So that is why you wrote 'symptoms most consistent with a viral illness'?"

"Yes. As is often the case in medicine, in the early stages of an illness you are often forced to make a presumptive diagnosis based on what is statistically most likely until the nature of the illness becomes clearer."

"What about the role of the white blood cell count in your evaluation?"

"Usually there is no significant white blood cell count elevation in a virus of the gastrointestinal tract. However, when there is a bacterial infection, as with appendicitis, the white blood cell count typically rises. About two-thirds of the cases of appendicitis have an elevated white blood cell count."

"So would it be correct to say that a normal white blood cell count does not rule out appendicitis, but *does* make appendicitis less likely?"

"That is correct."

"And how about the urinalysis?"

"We do a urinalysis to make sure that a urinary tract infection is not the source of the abdominal pain and vomiting."

"And in this case, Robert's urine was normal?"

"Yes."

"You next wrote, 'Doubt appendicitis, but needs to be watched.' What did you mean by that?"

"Robert had had symptoms for only about eight hours when he presented to the ER. His illness was early, and even though he did not have evidence of appendicitis at that time, I was still concerned that appendicitis was possible. So we needed to watch him over coming hours to see if his symptoms and his physical examination became more consistent with appendicitis."

"What symptoms are consistent with appendicitis?"

"In the typical evolution of appendicitis, pain starts somewhere in the central abdomen and migrates over a period of time to the right lower quadrant—just above the hip bone. On examination, there is prominent tenderness when you press on a spot called *McBurney's point*, right over the appendix."

"And am I correct that Robert was not tender over this part of his abdomen?"

"That is correct. When I worked my way around his abdomen—pressing in all four quadrants—he would nod his head that he was tender here and there in scattered places, but never over McBurney's point. When I re-examined him before he left the department, he again nodded his head that he was tender in scattered places, but they weren't the same places as on the first exam. In other words, his reporting of the location of pain was inconsistent. In addition, he never grimaced, or made a face, or cried, which indicated to me that the tenderness was not severe."

"But in neither exam did he claim tenderness over the right lower quadrant where the appendix is located. Is that correct?"

'That is correct."

"So I take it that the diagnosis of appendicitis is not always easy, Dr. Randolph?"

"Difficult enough that studies have shown that in children, the appendix has already ruptured about one-third of the time before the diagnosis is made."

"So tell us Dr. Randolph, what is the most accurate study that can help you make the diagnosis of appendicitis?"

"A CT scan, or CAT scan as they are often called."

"Can you tell us exactly how they are helpful?"

"CTs are wonderful tools. They give a high resolution, three-dimensional view of the abdomen that is successful at identifying appendicitis in over ninety percent of cases."

"And yet you wrote, 'Radiation from CT not justified at this time. Recheck in eight hours.' Why didn't you do a CT at that time?"

"As in often the case in medicine, studies come at a price, and not just a monetary price. They come with a price in terms of risks to your health from the study itself."

"What are the risks associated with CTs?"

"The risks of radiation exposure. One CT of the abdomen delivers an organ radiation dose of between ten and thirty millisieverts which is equivalent to the radiation from about four hundred chest x-rays."

"That's a lot. Can you tell us why we should be concerned about radiation exposure?"

"The biggest concern is that radiation damages the DNA in our cells, which can result in the development of various forms of cancer later in life. Over seventy million CAT scans are performed in the United States every year. It is estimated that about two percent of all future cancers are going to be the direct result of radiation exposure from CAT scans."

"Is there a particular group of patients in which exposure to radiation is of greatest concern?"

"Yes, in children, for two reasons. First, radiation damages cells that are rapidly dividing more than cells that are not dividing. That's why radiation will kill rapidly dividing cancer cells without producing as much damage to other tissues whose cells are not dividing. But a child's cells are dividing continuously because they are growing, so there will be more damage from radiation to a child than to an adult.

"Secondly, a child has many more years to live than an adult, so there will be a greater lifetime opportunity for a child to develop cancer than for say a fifty-year-old patient."

"So, Dr. Randolph, are the risks high for an individual child?"

"No. The risk of an individual child developing cancer from a single CT scan is about one in a thousand, so when the risks of an undiagnosed illness are high, it is worth doing a CT.

"However, when you multiply one in a thousand by seventy million CT scans a year, that's a lot of cancers. It becomes a significant public health issue. So in recent years many different academic medical societies have begun to develop programs to try to reduce radiation exposure to our population, and decrease CT usage to only those cases where there is a very clear indication, especially in children."

"Are there any other concerns in the medical literature regarding CT scans in children?"

"Yes. There are concerns about the potential for radiation brain injury in children and an adverse effect on cognitive function. This is a very difficult subject because direct studies have not been done and probably never will be done.

"But there was a Swedish study several years ago that looked at children who had received radiation for treatment of hemangioma facial tumors. In that study, children receiving radiation doses roughly equivalent to a CAT scan were fifty percent less likely to graduate from high school."

"Objection!" roared Franklin Stern, as if an enormous travesty of justice had just occurred. "That is hearsay and without foundation in the record."

"Ms. Stefanik?"

"The study to which Dr. Randolph is referring is cited in our expert witness's report," said Kathleen, "but we will agree to defer reference to that study until I have called our expert witness."

"All right, Ms. Stefanik," said Judge Bower. "Please strike the defendant's last paragraph from the record."

"So in your opinion, Dr. Randolph," continued Kathleen, "Robert's symptoms and examination at eight hours into his illness were not far enough along to warrant exposure to the radiation in a CT?"

"That is correct. I favored a re-examination in eight hours at which time a CT could be performed if Robert's symptoms and examination were becoming more suggestive of appendicitis."

"How much time do you have in which to evaluate a patient before it becomes risky to wait and watch?"

"The major concern is that as the appendix becomes swollen and filled with pus that it will rupture, spilling pus and intestinal contents into the abdominal cavity. Rupture can occur as early as thirty-six hours from the time of onset of pain. About eighty percent of children will rupture within forty-eight hours."

"So seeing Robert again in eight hours would be a total of sixteen hours from onset of his symptoms, a period of time that you felt it was safe to wait to perform a CAT scan if necessary. Is that correct."

"Yes. That is exactly correct. Actually we don't even always do a CAT scan. If a child's symptoms are highly suggestive of appendicitis and he or she is very tender over McBurney's point, the surgeon will often decide to do an appendectomy without a CAT scan because the clinical diagnosis is so clear at that point. This spares the child a significant dose of radiation."

"Dr. Randolph, it has been suggested that you might have obtained an ultrasound examination when you saw Robert. Why did you not do that?"

"Robert's visit to the ER was three years ago. That was in the early days of ultrasound studies for appendicitis, which were for the most part only being done at certain university hospitals. Our hospital did not offer ultrasound for appendicitis at that time."

"I see. And how about a surgical consultation? Do you think that would have been of value?"

"There were literally no indications of a surgical problem at only eight hours into Robert's illness. Specifically, he was not tender over his right lower quadrant, and he had a normal white blood cell count. Any surgeon I could have asked to see him in my hospital would have recommended a period of observation, which was exactly what I did." Here, I finally decided to elaborate a little.

"I think it's important to recognize that in our ER we see as many as six, eight, or ten kids a day with Robert's initial symptoms— vomiting and mild abdominal discomfort. Among all these kids, perhaps only one child every three or four weeks has appendicitis. Doing CAT scans on all those children would be irresponsible. Getting surgical consults on all those children in a community hospital would be nearly impossible."

"So, Dr. Randolph, the bottom line is that based upon Robert's symptoms and examination you thought it statistically most likely that he had a gastrointestinal virus, but you were concerned enough about the possibility of appendicitis that you wanted him to return to the ER in eight hours to be re-examined. Am I correct in that?

"Yes."

"And in addition, because at the time of the re-examination Robert would only be sixteen hours into his illness, that was a short enough period of time that you considered that to be safe?"

"Correct."

"What were some of the possible outcomes of a recheck eight hours later?"

"At the time of his visit, it was statistically most probable that Robert's symptoms were due to a virus, so one of the possible outcomes would have been that his vomiting had stopped and that his abdominal pain had resolved by the next morning, in which case no further testing would have been necessary and we could have sent him home.

"A second possibility would have been that Robert's pain had intensified, that he would have become more tender in his abdomen, or that he would have developed fever, an elevated white blood cell count, or other symptoms of progression of a more serious illness. In that case, we could have done additional testing, including a CAT scan if necessary."

"So tell us please, what you communicated to Mr. and Mrs. Straley at the conclusion of Robert's visit."

"I told them that the most likely diagnosis at that time was a gastrointestinal virus, which could last as long as a week. If that was the case, he would be fine and need no medicine. However, I could not be completely certain that Robert didn't have appendicitis or some other more serious intra-abdominal problem, so I thought that we should see him again in eight hours for a re-examination and perhaps further testing."

"And then you followed up that conversation with a set of printed instructions, is that correct?"

"Yes."

"Could you please read for us, Dr. Randolph, what you typed in that set of instructions?"

"Certainly." I said, referring to the set of discharge papers. "'Stay on clear liquids only. No solid food. Return to ER in eight hours for re-examination. Return earlier if pain becomes more intense or localizes to the lower right side of Robert's abdomen.'"

"Why did you instruct the family to keep Robert on just clear liquids and no solid food?"

"For two reasons. First, he would have less vomiting if he put no solid food in his stomach. Second, when we put people to sleep for an operation, we like to have their stomachs empty so there is no problem with vomiting while under anesthesia. If Robert displayed evidence of appendicitis the next morning, his stomach would be empty and we could take him immediately to the operating room."

"Did you expect the Straley family to return to the Mason-Dixon ER the next morning, Dr. Randolph?"

"Yes. I thought that I was clear in my instructions. In fact, I left a handwritten note for the next morning's oncoming physician outlining the case. My sense was that the Straleys were responsible parents and would follow up as requested."

"And did the Straleys give you any indication at the conclusion of their visit that they were unlikely to follow your instructions?"

"No."

"Your Honor, I have no further questions for my witness."

I glanced at the jury. One heavyset man puffed out his cheeks as if in a quandary, but most faces were impassive.

CHAPTER SIXTY-EIGHT

RAOUL WRAPPED THE LOADED BROWNING Mark III 9 mm pistol in a towel and shoved it behind the wheel in the spare tire compartment of the rental car. A Ruger SR45 automatic followed, along with two boxes of spare ammunition.

He closed the rear hatch, then tossed two duffel bags into the back seat of the Ford Escape which he had selected specifically from the rental lot because it was four-wheel drive and had Louisiana license plates. Four-wheel drive could come in handy if you got involved in a chase, and Louisiana plates would make it just that much harder to track him down if something went wrong with the operation.

Of course, there had never been any question about flying to Maryland with such a cargo, nor did Raoul much like airplanes, from which, once aboard, there was no escape. He preferred the freedom and options that came with a car. There were risks, of course, of random traffic stops, or an accident while traveling in a vehicle, but with those, he would take his chances. Careful driving at the speed limit went a long way toward minimizing risks.

He was not happy about the girl going along on this hit. Facundo, he knew, would not do anything stupid, but three people presented a whole new world of risk, not to mention that one of them was an amateur bitch who couldn't be trusted to take orders.

Actually, he still couldn't figure out why he had agreed to do this job. In the back of his mind he knew it was because the beautiful woman with brass balls intrigued him, but he was not yet prepared to admit that to himself. She better pray that nothing went wrong with this operation, because with the first false move, the cunt would be dead. Maybe she would be dead anyhow. He still hadn't decided.

Facundo hopped into the right seat, carrying a bag of Doritos. Raoul pulled the shift selector into drive, and the two brothers headed east across north Miami toward I-95.

~

Allison Becker paid cash for her ticket, upgrading to a Viewliner bedroom, and climbed aboard the Amtrak 98 Silver Meteor for the twenty-three-hour-and-fifty-six-minute trip to Baltimore's Penn Station. She would have preferred, of course, to fly, but there was the little issue of the Sig Sauer 38 caliber in her backpack.

Nevertheless, the train ride would be relaxing and offer plenty of time to review every detail of her plan—probably a good thing. She could sleep all night and arrive Thursday morning at 8:16 refreshed and ready to spend the day observing Penny Murray's movements.

Her little MS-13 team wouldn't arrive until early evening on Thursday, which offered her extra time to prepare for what she had come to think of as a mission. A reservation for the two brothers was on file at the Days Inn Towson on Loch Raven Boulevard.

She had already decided not to pick up her Saturn or go home to Ascot until the operation was over, so she, herself, was booked at the Towson University Marriott. There could be no question of letting the brothers know where she lived, what she drove, or where she was sleeping. A rental car awaited her arrival in Baltimore.

The final payment of twenty-five thousand dollars in cash to the two brothers would be stored in a public place—a locker with a combination lock at Penn Station. Only she, of course, knew the combination. This arrangement provided powerful motivation to Raoul and Facundo to keep her alive. Murdering her in a public place would be a bit awkward.

Mary Anne settled into the lounge chair of her sleeper compartment and picked up a copy of *Cosmopolitan*. With a soft jerk, the train began to move and she looked up to see the station platform slowly pass by her window with gradually increasing speed. Her carefully laid plan was finally in motion.

CHAPTER SIXTY-NINE

FRANK SPENT LITTLE TIME IN CROSS-examination, asking me only how many CT studies I ordered a week, which is plenty—more than I would like—and then suggested that perhaps I wasn't really so concerned about radiation to Robert Straley, but in truth was anxious to get home at near the end of my shift and didn't want to take the time to get a CT.

This was easily answered—to my mind at least—as at the end of a shift we routinely hand off incomplete workups to the oncoming physician. But perhaps his questions were enough to plant a seed of doubt in the mind of a juror or two.

The crush of journalists and photographers was not nearly as bad at the end of the day on Tuesday, although I expected worse at the end of the trial, which would hopefully be tomorrow. Penny and I had driven together and had no real difficulty reaching my Jeep.

"So, how are you doing?" she asked, reaching out for my hand.

"I'm fine."

"Well, what do you think?"

"I really can't tell. I think the jury's having a tough time with this. There really aren't any medical issues. I wouldn't change anything I did. It boils down to where the doctor's responsibility ends and the patient's responsibility begins. That's a societal issue. I don't know. Maybe I just wasn't forceful enough with the family."

401

"You gave them very clear instructions, Alex. How can that be malpractice? Bad things happen to good people."

She should know.

~

Wednesday morning Kathleen called Kevin Law to the stand, a professor of emergency medicine from SUNY—State University of New York—Stony Brook, who was an expert witness for the defense. I had never met him.

A trim, fiftyish man with a graying goatee, Dr. Law knew his way around a CAT scan. He was the author of numerous articles on methods to reduce radiation exposure to the American population, obviously with a focus on children since he was doubly board-certified in pediatrics and emergency medicine.

Kathleen led him through the science of radiation injury and then had him describe the magnitude of the over-utilization of CTs in American emergency departments, citing the enormous growth in the volume of CTs in the last decade and the fact that as many as one-third of CTs among the millions performed may be unnecessary.

One would like to think that the legal system is impervious to emotion, but when Law mentioned that a single CAT scan of the abdomen was roughly equivalent to the radiation received by the survivors of Hiroshima and Nagasaki, I saw eyes pop open on the jury.

An hour later, Kathleen finally reached the critical issue surrounding the Straley case.

"Dr. Law, after careful review of the records and given the undisputed facts of this case, what is your opinion regarding the appropriateness of the medical care delivered by Dr. Randolph."

"Absolutely appropriate. Given the unavailability of ultrasound at his institution, I would have managed this case in exactly the same way as Dr. Randolph. A CT was definitely not indicated at the time of the patient's first visit, and a period of roughly eight hours of observation is an approach that we often utilize at University Hospital."

"So you do not believe that a wait of eight hours for a re-examination was an unacceptable risk?"

"At the time of his visit, the patient did not come close to meeting the criteria for making the diagnosis of appendicitis and taking him to surgery. Eight hours would likely have been the least amount of time it would have taken for his disease process to become clearer."

"And you do not think it likely that Robert Straley's appendix would have been ruptured at the time of a re-examination sixteen hours after onset of symptoms?"

"Highly, highly improbable at only sixteen hours into his illness, particularly given the absence of surgical indications on the initial exam."

"And what about a surgical consult, Dr. Law? Would you have obtained a surgical consult at the time of Robert Straley's visit?"

"No. With no clearly localized tenderness, no white blood cell count elevation, and no fever, he did not meet criteria for a surgical consultation."

"In your opinion, Dr. Law, were the written discharge instructions issued to the Straley family clear and adequate?"

"I don't see how they could have been clearer."

"Thank you, Dr. Law. Your honor, I have no further questions for this witness."

"Mr. Stern, your witness," said Judge Bower.

I expected a cross-examination from Franklin Stern, but he said quietly, "I have no questions, your Honor."

There is some controversy surrounding the dangers of CT radiation, and I thought that Frank would jump on the differences of opinion, but he didn't. Taking on Dr. Law on a complex scientific issue about which Law was an expert might have gotten Frank in over his head. I guessed that he had so much money already invested in this case that he was reluctant to book yet another expert witness to counter Law's testimony. If he lost this case, it was already going to cost him a bundle.

~

Closing arguments, of course, were a summary of the evidence and conclusions each attorney had hammered home during the trial with a few emotional appeals thrown in. I was happy to finally be nearing the end of this ordeal.

Frank emphasized the needless suffering and enormous expense the Straley family had endured, leaving them nearly destitute and on the verge of losing their home and quality of life, all of which could have been so easily avoided had their physician met even the barest minimum of the standard of care for this simple diagnosis. The defendant's alleged concerns about radiation were nothing more than a smokescreen to cover up a grossly negligent workup for the most common surgical diagnosis in children.

"The Straley family trusted their physician," concluded Frank. "They deserved better."

Kathleen rose before the jury and in a clear, but calm voice said, "Ladies and gentlemen of the jury, we are all saddened that Robert Straley, Jr. suffered so much with this disease that nearly took his life. The plaintiff's counsel would have you believe that this outcome was the direct responsibility of a negligent physician—that Dr. Randolph missed a diagnosis that could have been made by any young medical student.

"But the evidence shows that the defendant, Dr. Alexander Randolph, was anything but negligent. In fact, he displayed uncommon thoughtfulness in trying to spare his patient the potential harm of perhaps needless radiation, all the while protecting him from the possibility that a more serious diagnosis was evolving by simply asking the family to bring him back to the ER the next morning for a re-examination.

"His instructions were clear and unequivocal, but the Straley family made a choice not to follow them, no doubt with the best of intentions for their son. In truth, this is not a case about medical malpractice. This is a case about personal responsibility.

"Dr. Alexander Randolph did his very best to balance potential harm versus risk for his patient. Will we as a society, hold the physician responsible for every single decision that a plaintiff makes? Where did Dr. Randolph's responsibility end, and where did the patient's or family's responsibility begin?

"Will we pronounce this highly capable and careful physician grossly negligent because we are truly sorry for the Straley family and their current financial position? I would assert to you that such a decision would in itself represent a gross miscarriage of justice."

~

At the conclusion of her hour-long instructions to the jury, Judge Bower said, "Ladies and gentlemen of the jury, thank you for your attention. Now that you have heard the evidence and have been instructed on the law, it is time for you to retire to the jury room and decide this case."

Turning to the tipstaff, she said, Mr. Singer, would you please escort the jury to the jury room." I glanced at my watch: 2:15. I would have killed to retire to the defendant's room and have a Grey Goose and tonic, but I don't think there *is* a defendant's room.

I turned to Joan of Arc and said, "Kathleen, you were fabulous. Win or lose, I'm going to ask for you on my next case. Now, how about if we run down to Souris' Tavern and have that drink we talked about? Joel can come too," I said, nodding toward her young assistant. "If we wait 'til after the verdict, I might drink too much."

Kathleen smiled. "That's kind of you, Alex. I'll take your next case. But this is not the ER. Right now, *I'm* still in charge and you have to do what *I* say. So stay put. Unfortunately, this will be the longest part of the trial. I'd love a Grey Goose myself—straight up."

~

The media was out in full force for the conclusion of the trial, so Kathleen, Joel, Penny and I made our way through the crowded hallway to one of the attorney's conference rooms where we could wait in peace. There we sat for the longest three hours of my life, awaiting the verdict of the twelve sworn jurors who would decide whether or not I was grossly negligent as a physician, the calling that pretty well defined my life.

About 4:30, long after we had run out of small talk, Kathleen looked at her watch and said, "The jury's having trouble with this one."

Just before five o'clock there was a rap on the door. Mr. Singer stuck his head in and said, "The jury is returning." Everybody glanced at each other as if our plane was on final approach and we couldn't get the landing gear down.

We sat at the defendant's table as the jury was filing in. I watched the five men and seven women take their seats—scanning each face for clues, but finding none among the taut expressions. Several jurors looked at me briefly and then looked away again. Several others sat with their heads bowed and grimly stared at the floor as if awaiting the holocaust. This was not a happy group of people. I suspected that for many of them, this was the greatest responsibility they had borne in their lifetime.

"Madame Foreman," commanded Judge Bower, "would you please rise?" A fiftyish woman, smartly dressed in a suit the color of red geraniums, rose from the first row of the jury and stood clasping a piece of paper.

"I understand that the jury has reached a verdict?"

"Yes, your Honor."

"Would you please read the questions posed on the jury slip and provide us with the jury's answers?"

The foreman unfolded the paper, her hands trembling ever so slightly. She cleared her throat and began to read.

"'Did the defendant's negligence cause the injury alleged?'" She paused and looked up plaintively at the judge as if to say *please spare me from this*, then down again at the paper. "To this question, the jury answers...'Yes.'" A murmur rose up from the packed courtroom and several reporters bolted for the door.

"Question number two. 'What amount of damages do you award?' To this question," she continued, "the jury answers one hundred and fifty thousand dollars."

CHAPTER SEVENTY

BY 9:30 THURSDAY MORNING, MARY ANNE HAD rented a black Toyota RAV4 SUV and was headed north on I-83. On the train last night her mind was churning so furiously that sleep came late, but four hours of sleep in a train bed was far better than she would have had on a bus, and was a lot more comfortable.

Exiting I-83 at Padonia Road, she drove one mile west and turned right into Penny Murray's development. One hundred yards from the townhouse she noticed the "for sale" sign in the small front yard. The venetian blinds were closed on all of the windows visible from the road, and the grass was high. The little bird had clearly abandoned her nest, but Mary Anne knew to where she had flown.

~

"Are you going to take a nap today?" Ruth inquired.

"I'm going to lay down about noon for an hour or two, then I'll go pick up the kids after school," replied Penny.

"I'll have dinner ready about 5:00, so you should be able to leave for work shortly after 6:00. Right now, I think I'll go to Graul's and get the shopping done for the weekend."

"So, do you think the kids like St. Mark's, Ruth?"

"When I pick them up after school, Catherine can't contain herself—it's talk, talk, talk. I think she loves it. Jack? Well, you can't tell so easy. He's usually in his own little world. But I don't have trouble getting him ready and loaded up in the morning, so, I think he likes it.

"He can't wait to get home in the afternoon, though. First thing he does is find Maggie, although he doesn't have to look very hard because she's always sitting by the driveway when I get home, waiting for him."

~

Mary Anne passed a faded maroon Buick on Monkton Hill, crossed Gunpowder Falls, and slowly drove the winding road through the hamlet of Monkton. It was strange to be back on My Lady's Manor. So much had happened in the last week that it seemed an eternity ago that she was last at Ascot Farms. She thought about calling Manuela at the mansion, but rejected the idea. So far it would be impossible for anyone to trace her movements to Miami, and she wanted to keep it that way.

She crested the hill by the small Isaiah Baptist Church and then continued straight ahead onto Shepherd Road. A few hundred yards further, Randolph's farm came into view. Both his Jeep as well as a new white Honda Pilot—exactly like the one in which the Murray woman had crashed—were parked in the driveway. Too bad that idiot contractor had happened by the crash scene. The fire would have been a nice way for her to go.

So, she liked that car—bought another one. Thinks it saved her life, I bet. Actually, it only bought her another opportunity to beg for her life. Before this is over she'll wish the car had exploded with her in it. Maybe I'll let Raoul and Facundo have their way with her before she dies. That would be fun to watch.

But what if Murray's kids were there? If so, they would be sleeping in other rooms. If they woke up, there was always the possibility that they could identify the killers. She hadn't told Raoul and Facundo that children could be in the house. This was the one element of the plan that she would have to play by ear. If luck was with the children, they would survive. If not…well, life was hard.

CHAPTER SEVENTY-ONE

THE LEAD ARTICLE IN THE HEALTH SECTION OF the Baltimore *Morning Sun* occupied a full half page. Breaking my personal vow not to read, watch, or listen to any of the media coverage associated with the trial, I sat in the sun on the patio Thursday morning sipping coffee, and reading the article carrying the headline, "Maryland Celebrity Physician Guilty of Malpractice."

Three large photos accompanied the piece: one a shot of Penny and me wearing stoic faces, descending the courthouse stairs arm in arm through a crowd, and another a head and shoulders shot of Franklin Stern speaking into a handheld microphone, looking very much like a no-nonsense defender of the little guy who might someday make a great governor.

The third shot was a large close-up of Penny's gorgeous face, since she was the real reason that this case attracted so much attention. I wasn't sure whether I was reading the entertainment section or the health section.

"Dr. Alexander Randolph, an emergency physician at Mason-Dixon Regional Medical Center, who came to national attention during a hostage crisis last year, was found guilty of negligence yesterday in a malpractice trial in Towson," began the article. "The case involved a failure to diagnose appendicitis during eight-year-old Robert

Straley, Jr.'s visit to the Mason-Dixon emergency department three years ago."

The article went on to describe some of the basic facts surrounding the case. A few paragraphs later, Frank got his day in the sun.

"This was a victory for the little guy," Frank was quoted as saying. "This physician's negligence cost the health care system a fortune, not to mention the enormous suffering endured by my young client and his family. His conviction is another small step toward improving quality and reducing the cost of health care in America. I am proud to say that this Maryland jury has put Big Medicine on notice that shoddy medical care will not be tolerated in our state."

I didn't watch any of it, but I heard that for the next thirty-six hours there were similar long pieces during the news hour on all three Baltimore television stations, until the story had finally run its course.

~

The trial screwed up our work schedules, of course, so I started making up for lost time by being scheduled for Friday day shift and then Saturday night. Penny was scheduled for Thursday and Friday night. I was not looking forward to my first shift after the trial, a time when all of my colleagues would surely feel obligated to say something nice.

Beyond that, I was not certain how the guilty verdict might erode my moral authority as chief of emergency medicine, or what impact it would have on the political power that I wielded within the institution—important if you want to retain control of your department. Certainly, at the very least, the administration would not be happy with the adverse publicity. Jacquelyn Ford and Dr. Myers were no doubt ecstatic.

I walked into the ER at 9:00 AM Friday hoping that the day would be busy as hell with no time for chit-chat.

Happily, when I arrived there were three new patients in line to be seen, and in the first hour everyone essentially left me alone, although I could notice people glancing at me from time to time, trying to assess my mood and perhaps struggling to decide whether to say anything to me or not.

The only person to say anything to me was Lynn Saylor, the 5:00 AM doc, who without looking up from her computer, upon my arrival said, "Fuck 'em all, Alex."

~

Lisa Turano walked into Bed Three and pulled back the curtain. "Hi, Trish. I'm Lisa Turano and I'll be your nurse today," she said cheerily. "The triage nurse told me that you're having some back pain. Is that right?"

"Two days," said the forty-two-year-old, wincing and holding the right side of her back at the belt line. "It's killing me."

"That's a bummer, isn't it? I remember when I was in the last month of my pregnancy and still working. My back hurt me so much I didn't think I could make it through the day. Have you had pain like this before?"

"Oh, yeah. Plenty of times."

"How long have you been having this pain off and on?"

"Since my automobile accident."

"And when was that?"

"Oh, maybe five years ago."

"Do you have back pain every day, or just intermittently?"

"It comes and goes. I'll be all right for a month or two and then it just comes back."

"Does it go down over your buttocks or into your legs?"

"Goes down my right butt cheek just about to my hip."

"Do you take medicine for your back?"

"Just ibuprofen, except when I get these spells, then I have to have something stronger."

Lisa reviewed Trish's past medical history, current medications, allergies, and other questions regarding her social history as she entered data into the bedside computer. Her tasks completed, she said, "OK, Trish, Dr. Randolph should be with you shortly."

As Lisa pulled the curtain back into place, Trish said, "Wait. Isn't that the guy in the news?"

Lisa hesitated. "Well, he has been in the news from time to time."

"Didn't he just get convicted of malpractice yesterday?"

"Yes. He lost a case," Lisa said quietly.

"I don't want to see that guy."

Lisa bit her lip. "Listen, I know that this may sound self-serving, but I know Dr. Randolph very well, and he's one of the best docs I've ever met."

"Well, apparently the jury didn't think so. Have them get somebody else in here. I'll wait."

Lisa pulled the curtain and left the room without further comment, suddenly struck with overwhelming sadness. Quite apart from the fact that Alex Randolph was one of her best friends, he was a fabulous doc—one of the smartest guys she'd ever met. He tried to do what was right for his patient—didn't try to cover his ass by getting a CAT scan on everybody who walked through the door like so many other docs she knew. And what happens? The system screws him.

She shook her head as she walked down the hall toward the nursing station, thinking about what to say to him. Poor Alex and Penny. They just couldn't catch a break.

~

Shortly after 10:00 AM I picked up the chart for my fourth new patient of the morning. Lisa Turano, standing nearby, put her hand on my shoulder and gently said, "Alex, this patient doesn't want to see you. She asked if there was another doctor available."

I looked up from my chair. "She saw the evening news last night, right?"

Lisa nodded. I handed her the chart and my eyes returned to my computer screen.

"Alex, look at me," she commanded, her blue eyes burning fiercely. "You're the best physician I've ever known. Forget it. This will pass."

CHAPTER SEVENTY-TWO

THE FIRST FEW DAYS AFTER THE TRIAL PENNY and I were pretty much like two ships passing in the night. She got up at noon on Saturday after her Friday night shift, and I tried to take a nap at 3:30 to get ready for my 7:00 PM shift. I was looking forward to Sunday afternoon riding lessons and then dinner as our first time together in several days.

I lay in my bedroom with the blinds pulled and a fan on for white noise, but I couldn't sleep. The outcome of the trial had had a bigger impact on me than I expected.

It struck so deeply at the heart of everything to which I had devoted my life in the last eighteen years that I found myself questioning if I really was who I thought I was. Moreover, more than a little cynicism was creeping into my attitudes regarding American society and its institutions, needless to say, particularly its institutions of justice.

"They didn't want to convict you, Alex," Kathleen Stefanik had said. "They just wanted to help the Straley's a little bit financially."

I was unaccustomed to any sense of depression, but the trial verdict was like a heavy gray fog that enveloped and penetrated every nook and cranny of my life, sucking away every trace of joy or optimism. I finally gave up on sleep about 5:00, crawled out of bed, and showered.

With the wedding date now exactly two weeks away from today, I couldn't wait. I desperately needed that week of honeymoon to escape from all of this, gain some perspective, and clear my mind.

Ruth had dinner ready at 5:45. The chatter of Ruth, Penny, and the children was a welcome distraction.

"Catherine, you haven't touched those green beans yet. You're not getting down from this table until they're gone," Penny warned.

"But they make me *gag*," Catherine pleaded with pouting lips, her blue eyes becoming liquid.

Penny sighed with exasperation. "OK, Catherine. One green bean. Eat it now."

Catherine picked up her little knife and ever so slowly began to saw a solitary green bean into five tiny pieces. Looking up to see if Penny was still watching, she stabbed one piece with her fork, put it in her mouth and immediately reached for her glass of milk, swallowing the microscopic bean whole, like chewing would release a deadly poison. A dramatic, Academy-Award-winning gag followed.

"Don't you dare throw up, Catherine," Penny said sternly. "You could have eaten that whole bean at one time and had it over with. Now you've got to do it five times. Look at your brother. He ate all of his."

"Jack likes green beans, don't you, Jack?" said Ruth. "He had two helpings."

I noted that Jack's macaroni and pieces of pork chop were also gone. "Do you want some more pork, Jack?" I asked.

Jack nodded and slid over from his booster seat into my lap. Reaching around his body with both arms, I cut five more small pieces off my pork chop. Jack stabbed one with his little fork, leaned back into my chest and put it into his mouth. I cut another piece for myself, popped it into my mouth, and we sat contentedly chewing pork chop together, his warm little body leaning into mine emitting a powerful, light that pierced the gray fog with its brilliance.

I kissed Penny and the kids goodbye, hugged Ruth's bony body, and hopped into my Jeep, heading off for Saturday night in the ER. Taking action, the psychiatrists keep telling us, is the best antidote for depression. Maybe tonight would provide some action that would help to bolster my battered self-esteem.

~

At 6:40 PM, Mary Anne parked the Saturn in an empty space at the back of the ER patient parking lot, turned off the ignition, and lowered the sunglasses from her hair. Her wait was short. Five minutes later, a white Jeep Wrangler pulled into the adjacent employee lot. Alex Randolph exited the Jeep, flashed his badge at a wall reader by the sliding glass doors of the ambulance entrance, and walked into the building.

He's working the 7:00 PM to 5:00 AM shift. Tonight's the night.

CHAPTER SEVENTY-THREE

RUTH HEARD THE GRANDFATHER CLOCK IN the foyer downstairs strike three AM. She was never a good sleeper, but the last several weeks the nights had been long. Since the death of her husband five years ago, Alex Randolph and his new little family had been a godsend—returning joy to her life and giving her a reason to live in these twilight years. They depended on her—needed her. But she was worried sick about them.

Since the end of the trial, Alex had been uncharacteristically quiet. Usually he teased Ruth unmercifully, but in the last three days his mood had been somber. She had tried ordering him around—Alex liked that. Usually his eyes would twinkle as he came back at her with some witty comment of the kind that Ruth could never think of, but the house had been mirthless the last few days.

Nevertheless, intuitively Ruth thought it likely that Alex would soon snap back. He was the smartest, most competent man she had ever met, and she couldn't imagine that evil attorney keeping him down.

But Penny—a surrogate daughter who Ruth had come to love as if she were her own—was another story. Somebody had tried to kill that sweet girl in a horrible way—she had almost burned to death—a fact that was completely incomprehensible to Ruth. The world was filled with unspeakable evil.

That Stine man might be dead, but the woman who put him up to it was still out there someplace…and missing. Every time Penny left the house, Ruth held her breath until Penny's return. Daily she prayed that the police would find that despicable Williams woman and that this family could finally go back to a normal life. It would be such relief.

In a preview of fall, happily tonight was cool. It was the first night in weeks that she had not turned on her window air conditioner. Through the other open window in her bedroom, the peaceful chorus of the cicadas kept her company.

In the distance, Maggie began to bark ferociously for perhaps a full minute, then abruptly stopped. Ruth listened intently for several minutes but heard no noise or further barking. She turned on her pillow to check the time. Struggling to focus without her glasses, she was just able to discern a blurry 3:12 when the red LED lights on the clock went black.

Ruth rose from her bed and quietly walked down the hallway to the top of the stairs where she stood listening.

~

Facundo swung the white rental car into the small parking lot of the little white clapboard church on the hill in Monkton, seventy-five yards west of Shepherd Road. He parked behind the church where the car could not be seen from the road, got out, and climbed into the waiting Toyota SUV. Having two escape cars was just good planning.

Alice Cooper drove east onto Shepherd Road. One hundred yards past the Randolph farm she doused the lights and turned right onto a tractor path leading into a hay field of orchard grass. Engaging four-wheel-drive, she turned the black SUV off the dirt road into the grass and parked behind a stand of trees and honeysuckle. She checked her watch: 2:40 AM.

Drawing equipment from their fanny packs, the three SUV occupants first pulled out headsets with mics and earphones. After radio checks, they pulled on thin rubber gloves, donned night vision goggles, checked their weapons, and beneath a quarter moon sky, silently walked through the field toward the Randolph farm.

Climbing through a hedgerow onto the Randolph property, they walked between the barn and an outbuilding, hugging the side of the barn for cover. Between the barn and the house there was no cover but darkness.

Facundo marveled at the clarity of vision with the goggles. It was like mid-day, only green. But the clarity of the goggles also made him feel exposed, like he was walking around in broad daylight.

Bending slightly at the waist to minimize their profile, the trio began to run toward the brick farmhouse. Raoul immediately noticed a second car in the driveway: an older model Buick. *Mierda! Who the hell else could be here?* he wondered. For a split second he considered aborting the mission.

Alice Cooper spotted the Buick as the same moment as Raoul. *Shit! Whose car is that?*

Out of nowhere, with a ferocious roar, a large dog charged from the house at top speed, sliding to a stop not ten feet from the trio. Hair standing up and fangs bared, the animal made enough noise to wake the dead. Shooting the dog would make even more noise. Raoul issued an order. "Facundo, take him! Your knife!"

His eyes never leaving the dog, Facundo reached under his right pant leg and pulled a five-inch blade strapped to his leg. With a smooth, practiced motion his arm whipped and the blade sunk deep into the animal's chest. The barking stopped, and the dog slowly sank to the ground, his front legs collapsing first. Facundo circled the dying animal, pulled out the knife, and lifting the dog's head by his fur, slit its throat, jumping back to avoid the gush of blood.

Raoul didn't like this. There was an unknown car in the driveway and the dog may have awakened the woman. "C'mon. *Rapido!*" he commanded. The three sprinted to the cover of the old brick house.

Splitting up, Raoul and Facundo began a systematic search for a power breaker box. "Here it is," came Raoul's hushed voice over the radio, "on the back side of the house." He pulled the lever on the box, and through the windows of a set of French doors, saw the LED lights on a microwave go out.

Reaching into his fanny pack, he pulled a pair of wire cutters and snipped a thinner cable entering the house beside the breaker box. "Got the phone line, too," he whispered into the microphone.

Alice and Facundo appeared on the patio. "You stay here and stand guard," Raoul said to Alice, "I don't want you in that house."

"No!" said Alice vehemently. "I'll stay here until you find her, but keep her alive until you come get me. If you let me kill her, I'll let you have your way with her before she dies." Raoul silently looked at Alice for a long moment, then said, "Facundo, open the door."

Pulling a small tool from his fanny pack, Facundo worked on the lock for perhaps a minute and a half before he felt, as much as heard, a click. Looking at the other two team members, he whispered, "OK. That's it. Here we go." The hinges gave out a long, low groan as the French door swung inward and the two brothers carefully entered the house.

~

Penny awoke with a start to the vise-like grip on her arm. She popped up onto her elbows and blankly looked around the room for the digital clock, but couldn't find it. In the dark room she could make out only the faintest outlines of someone standing over her.

"What...?" she mumbled. A bony hand clamped over her mouth and Ruth's voice hissed in her ear. "Quiet! There's somebody in the house! The power's off. Take the kids and get in the closet room, quick!" Ruth's commands produced instant clarity.

Throwing back the covers, Penny scrambled across a child's sleeping body, nearly falling as she reached the edge of the king-sized bed. Finding one arm in the darkness, she yanked Catherine to the edge of the bed, effortlessly lifted her limp body and stumbled the short distance to the open closet bordered by two sets of folding louvered doors.

Oh, God, please! she silently pleaded as she fumbled through the hanging clothes, fingers frantically searching for the tiny hole in the cedar-paneled rear wall that would release the door to the small hidden room. In answer to prayer, a finger sunk into a hole, the latch clicked, and the door swung open. Blindly, she lay Catherine on the floor, who began to stir and said, "What Mommy?"

"Sshhh, Catherine, don't say a word!"

She turned to retrieve Jack and bumped into Ruth holding him out among the hanging clothes.

"My cell phone! Get my cell phone beside the bed!" she whispered, pulling Jack into her arms. Groping in the darkness, she found Catherine on the floor. "Catherine, hold Jack!"

A second later, she heard Ruth's raspy whisper. "Here!" Penny reached out, found Ruth's arms and took the cell phone. She grabbed an arm and pulled. "Come on in. Hurry!" With incredible speed and strength, Ruth jerked her arm out of Penny's grasp, and in an instant had closed the small door. Penny could hear the clothes being re-arranged on the hangers and then the louvered doors quietly snap shut.

In the blackness, suddenly all was quiet but the pounding of Penny's pulse in her ears. "Mommy, I can't see. I'm scared," Catherine whimpered. Penny's hand clamped over her daughter's mouth.

Oh my God! How am I going to keep these kids quiet?

CHAPTER SEVENTY-FOUR

SATURDAY NIGHTS ARE FUNNY. WHEN THE moon is full, all the dysfunctional brains in the county seem to go into overdrive and an endless procession of overdoses, panic attacks, sucker-punched bloody faces, and motor vehicle accident victims flood the gates of our we-can-solve-all-problems public institution. The security guys like these nights because they go much faster than a boring Monday night.

On the other hand, sometimes Saturday nights are remarkably peaceful. Nobody has to go to work on Sunday morning, so we don't see drunks looking for a work note at 4:00 AM, and the kids with fever can wait until morning because mom and dad will both be home. So you never know what a Saturday night will bring.

Tonight was only a quarter moon—patient flow was steady, but manageable. Scott Foreman was the 3:00 PM to 1:00 AM doc. He and I chatted about the U.S. Open tennis tournament between patients.

The major bummer about working tonight was that had I wanted to see the third round match between Serena Williams and Victoria Azarenka, which obviously wasn't going to happen, so I settled for the next best thing. I pulled up the U.S. Open app on my iPhone and laid it beside my computer so I could at least watch the scores in real time.

Azarenka was down 3-0 when I went in to see Cory Burkholder, a slender ten-year-old boy who had wrecked his four-wheeler riding in the dark. By the time I had finished cleaning dirt, leaves and pebbles out of the six-centimeter laceration on his knee, Williams had cleaned Azarenka's clock in the first set 6-1.

~

"How's it going in the second set?" Scott asked.

"Azarenka must have regained her footing. They've traded a couple of service breaks and it's 6-6. They're just starting the tiebreaker."

I desperately wanted to watch the tiebreaker evolve, but, of course, that was not to be. It was near midnight when I finished up with Cliff Stover, a very nice elderly gentlemen whose heart had decided to do a little jig at a hundred and fifty beats a minute—atrial fibrillation we call it—and the match was long over. Serena won in the second set tiebreaker 7-5.

I suspected that Serena would take the whole tournament. Only Australian Sam Stosur posed a significant challenge in the remainder of the draw, but her record against Serena was not good. Williams was likely to hoist another silver cup.

Shortly after midnight the doors to the ER magically slammed shut, and Scott was able to leave on time at 1:00 AM. By 3:00 I had gotten most of the remaining patients processed and was down to just two in various stages of workup.

I heard my iPhone vibrate and glanced at the screen. A wave of nausea swept over me as I read the text from Penny:

someone in house call 911 hiding in closet

It took a second for my brain to shift gears. I tapped back:

on my way

"Pat!" I said, grabbing the shoulder of the charge nurse sitting at the computer to my right, "Listen carefully. I just got a text from Penny. Call 911 and tell them there's a home invasion at my house. I'm leaving." I scribbled the farm address on a piece of scrap paper and handed it to her. "Here's the address. Call Scott back in. And call Lisa Turano and tell her to send Frank to my house."

I slammed through the ER door, grabbed my keys from my shorts in the locker room, and tore out to my Jeep, my shoulder hitting the edge of the sliding glass doors at the ambulance entrance when they didn't open fast enough.

Running across the parking lot I glanced at my iPhone message page and saw *Read 3:16 AM* under my message to Penny. She got it.

It was exactly six-point-five miles to the farm on Shepherd Road. Although Lisa's husband, Frank, a Baltimore homicide detective, lived on Corbett Road—about the same distance from the farm—I had a major head start, and he would have to rouse out of bed and get dressed. I knew there was only one Baltimore County patrol car in the northern part of the county, and Lord knows when they would arrive. I would clearly get there first.

The narrow Wrangler briefly went up on two wheels as I rounded the curves down the hill from Middletown Road to the Gunpowder Falls bridge, but the Jeep mercifully clung to the road.

As the four cylinders painfully and slowly climbed the long hill to Hereford High School I began to formulate a plan. I had no weapon, but Sally Horn kept a .22 rifle in the barn that she used on groundhogs in the pasture. It had no stopping power on a man, but it would have to do.

I debated whether to stop short of the farm and go in on foot, but decided that time was almost certainly critical. I wanted the invader to be distracted by my arrival. I would go in by the driveway, pull up to the barn, and grab the rifle. I rolled through a red light at Mt. Carmel Road in Hereford and made the left turn onto Monkton Road at twenty-five miles an hour.

CHAPTER SEVENTY-FIVE

PENNY PUT HER LIPS TO CATHERINE'S EAR AND stroked her hair. "It's OK, baby," she whispered softly. "Ruth thought there was somebody else in the house so we're just hiding here until she checks and we're sure. We're going to be fine here. Alex is coming. It will only be a little while, but you must be very quiet so they don't hear us. If you want to whisper something to me, tap me on the arm, but don't talk unless I say it's OK." Penny could feel Catherine's head nod under her hand.

A minute passed with not a sound except Jack's slow deep breathing, who blessedly remained asleep in Catherine's arms. Penny began to wonder if Ruth was hearing things, but it was true that the power seemed to be out.

In the distance a woman's screaming voice broke the silence, followed by a powerful crack that Penny could feel through the floorboards. It was unmistakably a gun. Silence again. Terror flooded the young mother's heart. She gagged and then swallowed the vomitus that welled up in her throat.

"What was that, Mommy?" came Catherine's voice. Penny's hand viciously clamped over her daughter's mouth for the second time.

~

Alice watched as the brothers crept through the patio doors into

425

what appeared to be a family room that transitioned into a kitchen at the front of the house. On the far left of the kitchen was an opening that led to another room or a hallway. The stairs would be in that direction.

To the right of the kitchen was a closed door that likely led into a mudroom or laundry. Working as a team, Facundo quietly turned the knob and pushed open the door while Raoul rushed the doorway with both hands on the Browning. Both men reappeared a moment later with weapons at their side.

In an instant, a skeleton-like screaming banshee with wild green hair appeared in the kitchen holding a butcher knife in one raised arm. "What are you doing here? Get out!" she wailed.

The two brothers stood motionless for a moment, paralyzed. Through the open patio doors, Alice calmly raised her Sig Sauer P238, placed the red dot on the woman's forehead and squeezed the trigger. In an instant, the banshee collapsed to the floor.

"Get upstairs," Alice ordered the two shocked brothers. Weapons out in front, they disappeared through the opening to the left of the kitchen.

Walking to the body in the kitchen, Alice surveyed her handiwork with satisfaction. The shot was perfect. The slug from the Sig Sauer had entered the middle of the old woman's forehead and exploded out the back of the her skull, leaving a giant hole oozing with blood and brain matter.

Dipping two fingers into the exit wound, she walked back into the family room and knelt on a leather sofa, drawing a crude hand in blood on the wall above, signing the letter "C" between thumb and index finger. From her fanny pack she fished a blue bandana, wiped the blood from her latex gloves and dropped the bandana on the carpet by the patio doors.

~

Raoul entered a dining room, spotted a hallway to the right and quickly moved into a foyer at the bottom of a main staircase. The brothers took the stairs two at a time. At the top of the stairs they paused in a hallway that ran nearly the length of the house with about six doors.

Straight ahead was an open bathroom door. Down a hallway to the left was an open door that appeared to lead into a bedroom on the east side of the house. To the right on the west side, all the doors were closed except one.

Raoul tapped Facundo on the shoulder and pointed to the open door on the right. Raoul himself turned left toward the open door at the east end, raised his gun and popped into the room in a crouch. The room appeared empty, but the covers were thrown off the bed and the sheets in the middle glowed with warmth in the green light of the goggles. Raoul placed his hand on the sheets and confirmed the warmth. Someone was in this bed moments ago. He dropped to one knee and searched under the bed, then stood.

This is a master bedroom, thought Raoul. *I bet the girl was sleeping in here. The old woman must have been a housekeeper or relative.* He cursed the old woman for broadcasting a warning. Now they'd have to find the girl and that could take time. This wasn't what he had bargained for.

What if a neighbor had heard the shot and called the police? That bitch, Alice—or whatever her name was—had held out on him. She seemed unsurprised by the old woman. He silently vowed to kill her after they were paid. Maybe he would have his way with *her* before he killed her.

To the rear of the room was another open door, undoubtedly a bathroom. Raoul rushed the doorway and snapped back the shower curtain, but the bathtub was empty. Adjacent to the bathroom was a pair of narrow stairs that curved and led to somewhere on the first floor. Raoul decided to check them later. Only the closet remained to be searched in this bedroom.

Standing in front of the louvered doors, gun extended, he whipped one spring-loaded door open on its tracks: nothing. He pushed the second door open and searched through the hanging clothes, but the closet was empty. Tank tops and sun dresses hung from the metal rod. These were the clothes of a younger woman.

Pushing the transmit button, he whispered, "The master bedroom is empty, but she's here. The bed is warm."

"My room's empty, too," responded Facundo. "This one must have been the old lady's room."

Meeting again in the hallway, the two began a methodical room-to-room search.

~

It had taken a little time groping around in the pitch black tiny room to find the box containing the Glock, and even longer to find the clip and box of ammo high on a narrow shelf. With trembling hands, Penny loaded the weapon by feel, dropping two shells in the process and wincing at the sound as the casings hit the wooden floor.

She sat cross-legged on the floor in front of the door, listening intently, holding the Glock in her lap and one hand gripping Catherine's leg who sat holding Jack in the corner behind her.

Faint sounds of someone moving around the bedroom reached her ears. Quietly she rose to her feet, crouched, and held the Glock in front of her with two hands. Her body jerked when the louvered doors snapped open, her finger almost pulling the trigger. With her heart in her throat, she listened as someone pushed the clothes on hangers from side to the side, searching for her and her babies.

~

Mary Anne heard a vehicle approach at high speed and then saw headlights sweep across the barn as Alex Randolph's Jeep roared down the driveway and slid to a stop in the grass by the barn.

She smiled. *Well, well...it's dear Alex. I don't know who invited you, lover, but welcome to the party.* "We've got company," she whispered into the microphone. "It's the boyfriend. Keep searching. I've got him covered."

Alex leapt from the Jeep and ran around the corner of the barn, disappearing inside. Mary Anne sprinted to the cover of a large maple halfway between the house and barn to get closer to her target. Beyond thirty or forty feet, the accuracy of her Sig Sauer was not good.

A moment later Alex reappeared, carrying a small caliber rifle and unknowingly ran directly toward Mary Anne. Fifty feet from the tree he tripped over the body of the dog and violently sprawled forward, the rifle flying from his hands. As he rose to his knees Mary Anne placed the red dot on his chest.

CHAPTER SEVENTY-SIX

THE HOUSE WAS DARK AS I TURNED INTO THE farm lane, although the dawn-to-dusk light on the barn remained illuminated. Only Penny and Ruth's cars were in the driveway. There were no visible signs of activity.

I angled off the driveway, sliding to a stop on dew-covered grass at the far end of the barn. I ran around the corner through an open door facing the paddock into a tool storage area.

Sally's rifle hung from two nails high on the wall just inside the door. I quickly found it by feel, then groped on an adjacent shelf for the box of ammo. Fifteen seconds later, I peered around the open door toward the house, but could see no movement. Exiting the barn, I ran at top speed along the paddock fence for the patio.

Twenty feet from the barn I tripped over something large and soft and went sprawling, landing on my chin with a force that made me see stars. I tasted blood, spit sod from my mouth, and rose to one knee, looking around for the rifle. In the dim light, my eyes alighted on Maggie's dead body. A brilliant red dot erratically played across the grass in front of me and then rose to my chest. I recognized it instantly and violently dove to my left toward the paddock fence.

The shot rang out as I was in mid-air. I hit the ground and rolled three times under the bottom rail of the fence. As I tried to stand, my right leg collapsed and I fell in a heap. I heard the snort and whinny of agitated horses and dragged myself around the rear end of Abigail, whispering to her and praying that she would not smash my skull with a powerful kick. Using the horse for cover, I carefully rose to my feet again, keeping weight off my right leg as much as possible and hopped around General Lee toward the barn, rolling again under the fence and through the open door into the tool storage area.

I stood gasping for air with my back pressed against the barn wall just inside the doorway. My hands reached out, groping among the tools leaning against the wall until I found the handle of a pitchfork, now the only weapon available. I held it in both hands with the tines pointed toward the doorway.

Increasingly aware of vague pain, I reached down to my right thigh and felt sticky wetness on my scrub suit pants. This was no doubt a bullet wound. Gradually, I placed increasing weight on the leg and it held. At least the slug had missed the bone and there seemed to be no fracture, but I couldn't tell how fast I was losing blood.

~

Terror stricken that Alex would arrive—unarmed—before the police, Penny's body shook so violently that it took several seconds to find the button on her iPhone. Shading the screen to minimize light that might be seen through cracks in the door, she checked the time: 3:23—eight minutes since Alex's text. He would likely be here at any moment.

Holding her breath, she listened intently, but only Jack's steady breathing could be heard in the isolated little room. Another endless minute passed, and then the unmistakable muffled crack of a second gunshot reached her ears.

~

In the upstairs hallway together at the top of the stairs, Raoul and Facundo heard the gunshot and froze. Alice's cryptic voice came over the radio a moment later. "He's wounded. He ran into the barn. Keep searching. I'll finish him off."

"Fuck!" swore Raoul. "This cunt is getting us in deep shit! Five more minutes is all she gets and we're outta here! One more quick search of the rooms!" The brothers split once more to opposite ends of the hallway and resumed the search.

What could I have missed in here? thought Raoul as he re-entered the master bedroom. He rapidly descended the narrow curving stairway and found himself in the kitchen. Nothing there but the body of the old woman.

Climbing the stairs back to the bedroom, he walked again to the closet. The back wall was unusually far away from the clothes rod and constructed of vertical wood boards. Carefully, he began a systematic scan of the paneling. At waist level he found a round hole. Two feet above the hole was a faint horizontal line. *Is that a seam?* He ran his fingers along the line. Raising the Browning with his left hand, he slipped his right index finger into the hole.

~

"Hello, lover," came a sweet voice from the darkness near the doorway. I recognized it instantly. "Don't think about using that pitchfork, darling. You'll be dead before you can blink."

She can see me. How...? She must be wearing night vision goggles. But her voice is close. She can't be more than eight or ten feet away.

"You had to come, didn't you? It's a shame, you know?" she continued. "You and I could have had a wonderful life together."

I need to buy time.

"Why...?" I asked. "You have everything."

"It was for us, of course," she answered with incredulity. "I loved you! I've dreamt of you day and night for months. If your bitch had been killed in that accident we could have been the perfect couple, with money and power and fame. You could have been the master of Ascot Farms."

I have to distract her! Vague pain registered in the periphery of my consciousness. Something was boring into my back below my shoulder blade. *The light switch!*

"I begged you. But you were pussy-whipped by that blond whore, weren't you, Alex? You humiliated me—blew me off and threw her in my face. And now, it's come to this, my dear, dear beautiful man. So sad…so needless. Now you have to die, my love."

Pushing my back against the switch, I slowly rose on my toes. A red laser dot played erratically on my chest. With a click, the barn was suddenly flooded with blinding light. In an instant, I had hurled the pitchfork with all my strength toward an amorphous black figure standing to my right.

Mary Anne's body rocked back against a wooden stall, her gun dropping to the dirt floor. Still standing, she slowly reached up and pulled the goggles from her eyes, then grasped the pitchfork that bobbed from her chest with both hands. She raised her face and looked at me blankly. "My breasts…" she said.

I stood and stared as my breathing slowed, suddenly appalled at the damage I had done to this sentient, living creature.

My eyes fell to her chest. The tine pattern had entered her thorax horizontally. It was impossible to tell whether her rib cage had been penetrated. Two tines had entered to the left of her sternum. Had they punctured myocardium; aorta; lung? How fast was she bleeding internally? Instinctively my hands reached out to stabilize the oscillating pitchfork handle in an effort to minimize the damage of moving tines tearing through tissue.

Behind me, a muffled shot rang out from the direction of the house. A wave of nausea washed over me. Mary Anne's eyes widened and then in recognition, she briefly laughed, triggering a violent coughing spell. When the spell subsided, she looked at me again and smiled. "That was your girlfriend, Alex. She's dead."

~

As the door to the secret room swung open, Penny's finger tapped the camera icon on the iPhone and, in a brilliant flash, illuminated a black alien with huge bulging eyes. A microsecond later, her right index finger squeezed the trigger on the Glock and a powerful explosion deafened her. Miraculously, the alien vanished from view.

Rising slowly from her knees, Penny took a step forward and leaned against the clothes rod. As she violently emptied the contents of her stomach, the fingers on the Glock slowly uncurled, and the gun clattered to the floor.

"Mommy!" screamed Catherine. In a daze, Penny wiped her mouth with the bottom of her tank top, turned, and reaching through the door, illuminated the little room with the flashlight app on her iPhone. Bending at the waist, she lifted Jack—now wailing—from her daughter's lap, and then reached out for Catherine's arm, hugging her daughter to her leg.

"Ssshhh…ssshhh…it's all right, babies. It's all over. We're safe now."

~

Facundo froze at the sound of the shot. It was different. *Was that the Browning?* He waited a moment for a radio transmission, but there was none. He pressed the transmit button. "Raoul?" Silence. "Alice?" A nauseating fear welled over the hunter. He suddenly felt very much alone. *I need to get out of here!*

Heart pounding, he tiptoed to the doorway of the child's room he was searching and carefully peered down the hallway. A light was on in the master bedroom. Mustering all of his courage, he crept down the hallway, astonished to hear the wail of crying children. *The light's too bright*, he thought, ripping the goggles from his eyes.

He dropped into the room on one knee, gripping the Ruger automatic in both hands. In his sights, stood a blond woman looking directly at him, holding a crying child in her arms, with a second clinging to her bare leg. On the floor lay the body of his brother.

CHAPTER SEVENTY-SEVEN

IT HAD NOT OCCURRED TO ME THAT THERE would be more than one assassin at the farm. Terrified at what I might find and cursing my leg, I grabbed Mary Anne's pistol from the dirt floor and hobbled to the patio as fast as my body would carry me.

One of the patio French doors hung open. I crept into the darkened family room. As I rounded the granite counter that divided the kitchen from the family room, I could just make out a form lying on the floor of the kitchen. When I knelt to the floor it became obvious that it was Ruth's body. A violent, all-consuming rage rose like Vesuvius in my brain. There was someone else in this house and I would kill them.

From Penny's text. I knew that she and the children were in the secret room. As I approached the sneaky staircase, my heart leapt at the sound of Jack and Catherine crying. I prayed to God that they were not crying over their mother's dead body. I forced myself to go slowly, knowing that the danger was not over, holding my breath for a creak on the staircase that would betray my presence.

As I reached the top stair and peered around the corner, overwhelming relief washed over me. In the ghostly light provided by her iPhone, Penny stood with Jack in her arms and Catherine at her side looking toward the bedroom door. To my right, movement caught my eye as a black figure dropped into the room on one knee, the gun in his arms rising as if in slow motion toward the gathered mother and children. Without conscious thought, my gun aligned with his torso and fired. The man jerked violently, then awkwardly tried to stand. A second explosion ripped the air and he fell forward, sprawling onto his face; the gun clattering from his hand to the floor.

I limped to his side and kicked away the gun as he slowly struggled to rise again to his hands and knees. Stepping on his back, I violently slammed his body to the floor. Blood poured from his nostrils, pooling on the wooden floorboards.

"Alex! You're alive!" Penny cried. "But you're hurt!" I looked down at my scrub suit, covered in blood and dirt.

"Get me the lantern from the little room," I said. With her flashlight Penny quickly found the battery-powered lantern and flicked the switch, its small florescent tube bathing the grisly scene in cold white light.

"Take the children to another bedroom," I ordered quietly, "—not downstairs."

"Alex! No!" she screamed.

"Go, Penny!" I said without looking up.

She fled from the room sobbing, carrying Jack and pushing Catherine along. Kneeling beside the man, I ripped the black knit cap from his shaven head. He appeared young—maybe early twenties. I put the barrel of my gun to his temple and my mouth to his ear.

"Who are you?" I whispered.

"Facundo...Facundo Ramirez," he choked. "Please, I kill no one. It was the girl. She kill the old woman. Please...please help me."

I applied pressure to the trigger for several seconds, hesitating as powerful conflict raged within me. In the end, my index finger slowly relaxed.

"Where are you from?" I barked.

The young man coughed violently, spewing more blood across the floor.

"Where are you from?" I screamed again, brutally pressing the gun barrel into the skin in front of his ear.

"Mi…Miami…" he whispered, his eyes growing distant. Deeply ingrained instincts rising, I released his head and began to search for entrance wounds in his chest. I found blood seeping through his jersey, just below the left armpit and a second wound three inches lower. There were no visible exit wounds on the other side.

The slugs had travelled through his thorax from left to right, transiting the mediastinum where lay the heart and great vessels. perhaps hitting a rib that dissipated energy, but in the process, flattened the bullet, causing it to tumble and producing enormous destruction in its wake. My fingers went to his neck, searching for a carotid pulse, but I could feel nothing.

I rose and stood over him with the gun at my side, watching the color visibly drain from his face, and his breathing become shallow and irregular in the dim light. He was dying and I could—would—do nothing to save him.

I heard movement in the hallway and turned to see Frank Turano burst into the room with his gun raised. We stood and stared at each other for several seconds.

"Come on, Frank," I said, hobbling slowly to the door. "We need to search the rest of the house."

CHAPTER SEVENTY-EIGHT

AS THE INTIAL SHOCK OF THE INJURY SUBSIDED, lightning bolts raced through nerves to Mary Anne's brain. Each tiny movement of the tines and every short, shallow breath was agony.

With enormous strength of will, she slipped her fingers through the tines, screamed, and gave a mighty heave, the pitchfork popping out of her chest and clattering against the stone foundation wall of the barn. She stood holding her chest with both hands, bending at the waist and gasping for air as powerful electric waves of pain jolted her slender frame. Abruptly, another violent coughing spell wracked her chest and she tasted blood in the sputum that rose into her mouth. Her vision became dark and she slid to the dirt floor, leaning back against the wooden stall boards.

I'm still awake and I can still breathe. I have to get to the car! Slowly her vision began to clear and the wooziness in her head subsided. Struggling to her feet and supporting herself with one hand on the wooden stall she walked to the doorway. *I'm on my feet and I haven't passed out.* To the right, faint light glowed through an upstairs window of the darkened farmhouse, but no movement was visible.

As she exited the tool room and rounded the corner of the barn, another muffled gunshot boomed from the house, the clanging alarm of danger in her brain providing a surge of strength. Still holding her chest, she broke into an agonizing slow jog along the side of the barn and then turned east toward the hedgerow.

Within four minutes she had reached the black SUV just as the warble of an approaching siren gradually became audible amidst the night sounds. With headlights out and wheels spinning in the grass, Mary Anne reached the hard pavement of Shepherd Road in time to see flashing red and blue lights turn into Randolph's lane one hundred and fifty yards to the west.

Ten miles later, having crossed the Baltimore County line into Harford County, she finally felt safe enough to pull into a 7-Eleven parking lot in Jarrettsville. The police would assume that she had escaped in a car, but would have no way of identifying the vehicle she was driving. So, as long as she drove carefully and stayed within the speed limit, she should be safe.

Although she winced with each turn of the steering wheel, the searing pain in her chest was gradually subsiding. *I can live with this for a while.* The sudden spasms of coughing continued, but she could no longer taste blood. Remarkably, she felt no real shortness of breath. These were all good signs, she thought.

Nevertheless, even if the tines had produced no fatal injuries, infection from a pitchfork wound would surely set in rapidly and she knew instinctively that would kill her without treatment.

Under the light of a lamp post, she unzipped the black running jacket and pulled up her sports bra to survey the damage. The pointed metal tines had first passed through both pieces of clothing, perhaps at least cleaning off some of the dirt before entering her skin…she hoped.

In the dim light she could see five small puncture wounds evenly spread horizontally across her chest along the top of her breasts. Only a few traces of congealed blood could be seen on the surface of her skin, but there were half-dollar-sized bruises surrounding three of the wounds.

The worst of the pain seemed to come from under the last wound on the left above her nipple. She reasoned that at least one of the tines must have penetrated deeply enough to puncture a lung, because she had coughed up blood.

She licked dry lips, suddenly aware of a raging thirst. Reaching for the water bottle in the console cup holder, she drank deeply. With thirst quenched, she fought to force the pain from her mind and focus on a plan.

Two things were clear: she needed treatment for her wounds and she needed to get out of the country. Without doubt a massive manhunt would be launched and perhaps was already mobilizing.

When she escaped, she had instinctively turned east away from the approaching police car. But that was probably a fortunate happenstance. Already she was in another county, and Philadelphia would certainly be a better place to try to catch a flight than Baltimore. Continuing to travel northeast made sense. But where to get treatment?

Pulling out her smart phone, Mary Anne logged onto Mapquest, pulled up a map of northeastern Maryland, and typed "hospital" into the search function. In an instant, eight blue pins populated the map. She zoomed out until Philadelphia, too, was on the map, and more pins appeared.

The Delaware state line was less than an hour away up I-95. A Delaware hospital would be better than a Maryland hospital. *I can make it that far.* She placed the little hand cursor over the first hospital pin in Delaware and a little box appeared that read "Christiana Care Health System, Newark, DE." A minute later, she had driving instructions.

~

Maryland State Police helicopter *Trooper 3* arrived from its Frederick base on-scene over Monkton at 4:12 AM, adding its F.L.I.R. forward looking infrared system to the hunt as well as its massive thirty-million-candlepower *Nightsun* searchlight—powerful enough to light up an entire football field.

It was not until 4:37 that a ground search team discovered the fresh tracks of a vehicle in the hayfield adjacent to the Randolph farm. Skid marks and grass spun into mud indicated a hasty exit. Thirty minutes later the incident commander called off the ground search and then made a phone call to Sergeant Dan Fry, the investigative officer on the Mary Anne Williams case. Fry, in turn, roused Calvin Bacon out of bed.

Mary Anne Williams had obviously escaped by vehicle—possibly a smaller SUV by the look of the tracks—but with significant injuries according to Dr. Randolph.

At 5:45 AM, a team of senior officers from Baltimore County and the Maryland State Police, as well as a representative from the FBI, met in the Randolph kitchen to plan the manhunt. The media would be all over this case, everyone knew, so this would be a massive effort. Fry asked Calvin Bacon to sit in on the meeting because, although a junior officer, Bacon knew Mary Anne Williams better than anyone else on the team.

Unaccustomed to participating in such a high-level meeting, Calvin was uncharacteristically quiet. Assignments were made for contacting all hospitals in the Baltimore and Washington region as well as York and Harrisburg, Pennsylvania, followed by assignments to all transportation hubs including the Baltimore and Washington airports, Harrisburg airport, and all train and bus stations—a massive undertaking made all the more difficult by the fact that it was a weekend.

Calvin squirmed on his stool by the granite counter, the round wooden seat no match for his considerable weight. *This won't work. She's too smart and careful,* he thought. *They'll never find her.* But he said nothing.

Two officers were immediately dispatched to Ascot Farms, and an APB was posted along with a file photo of Mary Anne obtained from the mansion during Fry and Bacon's initial missing-person meeting with Williams's housekeeper.

When the meeting broke up, Bacon, dressed in civilian clothes, stood near Fry as he finished a conversation with Scott Tinley of the Maryland State Police. As Fry gathered up his papers, Bacon finally spoke for the first time. "You're not going to find her, Sergeant," he said quietly.

"Why not?" Fry asked without looking up.

"She's not going to Baltimore, or Washington, or York, or

Harrisburg. She's too smart for that. She's going to Philadelphia so she can get a non-stop either out of the country or to Miami, and she's going to stop at a hospital along the way.

"Let me go to Philadelphia," Bacon said earnestly. "I've studied more photos of her more times than anyone else. You don't need me here. If I'm right, I can find her. But I have to leave right now, and you have to have someone else call all the hospitals enroute, and someone else set up a liaison with the airport police."

Fry stared at his subordinate for a long moment and almost laughed. Without a shower this morning, Calvin's cowlick had hair going in all directions. He was big—probably six-three and three hundred pounds—not exactly the picture of a deadly SWAT team member. But Bacon had good instincts. Dispatching him to the Philadelphia airport would only cost Fry one man from the local search. It was worth a shot. "OK, Calvin. You're on. Get moving."

Fry looked at his watch: 6:18. "Lights and siren to Philadelphia, Calvin. She's got a big head start on you."

Calvin turned and headed for his cruiser. "And Calvin," Fry called out behind him, "comb your hair before you enter that airport, or else don't tell 'em you're from Baltimore County."

~

At 5:58 AM Dr. Robert Stanton stood at the PACS screen scrolling through the chest CT on Olivia McDonald. *This was one lucky little horsewoman*, he thought. The only significant abnormality in her chest was a ten percent pneumothorax—a partially collapsed left lung—and a thin black line evident in the upper third of her sternum that was probably a non-displaced fracture. A minimal amount of fluid—probably blood—was present at the bottom the left hemithorax, but that was of minimal significance in the absence of further bleeding.

Almost all accidents involved some minor error in judgment, and in her case, leaving a pitchfork lying on the barn floor with the tines pointing upward set her up for a near fatal accident when she tripped over the hay bale, landing on the pitchfork. The sternum that was fractured had probably saved her life by preventing the tines from further penetrating her chest.

But she was one tough girl… and beautiful too. She had refused all pain meds, saying that she hated narcotics—knew too many people with drug problems. He had to admire her for that.

He debated whether or not to insert a tube into her chest to suck out the air that had escaped from her lung into the chest cavity, partially compressing her lung. But if the puncture wound in the lung had sealed, that may not be necessary. Her body would reabsorb the air within a week or so, and her lung would re-expand on its own. He decided to leave the decision to the surgical consultant, who would no doubt want to admit her for at least twenty-four hours of observation, if not put in a chest tube.

Within the first hour she had received a liter of IV normal saline and her first dose of IV antibiotics. He walked back into her room to report the results of her CT.

"So that partially collapsed lung will heal on its own?" she asked.

"Well, I said it *may* re-expand on its own without intervention. We'll have to watch you for a day or so to make sure it doesn't get worse. You may or may not need a chest tube."

"Great. So how soon can I leave?"

CHAPTER SEVENTY-NINE

MARY ANNE PULLED A FRESH ORANGE TEE shirt from her backpack to replace the black jacket, dressed, and signed herself out of the hospital against medical advice. By 6:45 AM she was back on I-95 with prescriptions filled for the antibiotic Augmentin and the painkiller Vicodin at a nearby all-night pharmacy. Thirty minutes later she took the exit for Philadelphia International Airport and pulled into the daily parking lot closest to the terminal.

Carrying just her backpack, she stood in front of the big departures board and searched for a destination. Her preference would be Antigua, but it was unlikely she could get there today. She knew that the last Antigua flight left Miami at 10:55 AM. The best that she could probably accomplish was to get to Miami. From there she could choose from a host of Caribbean flights.

She checked her watch: 7:20 AM. Her eyes ran down the departing flights until they alighted on Miami: US Airlines, departing at 7:50. *I'll never make it.*

The next Miami flight was 9:55 AM: US Airways Flight 2051. Two hours. That was longer than she wanted to hang around the airport. *But how would they find me?*

She had her new IDs and credit card in the name of Allison C, Becker. It was impossible that the authorities could track her by that name. Someone would have to recognize her on the basis of physical appearance. Maybe the police would circulate an old picture, but with her black hair and sunglasses, finding her among the masses would be a stroke of pure luck.

She suddenly coughed violently, sending fresh waves of intense pain coursing through her chest. She dropped her backpack and held her chest with both hands until the pain gradually subsided. She thought again about taking a Vicodin, but decided for the fifth time against it. Sedation was out of the question. She had to have her full wits about her until her flight was wheels-up.

She looked at the board again. There were flights to Chicago, LA, and Palm Beach leaving in about an hour. She might make one of those. In the end she decided that the risk of waiting for a Miami flight was small and she desperately wanted to be on familiar turf. She would wait for the 9:55 flight.

~

At 7:42, as he neared Chester, ten miles south of Philadelphia International, Calvin's cell phone buzzed. He turned the siren switch to "OFF" and slowed to seventy.

"Bacon here."

"Calvin, this is Marjorie."

"Marjorie, what the hell are you doing in the office? It's Sunday morning."

"Well, you're the problem, Calvin. Fry called me in to make phone calls for you."

"OK, Marjorie. I owe you one for that. Ya got anything for me?"

"Yeah, you owe me big-time, Calvin. A twenty-eight-year-old horsewoman who identified herself as Olivia McDonald checked into Christiana Hospital at 4:58 this morning after having fallen on a pitchfork. She had five puncture wounds to her chest, a fractured sternum—that's a breast bone, Calvin—and a partially collapsed lung. She got IV antibiotics but refused to stay and signed out against medical advice at 6:23."

"I *knew* it!" shouted Calvin. Marjorie pulled the phone back from her ear.

"Where's Christiana Hospital?"

"Near Newark."

"Do you have liaison set up for me with the airport police?"

"An officer will meet you at the US Airways departure entrance. You can leave your patrol car at the curb."

"Marjorie, I'm gonna kiss you when I get back."

"Calvin, you do that, and I'm gonna tell the captain that you patted my ass."

"I'm gonna do that, too, Marjorie. Get a description of what that girl was wearing. Call the airport police back and tell them to start looking for a passenger ticket issued to Olivia McDonald—probably to Miami or the Caribbean. And tell them I'll be there in ten minutes. I love you, Marjorie."

"Goodbye, Calvin."

Allison Becker handed her driver's license and a credit card to the US Airways ticket agent.

"OK, Miss Becker. Are you checking any baggage?"

"No, I just have a carry-on."

The agent placed Miss Becker's ticket in a folder, scribbled on the outside of the envelope, and handed the young woman her ticket, license, and card.

"Flight 2051, Concourse B, Gate 10. Your flight should start boarding about 9:30. Have a nice flight, dear."

"Thanks." Mary Anne took a deep breath and winced. Only one more major hurdle: getting through security. But since no one would recognize the name Allison Becker, her only real concern was that someone would see the bundles of cash in her backpack on x-ray and decide to check the bag. She could think of no way around that risk.

The middle-aged TSA agent peered at Allison Becker's driver's license through glasses on the end of her nose, looked up at Becker twice, then scribbled on the ticket and passed her through.

Allison stepped out of her sneakers, placed her backpack on the conveyor belt and walked through the metal detector without difficulty. As her backpack went through the machine, the conveyor belt stopped, backed up, and several seconds later went forward again, dumping the backpack onto rollers. It's owner exhaled a sigh of relief.

Mary Anne looked at her watch: 8:09. *Plenty of time to buy new luggage—something with wheels. Every time I lift this damned backpack it kills my chest.*

I need to get fresh clothes, too, she thought, looking down at her dirt-streaked black tights. I need to leave that girl in the tights and orange tee shirt behind.

~

Calvin slipped on a nylon jacket to cover the gun holstered on his belt and walked into the packed US Airways departures entrance in the company of Corporal Salvatore Benanti. He stood for a moment and with a sinking feeling watched the crowds of people snaking their way through mazes to the ticket counters like ants returning to the nest.

My God. She's here...I know it. But how in the hell will I ever find her among all these people? And for sure, she's not even gonna look like any of her pictures.

"Where's a departures board, Sal?"

The young uniformed airport policeman led the way, motioning with his index finger for Calvin to follow. A hundred feet away, they stood side by side looking up at a big electronic board.

"Miami, Salvatore. That's where I'm betting she's headed," said Calvin. "Looks like a US Airways flight left two minutes ago. If she's on that one, best of luck to her. But I don't think she likely had time. The next one's at 9:55, Gate B-10. That's where we'll look for her first."

Calvin turned and looked down at the young cop with an Italian name. "You got any civilian clothes, Sal? She'll spot you a mile away."

"Yeah, sure. But we're required to be in uniform...I don't know if the sergeant will let me—"

"Fuck policy, Sal. That girl killed an old woman in cold blood four hours ago. Put a bullet right here," Calvin said, placing his index finger on his forehead between the eyes. "You wanna send her a

Valentine's card telling her we're about to arrest her? Let's go talk to your sergeant."

~

At Brooks Brothers, near the entrance to Concourse C, Mary Anne selected a navy blue Tiger Lilly print silk dress, a pair of plain navy flats, and a wide-brimmed woven straw hat with a navy blue band. To these, she added a simple navy purse and several articles of jewelry.

After paying with her CardOne debit card, she exited the store and walked to Gap at the far end of *Marketplace*, where she purchased a snug pair of white shorts and a Gap tee shirt. Two doors to the east, at Roster, she bought a baseball cap.

In a nearby ladies room, she scrubbed her hands and face, painfully wriggled into the shorts and tee shirt, then slipped the elegant dress over her head. *Awesome! If I need to lose a tail, I just walk into a restroom, pull the dress over my head, and the girl in the navy blue dress disappears!* The tights, orange tee shirt and sneakers, she dropped into a trash can. The baseball cap, she folded and tucked into her left-hand dress pocket.

Standing in front of a mirror, she watched herself brush out long, shiny locks of brunette hair, wincing with the movement of her chest muscles. *Hasn't been washed since yesterday, but it'll do. Overall, not bad...a young Philadelphia matron headed to Miami.* Picking up her backpack with a groan, she lowered her sunglasses, adjusted the angle of the straw hat, and emerged from the restroom a new woman.

At TUMI leather goods directly across from Brooks Brothers, she purchased a tasteful carry-on bag. Returning to the same restroom, she transferred the contents of her backpack into the new bag and tossed the backpack into the same trash bin with the rest of her discarded clothes.

I love this! They'll find all these clothes and realize that I was right here under their noses.

Much better, she thought as she pulled the wheeled bag back toward Concourse B. *This isn't killing my chest.*

~

"OK," said Sergeant O'Donnell, waving to Corporal Benanti, "get into your civies. We'll do this as a favor to Baltimore County," he said pointing his index finger at Calvin, "but we make any arrest that occurs. Understood?"

Calvin held up both hands. "Hey, it's your turf, Sergeant. I'm just here to help you look good. You got any girls workin' here?"

"You mean hookers, or cops?"

A broad smile spread over Calvin's huge face. "Cops."

"Yeah, I've got a couple."

"How 'bout you give me one of them in civilian clothes, too. I wouldn't want to scare any of your female passengers running into a ladies room after our little honey."

O'Donnell smiled. "You're very persuasive, Officer Bacon. All right. I'll give you one of those, too."

~

Despite the constant pain, it suddenly occurred to Mary Anne that she was having fun. She *loved* this cat and mouse game—this matching of wits. The high stakes made it all the more exhilarating. The police were still no match for little Mary Anne Hampton from the Everglades.

Nevertheless, she needed to be careful. *If* the police were looking for her here, they would likely be watching boarding areas. Loitering in shops would be safer than sitting in a boarding lounge. She decided not to approach her gate until the last minute when most of the passengers had already boarded and it would be easier to spot the police.

But by now they may have figured out that there was a Miami connection to Mary Anne Williams. What if they were watching only Miami-bound flights? Suddenly she felt less confident. A shiver rolled through her. *I need a Plan B.*

Stopping in front of a departures board she ran her eyes down the list of morning departures and found exactly what she was looking for. *Perfect!* US Airways Express Flight 3315 to Atlanta departing at 9:50, Gate C-22—five minutes before her Miami flight at Gate B-10.

If she bought a ticket to Atlanta, she could check out the Miami flight gate for cops—say twelve minutes before departure—and at the first hint of trouble run straight to Concourse C and immediately walk onto the flight to Atlanta. *I'd disappear just like that,* she thought, snapping her fingers. *Poof!*

It was 8:40. She would have to exit the secure area, buy a ticket to Atlanta, get back through security and make it to Gate B-10 by at least 9:35. *Wow! That might be tight. And what if the flight to Atlanta's full? But it's Sunday morning—no business travelers. It's worth the risk.*

~

Calvin paced outside the airport police office just off Concourse C, checking his watch every minute as he waited for his little team to change into street clothes. Across the concourse was an Au Bon Pain bakery—irresistible. Calvin was famished. He bought a coffee and a croissant smeared with chocolate, and stood scanning the expansive *Philadelphia Marketplace* mall of airport shops between Concourse B and C.

Forty feet to his right, anchoring the eastern end of the marketplace was Brooks Brothers, and to his left, a small, high-end watch shop and a leather goods store. *Why would people shop in an airport?* he wondered.

He felt a tap on the shoulder and turned to see Sal Benanti in jeans, a black tee shirt, and a leather vest, standing beside a short Hispanic girl of maybe twenty-five.

"Officer Bacon, this is Maria Esposito."

Calvin stuffed the remainder of the chocolate croissant into his mouth, switched his coffee to his sticky left hand, and reached out with his right. "Hi, Maria, I'm Calvin," he said unintelligibly. "You have good croissants here in Philly. Hang on just a second."

Licking his sticky fingers, Calvin hustled to a napkin dispenser and dried his fingers, then reached into his jacket pocket and pulled out a large-screen smart phone.

"OK, guys," he said, bringing up a photo album, "our suspect is a very wealthy and very beautiful little psycho who should be considered armed and dangerous. She already whacked a little old lady this morning with a .38 between the eyes, and she's a suspect in another murder a month or so ago."

"Here's a few photos of her," he said scrolling through the album, "but she won't look like any of these photos, she's too smart for that. People who know her say she very hot—you know, slender and good looking—and she's about twenty-eight.

"This sounds unbelievable, but she got stabbed in the chest with a pitchfork this morning and stopped at Christiana Hospital for treatment on her way here, so maybe we'll see some evidence of incapacitation, or bandages under her clothes, or something.

"If we catch somebody that we think is her," he said turning to Maria, "we'll just have you take a quick look at her chest and that will tell the story. I'd do it myself, but my sergeant probably wouldn't approve," he said chuckling. Maria rolled her eyes.

"She's originally from Miami, and brought two goons up here to help in a home invasion this morning. Well, she picked the wrong home, because they're both dead, and she almost got whacked herself. Anyhow, we think she's most likely headed to Miami, so, since we can't cover the whole airport, we're gonna just cover the Miami flights this morning.

"First flight is US Airways 2051 at Gate B-10. I'm gonna sit in the seating area as a passenger. Sal, you sit someplace where you can move in for an arrest from the other direction, and Maria, I'd like to have you further up the terminal to cut her off if she tries to run."

"I'll sit across the corridor in B-11," said Sal, "and Maria can sit further up the concourse in B-8."

"OK," said Calvin, checking his watch, "it's 8:20. Let's exchange phone numbers so we can text each other, and then go get familiar with Concourse B. Everybody's got a radio, too, right?"

After the exchange, the trio set off to the east through the mall. Forty feet behind them a young woman in black tights and an orange tee shirt exited Brooks Brothers and followed them the length of the mall until she turned right into Gap.

~

Ted Sloan sat alone at Gate B-1 working on his laptop, early for his 10:30 flight to Dallas. Vaguely aware of someone taking the seat next to him, he felt a hand on his arm and looked up.

"Would you mind terribly watching my bag while I run to the restroom," said an elegant young woman in a straw hat. "It's such a pain to lug a suitcase into a stall, if you know what I mean," she said, her lovely smile revealing rows of even, white teeth.

I'll even help you in the restroom, if you like, thought Ted. "No, of course not. Take your time." He watched her lovely hips sway as she briskly walked away toward the shopping mall until he lost her in the crowd. This flight was getting off to a good start.

Now I won't have to bring that bag back through security with all that money, thought Mary Anne.

~

On the way to Concourse B, Calvin purchased a black duffel bag at Brighton and a *Philadelphia Inquirer* at CNBC News. *I need to look like a passenger.*

Walking separately, the three officers leisurely began to make their way down the four-hundred-foot concourse. At the far end of the massive corridor the concourse turned right into a separate limb housing gates B-10 through B-16. B-10 resided inconveniently out of sight just inside the limb, from where it would unfortunately be impossible to see passengers approaching down the concourse.

Eyes memorizing every detail, Calvin pretended he was Mary Anne Williams on the run—albeit two hundred pounds lighter—making note of every location on the long concourse where she could disappear from view in a bar, restaurant, or shop. Only one set of restrooms was present on Concourse B, between gates B-5 and B-7. That, at least, was helpful.

Maria Esposito split off at Gate B-8, taking a seat from which she could view both directions on the long concourse. But, of course, she could not see around the corner to B-10.

At the far end of the concourse, Sal chose a seat in B-11, the gate with the best view. From this seat he could see every approaching passenger coming down the concourse, as well as Gate B-10, just across the hall diagonally to his left.

Calvin wandered into B-10, lowered his considerable weight into a seat on the back wall, and surveyed the seating area. *This sucks.* Because B-10 was around the corner from the long concourse, he couldn't see a single damned approaching passenger until they actually walked into his gate. But since he was the only one who could likely identify Mary Anne Williams, there was really no other choice.

This was the highest stakes operation of Calvin's career—one for which he bore total responsibility. Already sweat was beading on his forehead. He didn't fear Mary Anne Williams, but he feared her brain—he was afraid she would outsmart him.

In addition to Calvin's team, Sergeant O'Donnell had two unformed officers loitering at the Dunkin' Donuts kiosk at the entrance to the concourse. All three officers on Calvin's team had concealed radios linking them to the two uniformed officers on a discrete operations frequency.

They had constructed a net which would be difficult to escape, but if anyone could make them all look like fools, Calvin knew, it would be Mary Anne. The big hole in the plan, of course, was that nobody had a clue what the hell she would look like when she appeared...*if* she appeared.

A few Miami-bound passengers began to drift into B-10, but none remotely resembling Calvin's quarry. He glanced at CNN on the ceiling-mounted TV: 8:42 AM. The next hour would pass like ketchup from a Heinz bottle.

CHAPTER EIGHTY

TICKET IN HAND, MARY ANNE EXITED Terminal C security and checked the time: 9:19—*could have been worse. Lucky this was Sunday morning.* Lifting the hem of her silk dress, she stuffed the Atlanta ticket into the back pocket of her white shorts, and briskly headed for Terminal B.

Less than twenty minutes now remained in which to scout the concourse for anything peculiar that might indicate a trap before she would have to make a decision whether or not to take the Atlanta flight. Near the concourse entrance, two cops stood chatting and drinking coffee at Dunkin' Donuts, but they seemed oblivious to the rest of the world. *That's a good sign*, she thought.

She flashed a smile at a disappointed Ted Sloan, retrieved her luggage, and began to walk down the concourse toward Gate B-10. *This is it*, she thought. *The next twenty minutes will tell the story. If they try to arrest me it will be at the gate. I need to stay focused.*

Scattered along the concourse were perhaps a dozen restaurants, coffee bars and pretzel kiosks, as well as three or four bookstores. With every sense on high alert, Mary Anne forced herself to walk slowly, her eyes continuously scanning the crowds ahead for anything that didn't look right.

As her mind catalogued every hidden recess, unmarked door, and potential escape route, she suddenly stopped dead in her tracks. *Oh my*

God! My driver's license and credit card are in my purse, and I've got documents in my luggage in the name of Allison Becker. If I had to run for it and lost either one it would be disaster! They'd be able to track me!

Now halfway down the concourse, she walked into the women's restroom between B-5 and B-7, memorizing the location and the layout of the facilities. There was one curving passageway in and twenty feet to the left—further up the concourse—another separate curving passageway out. No doors.

Slipping into a stall, she winced as she lifted the carry-on, then removed the better part of twenty thousand dollars and stuffed the packets of hundred-dollar-bills into her shorts.

She slipped the bottom of the full-page documents pertaining to her offshore accounts into the waistband of the shorts and secured the top of the papers under the elastic bandages that encircled her chest.

The only other identifying documents were her driver's license and credit card, and the US Airways Miami ticket in her purse. She slipped both plastic cards into a front shorts pocket, and tucked the airline ticket into the pocket of her dress. Satisfied, she zipped closed the carry-on bag and exited the restroom. Her watch read 9:26.

Mary Anne had decided that the very latest she could make the decision to head for the Atlanta flight on Concourse C was twelve minutes before departure, which would be 9:38. Now her heart pounded as she approached the end of the long concourse before it turned right to Gate B-10. Straight ahead was a CNBC News stand. From there she hoped that she could see into the B-10 seating area.

~

Calvin looked up from the paragraph in his newspaper that he had read thirty times without a glimmer of comprehension, and once again surveyed the large crowd that was now gathered at Gate B-10. Only three young women met the category of beauty and body type of Mary Anne Williams.

The Maryland DMV had provided a copy of her driver's license which listed her height as five-eight and her weight as one hundred and twenty-one pounds. Two of the three young women he had been watching were four inches too short, and the third was obviously married and with her husband. *Maybe she's not going to show.*

Popping a Rolaid into his mouth, he mopped the sweat from his forehead with a white handkerchief. He would have given a box of Dunkin' Donuts holes to get rid of the nylon jacket, but it covered his gun and a radio. Some passengers were already standing in line near the walkway entrance and it was getting more difficult to keep the entire gate under observation from his seat.

"Ladies and gentlemen," came an overhead female voice, "we are now ready to begin the boarding process for US Airways Flight 2051, nonstop service to Miami. Passengers with young children or those in need of assistance are now welcome to board, Gate B-10."

Calvin folded his paper, reached for his duffel bag and stood, his eyes scanning the outer fringes of the crowd but finding no targets. He walked to the periphery of the seating area near the end of the forming line, and leaned against a pillar, his face the picture of boredom.

Diagonally across the wide corridor in B-11, adjacent to CNBC News, Sal Benanti's eyes immediately latched onto an elegant young woman emerging from the crowd one hundred and fifty feet up the concourse. It was her walk that first caught his eye—confident and seductive. Slender and stylishly dressed in an expensive blue dress and straw hat set off by a pair of dark aviator sunglasses, she could have just walked off the cover of *Vogue.*

Wow! That one's gorgeous, he thought. *Maybe that's her— no...couldn't be.* Walking straight ahead to the end of the concourse, the woman disappeared into CNBC News. *I better let Calvin know about her.* Both thumbs a blur of motion, Sal tapped out a message on his phone:

brunette blue dress straw hat cnbc news right height weight

A reply came almost immediately:

let her approach the gate

456

Three minutes later the woman reappeared, pausing just outside the shop entrance to stow a book in her purse as her head swiveled and her eyes obviously scanned the concourse. She took two steps in Sal's direction and suddenly stopped, her body wracked by an explosive coughing episode. Bent forward at the waist, she held her chest with her right hand until the spasm finally stopped. As she stood fully upright again, she made eye contact with Sal who immediately looked down and tapped out another message:

bad cough holding chest

When he looked up again, the girl was gone. Frantically he scanned the crowd and saw her back disappear into a group of passengers ninety feet away headed back up the concourse. Sal could see Calvin standing on the edge of B-10 and shouted across the concourse. "Calvin, she bolted! Up the concourse!"

Calvin reached inside his jacket for the radio. "All units, subject is headed up the concourse. Blue dress with straw hat. I think she spotted us. She's probably close to B-7 right now."

Maria Esposito was immediately on her feet, standing on tiptoes, searching the moving river of passengers flooding out of the B-7 gate from a newly arrived flight. For an instant she thought she caught a glimpse of a rapidly moving blue dress and then lost it. She turned left, ran at top speed up the concourse to one hundred feet above the women's bathroom and then began to work her way back down the concourse through the dense crowd. By the time she reached the restroom entrance, Sal ran up from the opposite direction.

"She's gotta be in the bathroom!" he gasped. Drawing her gun, Maria cautiously made her way along the curving entrance while Sal covered the exit. Calvin arrived a moment later, waving away scores of women from the entranceway.

The first woman to notice Maria's drawn gun began to scream, followed by another, and then another. "Police! Everybody out!" Maria shouted above the din. Sal stepped aside as women in various stages of undress began to pour out the bathroom exit.

Inside, the enormous restroom space was divided by a central wall into two mirror-image rooms with rows of sinks on both sides of the central wall and stalls on both outside walls. Within thirty seconds the restroom had substantially emptied. Along the right hand wall, three stall doors remained closed. Feet could be seen under each door.

"Police!" screamed Maria. "Open your stall door *now*!" She stood crouched off to the side with both hands on her gun as one by one the three doors opened revealing one white-faced elderly woman, and two middle-aged females sobbing uncontrollably.

"Shit!" Maria whipped around the wall to the other side and repeated her clearing technique. Three minutes had elapsed by the time the restroom was cleared.

~

Mary Anne grabbed her chest with her free hand as violent spasms of pain coursed through her chest with each uncontrollable cough. *Shit! This is a dead giveaway!* she thought, but she was helpless to stop the coughing.

When the spasm finally subsided she looked up directly into the eyes of a thirty-something man sitting at the adjacent gate in a black tee shirt and leather vest. Immediately, he averted his eyes and began tapping on his phone. Something was wrong about this. *His eyes didn't try to flirt with me. He's a cop...I know it!*

As fast as she could walk, Mary Anne headed for a cluster of people one hundred feet up the concourse. When she was through the knot she looked back and saw the man on his feet. Throwing the straw hat to the floor, she broke into a run along the right side of the concourse, ignoring the searing pain in her chest.

Ahead, a throng of people was exiting Gate B-7 just before the women's restroom. As she ran, she unbuttoned the top of her dress with her free hand, shoving aside passengers in her way and eliciting shouts of anger from the crowd.

Slipping inside the restroom, she turned left toward the exit, whipped the dress over her head and stuffed it into the trashcan. Ten seconds later a girl in white shorts, purple tee shirt, and a baseball cap casually walked out the restroom exit passageway and joined the crowd departing the concourse.

Twenty feet ahead a young Hispanic woman frantically fought her way through the dense stream of passengers toward the restroom. *She's a cop, too,* Mary Anne smiled to herself.

Three minutes later Mary Anne reached the head of the concourse where two alert, uniformed policemen now stood on either side of the wide corridor, eyes searching the crowd. Ignoring them, Mary Anne turned right and began to walk briskly through the retail mall toward Concourse C. She checked the time: 9:37. *Perfect!* She would reach the C-22 gate just before the door closed on Flight 3315 to Atlanta.

~

Calvin cursed. She had vanished again into thin air. He ignored the raucous voices around him and tried to concentrate on putting himself in Mary Anne's shoes. She was very careful. Always seemed to have a backup plan. He was sure that she still desperately wanted to get out of the mid-Atlantic region to safety.

"Where's the nearest departures board?" he barked.

Near the head of the concourse Calvin stood towering over the four airport police officers and looked up at the big board. Seconds later he said, "C'mon. We don't have much time."

~

Swearing at the pain, Mary Anne stowed her carry-on in the overhead bin and settled into her window seat. Thankfully, the flight to Atlanta was relatively empty on this Sunday morning, and the seat beside her on the *Embraer 170* regional jet was empty.

Heart still pounding she looked at her watch: 9:52. The doors should be closing momentarily.

Overhead, a voice said, "Ladies and gentlemen, please take your seats as quickly as possible and fasten your seatbelts. Make certain that all carry-on items are securely stowed in an overhead bin or under the seat in front of you. The doors are closing and we should underway in just a few moments."

Mary Anne held her breath and crossed her fingers. A last passenger walked down the aisle, puffing and sweating, holding a black duffel bag out in front of him. The enormous man paused by Mary Anne's seat. *Oh, God, no. This airplane's almost empty. Tell me he's not gonna sit beside me. He'll spill over into half my seat! I won't be able to breathe!*

In direct confirmation of her fears, the man pushed his duffel bag under the seat ahead, struggled to turn his massive butt in the narrow aisle, and plopped down beside her with a *whoosh*.

He wriggled around to get comfortable, then said "Whew! Made it!" Turning to the girl beside him, he stuck out a monstrous sweaty paw. "Hi. I'm Calvin Bacon," he said with a huge smile. "Good to finally meet you, Mary Anne. You look just like your pictures."

EPILOGUE

PENNY'S PARENTS ARRIVED WITHIN AN HOUR and a half of the police and whisked Catherine and Jack away to Annapolis. The bleeding in my thigh had slowed of its own volition. I permitted the ambulance crew from Hereford Station 53 to cut off the leg of my scrub suit and bandage the wounds, but refused transport to the hospital until the children were gone.

By 6:30 AM the police had finished interviewing Penny and me, and I finally consented to being loaded in the ambulance. At Mason-Dixon, Phil Timmons took me to the OR and cleaned out the wound that thankfully had been confined to muscle and involved no bone or major arteries.

Shortly after noon, as Penny sat beside me in the recovery room, we received word that the police had captured Mary Anne Williams at Philadelphia International. I refused admission, and at 4:00 PM Penny and I climbed into her SUV and followed the children to Annapolis, arriving at Buchanan House exhausted, just before dinner.

~

Tom and Denise Murphy asked us to stay at Buchanan House as long as we were comfortable, and we took them up on that offer. Psychologically it couldn't hurt for Penny and the kids to know that there was a guard at every entrance to the enclave where they slept.

461

Complete protection from the media was an added benefit. It was the perfect cocoon in which to heal.

At the end of the day, I could not imagine the children ever again having dreamless sleep at the farm. When Penny and I returned to the farm to gather our personal belongings, the reminders of Ruth at every turn in the house brought profound sorrow, not to mention the absence of Maggie who would never again tumble in the yard with Jack.

We spent nearly two weeks giving things time to settle as we debated whether or not to leave the farm, but by the end of that period it was clear to both of us that the dream was over. A realtor's sign went up at the end of the lane the next day—the same day as our cancelled wedding. Astonishingly, once the decision was made to part with the farm, neither of us ever looked back.

On the sixth day, the medical examiner released Ruth's body. Her funeral was held the next day at Hereford Methodist Church, exactly one week after her death. Perhaps thirty people were gathered in the sanctuary to mourn her passing, most of whom were elderly, and most of whom I did not recognize. It was the saddest day of my life.

As the service progressed, the minister reached the pertinent scripture reading: "Greater love hath no man than this:" he said slowly, "that a man lay down his life for his friends."

Penny had wanted to speak, but could not find her voice through the tears. I rose in her place, but she laid her hand on my arm, stood, and I took my seat again.

"What do you say about someone who has given their very life for yours?" she finally began in a remarkably clear voice. "Not only for you, but for your children, too?

"Most of you, I think, are aware of the circumstances that led to Ruth Hollens' death. Unless you were there, as was I, it is impossible to conceive of the courage that resided in her frail body in the most terrifying of circumstances.

"I...I wanted to publicly thank Ruth—perhaps in the hope that she could hear me—for consciously sacrificing her own life for my life and the lives of my two children, Jack, four, and Catherine, seven, who she loved as if they were her own."

Here Penny paused, her voice faltering. "But the enormity of Ruth's sacrifice is utterly overwhelming to me. Saying *thank you* seems such an impossibly small gesture."

She looked down at me, tears drenching my jacket sleeve. I squeezed her arm and nodded.

"Ruth devotedly served my fiancé, Alex Randolph, as a housekeeper and surrogate mother. Alex, the children and I became Ruth's family, and she, our family member. She lived for the day that Alex and I would marry. We have no conception of how to thank her, except by living our lives to the fullest together, a dearly-held dream of Ruth's that Alex and I will soon consummate."

She paused and took a deep breath. Raising her eyes she said softly, "So Ruth, thank you for our lives. We will never, never forget you. You will always be part of our family."

For most of the trip back to Annapolis we were silent, both lost in our own thoughts. Finally I turned to Penny and said, "That was the most eloquent eulogy imaginable."

~

I awoke to distant crying, and looked at the clock: 2:58 AM. Throwing back the covers, I padded down the hall to the room where Catherine and Penny slept. A nightlight plugged into a receptacle bathed one side of the room in subdued light.

Penny lay with her arm around Catherine who was curled up with her face buried in Penny's shoulder, whimpering softly as Penny stroked her hair. "Sshh, sshh, sshh," Penny whispered. "It's all right, baby."

Tom and Denise Murphy had been a godsend for the children, showering them with love and security. Jack seemed to almost not skip a beat, spending hours with Tom climbing the statues of John Paul Jones and Tecumseh, or saluting the midshipmen as they marched through the quadrangle. The midshipmen all knew Jack, of course, because he was always with the superintendent.

Catherine, however, was a different story. The joy seemed to be gone from her eyes. I would often catch her staring off into space and nothing captured her attention for very long.

Never a clingy child, every time I saw Catherine these days she was standing beside Penny with her arm wrapped around her mother's leg. We were usually able to get Jack to sleep alone without much difficulty, but Penny had to sleep with Catherine every night.

She spent hours rocking Catherine in her arms, answering questions about Ruth or Maggie, or more disturbingly, about *bad people*. If you are prone to question the presence of evil in the world, you should talk to us.

I sat on the edge of the bed and lay my hand on Penny's thigh. "Did she hear a loud noise again?"

Penny nodded. "It's about the same time every night," she whispered. "From a dead sleep she suddenly sits up in bed and asks, 'What was that? What was that?' She looks around the room for thirty seconds, lies down and cries, and in two minutes, she's back to sleep."

Penny is always teaching me lessons. I watched her carefully in the first several weeks after our night of terror. There is no question, of course, that she was less animated and joyful. Especially in the first week, her face was strained, and she was often quiet and distracted. But amazingly, I could see little trace of anxiety, or even depression per sé—great sorrow, for sure, but none of the clinical signs of depression.

It was obvious that her overwhelming focus was on getting the children past this trauma. Penny lives to love, a preoccupation that I have slowly come to recognize in a very unscientific way as being the only path to happiness.

~

As the days wore on, it became clear to me that Mason-Dixon Regional Medical Center had lost its luster in my life. Perhaps it was just the whole association with sequential horrors. But the trial had taken its own toll as well, and I no longer had the heart for administrative battles.

In late September, I resigned as chief of emergency medicine and gave my three-month's notice. Three days later I signed a contract to do *locum tenens* work for a company that supplies temporary emergency docs to hospitals. I would start when my three month's notice was over.

Penny, herself, never returned to Mason-Dixon. She tendered her resignation from the nursing staff and used up her remaining paid-time-off, devoting her full attention to the children.

~

On October eighteenth, Penny, I and the children traveled to the White House, accompanied by Tom and Denise, for the posthumous awarding of the Congressional Medal of Honor to Patrick Murray. I offered to stay at home, but Penny had insisted that I accompany her.

It was a tearful day. Penny hugged Patrick's parents and I shook hands with them. The awkwardness of the moment was relieved by the graciousness of Andrew and Liv Murray, who congratulated me on my engagement to Penny and wished us many happy years together.

"We're all related through the children," said Patrick's mother holding my hand in both of hers. "I want you to always feel completely comfortable with Andy and me. Penny has told us how close you are to the children. We're so happy that she found you and that Catherine and Jack will have a loving father in their life." Somehow her graciousness made the day all the more poignant and painful.

I stayed in the background as much as possible during the brief meeting of the families. It was not my day, but Patrick's.

Jack paid no attention at all during the ceremonies, apparently unimpressed by the President of the United States, but Catherine seemed to absorb everything that was said. I hoped that she was old enough to remember for a lifetime this tribute to the brave man who was her father.

~

Autumn in Annapolis was glorious, filled with color, crystal clear azure skies, warm days and brisk nights. My leg healed. Slowly but surely, laughter began to make an appearance at Buchanan House. More importantly, Catherine began to sleep through the night.

It took the police weeks to track down the Miami connections of Mary Anne Williams, but finally most of the pieces of the puzzle fell into place. Whether or not Williams had killed Stine remained a mystery, but thankfully it became clear that the threat to the family had ended with her capture. Her trial for the murder of Ruth Hollens would not occur for months.

From the beginning, the police and state's attorney took the position that the death of the two Miami brothers was justifiable homicide. No charges were filed against Penny and me for killing two people that night.

Our final meeting with Calvin Bacon was therapeutic for Penny. At the end she gave him a huge hug and a kiss on the cheek, her arms barely reaching his back. Calvin's smiling face turned crimson.

Later that evening, we went out by ourselves for the first time since leaving the farm, walking hand in hand through fallen leaves under the Academy streetlamps to a quiet dinner together near the harbor.

A briskness had returned to Penny's step that I hadn't seen in weeks, and she chatted nonstop on the way to the restaurant. I leaned back in my chair and from across the table watched her animated eyes flash. Broad smiles once again graced her lovely face.

For weeks, my one recurring fear was that the impact of the sequential tragedies of the last two years would doom Penny's and my relationship. Between nearly losing her life in the hospital hostage event and the terror of the Mary Anne Williams episode, her life had gone to hell since she met me.

I wondered from time to time if subconsciously she would somehow hold me responsible, or at least associate my presence in her life with death and profound sadness.

Midway through the salad, she lay down her fork and wiped her lips with her napkin. Reaching out for my hand, she cocked her head to one side, the picture of loveliness; soft light glinting off silky, flaxen hair. "OK," she said with great decisiveness, "there are some things we've got to get going on."

This is good sign...I think. "You have a list for me?"

"First, we've got to finally get married. I'm so tired of sleeping without you. I don't think I can stand it another night."

"How about tonight?" I scratched my head. "Wait, have we had this conversation before?"

"We can't do it tonight, silly. Jack has to be the ring bearer, and he's already asleep. Besides, Catherine would never forgive me if she didn't get to wear her purple dress in the wedding."

"OK. What's the second?" I asked.

"We've got to find a place to live. It's time we got our own place. Maybe a cottage on the water, with a little boat slip! We could get a black lab, and the kids could throw sticks off the dock into the water." She leaned forward in her seat. "What do you think?" she asked, her green eyes glittering.

ABOUT THE AUTHOR

D. Bruce Foster is a native of northern Baltimore County, Maryland, the location of the novel *This Way To Paradise*, where he grew up observing the cultural milieu of My Lady's Manor steeplechase country. For twenty-five years he has been chief of emergency medicine at a Pennsylvania hospital, and is the medical director of an aero-medical helicopter service.

He has two published medical textbooks: *Twelve Lead Electrocardiography for ACLS Providers* published in 1996 by W. B. Saunders (Harcourt Brace), and *Twelve Lead Electrocardiography- Theory and Interpretation* published in 2007 by Springer. The former, now out of print, sold seven thousand copies, a significant performance for a medical textbook, and the latter earned a four star "Outstanding" rating from Doody's Book Review, a review service for the medical publishing industry.

This Way To Paradise is Foster's second work of fiction, continuing to follow the life of ER doc Alex Randolph, introduced in his widely praised debut novel, *Kiss Tomorrow Goodbye*. He lives with his wife on a farm in southern Pennsylvania in a lovingly restored pre-Civil-War brick farmhouse. You can learn more about Bruce Foster at www.dbrucefoster.com.